CULLING

LOWER EARTH RISING: BOOK 2

EDEN WOLFE

ESN INK

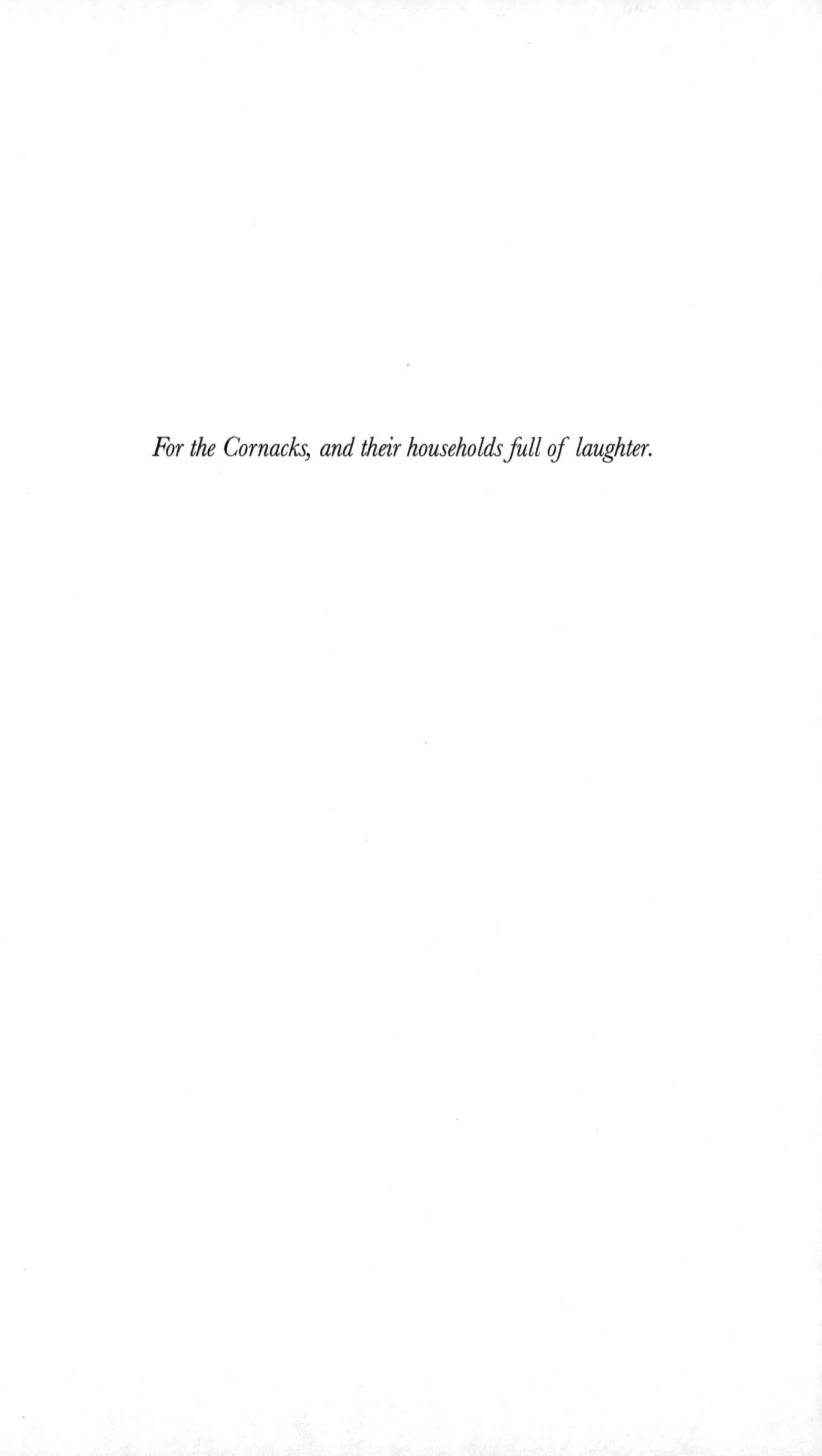

For the Cornacks, and their households full of laughter.

FROM THE AUTHOR

This story is the second novel in the Lower Earth Rising Series, and it was drafted entirely during the initial lockdown of the Coronavirus pandemic.

I'm so grateful to have the Selfsame Readers Club, a place where we can talk about the series, the world, and the madness which is the dystopia of everyday life.

Also, I share exclusive material with Club members, like short stories and unpublished material, as well as first-notice of any free book promos.

When you join, you get "Deviants", a novella about Rose's struggles in Cork Town, as my gift to you.

Our world is a wild place; Lower Earth is my escape from the madness. Come join me on a voyage into *what if…*

~Eden Wolfe

www.edenwolfe.com

Rainf
Strangelande
West fields
Leeside Mountains
Lakes Region
Minor Rainforest

FORGOTTEN iSLANDS
WEST GANA
EAST GANA
inforest
CENTRAL Mass
EAST FIELDS
GeB

LOWER EARTH DIRECTION, YEAR 407

FIFTEENTH GENERATION
SINCE THE DUST
UNDER THE REIGN OF QUEEN ARIANE I

GEB COUNTY DIRECTION

Commandante - Irene (Irilena), warrior priestess of Gana
Great Geneticist - Roman of the first line
Primary Overseer - Uma of the nineteenth line
Senior Overseer - Carole of the fifth line

GANA PROTECTORATE

Chief Priestess - Habana, warrior priestess (deceased)
Keeper of the Chief - Batrasa, warrior priestess

OUTER COUNTIES MANAGEMENT

Prefect on Three-Year Cycle

DARK COUNTIES PROTECTORATE

Prefect on One-Year Cycle

CENTRAL MASS PROTECTORATE

Under Command of the Queen's Guard

STRANGELANDS SECT

Head Sister - Daphna, former employee of Central Tower

CULLING

YEAR 407

FIVE YEARS SINCE QUEEN ARIANE WAS CROWNED

1

———

Leadon's throat was dry with ocean air. Empty boats bobbed on the ocean, gently rolling over the waves as the tide moved in. Fishing rowboats ducked alongside sky-high ocean vessels built in the generations before the Mist. Leadon watched them dancing on the water, but her mind was off in the heavens. Her heart ached for her absent friend.

Five years had passed since Aria had been declared Queen. For Lea, it was a lifetime ago.

She walked away from the ocean, toward the river that ran up alongside the main village.

Aria. Give up on the Aria of your memories, Lea. She is Queen Ariane now. And she has no time for the likes of a mere subject like you. Know your place.

Leadon sighed into the river, watching it rush on. She kneeled for a moment, remembering how she'd watched Aria rearrange the stones so that the currents would invite the fish back.

Her boots nearly soaked through but she didn't see a single fish. She walked on, following the twists and turns of the riverbed. It wound along and up, rounding the hills before reaching its destination. Lea approached the end of the town limits, the low wood fence the sign that she ought to turn around. But she wasn't ready to go home yet.

Her fingers ran along the wood fence, little splinters catching in her skin, then falling aside. The fence was as old as the new world. More than four hundred years had passed since the settlers after the Final War had laid down borders in Lower Earth. The warrior priestesses had been on the land for generations before and had never needed borders to know where they lived. Then a wooden fence became all that created peace between them and the settlers' society. It had worked.

And then it didn't.

No fault of the fence, Leadon thought, *People were the problem.*

She wasn't sure who had been the first to negotiate with the new peoples. Nor why. These weren't the stories recounted over fires in midnight rituals. They could begrudge those forbearers all they wanted. Nothing had changed since the first warrior priestess had started making concessions. Maybe it was during the wheat shortage. Or the period of the locusts. All of Lower Earth had suffered then. Desperation was a powerful driver for change. For loosening limitations. For giving in.

Now the Ganese weren't allowed to leave the broader Gana limits. At all. East and West Gana, despite their cultural differences, were united under this decree. Only travel allowed that didn't require written authorization was to the capital city via the Geb Free Route. And the Ganese leaders had all but forbade the warrior priestesses to go, even though they were allowed.

The short wood fence turned to stronger timber as Leadon reached the border of Gana proper. It didn't look like much. A wooden gate, unlocked. Tall and crooked. Unprotected wood making a hatch that didn't keep anyone or anything out.

But it kept her in.

If only Leadon could get permission from the Keeper of

the Chief. But Batrasa had held the role for several years, and Batrasa would never let Leadon go. Not even if she explained why. Batrasa had been skeptical of Leadon from the start; maybe even since before she was born.

So she didn't ask.

She put her hand on the wood of the gate that was latched in diamond shapes. She could see through to the plains. A couple of days' journey to Geb. How different the world was there. Twenty-four years she'd lived, confined in Gana's borders. Two days' journey was all it took to change worlds, though Leadon had no idea what that would look like. It only came to her in stories from the few who'd traveled to negotiate new terms for Gana with the capital. She dreamed of one day taking the Free Route to Geb, to follow the steps of her people when the settlers had first established the city.

"Leadon!"

"What? What?" Leadon felt like she'd been caught, though she wasn't doing anything wrong. Only in her imagination was she breaking the rule. She couldn't be persecuted for what happened in her imagination. Not yet anyway.

The woman cocked her head as she led a horse toward the stables on the edge of the village. "Why are you so startled? It's almost time for the quorum, we've got to prepare."

Leadon closed her eyes. She would one day find herself in real trouble if she missed the third-day prayers quorum.

"I'm coming. Of course, I'm coming. Just doing some morning exercise," she lied. "Cooling down from climbing." She mustered a smile, "Thanks, Miliah."

"Nothing to thank for," she patted the wide neck of the deep chestnut-colored horse. "We have a responsibility to each other."

"Indeed."

Miliah nodded and turned, the flaps of her leather tunic slapping her sides as she went, the Ganese steed walking proud at her side. Her breastplate was ceremonial; Lea couldn't see why she'd be wearing it for third-day prayers. This wasn't a special day.

Or is it? Where is my mind? No, today is not a skills parade, nor a sacrifice. But I'm missing something.

She left the gate out of Gana behind her and walked towards the village center. Even though they still called it a village, it had the population and activity of a city. More than a hundred thousand of them now, ever since the Willing Woman program had been more accepted among the priestesses. As she arrived, the city was already bustling. She had to find her quorum quickly.

"Lea, thank heavens! Get in here and prep the stew." Her quorum lead, Shyanne was running between a boiling pot and sizzling root vegetables on the fire.

Lea walked to the pot and gave it a stir. "Goat? Today? What is going on?"

"Where have you been, Leadon?" Shyanne came over and put her hands on Lea's cheeks. "Incredible how you live in your own head. The whole morning has been buzzing with it. Batrasa has called a full quorum."

"A full quorum? What? Why? We haven't had one since Habana died."

Shyanne lifted her hands, urging Lea to recognize some seemingly obvious fact.

Lea shook her head. "Batrasa - is Batrasa dying?"

"Why else would we have a full quorum? Stir the pot, for heaven's sake!"

Leadon stirred but her mind was absent. Batrasa, dying. If true, it could throw all of Gana into disorder for a period. No one expected it this soon. Habana's successor hadn't even been announced. Batrasa may have been the Keeper of the Chief, but she was no Chief. How could this happen? And who would step in next?

Anyook is too rash. She's probably the most likely selection, but we'll end up bandits and thugs if she has her way. Just because she exudes power doesn't mean that she has the makings of our leader. Priyantha? Possible, but she is too concerned about her inner circle. Mitam? Maybe, she's a bit young, just had her woman's day. But she's promising. If only she had more experience. If only Batrasa could hold on a few more years - announce Habana's successor and provide training. Look how her training of the Queen has worked; Aria will likely be the greatest Queen Lower Earth has ever seen. Much of that must be due to Batrasa. How I miss Aria. If only Aria would step in and help decide.

"You're letting it burn, Lea. I can smell it from here."

"Sorry," she picked up the pace of her wrist's twisting. It was a large pot. They'd be responsible for feeding three hundred mouths. Every feeder house would be.

Maybe I can get a few moments with Batrasa. Perhaps she would listen to me, given my background. I could convince her to ask Aria. I mean, Queen Ariane. If the Queen made the announcement, then everyone would have to follow. Habana had always been attentive to my ideas. I know that I was a genetic curiosity for her, but still, she seemed to appreciate my insights. Maybe Batrasa will do the same.

"Leadon! The stew, for heaven's sake!"

Leadon and Shyanne bumped through the growing crowd as they took the cart of stew into the center of the village. Most Ganese would be there, except for the very ill and those overseeing the borders. The lookouts were more ornamental now than anything else, their roles nearly defunct. But when Leadon looked up and saw them at their stations, she felt a puff in her chest. They stood as still as statues, a message facing the rest of the world, an enduring message. The border lookouts had been there since the outbreak of the Final War. And they'd be there until the next assault on their tribe, whatever that may look like.

But the lookouts couldn't do anything about the water sickness, the drought, or the crop viruses. Their skills fell far short of the threats in their modern world.

For all those microscopic invasions, Gana was reliant on Central Tower in the capital. The researchers of Central Tower were revered throughout Lower Earth. Without them, all society would have died off in the second generation after the Mist. The Mist had already killed most of the habitable land on the planet. How blessed they were that Lower Earth survived the worst of it. Their native home. One of the last strongholds on Earth.

Their enemies weren't biological weapons from a far off enemy or adversary, but rather the land on which they lived, which seemed to be in a constant state of flux. Invisible enemies in the shape of bacteria, parasites, viruses from the old world that had managed to travel on the Mist's back, surrounding the planet in places they never belonged. The Ganese had been gifted in finding ways to overcome them, but they had their limits. Some illnesses they just couldn't outsmart.

"Look out, coming through," Lea led the cart through the first few hundred who'd arrived. Some wore the garb of West Gana. Lea loved how the long, white tunics flowed from their shoulders to their waist to the ground, how it caught the wind and flew like clouds behind them. Under the translucent cloak were the standard leather tunics, bodices with iron rings for attaching weapons, and the fur hangings to cover their legs. But the white over-layer caught Lea's breath every time. The West Gana population was fewer now; most had been called back to East Gana for agriculture. But the old theology was alive in the West. Lea thought they were more connected to the earth than the Easterners who looked out at the ocean and dreamed of something more, something greater. The Easterners had kept up the ways of sailing like the old genera-tions, the boats maintained, especially for the management of the Forgotten Islands Prison. Certainly, there was good in the ways of the East and the dreams of what was out over the water.

But Lea admired how the Western theology focused on the here and now. They were grounded and realistic. They favored plans over dreams.

The crowd grew; Lea couldn't see across the central meeting point, there were too many women in the way. Their skin rich and dark like their land, hair long and woven. Most had taken the time to prepare for the full quorum. Leadon felt a sting in her stomach and tried to flatten her hair. She too was a natural Ganese, even if she was different from all of them. Those who knew her genetic background gave her sideways looks, always second-guessed her motives. They treated her as though she was never supposed to have happened. As though Ganese should not play with genetic codes the way the settlers' descendants did. But Leadon had been given no choice in the matter. She'd just been born that way. A genetic design, an intentional copy. The only one in Gana. Warrior priestesses like Ahnira made their disdain known.

Lea saw Ahnira coming toward her, and she mustered her nerves. She inhaled deeply, trying to calm her breathing. Ahnira pulled her cart up alongside Lea, her lips taught.

"Aren't you supposed to be setting up on the fourteenth corner, Leadon?"

"That's where I'm headed."

"Get moving then."

Ahnira pulled her cart away without waiting for Leadon to give any kind of response. A call came across the shell horn. One long, two short. They had only a few more minutes before Batrasa would appear.

"Go, go!" Shyanne pushed the cart forward.

"There's people there, stop pushing!"

"No time, Lea, no time."

Lea eased the cart into the fourteenth corner and joined

the crowd in the center. The clinking of iron on tunics clanged as bodies turned to look for Batrasa, though she hadn't yet emerged from her hut. The sound of the iron was musical, and despite the charged ambiance, Leadon found herself grinning at the excitement of it all.

"What are you smiling about? Don't you know this is a full quorum?" a voice assaulted her, a shoulder bumping into her. The woman was tall, broad. Strong shoulders and glaring brown eyes. Judging eyes. Leadon refused to feel shame.

"A full quorum is not by its definition a sad occasion."

"You inherited something funny in that blood, replica."

"Replica?"

Shyanne's voice pulled Lea out of the conversation. "Leadon! Over here, I found our quorum house."

Lea watched the woman and the woman watched Lea for a few steps, and then she was in the crowd.

Replica? They call me that?

The noise of feet stepping and iron chinking and nervous conversations surrounded Lea as she tried to follow Shyanne's path. She picked up pieces of other peoples' exchanges as she went.

"Do you think she identified someone?"

"I thought this would be a council decision."

"Upper Earth attack maybe?"

"Not a chance, we have haven't seen sight or sound of them since the scout removal."

"But they could, theoretically."

"Who's accompanying Batrasa? Could this be her final rite?"

"No, she wouldn't leave it for the last second."

"Maybe she didn't know, maybe she-"

"Wanalia, over here! Our quorum's near the ninth corner!"

Lea and Shyanne reached the other women from their

quorum just as the shell horn called out for silence. One long signal, no mistaking it.

"Where were you?" Niapal hissed.

"Where were *you*? I was setting up the cart. You were probably off at the boats again."

Niapal lowered her voice. "Of course I was at the boats. We had no warning."

Lea sighed. "I know. I was caught off guard too."

Niapal took Lea's arm. "We might need the boats more than ever. We could be at the beginning of very difficult times."

"We could be."

"Hush, you two," Shyanne gave them each a light slap on the back, "She's coming."

All sound flew away on the wind as the horn echoed out to the forest beyond the village. Slapping leather against bodices and legs were the only sound as the fur door covering of the hut pulled back. Batrasa stepped into the light.

"She has no accompaniment," Niapal whispered.

"Maybe that's promising," Lea replied.

"Hush."

Batrasa looked out over the thousands of gathered women, seemingly still in her thoughts, not looking at anyone in particular. She closed her eyes and inhaled, her ribs expanding under her ceremonial priestess robes. No sign of the warrior she'd always been. She'd abandoned the leather and iron for softer custom.

Lea could tell this full quorum would not be what any of them had thought.

Batrasa exhaled and finally set her eyes straight. She looked at the women, one by one, those in her immediate radius. The women parted, giving her a pathway through the crowd, but Batrasa lifted her hand.

She walked first to the left, following an imaginary labyrinth. She then turned right, into the crowd, women stepping aside as she came. Those she passed absorbed the sight of her, she who had led them for the past few years, since just before the coronation of Queen Ariane. Habana had been Chief for two generations, more than eighty years. She and Batrasa had quarreled, all of Gana knew it. Habana had wanted Batrasa to lead until her death, to take over the role as Chief. Batrasa insisted it had to be someone of the next generation. The fight had lasted days. Two elderly women with voices that echoed through the village. They let everyone hear their argument; they hadn't tried to hide it.

Batrasa began to speak, still from within the crowd. She was far from the podium in the center of the square. Her voice carried through the village square to waiting ears.

"Warriors. Priestesses. We of Gana are women of many faces."

She continued her spiral through the crowd, inlets opening before her.

"I have many secrets. They inform my ways. To you, I might look erratic. Obscure. Maybe even senile." She touched the face of a woman as she passed. "Glowell, how tall you've become." Batrasa stopped, taking in the woman's height, her breadth, her muscled arms, and chiseled face. "How you've changed." She carried on walking. "We are all changing. Lower Earth is changing. I will soon change. I will pass into the world beyond this one, where our ancestors will greet me. I can only hope they will be pleased with what I've done." She stopped and let out a sigh. "I did what I could. I failed many times, I know." She nodded her head to the beyond, her eyes set on the clouds above.

Lea couldn't unhook her eyes. They were held captive on the sliver of Batrasa she could see through the crowd. She felt the eyes of everyone cast in that direction, through Lea, through everyone. All eyes pointed at Batrasa, waiting.

"You've seen I am unaccompanied. I am not the Chief. I

was only ever the Keeper. I have asked the souls of Habana and those before her for guidance. Habana, who went just before Lower Earth's transition in power. Her judgment was already foggy with oncoming death. You were there, you recall. Only a strong leader can admit when she doesn't have the answer. And so we find ourselves here today."

"Is she going to say who the successor is?" a voice behind Lea asked.

"Today is a day of reckoning. You all expected an announcement, I'm sure. But I will not give you such relief." Gasps emerged from the crowd. "There is a reckoning to be had. Humility. Shame." Batrasa stopped. "Women of Gana, you have become too proud."

"How can she say that?"

"Does she have any idea what we seek?"

"How can we be proud when we remain tethered under Geb?"

"Stop!" Batrasa raised her hand high. "Your very words are your condemnation! Think on this, women of Gana. Who among you is the least? Who among you have you most cast away? Who is she that will stand forth when you have fallen under righteous weakness?

Leadon felt her heart racing, as though Batrasa was speaking directly to her.

Batrasa arrived in the center of the village square, stepping onto the podium without use of the many hands which offered support.

"You might call me hard for these words, but truth is hard to hear." She looked out, no one dared to speak, lest they be labeled for the rest of their life. "I will announce nothing today but this: she who will lead you must be prepared to be hated by you. She who can withstand such hate and ostracism is she who will stand when you have fallen. It is she who will find you justice, liberation, fair negotiation, and honorable position."

Batrasa stepped down from the podium, her cadence like a conversation with their society. "Do not speak to me of this. Do not ask. Do not parade your feathers like a proud peacock." She wafted her hand as though swatting the thought away. "I must rest now. I will call upon those with whom I must speak, but make no assumptions. I hate your useless assumptions. Dangerous assumptions."

Batrasa reentered her hut. The electricity that had run through the crowd before her arrival dulled into a charged hum. Lea served the stew as the line of women passed with only nods of thanks as they went by. Lea looked over to Shyanne who kept her eyes on the serving spoon. Lea's mind ran a thousand miles a minute.

No announcement? Too much pride? If only Aria were here. She could talk some sense. She could influence Batrasa.

Lea sighed as the spoonful she served splashed out of the bowl.

"Watch what you're doing," the woman snapped in a low voice. " You'd better not have tainted the food. I've always wondered if you're a spy for the Sisters."

"Tainted the food? Why would I even do that? Your tongue is sharp but your wit is dull."

"Lea!" Shyanne hissed.

She spooned a second helping as the woman glared at her.

"Move along," Lea said. The woman turned, shaking her head as she went.

"Mind yourself, Lea." Shyanne kept serving but spoke to her. "You walk such a thin line."

"And why is that, Shy? It's not because of me, it's because of what I represent. And how is any of that my fault?"

"Don't speak of it. That only makes it worse."

"I've been silent for twenty-four years. Don't you think the time has come for us to speak of such things?"

"Hush. Damn it, Lea. Clear up here. I'll go back and start in the kitchen."

Lea let the air huff out her nose. Speaking to Shyanne wouldn't change anything. But she was tired, so tired, of having to stay silent.

THE NOTE SLID ACROSS THE DIRT FLOOR OF THEIR QUORUM house. The curtain flapped in the doorway as the messenger passed by. Niapal and Lin were closest and jumped upon it.

Lin was always fastest and she snatched up the paper as Leadon put the last of the kitchen implements away.

"Leadon," she whispered. "It has your name on it."

"Me?"

Lin nodded and passed the paper. Leadon looked at it for a moment before reaching out. She'd never received a message before. She was second cook in a feeding house and tried to keep out of the way. There had never been a reason for anyone to send her a message, and she'd always been glad for it.

She touched the paper and her stomach sank.

Is it Aria? Has something happened? Or could it be Irene? She hasn't been back in so long.

Irene. The Queen's Commandante. Dedicated servant to settler Queens. Irene was well into her fifty-fifth year but remained as true as ever to her warrior roots. She took no prisoners. She led the Queen's Guard and enforced the disappearances. She was revered and feared across Lower Earth, the only Ganese of high position in the Fortress.

And despite more than thirty years between them, Irene was Leadon's genetic twin.

Leadon was the first genetically-designed warrior priestess in Gana. A fact too well known across their land, where native blood was their pride in the aftermath of the Final War. Leadon was the first, the only, the outlier of Gana.

A replica.

"So," Lin stepped beside Lea, "What does it say?"

Leadon stepped away from Lin, desperate for a little space.

The note was folded twice over. The paper was crisp under her fingers and cracked as she opened it.

Lea read its contents and looked up to Lin's and Niapal's waiting faces.

"It's Batrasa. She wants to see me."

"You?"

"When?"

"Tonight."

"Tonight!" they both said at once. The weight of it fell softly over all of them like a wool blanket and they said no more.

Lea looked in the mirror as she prepared for the meeting.

How do I dress? Ceremonial garb? Or do I go as I am, natural? What does she want?

She smoothed her hair in the reflection and ran her fingers under her eyes. Her eyes were looking more tired than usual, dark circles underneath them. She pulled the sides of her face back, but instead of looking fresher, she looked contorted. She scratched her shoulder as she looked at the different clothing options laid out on her bedplate.

"Can't decide?" Shyanne poked her head through the curtain.

"What is someone supposed to wear to a meeting with the Keeper of the Chief?"

"I don't think there's anything 'supposed' in it."

"Then I should just go as myself?"

Shyanne backed out of the room, "It's not for me to tell you."

Possibly the most important moment of my life, and I'm worried about what I ought to wear? I've got this all backward.

She sat on the edge of her bedplate and closed her eyes.

I've got to be clear in what I want to say. I may never get another chance in my life like this one.

Lea walked into the fresh night air. Autumn was coming in, and the smells of transition were swirling in the air. Cooked root vegetables. Leaves fallen and moist from morning rains. She inhaled deeply, the cool air feeling like a cascade into her lungs. She tuned in to the slightest of changes, the air warming inside her. She let the air fly out, her shoulders relaxed. And she knocked on the hut's pillar.

The fur curtain moved slightly but Lea couldn't see who was behind it.

"*You* received an invitation?" a voice spoke from behind it.

"Yes," Lea lifted it in her hand. She'd guessed she might need it. As proof.

The woman led her in, each step intentional and heavy. The air in the hut was thick with smoke and incense. Lea felt a tickle and swallowed hard to make it go away. She intended to make an impression. A lasting and deep impression. This was her moment to impress upon Batrasa the need to bring in the Queen to help decide Gana's future. Lea believed it with her whole heart, growing in conviction with each step.

The woman pursed her lips and then spoke quickly to Lea. "It's through there. Wait to be addressed. She's in a time of deep prayer. She'll speak to you when she's ready and not before. Understood?"

"Yes."

The woman lingered a moment longer, looking Lea down and up. Lea took in a deep breath and forced herself to give a nod to the woman, hoping it looked like she was dismissing her.

Then she turned her eyes to the little fire in the middle of the room.

It crackled, small twigs and embers waving smoke streams into the hut. The roof hole was closed, forcing the smoke back in, rounding down the sheep-skinned walls. Lea felt a layer of sweat start to gather in the small of her back and a trickle down the side of her face. Batrasa sat on a small stump at the edge of the fire, her prayer stick thrust into the middle of it all. Dried leaves and feathers caught the flames and sizzled out; Batrasa re-fed it, nodding at the little sounds. A crackle of ember shot up, landing on Batrasa's wrist. She put down the prayer stick and slapped out the glow, a black char of her skin left behind. Batrasa inhaled deeply and looked up to Lea at last.

"Thank you for coming."

She's thanking me?

Leadon began the greeting prayer, hoping it would set her on the right foot.

"Lassa Batrasa weh."

"Pona sebana weh" Batrasa replied.

"Lassa mokha wanna weh."

"Haffaah."

Lea nodded slowly in response.

"Bring over that stool, sit across the fire from me."

Lea did as she was told. She set down the wood stool, low to the ground as it was, and crouched onto it. The single flame of the fire licked up and interrupted Lea's view of Batrasa. She struggled to keep her eyes focused on the old woman through the light. Batrasa had changed so much, and it had happened so quickly. Just a few years earlier, just before Aria had left. It had begun not long before the coronation and since then had been a steady step closer to the next world. White hair, hunched back. Muscles turning into hanging flesh.

But her voice remained as strong as ever.

"Leadon. What have you to say?"

Lea shifted on the stool, unprepared for a direct question.

"I have come as you asked."

"Is that what you have to say?"

She was making a mess of it already.

Focus, Lea. Focus. Do not be intimidated, do not let her cast you off balance. She is just a woman like you.

"It is but the first thing I have to say."

Batrasa smiled and tilted her head to the side.

Lea inhaled deeply. "Indeed, I have much to say, but I have distilled it into this first statement so that you can then hear the rest with the right intention. Gana is my heart, my soul, my love. There are many who look at me and doubt me, but they are wrong and have always been wrong."

"And what have you to say to them?"

"Nothing. They must make their own judgments. I only ask that their words not taint your impression of what I have to say. My motives are good, sincere."

"Yes, you strike me as sincere."

"You face a critical decision, Keeper of the Chief." Batrasa nodded at this, and Leadon suddenly felt encouraged. "And I am not one to advise you on that, not me. Many others may try and they will fail because of it. I do not want to influence you. Instead, I come to implore."

"Implore? I see." Batrasa's wrinkled forehead pulled into an even more severe expression. Lea wasn't sure if the look was one of sincerity or bemusement.

Focus.

"I implore for our friend, Batrasa. Our friend and protector. Aria. Now Queen Ariane."

Batrasa sat up, her back snapping to attention. "The Queen? I did not expect such a request. Explain."

Lea steadied her voice. She had to get it just right. "I know she has not returned since she left, her absence more telling than her decisions from Geb. But I cannot believe she has abandoned us in heart." Batrasa didn't speak, so Lea continued. "She is active in the Direction of Lower Earth. The urges of Lower Earth are demanding; we see but the tip of it here. But I'm saying things you already know. What I came for, what I implore, is that in the process of your sacred discernment, which will determine the course of Gana for generations to come, that you seek out Aria's insight. That we go to her with humility, and on behalf of the people who hosted her before she took the crown. She has abilities, Batrasa. You know many of them. I, too, saw more than most. She was my good friend. And she spoke to the earth like no other. We can rely on her, Batrasa. She will be there for us in our time of need. Consult with Aria," Lea corrected herself, "with *Queen Ariane*, and we can guarantee a cohesive future, one which will not divide Gana against itself."

Lea sat back on the stool, the weight of her words sitting heavy on her chest. She waited for Batrasa to respond.

Instead, she got no reaction at all.

Batrasa appeared frozen, unmoving, eyes fixed on Lea as though she continued to speak. Lea's breathing became shallower and she shifted under Batrasa's gaze.

Have I displeased her?

Batrasa inhaled sharply through her nostrils, looking up at the smoke-filled ceiling of the hut.

"You are most unexpected, Leadon."

"Unexpected?"

"Your words - they give me pause."

Lea's heartbeat increased. "Have I spoken out of turn, Keeper?"

"Indeed not, I invited you to speak. But your choice of words has rendered me speechless. It's unusual as an experience." Batrasa looked back down at Lea. "Have you ever been speechless?"

"I think I am, right now."

Batrasa smiled and then collected her prayer stick and a fresh set of leaves from the shell beside her. She pressed three leaves onto the end of it and wafted it over the flame, too high for it to alight.

"What do you know of Queen Ariane, since she became Queen?"

"Very little. Like most of us, I haven't seen her. She hasn't sent for me. Not a message either. I wrote to her, a few times. But no reply." Lea quickly corrected herself, "Not that I expected one. I wanted her to remember that she was still loved here, that she still had a place in Gana should she ever wish to return. I know not all Ganese feel the same, but I - well, I think Gana is better for having had her in its charge for those years."

"And you?"

"And me? What about me?"

"Is Gana the better for having you as its charge?"

So she's coming to it. I could have expected she'd challenge my authenticity.

"Batrasa, I know there are many who speak of the dangers of genetic design, but as sure as I sit here across from you now, I am true and I am honest. Those who speak otherwise are wound in wretched stories from my birth and early years. None of them are true. I never sacrificed any creature for my own domination, I never had designs on the Fortress. I may be of the design of the Commandante, but I am no Irilena. I am Leadon, born of my own skin, beating my own heart, and despite their words - venomous though they have been - they are only words. I am flesh and blood, and I am as much Ganese as any one of them. My heart beats for this nation and I call to our ancestors with the same fervor as any warrior princess. Anyone who speaks otherwise has not seen the truth within my heart."

Leadon felt her heart beating out of her chest, the flames licking so close to her cheeks that it burned, but she had to know that Batrasa had heard her, heard the truth in her words, in her voice, and in her soul.

"Calm, child." Batrasa stood, laying the prayer stick again on the ground. She walked around the little fire and kneeled at Lea's side. She took Lea's hand in her own. Lea felt the bones thrusting through the skin, like wet paper. So delicate. Lea feared the skin would tear at the slightest upset. The sight of Batrasa stroking the back of her hand and then holding it tight brought a wave of relief over her. Batrasa turned Lea's hand over and pressed her forehead against the palm. Soft, warm, snakelike skin under her fingers. She never could have imagined that she would find herself above Batrasa, the Keeper of the Chief lowering herself before her.

Batrasa raised her eyes, which were relaxed and calm. The old woman's face took on a different quality, somewhere far off. Batrasa wet her lips and whispered.

"Forgive me."

Lea could only shake her head in disbelief.

Batrasa bowed her head. "I, too, was one of those voices. I was wicked. I was wrong."

Lea had no words. All words disappeared. Every cell in her body felt electrically alive, rushing. She swallowed.

"Of course I forgive you."

Batrasa squeezed her hand. Lea felt she might disappear, so unreal was the scene before her. Like a dream or an apparition.

"You will have to forgive many," Batrasa stood. "Even if they cannot ask for it. Many do not have the words to ask for forgiveness. It is a skill we've lost in the way of our new world. Forgiveness is worthy of being reborn among us. But it cannot be me, though I'll try. Our ancestors forgave. How else could we have found peace in this, our old world, with their new world ways? We all forgave the settlers a long time ago. But those were days before birth rites and crop disease. Before genetic design. We still have much to learn and re-learn." Batrasa stood tall, her spine bringing her upright, the full height of the Ganese warrior priestess she used to be. "Leadon, you thought you were coming here to implore me."

Leadon had forgotten why she had come at all.

Batrasa continued, "In fact, it's me who will implore you."

How has this come to be? Have I been here a lifetime already?

"Please, Batrasa," Lea found her voice, "Anything."

Batrasa looked up at the smoke swirling over their heads. "You will go to Geb. By mule, no horse. You must blend better than that, and as it is you will stand out for the color of your skin against the majority of Geb women. There, you will find your Queen. You will watch her. You will not approach her. You will see if she remains the girl you once knew. And then you will return. If you see your Aria, this Queen Ariane, and if you believe she can influence my decision into what it must be - then I will follow your request. I will. But first, you go to Geb."

"As you wish," Lea managed to breathe out the words.

"Now leave me. I have much to consider."

Lea stood, bowing low and hoping her legs would sustain her until she reached the front of the hut. She paid no attention to the woman at the front; her mind was full of Geb.

Geb. The capital. To see Aria again.

The fear and excitement of the journey ahead rose in Lea's throat and she ran back to her quorum house, not caring who saw her or what they thought. She had to be in her room, on her bedplate, crunched in a ball as she made sense of the mad scene she just lived with the most important woman in their society. Everything just became more important.

Leadon felt like her destiny was being laid before her.

2

The two-day journey went by fast and slow. The mule was a steady companion; often Lea chose to walk alongside him rather than ride. She was restless and eager. But when her legs grew tired she happily hopped onto the mule's back. Despite her height and weight, he didn't seem to mind.

The Free Route was well worn; the few forks in the road were well marked. She saw signs belonging to the first settlers, carved stones with symbols whose meaning had been lost over the four centuries that had passed. They were simple geometric shapes: tilted triangles, dots within a circle, diamonds.

The first settlers. Who knew these childlike symbols would give rise to the powers of Central Tower? 'First settlers', what a terrible term. As though we weren't already here.

She meditated on the idea of first.

First settlers, first viruses, first genetic duplicate. One word, so many applications; its meaning different in each one.

She approached the checkpoint on the Geb Free Route; the Ganese had managed this one since the second generation. She hoped she'd recognize someone there. The initial excitement was wearing off, and left behind was a knot in Lea's stomach.

She was used to being alone, but this trip was nothing like anything she'd ever experienced. She suddenly wished she could share it with someone.

The checkpoint was a hamlet, the point almost halfway between Gana's gate and Geb. A Ganese woman took Lea's papers without as much as a greeting and showed her to her tent. The woman took the mule to the stable, leaving Lea and her bag at the tent's entry.

"Dinner at eighteen hundred. We practice old rites. Be on time."

Lea nodded and watched the woman leave with the mule plodding beside her.

Old rites. She's a West Ganese. The meal will be plentiful, but I better not expect lively conversation.

LEA AWOKE THE NEXT MORNING WITH THE SUN. THE THOUGHT of the journey and the arrival in Geb whirred her to life. She nodded in thanks to the woman and walked out along the main track. But something told her to stop. She dropped the reins of the mule and returned to the woman.

"Before I go, I wish you the will of the old gods with the blessings of the ancestors." Lea put her hand on her heart.

The woman opened her palms before her, her eyes softening. "I accept their will." She let her hands come to her sides and her face changed to one of surprise. "It has been a long time since I heard the prayers of West Gana here."

Lea loved the blessings from West Gana, even if most Easterners thought they were archaic and misplaced. Lea bowed to the woman and took up the mule's reins. She smiled as the pines turned to brush and the brush to rust-colored gravel.

.   .   .

SHE SAW CENTRAL TOWER BEFORE SHE SAW ANY OTHER SIGN OF the city. In absolute terms, the fortress was higher, built into the cliff hill at the city's far eastern border. But Central Tower rose like a phoenix from the dark concrete blocks below it. A vision of steel and glass, of what the settlers could accomplish, even though it pre-dated their arrival. It stood as a sign of success in architecture and in research. So they'd all been told. A symbol of humanity's revival when it had reached the edge of extinction.

Lea had heard it described by the few Ganese who'd traveled to Geb, but their words of 'grandeur in simplicity' didn't capture what Lea saw before her. Cylindrical, it reflected the sky in every direction. It was as though the Tower was the sky itself brought down to the city, and not the city extending into the sky.

She halted the mule a few hundred feet from the place where gravel became asphalt. She would walk into Geb on her own two feet. She tied up the mule and set forward, her only information being the name of the rooming house and the name of a "friend to the Ganese" that Batrasa had given her.

Her senses were overwhelmed. The streets were straighter than a crow's flight, apartment blocks of three four and five stories nestled side to side but each one an individual in its own right. Some were simple flat squares while others had winding designing carved and creeping up the walls. Lea's curiosity grew.

Why wouldn't they use the same design throughout the city?

Screens were fixed to several street corners, but all of them were black. Lea had heard tales of a woman who rang out over the city streets at certain hours of the day, but she didn't know the times to expect it.

Green spaces popped up between blocks where girls played under the direction of housemothers. The ways of Geb came in sharp contrast to Gana, where those who gave birth kept the child with them in their quorum until death. Here the children were mixed around, moved out of the home of their Willing Mother into larger Girls Homes, and later to boarding schools.

Lea felt a shiver. It wasn't that seeing the children in their mass reinforced her belief that the process was a cold, impersonal way to raise children, though that had weighed on her conscience since she'd heard of the Willing Woman rules.

It wasn't that. Her stomach tightened.

They all have green eyes. How can they all have green eyes?

A girl, perhaps four years old, marched over to Leadon, a lava rock bouncing against her chest. Lea felt glued to the spot. Her own interest was as powerful as the child's.

"Who are you?" The girl put her hands on her hips.

"I am Leadon. Who are you?"

"You are very dark. Where are you from?"

"I'm from Gana."

"There are rebels in Gana."

"We are faithful in Gana."

"But you don't wear the lava rock of the settlers."

"We were here before the settlers. Therefore, we don't worship them."

"You look strange."

"In truth, you look strange."

"I do?" The girl started.

Lea forced a smile. This was not the conversation to be having with a child.

"Strange in a good way. You are your own person. Just as I am."

"I think you're right. We are both ourselves. There's no one else just the same as ourselves, right?"

The child couldn't have known that Lea was a genetic copy. All she saw was a dark-eyed, dark-skinned foreigner. Lea was happy to be the odd one out if it was only for those reasons.

"You'd better get back to your housemother."

"Yes," the child leaned forward to whisper. "Mother gets very angry when I speak to strangers."

"Off you go then, quick."

The girl turned and ran with the fervor that only four-year-olds can have.

Lea continued walking, but with every woman she passed, the reality became more and more evident. She looked at the women, their hair, their eyes, their skin, their mannerisms, their jawlines. Each of them wearing the lava amulet, the symbol of the settlers' first arrival at the Rainfields cliffs.

It's not that I'm different, Lea took in the sights of a market in full swing, women selling oranges and beans, bags of rice and wheat. *It's that they all have brown hair. Olive skin. Differing shades but all green eyes.*

She looked around, seeking the eyes of every woman who passed by. It wasn't difficult, they were all staring at her.

How does no one speak of how they all have green eyes?

Aria's eyes were brown. Beautiful deep brown with flecks of green. Lea had assumed there was the mix of colors in Geb as they'd heard of in all the outer counties: brown hair, blond, grey, and some red. Blue eyes, brown eyes, hazel, and green. Olive skin, brown skin, darker skin, pink and white.

But no. Not in the Geb she saw.

She turned her head in time to see a man across the market.

She'd only ever seen one man in her life, a tall and broad man, Archer, who was responsible for reporting on Aria's well-being in Gana. But this man in the market was completely different. He was shorter than most of the women. He was sweating, despite the relative autumn cool in the air. His gut reached outward, hanging. Lea wondered how he moved at all; he seemed to defy physics.

He's degrading. She blinked her eyes to take him in with more detail. *So that's what it looks like to degrade as the men have done since the Mist.*

She'd learned of it in classes, the virus in the Mist that broke down the Y-chromosome. The same virus that attacked lands and rendered them poisonous. The Mist that consumed most of the planet, and she was witness to its effects before her very eyes in the market in the middle of a weekday morning.

She pretended to shop at the market, trying to get closer to the man. Her curiosity made her tremble. Something in her was fearful but she couldn't name it. She stayed across an aisle from him, looking over the wheat, pretending to inspect its quality. Watching his every move. His legs could barely stand him up. He'd have to be in a wheelchair soon.

"You buying it or not?" The vendor had her hands on her hips. "You've been staring at the buckets for ages now. Are you buying or are you contemplating the meaning of wheat?"

"Sorry," Leadon shook her head to bring her back into herself. "Yes. Some fruit?"

She pointed to the oranges. "These are good ones. Fortified. Less flavor but better for you. It's the best they can do in the East Fields these days, what with the crop killers."

"I'll take two oranges." She passed a bill from the pouch Batrasa had given her. The ways in Geb were not like Gana. She'd have to pay for everything she needed. In Gana, food was for all to eat.

The woman put the oranges in a paper bag and handed them across the bushels. "Thank you," Leadon smiled, "I haven't had oranges in years."

The woman screwed up her cheeks. "In years? Where *are* you from, foreigner?"

"Gana."

"Ah, Gana. Like the Commandante."

"Yes. Like the Commandante."

"I can see the resemblance."

Lea felt her heart flutter. "Thank you, goodbye."

The man had disappeared, remarkable considering his slow stride, but Lea had been completely consumed by the vendor.

What if they find out I'm her genetic duplicate? I already stand out like a goat in the pigpen. This task may not be as easy as it seemed.

She continued her walk deeper into the city. Concrete blocks rose high to her left and her right. Variances in each of them. The occasional balcony, one with a terrace, one with large windows, one with full-size doors made of glass. Not a single one was beautiful, all looked rushed. Even the huts in Gana had some decoration, usually sacred, to give some color and texture.

The fox skin on the roof of her quorum house was Leadon's most precious. She'd known that fox from birth, watched the little litter emerge in the forest that ran along the Gana River's edge. Hers was the runt, left behind for the most part, though he wound his way every time back to the troop. He had a white strip down his side, a marking for life of his inadequacy. He couldn't hide it; it was on parade for all to see. But it didn't seem to bother him either. He carried on with his little wild life, killing smaller forest creatures, creeping about the Gana protectorate. He must have been about fifteen years old when he died. Leadon had been sitting by the river when his red muzzle peeked out from the trees. He stepped, slow and gingerly toward the river. Leadon knew his time was coming; it had been for a while. He'd gotten slow and his back hip gave out on him. He took one step, and then another, each one gingerly appointed, each one painful to his aching body. He trembled with it. Leadon didn't dare move. He arrived at the river's edge and lay down. He was directly across from her. He was on his right side, so she could see the full length of his white stripe on his left. It extended from ear to the end of his tail, like some heavenly being had taken a brush and held it in place as he'd pushed out the womb.

His breathing calmed and slowed. Deep breaths, his chest lifted and fell, the sound of the river masking any noise he might have been making, any wheeze or whistles was lost on the rapids that separated Leadon from him.

In. Then out.

In. Then out.

Leadon lost track of time, perhaps an hour or two or three had gone by, when at last his chest was still, the last exhale emptying his soul to the river.

She waded across. The water came to her waist but the current was gentle that day. She lifted his body and turned back, carrying him through the village. Eyes poked out from huts to watch her pass, brows furrowed in question, though no one dared ask her. They always kept their space but for an occasional spiteful remark.

But as she held him through Gana village, not a voice stirred her from her death rite. She laid him down in front of her hut, chanted over his beautiful limp body, and dutifully skinned him in the way of their ancestors.

He was her welcome, the white-streaked fox that laid over her entry. He'd survived against his litter's abandonment. She would survive against her tribe's judgment.

We each have our battles of body and mind.

Leadon whispered the prayer again as she walked through Geb city center. So far from home. So far from her streaked fox. The asphalt under her sandals was rough, the air more humid than Gana.

Beside her, a screen buzzed to life, and Leadon nearly jumped. The streets were mostly empty, middle of the week nearing mid-afternoon, and she was glad for the solitude. She knew that when more of the women emerged she'd find herself the center of attention. A visitor from Gana, and what was she there for? Why had she traveled so far? Did they give free leave to the women or were they kept like caged animals as the old tales went? The questions would come. Leadon heard the other women tell their own stories, the few who had made the trek to Geb. In the city of brown-haired, green-eyed, olive-skinned women, Leadon's stature, her deep brown skin, her near-black eyes, and feminine form would stand out even more than the fox's white streak. Leadon realized that she couldn't just slide in amongst the women of Geb; she needed to change her strategy.

She needed a better story.

To state she was simply on a visit to the capital would be insufficient, she now understood. Batrasa had tried to explain it to her, but Leadon's ears were naive. 'Prepare for any eventuality,' Batrasa had said. Leadon had thought that meant scorching heat on the journey, or crossing a pack of wild dogs. Or losing the money Batrasa had given her to survive in the city for her few days' stay.

Now Leadon saw it all much more clearly. She had to find Queen Ariane – Aria – in a city so foreign to her, and then get close enough to assess whether Aria really could help the Ganese determine the next Chief. Who knew how much Aria might have changed since she left Gana? Certainly her role as Queen would have changed her. Had Leadon been too foolish and naïve in her plea to Batrasa. Nothing was as clear as she'd thought it would be.

Twenty-four years and there's so much in me that is still a child.

A face came on the screen. A woman. Likely Lea's age, with brown hair, olive skin, and green eyes. Crystal green, powerful eyes. Even on the screen, her eyes shot out across the distance. The screen rose two stories against the building on which it hung. Her face took up the full height of it.

"Citizens of Geb, I greet you with appreciation during this 'Week of Industry'. I speak for Queen Ariane when I say we are humbled by your commitment and dedication to your service. Your production this week has outstripped the last three years!"

Mary. So this is Mary. How can she be so young? She's been in place for two generations. Is there more than one Mary? How can they do that?

Lea felt Mary's eyes come to rest on her, even though she knew it wasn't possible. Her heart began beating between her ears at the sight of the green eyes that scanned the city streets from the screen.

Does she see me? Is this some kind of magic?

"As per Directive, you'll stay in Industry until three in the afternoon, when I shall call you with the sound of the flute to join in Central Square for a briefing with our beloved Queen. Continue, women of Geb! You are the generation to take our world further than we could have imagined."

The screen buzzed to black.

Leadon's heart wouldn't slow.

Week of Industry? Is that why there's no one? Where are they? What are they doing?

Leadon walked slower, staying towards the edges of the center. Her timing was poor. Week of Industry? She'd stand out even more than she did already. But a briefing in the after-noon - that would be a unique opportunity.

Perhaps it's not as lost as I thought. If I can stay in cover until then, I will have a chance to catch sight of Aria. Perhaps she'll recognize me. Perhaps she'll call me to the fortress. Perhaps we can discuss. Batrasa doesn't want me to bring up the process for deciding on a new Chief, but if I can get Aria alone -

Leadon stopped. Reason struck her like a brick. She couldn't just stay where she was and rely on no one reporting her presence.

I have to get out of the city until then. If I'm called to report, if the Queen's Guard pulls me aside, I might miss my opportunity to see Aria.

She walked, swiftly but not quickly, so as not to draw any further attention to herself, back to the main entry of Geb and back to the mule. She didn't need to explore the city now; there would be time for that later. Now she just needed to wait out the time until Queen Ariane would give her briefing. She mounted the mule and headed west towards the city's edge. She'd go unnoticed there.

The mule plodded and Leadon reflected. How could the Geb of her childhood musings be so different from the city that rose before her? How can the imagination be so wrong in its drawing up of descriptions? Central Tower, the fortress, the roads, the women. The city was a stranger to her. She'd been operating off a lie of her imagination.

She approached a tall metal gate enclosing a large block of machinery. It was still too far to see the detail, but the sound of the hum and vibration of the ground reached the mule's hoofs. He was not pleased about continuing in that direction, and Leadon had to give him a sharp kick to keep him moving. She made out a sign in the distance as they approached: Power Hub.

The generator for Geb. No wonder it's so loud.

She let the mule take a wide birth around it and walk on. As they reached the northwest corner, Leadon thought she heard voices. They passed the edge of Power Hub, and on her left two women were standing close to each other, handing something between them. Leadon couldn't see what it was.

"You still owe me for the last time."

"I've got a payment coming; Central Tower only pays monthly, I'll have it. I'm good for it."

"You'd better be."

Both women had the common brown hair and olive skin color, but while one woman was dressed in matching jacket, slacks, and boots, the other was hunched, a scramble of fabrics tied over her body. Part of her face drooped and her hair was matted in places. She lifted a little bag in the air.

"You don't know what it takes to produce this. You and

your Central Tower buddies swoon over sequences and enzymes. I'm slaving in a basement in the heat of hell for you."

"I know, I know. Look, I've got to get back before they miss me. It's Week of Industry. I'm already taking a risk by being here."

"You're the one who came to me."

"I know, now let's be done with this and I'll find you when I have my pay."

"You'd better."

"I will."

Leadon made sure to stay far enough away that she appeared uninterested, but every word the women said ran questions through her mind. The clean and proper woman turned, seeing Leadon and the mule. The woman's face flushed with panic, and then reset itself, appearing as though everything was perfectly normal.

The other woman hadn't paid Leadon any mind at all. She'd turned and skittered through a door past the Power Hub into the commune behind.

Opie dealers. Just like the warrior priestesses warned. So it's still being produced in the capital. The Guard can't be pleased about that.

Lea wound around the western edge of the city, wire fencing rising high along the city's border. It was out of place. The rest of the city was open, except for Power Hub, which was to be expected, given the risks.

But here?

Leadon couldn't see a reason for enclosing a commune. Unless it was prison? She continued on, but stayed carefully aware of the position of the sun. She couldn't bear to miss the briefing.

Mule attached and nearing the time of the briefing, Leadon calmed her steps as she reentered Geb center. She had to play her role. Visitor from Gana. Sent by Batrasa for reports on the West Fields as the East Fields hadn't yielded as previous years and the stores in Gana were getting low. It was viable. More than viable, it was true. But it wasn't the purpose of Leadon's journey.

The pace of the city had changed since her earlier visit. Women bustled, smiling, eyes curled upward.

Relief? The end of the workday?

They scattered but everyone was heading in one direction: the central square. Several thousand could fit in the square, and even more in the adjacent parks where the screens broadcast the fortress' balcony. The screens were already alive, alit with the image of the balcony, still empty.

"Watch your step," Lea heard a woman say.

"Sorry, sorry," the voice was low.

A man.

Leadon sought him out but couldn't see him in the crowd.

A man. Another man. So few left and yet here there were more than she'd ever seen in Gana. Her whole life there had only been one man who came, the one called Archer. When he had come, it was always brief. And it was only ever to see Aria.

"Come, children, quickly now. Queen Ariane will be up on that balcony soon."

"I hope she's wearing the robe she wore last week. I love how it captures the sunlight."

"I hope she sees me."

"She can't see you, stupid, there are thousands and thousands of people coming."

"Don't you know, *stupid,* she sees everyone, all the time."

"Not all the time."

"Yes, *all* the time."

"Quiet!" the housemother walked over to the two girls who'd been talking. "You watch your mouths now. We're almost there."

Leadon looked up from the entry of the main square, the fortress rising high in front of her, Central Tower rising high behind her, and she suddenly felt claustrophobic. Women pushed to advance, hardly seeming to notice that she didn't belong. They were almost trance-like in their approach, pushing, moving forward, advancing. Leadon closed her eyes for a moment and tried not to lose her balance as others came and pushed, twisting her so they could pass. She inhaled deeply through her nostrils, letting the air filled with the smell of bodies sink deep into her lungs. She opened her eyes and set them on the balcony. She joined the women, advancing, moving closer, having to get the best view possible of Aria.

She's Queen Ariane here. I must burn that into my mind. She's no longer Aria in this place.

The screens on three sides of the square made a prism of the balcony. Leadon looked up, eyes locked, waiting to see her emerge.

The crowd hushed. The time had just ticked three in the afternoon.

Every eye turned to the balcony and waited.

Leadon felt paralyzed. She held her breath.

The left door of the balcony opened, then the right.

The Queen stepped onto the balcony and lifted, at the speed of a drifting feather, her arms towards the sky.

The crowd burst.

"Queen Ariane!"

"Long live the Queen!"

"Hahlah! Queen Ariane!"

Leadon broke into a wide smile at the sight of her and waved from her crushed spot in the middle of the square, "Aria! Aria! Queen Ariane!"

The Queen started at the south edge of the square, running her eyes across the crowd and the people settled, an occasional whistle and some clapping as it slowed back into quiet.

Look at me, Aria. Rest your eyes on me. How good it is to see you. See me, Aria, see me -

The Queen's eyes reached the center of the square and Leadon gasped, her breath punched out of her. The Queen scanned the middle of the crowd, up and down, seeing Leadon, and nodding in her direction, but it was a nod of greeting.

Not of friendship.

Leadon saw it immediately, and she couldn't breathe. She was drowning in the crowd and couldn't will her lungs to open.

The Queen's eyes, green.

Her skin, smooth.

Her gaze, proud and aloof.

It's not Aria. It's not Aria.

The Queen isn't Aria.

Queen Ariane isn't Aria.

She couldn't move. Leadon knew if she tried to leave, she'd be caught out and questioned and she couldn't have that now. She had to stand and wait it out. Dead still, dead eyes. She had to hold the terror inside. It grew like a fireball from the center of her chest.

She listened without hearing, desperate for the time to pass. Desperate to escape.

The Queen's words slide off her like oil on rubber, Leadon made herself a vessel, empty. She didn't hear the announcements, only vaguely aware of the pronouncements of success by Central Tower, overcoming hardship, binding together as a society.

Applause. It was over. Leadon made her hands hit each other, her eyes vacant, pointed up at the imposter.

The minute the crowd broke, Leadon was running. She ran to the mule and hopped on, desperate to think, desperate to understand how any of this was possible. Her childhood friend, gone for five years, gone to rule their nation, gone to lead them through the next generations.

And yet it wasn't her.

The mule took step after steady step as Leadon sought the words to tell Batrasa.

The Queen is not who she's supposed to be. The Queen is not Queen Ariane. Aria. What's happened to Aria? What is happening to Lower Earth?

She rode the mule back to Gana pausing only for a short rest at the checkpoint.

This couldn't wait. Batrasa had to know.

This would change everything.

3

Irene's eyes closed. Her hand clasped her long braid, pulling it forward and wrapping it under her the fold of her arm. She inhaled, letting the cool fortress air calm her. When she opened them again, the Queen was leaning on the armrest of her velvet desk chair, head cocked, staring at Irene. And she did not look amused.

"Are you finished?"

"I was just thinking."

Queen Ariane sat back in the chair, tensing her lips. "You've been distracted, Irene. I want to know why."

"There isn't a particular reason." Irene sighed, "Trying to assess the landscape. The unrest in the Dark Counties has been weighing on me."

"Because of the boy disappearance? That was just an inciting event. There's been an undercurrent there for some time."

"Exactly. We knew the boy birth was coming at the time, has it been seven years already? They should have been elated to host the child. And they weren't. Why? They should have felt honor and pride. It should have been the moment we saw a turn for the better up there. And we didn't. And then the disappearance... and now the riots..."

"Likely the boy died. That could be sufficient enough explanation."

"No, I don't think so. If he'd died, they wouldn't have been ashamed to say it. That would have played into the bigger narrative very well. And we both know he shouldn't have died naturally."

The boy had the code of Kings past running through him. He wouldn't have degraded like the others.

Irene's mind circled around and around on it. More than a year had gone by since the boy had vanished, and it hadn't been the will of the Guard. Only the Guard was sanctioned to see people disappeared.

Someone took the boy. Or else someone killed him.

It ran shivers down Irene's spine. If someone killed the boy, then they had wrongly assessed the values of those living in the Dark Counties. And Irene hated to be wrong.

Now they'd have to see another boy born, somewhere, as the Directive demanded the King's line continue. They had to study his behavior, read his nature.

And make sure that men like him never ruled again.

The Queen stood. "So you're concerned still about the boy disappearance. Riots in the Dark Counties. What else?"

"What else what?"

The Queen raised her chin, "You haven't mentioned Gana. Given all the change underway there, I am surprised you wouldn't bring the subject to me."

"It'll be a complicated period. But Gana has lived through worse. Transition of leadership is not the greatest cause for alarm. Not to them."

"You might be out of touch."

Irene grimaced. "Out of touch? With my people? No."

"Then why was your double in the crowd today?"

"Leadon? She was here?" Irene couldn't hide her surprise. That made no sense. Leadon would be the last one Batrasa would send to Geb. From the beginning, Batrasa didn't trust Leadon for the mere fact of her birth as a genetic duplicate. Never mind that Irene and Batrasa had their own - complicated - relationship. Ever since Batrasa had called her a watered-down sellout for having taken up the role at the fortress, Irene didn't much care to interact with her.

"So Leadon didn't come to see you." The Queen's eyes were evaluating her, Irene could feel it.

"Of course not, I would have told you."

"And you didn't see her."

"Had I seen her, I would have sought her out for an explanation. And then, again, I would have told you."

"Seems there's much you would have told me."

Irene didn't know how to respond. Five years she'd been in this Queen's charge and she still didn't know how to read her.

When Maeva had been Queen, they'd been more like sisters, even if Maeva had been given to moments of authoritarian rule. Still, they'd always had a rich relationship.

But this Queen was not her sister. This Queen was her master.

Queen Ariane inhaled deeply through her nose and squinted her eyes at Irene.

"You'll go to Gana. On your way, you'll prepare ideas for cleaning up Cork Town. That commune has caused nothing but trouble while sucking away at resources. The Guard must be a combination of subtle and strict. I'm tired of shoddy implementation. On your return, I'll hear your ideas and we will make an appropriate plan. Assuming you have heeded my instructions." Ariane walked to Irene. While she did not reach Irene's height, Irene could tell that the Queen was more assured than she could ever be. Her whole life, Irene had believed she was the one with nothing to lose. But looking at Ariane, her own resolve shrunk.

Irene had never considered herself a citizen of Lower Earth. Gana was her land. But under Maeva's reign, she had changed. The lava amulet hanging around her neck had at first felt like a noose. Now she felt vulnerable without it, though she only removed it to sleep.

Which made this Queen's approach all the more difficult to swallow.

"Before I go, I want to be sure I've understood these instructions for Cork Town. What is it exactly you want done with these people?"

"Cull the population."

"Ariane - "

A voice came from the other side of the door as it creaked open a sliver.

"Enter."

Maeva stepped into the room, spine tall, but Irene saw the circles under her eyes.

"What is it, Mother? I'm preparing the Commandante for a mission."

"A mission. What mission is this?"

"The Cork Town culling."

"I see." Maeva turned to leave and stopped. "I thought you'd abandoned the idea. I thought we'd discussed it - "

"Circumstances have changed. Resources are being depleted. And we're propping up a population who never should have been born in the first place. Under *your* reign." Neither Maeva nor Ariane moved. Irene looked between the two of them. Such perfection, the people had been promised. Perfect Queens, naturally-born Queens. The DNA of the ages.

How little the people saw.

"Irene," the Queen looked to her, not dismissing Maeva away, "You'll start with any men who meet the selection criteria. There's already enough suspicion for their removal without much concern. Then the opies. Those women have been the bane of our society for a generation now. Haven't they, Mother?"

"Indeed."

"And why is it that we still face their destructive ways today? How is it that you couldn't erase this stain on our society?"

"Addiction is powerful, especially among those who've been cast - "

"Enough. Irene, the opies are next, particularly the dealers. Make it clear why. The good people of Geb will be glad to see them go."

"Yes, Queen."

"Then those who are already in advanced stages of degradation."

"Sorry?"

"That's right. Their deaths are imminent. We will save them from the pain, the humiliation. We will provide them with a dignified departure."

"You want me to round up the ill like cattle, and then slaughter them like dogs?"

"Your imagination is full with righteousness. Cast yourself in my role for a moment." Queen Ariane came nose to nose with Irene, leaning forward so her lips grazed Irene's ear. The hot breath ran a shiver down Irene's body. Her skin stood on edge. "We do not have enough to sustain everyone. The viruses in the fields are out of control. There will be death; it is inevitable. Do you kill the healthy women who have built our society from the ground up? Or do you escort the dying through a sacred rite to the afterlife? Cork Town bleeds our resources and in return for what? Drug-infused transgression? Backroom men who plot against those who try to keep them alive? They take and take, and we have little left to give. Their selfishness is insufferable. You will bring balance again; it is no more philosophical or political than that. Cork Town is where we must start."

The Queen stepped away, her breath stroking Irene's face as she passed.

Irene looked to Maeva who stood by the door, giving nothing away with her eyes. But Irene had known Maeva for thirty years.

She would not take the execution of Cork Town lightly.

"Off you go to Gana. Sort your people out. We'll discuss this when you return. You're both dismissed."

Maeva stepped forward, "Ariane - "

"I said, dismissed."

Maeva and Irene locked eyes and walked out in silence together.

They reached the east wing of the fortress before either of them dared to speak. Maeva opened her lips, though no sound came out.

"Maeva - "

"We cannot speak of it."

"But we - "

"Not a word. Too many ears. Hers especially. Go to Gana, Irene. Go with my blessing."

"Maeva - "

"Go."

Maeva turned and walked back towards the center of the fortress, but Irene saw the hunch in her back. From Maeva to Ariane, the contrasts were stark. The former Queen who only ever stood tall now lived in the shadow of her perfected genetic self. Irene felt the dread of all she was coming against, but she pushed it away.

She had to prepare for the trip to her homeland.

4

————

Maeva opened her eyes with the sound of the flute on the screen. Sleep. She had been sleeping again. She still wasn't accustomed to the sensation of awakening having lost hours where she could not recount all that had taken place. The dislocation, the shock of awakening. The gasp for air as she moved from one world of night to the next of day.

I will never get used to this. Not before I die. Since when did I have to sleep?

She rubbed her temples as the voices rumbled warning within her. They had become agitated of late, especially on her awakening in the morning. It was as if they too knew that she was going through a most unnatural transition. Sleep wasn't meant for their blood, the blood of Queens, and their ever-present voices in her veins. Sleep and unconsciousness were foreign. It had been designed out of their genetic code generations earlier. A simple way to readjust for the dangers of the modern world. Maeva used to close her eyes and await sunrise, her body and mind regenerating while alert.

Now she slept.

She walked to the window of the Queen Mother room.

Another thing she wouldn't get used to. She missed her quarters. The Queen's quarters. Missed the sunlight that rose from behind Central Tower. She was too low in the fortress now to see it before it was high in the sky. How she'd loved to walk in the morning in cold crisp darkness, the air brushing her skin with the nip of autumn and how she'd sat at that desk, that beautiful desk from the first settlers of Geb. How she'd pored over those files. The green files. The delivered files. The files which spoke of the future of Lower Earth.

The Ariane files.

Four files on her desk. Weekly they had arrived. How she'd obsessed over them, the decision looming, four files for four future queens, each with her perfect code, advanced code. Only their circumstances divided them. Each one extreme. Each one intended to bring the true next Queen into the light. And it was Maeva who'd had the duty to make the selection. The culling.

Apt that Ariane should call this Cork Town business a culling. She knows too well what goes with the word.

A cough rose from deep within her. She hurtled forward, the force of it knocking the wind out of her. She rested against the wall and coughed into her arms hoping the waiting women wouldn't hear. She hated their doting as if she was an ancient relic that might break.

When she regained her breath she stood straight and closed her eyes. There was a sensation on her arm. She looked down at it.

Blood.

She walked briskly to the washroom and rinsed it off. She didn't dare to use a towel lest the cleaning woman should see and report it. There was no room for weakness in Maeva. Not with her Daughter Queen tracking her every move. Queen Ariane thought her spies were shrewd, but no woman in Lower Earth could track Maeva without her knowing.

In some ways, Queen Ariane is still a child. A powerful, dangerous child.

A child, now twenty-three, now holding Lower Earth under her scepter. A Queen with no patience for substandard. No curiosity for the improbable. No love for the underdog.

Maeva wasn't sure she had love in her at all.

Certainly, the new Queen had passion, righteousness, even benevolence.

But love?

She hadn't demanded that Lucius code it in. He asked and she'd refused. She had been demanding indeed, but it was the needs of the times that had been foremost in her mind. That had been an era of intense fear, the threat of war was on their horizon, just off their shores – so it had seemed.

So it had seemed, and yet, never come to be.

And now this Cork Town culling? Culling. She might as well call it by its true name. A massacre. An organized and Royally-sanctioned massacre.

Hadn't Maeva demanded that the residents of Cork Town be secluded for their own safety? Hadn't that been her goal at the time? Hadn't the crime and accusations reached such a height that separation was the best option for everyone?

Maeva wasn't sure anymore.

My memory is tainted with the colors I've painted on them. How can I trust my memories when I was so diligent to remember them in my favor?

A knock on the door yanked her out of her thoughts.

"What?"

The door opened, revealing Maeva nude in the middle of the room.

"I'm sorry, your highness," the woman cast her eyes to the floor. "The Queen seeks your company."

"I find that hard to believe." Ariane might have been seeking her, but certainly not for her company.

"Madame, I promise, she's sent for you."

Maeva wafted her hand. "Yes, yes. I'll come. First, I'll dress. Wouldn't you agree?"

"Yes, madam. My apologies."

"Off with you, then."

The woman nodded, not lifting her eyes from the ground and backed out of the room.

This blasted tiny room. It suited Lucius better.

Maeva looked at herself in the full-length mirror. Her skin had only just begun to hang a little heavier on her. For her sixty-seven years, she remained in the condition of a forty-year-old normal design. Perhaps she was even younger if her physical training were tested.

But there were circles under her eyes. Hard-won circles, which Maeva read as the past five years of her life taking vengeance.

So many companions lost. Do I even have the right to call them that? I dare not call them friends. Much less the concept of family. But indeed, they all took a part of me with them to death. A part of me is dead already.

She inhaled at her reflection, her ribs extending, each bone catching the light. She swallowed hard at the sight, which reminded her of a prisoner's emaciated corpse and not a Queen's temple.

From across the fortress, the voice of Queen Ariane struck her; she still was not used to it after five years of commands. The voice of her Queen Daughter spoke in tones only she could hear.

"Come, Mother."

Calling, commanding, though the voice didn't speak above a whisper.

Maeva used to speak like that with Aria, across the Ganese fields. She didn't have to come any closer than that, and Aria would hear her coming. They spoke across the distance, their ears able to hear for a three-mile radius.

"Come now, Mother. Don't make me wait."

Queen Ariane had those same abilities, but there was never any conversation. Maeva was to wait until she was called. The communication was only ever to be one-way.

Maeva cast a disgusted look to herself and dressed faster than she cared to, all to meet the demands of the daughter she had selected herself for the throne.

"You take your time, don't you, Mother."

"I was not yet dressed."

"You were sleeping again."

"It is part of my evolution."

Ariane turned away from her, "An unfortunate part indeed. Your degradation will likely accelerate soon."

"Why would you say that?" It was the first time Ariane had brought up the subject of Maeva's degradation, a subject for which Maeva had been preparing for some time. But it caught her off-guard. There was no reason for that to be of concern, not with everything else happening in Lower Earth right now.

Ariane's eyes softened. "I've upset you."

"Not upset, no."

"What then?"

"Surprised me."

Ariane smiled, "I always thought it was impossible to surprise you. Growing up with the carers, it seemed you always knew before I did. Anticipated my move before I'd decided to make it."

"You were young. You were predictable."

"And now?"

Maeva chose her words carefully. "Now you are burdened with the future of our nation. You must run the scenarios and probabilities at a rate greater than I ever could have. It was what I designed you for – "

"You take the credit for my abilities?"

"Only for the genes that allow you to do as you do."

"And the rest?"

"There's a reason why I chose you, Ariane. Why you are now Queen, and not the others. If I cannot have faith in that decision, which was my decision alone, then I cannot have faith in my own existence. That decision will be the hallmark of my life."

"That decision, you call it."

"What do you call it?"

Ariane pursed her lips, her eyes looked into the rafters.

"I call it as you called it."

Maeva felt her heartbeat increase.

Ariane's eyes settled on Maeva. "The culling. You culled us, didn't you, Mother."

"If you ask closed-ended questions, I'll give you no satisfaction of a response."

Ariane walked toward the window. "You may wield what little power you have left. I already know the answer." Ariane touched the window with her fingertips. The heat of them made four fogged discs on the glass. "Have I lived up to your expectations, Mother?"

"You've exceeded them, Daughter."

Ariane looked back to Maeva, her head cocked to one side. "I can't be sure if you're sincere or cynical. But I suppose it doesn't make a difference anyway."

Maeva inhaled deeply. She listened carefully, the voices inside her whispered sounds, questions, signals of belief. "What is happening, Ariane? We have more walls between us now than five years ago when the worst of it took place. We were there together, you recall. We lived through your trials into coronation together. Why do we now have this distance between us?"

Ariane looked through Maeva, to somewhere far beyond

the fortress walls. She stayed there for a long time. Maeva waited. Ariane was on a journey. Maeva knew the voices were alive in her, more than any of the other daughters, possibly more than Maeva herself. She'd witnessed their carnage in the middle of dark nights when Ariane ran to the forest and on to Rainfields. Rainfields called them all back eventually. Meanwhile, the people slept, all unaware of their Queen's great flaw.

Maeva knew it too well.

It was the curse of an incubation birth; Maeva had known it would be when she first told Lucius the plan. He'd known the consequences too, but he didn't dare cross her then. He'd seen how far gone she was. And it had been his fault. He knew it. He knew it was his fault, and he knew he had to do the incubation birth, and he knew the child would be as affected by the voices or more. Such were the gambles they'd both made.

Those stakes played out in front of Maeva's eyes as she watched Ariane's eyes twitch with it. Reflections of the Queens past, all that was coded into her.

The sequence of Queens takes its course. Not one of us is exempt from its effects. None, except perhaps the first... Rose...

Maeva physically shook the thought away, not allowing her to take it any further. Ariane saw it and came back into the present moment.

"Come, Mother. Let's walk."

Ariane took Maeva's arm as she used to do in the days when she was first announced. In spite of herself, Maeva felt her shoulders relax and her heart calm. This was how it was always supposed to be.

They walked together in silence to the main gate of the fortress, out into the Geb City Square. It was relatively quiet. A morning soup seller in the corner and a small group of children taking lessons on the south side. Ariane led her towards Central Tower.

"How would you advise me, Mother?" Ariane asking, looking straight ahead toward the Tower.

Maeva thought carefully, her words would either grow their closeness or push Ariane even further. She had to start with something safe, something even expected. She could not jump straight to Cork Town; it would fall on deaf ears. Maeva knew it too well; she would have been the same.

In fact, she had been the same. When she'd been Queen.

Maeva started, "The Tuesday Briefings I used to give provided consistency for the people. They could rely on information and communion with their Queen at a specified time and place. The practice is outdated on some level, but on another, it is a tried and tested method for –"

"The Tuesday Briefing? I invite you to give me any advice on any subject, and that is your great counsel?"

"It is a starting point."

"A starting point for what? You had nearly forty years of reign. And Tuesday Briefings is what comes to mind? What about the scouts? What about the deviants? What about the traitors living within our own walls? Need I mention Archer, that dreaded code of kings? How close you came to complete failure because of a man, and not just any man, but the man you *knew* was designed to overthrow us?"

"He wasn't designed to overthrow. It was well within our scope of control. It had been from the time the Directive –"

"Don't throw these antediluvian Directives at me. They are as good as the wood chips on which those Queens wrote them. They are crude, and you know it as well as I. You bought into an ideology to which I cannot ascribe Mother."

I am offending her; she's right to be offended. She saw right through me. I must not try to outwit her. She sniffs it out like a lion to the deer.

"You are right, Daughter."

Ariane's head tilted, but she did not speak.

"Let me come right to the point. My advice is this: Listen

to the people. Listen to what they don't say. There is much unrest across this country now. The shortages have exacerbated it again, they always do. But if you hear what they don't say, and then speak it back to them in terms which show your solidarity, then you will find fierce loyalty even in the places where they have the greatest suffering."

Ariane re-took Maeva's arm and guided her again into a slow walk before Central Tower.

"This is worthy advice, Mother. Thank you."

Maeva nodded.

"I shall heed your advice."

Maeva smiled involuntarily.

"You shall go to the outer counties."

Maeva stopped, released Ariane's arm, and looking her in the eye. "Me?"

Ariane smiled. "It makes perfect sense. You have this experience. You are my most loyal subject, are you not?"

Subject.

Maeva felt the voices scratching at her throat.

"Of course, I am."

"Then you are best positioned for this most important act. You shall leave in three days' time; that's plenty to prepare. We'll make sure you have everything you need. I believe a voyage of three months should be sufficient, don't you?"

She's sending me away so that she can clear out Cork Town in peace.

Maeva saw the strategy in Ariane's eyes, and recognized it. The vision of her so clearly Maeva's own reflection.

Ariane placed her hand on Maeva's cheek.

"These are difficult times, Mother. Your act of loyalty will not be forgotten. Indeed, it may be the very spark the people need to light the fire of devotion in them again." Ariane brought her hand to the lava amulet around Maeva's neck. "They must remember where they came from. That we all landed on this rock, and that it's the Royalty who breathed life when they were all but extinct.

Maeva called on all her resources not to speak the words that were screaming inside her brain. She calmed her blood and brought her focus to a laser point in Ariane's eyes.

"Indeed, Daughter."

"You'll call me Queen on your travels."

"Of course, my Queen."

Ariane smiled but not with her eyes.

Maeva inhaled deeply to crush the rising anger. "I'll go prepare."

Ariane nodded in what Maeva understood was a dismissal. She left Ariane in the square, restraining her steps so they did not betray her emotion as the voices clawed at her veins.

5

———

Roman rubbed his forehead, the skin pulled forward and folded on itself. He'd become thinner since the incubation program had been in place. Anxiety. When he sat on a hard surface, he felt it through to his bones. He was into his fifties, without the signs of degradation that his contemporaries had shown at his age. But he didn't dare rely on that. He'd long ago learned now to count on anything. It could come any day for him; it didn't have to be a drawn-out process the way it had been for Isaac, or still was for Lucius. One day to the next, it could begin.

The fact that he was losing weight, despite it being for a side effect of lack of sleep and a tendency to skip meals, was actually a good sign. No one degraded by withering away. No, degradation was accompanied by muscle breakdown to fat. Obesity was the most powerful, visible indicator.

Roman looked down, remarking how his clothes hung on him as though he were made of sticks, and resolved to improve his nutrition.

Sunlight streamed into his office on the nineteenth floor of

Central Tower. He pulled down the shades and then went back to the report of the recent incubation program.

The figures before him made no sense.

The sequence they'd used was tried and true. They'd implemented it in phases, using best practices only, not taking any risks.

And yet there he was, staring five years of effort in the face, inching towards some kind of failure.

He stood up and paced the floor, rubbing the lava amulet around his neck. He used to believe that just touching it would channel some of the power of the settlers. But now that he was the Great Geneticist, nothing seemed to help. His office spanned the entire width of Central Tower, a quarter of the nineteenth floor.

Roman let out an ironic laugh.

Great Geneticist. I've been borrowing a title that never should have been mine.

It had seemed logical at the time when the new Queen had offered it to him. He'd occupied Lucius' office for many years by the time the Ariane instated him at the head of the Tower. He'd demonstrated his skill, his management, his loyalty. And he'd done it many times over. To his rational mind, the title came with the job description. Except for what he now saw was his greatest flaw. He walked to the small mirror near the door and saw the circles under his eyes that had developed in the past few years.

I'm not good enough.

He didn't hold a candle to Lucius. Lucius, stripped of the title or not, was even in his absence still the greater scientist. Roman returned to his desk, trying to channel some of the Great Geneticist energy at it.

Give me just a tenth of Lucius's skill. Is it even skill? It's as though he was born with it.

Roman paused.

Maybe he was born with it.

That would certainly explain it. Though he had no reason to believe Lucius had been designed from anything more than the common code of Man.

The reports continued to swim in front of his eyes. They'd used the strongest sequence they had for the incubation program. The best balance between intellect, physical endurance, and longevity. They'd applied everything he knew from their documentation on past incubation programs, limited though it was. There didn't seem to be anything exceptional about their newest efforts of implementation: a change of device, modification for first days' security. Feeding, comfort, and milestone monitors. The fetuses had all been born healthy in their glass wombs.

Everything had been done as it should have been done. Roman was a stickler for project management. The embryos developed as normal; became physically adept as expected. They'd met every critical development milestone.

And then it all fell apart. There had to be a solution for it; they'd adapted the sequence in small adjustments as necessary during the period between phases. They'd built that into their planning. Perfection in the first phases of implementation was unrealistic, but the results they saw now were unexpected. And alarming. The incubates, all female, simply weren't behaving the same as girls born through the Willing Woman program. They were insolent. Caustic. Rebellious. And they weren't yet five years old.

Unexpected, the report says. I can't stand unexpected. This whole incubation program has been designed for regular, ongoing, evolution. Not the unexpected.

A knock on the door caught Roman by surprise. He needed to focus before his briefing with the Queen.

"What? I made it clear I didn't want interruptions!"

"Sir?" Carole popped her head in the door. She was almost

the only person in the Tower who could bring Roman some good news.

"Carole. Fine. Come in. I'm looking at the figures, and I hope to the heavens you've got some way of explaining the behavioral variations."

Carole hugged the folder into her chest and made a sucking sound through her teeth. "I have *a way*. But I don't think it's going to help."

"Just give it to me, I'm exhausted of this. We're on ninth round implementation. What the hell is going on, Carole?"

She walked to his desk, her tight pantsuit making crinkling noises as she walked. Carole was always about practicality. Her hair cut to her shoulders, her nails cut short, her shoes always of the same practical style. She laid the folder on the stack of papers he'd arranged. She opened it, revealing several pie charts that compared the various behavioral markers widely accepted as the new normal.

There was no arguing with it. Fewer than ten percent hit the expected behaviors, despite exceptional cognitive development.

"Damn it, Carole."

"I'm just the messenger."

"Who's seen these?"

"No one."

"Are you sure?"

"Yes."

"How can you be sure?"

"Roman, no one runs these reports but me. They don't even have access to the software. It's safe. I haven't even shown it to Uma."

"Fine, fine." He closed his eyes. "I need to think this through."

Carole waited, but Roman had nothing more to say to her. He opened his eyes and looked down at the charts.

He heard her walking away. "I'll be on the twelfth floor, Cork Town blood processing, if you need me."

He gave a half-nod, keeping his eyes on the comparisons. The door clicked closed and he let out a sigh.

I'm going to have to be straight with the Queen. Give her the details, there's no point in keeping them from her now. We need a strategy that's beyond the bounds of the Tower.

He was relieved that he'd already raised the red flag nearly eighteen months earlier. The Queen appreciated early notification. Queen Ariane listened carefully and asked all the right questions. Roman watched as her eyes would process, ticking left and right before providing direction that was always precisely right for the moment. She exuded calm, remained collected even in the face of difficult news.

So much more reasonable than Maeva had ever been.

Maeva had been committed to results, regardless of the means. She demanded dedication and loyalty, but she didn't seem to understand what they were up against. New instructions would come from out of nowhere from Maeva, and the Tower was expected to do an about-face to meet her unrelenting demands. The incubation program was a perfect example of yet again how she had led him down a rabbit hole. Implementation *en masse* was premature, but she wouldn't hear of it. For her, there was no alternative. Maeva had to have what Maeva wanted. And if that was a massive program of incubation births, without testing, without control groups, without moderate phasing to ensure success – it didn't matter. She had to have it.

And look where that got them.

Thousands. There are thousands of them out there. And most without any sense of ethical barometer to guide them. How do you teach that? If morality isn't infused from the start... Cognitive and physical ability aside – there's no controlling a population who cannot recognize right from wrong.

He closed his eyes.

Maybe we're wrong. Maybe we've misunderstood the behavioral markers.

But he knew in his heart that it wasn't the case. The markers had been designed with pre-Mist inputs. The documentation went far enough back that they didn't have to recreate it from scratch.

If the subjects weren't meeting the behavioral markers now, all predictions were that they never would meet them.

That would create an exceptional problem during a period of military preeminence when they required all women to fall in line to protect Lower Earth against Upper Earth's attack.

And yet that's what they were born for.

Roman let out an audible groan.

What good is an army of rebels? I need the old team. Imagine us all… Lucius, Isaac, Adam, Uma, Carole, and Sara. We could have overcome this. We could have found the keystone in the genetic code.

He walked to the window; activity in the Geb City Square was light. He saw the Queen walking with Maeva nineteen floors below, unmistakable in their robes. He brought his hand back to his forehead, massaging his temples.

Queen and former Queen separated, each taking a different route back into the fortress.

We're only half a team now. Half a team, half the competence, half the success. Half the success is as good as no success at all. If only Lucius would hear me out —

He quit the thought. Lucius would never hear him out. Not again. Not after the "culling". Lucius had sent every message back unanswered, the closest thing to a slap in the face the newly appointed Great Geneticist would have.

Great Geneticist. I suppose there's no title for Mediocre Geneticist. I'm a manager, damn it. Hadn't I done well as the Primary Overseer of Central Tower? The keeper of the Great Geneticist, without taking the title myself? Expectations were realistic then. No one looked to me for a break-

through. If I can make it through this life and keep the title of "Great" until my degradation begins, I'll be the first one to admit surprise.

Mary's voice rang out on the screen, "Good afternoon, people of Geb! I bring a warning today of incoming inclement weather, so bring preparations - "

He glanced up at the clock, his throat tightening. He gathered up the charts and files, careful not to drop a page in the mass. The Queen would be waiting for him. He hated to keep the Queen waiting as much as she hated to wait.

6

Leadon hugged her knees into her chest, willing the river to swallow her up for a while.

Just until this madness has passed.

Three days had gone by since Leadon gave the news, the dreadful, shocking news to Batrasa. She'd prepared all her words in advance, knowing that this could be the last push to put Batrasa over the edge to the afterlife. Leadon didn't have any gift of life-giving. Not like Aria. Aria had understood the body so well, heard its inner workings. What a miracle when she'd saved Priyantha, everyone had borne witness to it.

Aria. Poor, abandoned Aria.

Batrasa had sat back against the hut wall as Lea recounted the story of all she'd seen in Geb. The imposter standing in Aria's place.

Batrasa had nodded, Lea had thought she was in some kind of shock, but when she'd spoken her words were measured and calm.

"You had to see it for yourself, my child. I'm sorry that this was how you learned of it, but there would have been no better way."

It didn't make sense.

Batrasa knew? How did she know?

"Let me explain."

The others in Gana didn't know. No one else had ever been close enough to Aria to recognize any difference, and those who were allowed to Geb at all certainly knew nothing of Aria's disappearance.

Disappeared. Aria. How much better she deserved than that.

Leadon took in the sight of the river. Blessed river. How many times had she spied on Aria as she sat by the river, her fingers in the currents, closing her eyes, interpreting them? The memory was so real, Leadon thought if she closed her eyes, she could reach out and touch her. Though she never would have. Even when Aria had been there, to disrupt her was to leash an angel in flight.

A thick raindrop landed on Leadon's hand. She let it come down on her, light at first, a gentle layer coating her skin. It intensified, the sky growing darker. Clouds swirled overhead in the growing wind, and Leadon watched as the wall of storm arrived upon her. She inhaled the smell of dust becoming mud, of leaves drinking, and the river hurrying against the banks. The rapids grew, and Lea had half a thought to move away, as the river was known to build to a roaring rush when the autumn flash storms came.

With regret, she stood and slowly walked with drenched heavy steps back to the village. She entered the warming hut to find ten or so other women there who'd come from the fields and forest having gotten caught in the rain themselves. All conversation stopped when they saw Leadon enter. They stood silent before the crackling fire, the rain beating down on the hut's roof around them.

"She can't wait much longer," a woman across the fire said in whispers to the woman beside her.

"Batrasa always does everything in her own time. There's

no point in fighting it," the other woman didn't move her eyes from the flames. "She'll do it when she does it and not sooner."

"She must be aware of our restlessness. You'd think she'd be more aware of our needs."

"Needs?" Another woman joined the conversation. "What do we need? We have everything. It's better she waits for the right moment, the right inspiration. We have no idea what's going on in her head."

The flap of the hut entry flew open and a gust of wind blew Lea's hair into her face. Priyantha came in, dripping.

"Hello," she said, nodding her greeting to the group.

"Priyantha," the first woman started, "Can you please help me talk some sense into these women? Do we or do we not need a faster resolution to the question of Chief?"

"How do you intend to speed the process? You know Batrasa."

"That's what I said," the second woman cast a glance in the first woman's direction. "You'll just have to be patient."

"Patient," the first woman shook her head. "You think our Queen is patient? You think she happily waits for her people to decide to admire her? To adore her? To humble themselves at her feet? Of course not. She makes demands and the people respond."

"What do you know about this Queen, really?" Leadon couldn't help but speak up.

"I know that since she left Gana she hasn't given us a second thought. Look how we struggle for basic supplies."

"That's the situation in the whole of Lower Earth, we're no exception." Leadon held back, uncertain of how much to say.

"And not a passing thought for us. She does as she pleases, rules as she pleases. It's time *we* ruled as we please. Our people have been here since before these so-called settlers. And don't you all look at me like that. You know it and you feel it, too. Priyantha?"

"You're not wrong – "

"And yet we're still dogs at her feet, begging for the slightest affection."

Leadon inhaled deeply, watching her words. Thunder clapped not far from their hut. "Aria was once with us, yes. Don't I know it better than anyone? Weren't she and I the most ostracized among you? Didn't you look at her and I, and see nothing more than strangeness in our blood? You said she didn't belong, she who was to be Queen – what insight did you have then? You thought she was an anomaly and you made her unwelcome, and yet look what she has gone on to do. She even resolved the latest wheat parasite that we saw in our own fields," Leadon fought with her conscience, knowing the Queen was ultimately not the Aria they knew, but she couldn't breathe that here. Not now. That would be too much fodder to their embers. The fire would blast Gana into civil war.

Leadon didn't know how she knew, but she knew.

And if they were to take on such a civil war, it couldn't be now. They still had so little information on their enemy.

Ariane, the enemy. How the world has changed before my eyes.

"For a replica, you have a lot of fine words," the woman said, "Who planted them there? Hmmm?" The woman walked around the fire to Leadon. "What treachery lurks behind those borrowed eyes?"

"What do you know? I've been here my whole life, as true a Ganese as you, and you know nothing more of me than the surface, you barely look beyond my skin. You've seen nothing of my heart."

"Can a replica have a heart? Or does it beat for the fortress, like your two-faced sister-mother-double self?"

"Ahnira, you're going too far," the second woman came around the fire.

Leadon didn't avert her eyes. "My heart is true. I have been breathing this air, the air of our ancestors, speaking the old rites and living in their midst longer than you have."

"You live with borrowed blood."

"My blood is Ganese."

"Your blood is false."

Priyantha stepped forward, "You may think you speak with common words, Ahnira, but you are crossing a line now."

"I say what all of you say behind her back."

"You say what you say without wisdom or restraint."

"You change your tune now? You're as false as she is."

"No," Priyantha turned to Leadon, "I can admit I was wrong."

Leadon blinked. She didn't know what to say.

"As was I. I was wrong," another woman joined.

"And I."

Priyantha crossed her arms over her chest in the way of the ancestors and bowed her head. "Leadon, I ask forgiveness. It was not until tonight I've heard my own words in another's mouth. I never before understood the venom in them. But we are Ganese, and these times are too trying for us crack down the middle. I will admit my wrong and fight to keep Gana as one."

Leadon stood, wordless. Three other women followed Priyantha, crossing their arms and lowering their heads.

"Not me," Ahnira leaned forward. "I regret nothing. I speak only what I see before me. I see a phantom, a fraud, a mistake." She walked out of the hut, two women following behind her.

The heads of the remaining women lifted. Leadon, in return, crossed her arms and bowed, accepting their humility and offering it back.

"These are trying times, Leadon," Priyantha let her hair down to dry, the length of it reaching to her waist, black as the night sky. "We must find ways to mend within Gana if we are to ever defeat that which is without."

Leadon lifted her arm, outstretched, and laid it on Priyantha's shoulder. "There is much to defeat out there. Perhaps as far as Upper Earth or as near as the Free Route to Geb."

Priyantha cocked her head, "I always thought you would be a defender of the Queen, we all did," the women in the hut nodded, "Your relationship to the Commandante, to Aria – we thought you'd be the first to turn."

Leadon shook her head. "So many things are not as they seem."

Thunder clapped and the hut's curtain again flew open, a gust flashing at the fire and throwing their hair into wild dances as the woman from Batrasa's hut entered.

"Leadon," the woman from Batrasa's hut spoke, "I've been looking for you all over the protectorate. They said you were at the river."

"I was, but the storm began."

The woman wiped the rain off her sleeves. "You are slippery, Leadon. Batrasa seeks you. Has been for hours. Get over there."

Leadon refused to accept the reprimand. A sensation was growing in her, something new and something she'd sought for such a very long time.

Conviction.

"I'll go right away."

LEADON OPENED THE HUT'S COVERING AND AT ONCE WAS overcome with a feeling in her stomach. The air was tense. The fire was out. She couldn't say why but in the flash of a moment, Leadon felt the conviction, of which she'd been so sure, turn fleeting in her stomach. She closed her eyes and inhaled deeply.

A wave of change is heading towards us. Raise your head to meet it, Leadon.

She stepped in deeper, Batrasa standing in full view, but looking to someone who was just out of Leadon's line of sight.

Batrasa turned her head, seeing Leadon, and a gentle smile came over her face.

"So there you are."

"I'm sorry to have kept you waiting, but I wasn't far at all."

"No apologies required. You couldn't have known I wished to see you. But your timing is surprisingly good."

Leadon stepped in further, through the second threshold where a second woman stood inside, to the left. Leadon inhaled sharply, she couldn't hide her surprise.

She was looking the older version of herself in the eye.

"Hello, Leadon." Irene's voice betrayed no emotion.

"Irene." Leadon bowed her head.

She didn't know what to say to the woman who had made no attempt to contact her in over a year. *The* woman, not just any woman. The woman on whom every aspect of Leadon was designed. A sister, a mother, a second self.

I am no replica.

The three women stood in silence. The Keeper of the Chief, the Commandante of Lower Earth, and Leadon.

Keep your conviction, Leadon. You belong here as much as they do. But her courage was waning. She needed someone to speak, but all ceremony required that it not be her.

Leadon looked from Irene to Batrasa and back to Irene, swallowing her questions and convincing herself to wait.

At last, Batrasa spoke, her voice low. "Leadon, Irilena has come at a most unexpected time, and yet I can't help believing there was something divine in it." Batrasa walked to Leadon. "You who wanted to consult the Queen," Leadon felt heat rising up her neck. How foolish she'd been, how little she'd known, "and instead you now have Irene to provide you with the answers I know you so desperately seek."

"From her?" Leadon noted the whine in her voice. Her feelings toward Irene had nothing to do with Aria. She had to keep her hurt at bay. Perhaps Irene had a good reason not to be in contact. Leadon exhaled and allowed her shoulders to relax.

Irene raised an eyebrow but waited for Batrasa to continue.

"Who else is better positioned?" Batrasa walked across the hut and put her hand on Irene's shoulder. "Irilena was there for Aria's birth."

Leadon looked over to Irene whose stance and expression had not changed.

"Few know," Batrasa continued, "of the workings within the fortress. But, Leadon, your curiosity, your insight, and most of all, your courage, has set you apart."

Leadon felt something flutter in her stomach. "Courage? Batrasa, I have only the greatest respect and admiration, and I have many qualities that I hope are becoming of our ancestors, our ways, and our future. But I'm afraid you might be misinformed."

"Misinformed?"

"I make no accusations, forgive me if I have offended."

"You have not offended, but you do assume much. In that way perhaps there is some power of genetics," Batrasa looked to Irene, who cocked her head and tensed her lips. Leadon sensed she was in the middle of a relationship that had more history than she knew.

Batrasa looked back to Leadon. "For example, you assume that I have not been following you, watching you, assessing you. You make a great assumption of your invisibility."

She's noticed me? More than that, she's been watching me? For how long?

Batrasa then came back over and placed her hands on

Leadon's shoulders. "You are not and never have been invisible. You were secluded, at times isolated, but always you were tracked. At first, it was out of fear. We could not be certain of what you would become."

Irene looked at the floor.

"And then," Batrasa tightened her grip on Leadon's shoulders, "and then your uniqueness became apparent. You have all that the ancestors bestowed upon us. You have an awareness of the women in Gana in a way few others have." Batrasa looked to Irene, "A very positive quality you share." She looked back to Leadon, "We are coming to a time when empathy must reign as strongly as the voice for Gana - a voice which honors the people from which we came, and which honors the women we are today. I said it at the full quorum and I'll say it again to you now. We need a Chief who isn't afraid of being herself when every mouth spews anger, resentment, and selfish greed in her direction."

Leadon felt her heart accelerate, the thumping near-deafening, but she remained transfixed, watching and listening to every sound that fell from Batrasa's lips.

"Leadon. You shall be Chief of Gana."

A WOMAN BLEW THE SHELL HORN, THE CALL OF URGENT FULL quorum - one low, one high. Leadon was in a daze. She hardly heard Irene and Batrasa arguing in low tones, hardly felt the warrior priestesses in full ceremonial garb dressing her, hardly felt the cool of the evening air as the dusk turned to night.

Warrior Priestesses, anyone within a half-day walking range, was there. They lined the pathways, the external perimeter, the space between huts.

Lea had tried to object to Batrasa, but only small sounds had emerged from her mouth, "Me? You can't mean me."

"I do."

"Not me."

"You, Leadon. *Because* you don't seek it. Because Gana needs a new position in Lower Earth. And most of all, because you are *you*, Leadon. I know you love this place and our people, our ways, and our history. Leadon, you are brave enough. You just have to believe that."

"What are you doing?" Irene had hissed from the corner.

Batrasa had turned to Irene, her wrinkled hands extending in the Ganese way of imparting wisdom. "Had you stayed, Irilena, it might have been you. But you didn't, and Leadon has qualities even you should learn. I'm not sure you've cared to see them in her before. But you will."

Now, after the hours had passed and the moment had settled in her memory, Leadon's mind was clear. She walked through the crowd warrior priestesses whose faces mixed between shock, elation, and disgust. But to Leadon's surprise, many, even most, of the women smiled as she passed. Gentle smiles, welcoming smiles, warmth, and deference across their faces. Leadon felt an urge to reach out her hands, to touch them, as much to give as to receive, wishing their confidence would infuse into her own skin.

They reached the fire in the center of the village. It burned high. Women lit their torches, the cool night having fallen quickly on them.

Batrasa stood on the small podium that had been placed for her near the fire. A warrior, wearing a mask in the symbol of the ancestors, brought a tray of ash. Leadon stood near Batrasa's waist, the weight of the leathers and fur pulling her toward the earth, the weight of the world on her shoulders. She began to feel it. The weight of all that was happening to her now.

Still, her mind was clear, no thought dared enter. She absorbed each moment. Batrasa dipping her fingers in the ash, the ash shifting, small channels in the wake of her fingers' movements. Some ash lifted into the air, floating in front of the fire, flying into the sky, freely floating in the sky and the fire crackled. Thousands upon thousands surrounded them, the sound of breathing stifled in the crackle of the fire. Lea didn't hear her own breathing but felt the weight of her chest as it lifted against the pelts, and then lowered again. Waves of air in and out as Batrasa lifted her fingers to the moon.

She broke into the chant, the old chant of ages, the sound stinging Leadon's ears, jolting her out of thought. The sound, so honest, so close.

And for her.

The warrior priestesses replied, the echo of the chant, the sign of dedication, commitment, and love for all they stood for.

Batrasa joined the women's voices and together they chanted, voices cutting across and lifting up, Leadon closed her eyes as Batrasa ran the ashes down her forehead, over her eyelids onto her cheeks and sweeping down her jaw.

Batrasa began stamping her feet in the rhythm of the song. Voices slowly died out as feet commenced. Stamping dust and dirt, stamping in the village, through the village, out the village into the perimeter, the lookouts and beyond. In rhythm, thousands of warrior priestesses stamping, demanding, calling the ancestors for their new Chief.

Batrasa stepped down from the podium alone, the large step perilous for her, but the symbol clear. Her time as Keeper passed, the Chief must take the step. The sounds of stamping feet filled Leadon's brain, her heart, her whole being, and in that moment she didn't question.

She knew.

She was the Chief. The sensation lived in the very center of her being. She took in the sounds, the faces, anticipating, the rhythm accelerating, and she kept her mind clear, commanding that her memory capture each split second.

She lifted her foot to the podium, pressed into it and pulled herself high, lifting her hands into the air, toward the sky, to the ancestors past and future to whom she owed her life, and the crowds erupted, stamping calling, whistling, crying out, arms lifted, and mouths opened in joyous sobs.

Gana's new Chief was declared.

As quickly as it had begun, the sounds suctioned into silence.

Two days of mourning for the death of an era passed. The ceremony called for it. Two days in silence, somber and isolated for every warrior priestess.

And then the celebrations would begin.

The women dispersed, those who'd traveled to stay in the temporary tents set up on the outskirts of the village before making their return home at sunrise. The fire was put out with several large buckets of water, the smoke sizzling into the sky. Leadon was now in her period of transition. She too would have two days of mourning for the life she had before. Everything was to be reborn.

Irene stayed close to Leadon. Not a word between them. But even Irene lowered her eyes in deference. Irene had always been as much a believer as any other of the ways of the ancestors; Leadon saw this had not changed during her absence. Irene escorted Leadon to Batrasa's hut, where Leadon would sleep the next two nights before her rule began. She slept on the hay mat in the front part of the hut, leaving Batrasa her privacy of the room behind. Batrasa entered the hut after Leadon, passing her, giving a deep nod of her head, and walked to the back room.

Leadon had just lowered her head to the mat, consumed by the fatigue of what had become the most important day of her life, when Batrasa came back out. She kneeled in front of Leadon, tears streaming down her face. She took Leadon's cheeks in her hands.

Leadon tried to read her eyes, but there was so much

anguish in them, pain, something resembling regret. Leadon leaned her head forward and the old woman did the same, their foreheads touching, the air from their mouths mingling between them. Leadon felt Batrasa's hands fall from her cheeks. She held back a sob without knowing why she felt so sad. Batrasa rose, not looking Leadon in the eyes, and returned to her room. Leadon let her head touch the mat, her eyes fluttered closed, and she was asleep in the same moment.

Shuffling feet, Leadon opened her eyes. The middle of the night. Movement in the hut. Leadon listened. She turned her eyes and saw Batrasa walk out through the curtain into the village.

She knew she shouldn't follow; she should have left the old woman to her ways. Batrasa probably had amends to make in the early morning moonlight. Leadon should have left her that privacy.

But she didn't.

The past day had alit too much in Leadon's heart; she felt a magnet calling her to follow the Keeper of the Chief. She didn't know why, but she heeded its message.

Out into the night, Leadon kept her distance, only the lookouts in place, facing out to Lower Earth, not in to Gana. No voice was allowed to speak this night, no movement in the village. It was the safest of all nights to be out in quiet isolation. Batrasa walked.

Through and out of the village.

To the river and across it at the rope bridge.

Leadon followed.

An hour's walk and they were at the sea's edge. Batrasa removed her shoes and let her feet stand in the small wake of a gentle wave. Her garb floated on the water's surface, swirling around her feet like a cloud.

Batrasa took another step.

Leadon stood between trees on the grassy knoll before the

beach began, the sound of her breath inside the sound of the waves.

Batrasa took another step.

And another.

Leadon watched in passive acceptance as Batrasa took one step after another into the sea, the moonlight washing over the old woman's white hair, until her last step when she disappeared from view entirely.

7

____

C arole crossed her legs and sat back in the chair. In her right hand, she held up the statistics of lodgings for the past four waves of incubation births. In her left was the list of anomaly reports made. She looked from one to the other.

There must be a pattern in it. It can't be as widespread as that.

But all the evidence showed that the behavioral anomalies were in nearly every phase, nearly every sequence, nearly every lodging type, and nearly every career channel.

Carole dropped her hands to her desk with a thud just as a knock came on her door.

"Yes?"

The woman held a large-format envelope in the air, "Another one, Carole."

"Detailed or single input?

"Detailed."

Carole sighed. "Fine. At least we'll get more data points from it." She beckoned with her hand and the woman entered, passing the envelope across the desk.

"Thanks."

The woman nodded and left. Carole stared at the envelope,

not ready to read its contents. When she'd joined the team managing the Willing Woman program nearly fifteen years earlier, she couldn't have imagined that she'd find herself overseeing an essentially anti-Willing Woman program. Incubation births involved no women in the reproductive process at all. In her new role, the only Willing Women she saw were those who took over the infants once they'd reached weaning age. It was a far cry from where she'd started: recruiting women, training women, campaigning for more women. Her heart and soul had been in the Willing Woman program since she was first channeled into genetics in her fifteenth year.

She'd welcomed the challenge five years earlier at the announcement of the incubation program. She'd grown tired of the Willing Woman campaigns, even if she still fundamentally believed in everything it stood for. It was exhausting to start anew with each season as new women came in. Carole grew older, but the Willing Women remained the same age. Always the same. Young.

Some were too young, but the policy had changed over time. Seventeen became acceptable. Carole had told herself that if the Queen had declared it so, then it had merit.

But with age, she became less sure.

When Uma offered her the opportunity to be at the helm of a new approach to sustaining life on Lower Earth, the offer was too good to refuse. She'd always been dedicated to their reproduction and continuity. So what if the means were different?

Now she knew. The means mattered.

I was hasty. And ambitious. And now look where we are. These are the consequences for mass incubation births; they are finally coming to light. So much for glory and fame, more like failure and infamy if we don't turn this around.

She grasped the lava rock dangling from her neck.

Imagine what the settlers would have to say about this.

With that, she tore open the envelope, wanting to get it over with. She scanned the cover page; it read the same as the others she'd received.

Uncharacteristic independence. Depressive episodes. Withdrawal.

Suicidal tendencies.

And all the subjects were five years old. Or younger.

This pattern is beyond all acceptable markers. Suicidal tendencies? They're not even five and they're throwing themselves off bridges, into fires, over cliffs. Something is horribly wrong in the sequence for the suicide rate to pass two in a hundred thousand. And this current rate? It's...

Carole turned the page and dropped the folder on her desk.

Suicidal tendencies in nearly a third of subjects. There's no precedent for this. It's worse than the pre-Mist period.

Carole grabbed the amulet tight enough that it left marks in her palm.

I have to get through to Uma. This isn't sustainable. We'll have a population that offs themselves before Upper Earth even gets here.

She stacked up the reports and marched to Uma's office, pausing before knocking. Uma would be infuriated, but Carole would just have to take the heat. Otherwise, they would lose the very women they were counting on to save Lower Earth when the enemy arrived on their shores.

8

Uma thought back to the blowout in Cork Town the night before.

The beating of the drums.

The bodies, undulating bodies. Faceless, soft bodies. How they rolled into each other. Deviants. Women from the outer counties.

And Uma.

No one would recognize her there. She was unknown, anonymous, nameless.

But the sound of the drum, the smell of sweat and skin, the smoothness of skin with flying hair as bodies danced into the night consumed Uma's memory.

She was sitting at her desk but her body relived each moment of it. The buildup, the tension, the physical *need* to move into, against, and along other bodies…

She caught her breath.

Someone was outside her door.

She turned her eyes back to her desk where the brief for the Queen waited for her. There really wasn't time for the distraction of memories. Otherwise, she'd lose hours in daydreams. Daydreams that were intoxicating.

And forbidden.

The door creaked open. "Uma?"

"Not now. I'm working on the Queen's brief."

"It has to be now."

Uma looked up. Carole had one hand on her hip, the other holding a thick folder.

"Cut the dramatics. What is it?"

"The suicide rate is through the roof."

"Even beyond the second phase births? You know we expected it up until the second phase-"

"Way beyond second phase. We've gone way beyond it now."

Uma rubbed her forehead. "Leave me just those reports which indicate suicidal tendencies or fulfillment, take the rest with you, I don't have time for all those."

Carole entered, laying the thick file on Uma's desk.

"I said, only the suicides - "

"They're all suicides, Uma. All of them."

Uma looked at the folder, thicker than the file on West Field viruses.

"All of them?"

"All of them."

"I see."

But she didn't. It didn't make sense; they'd identified signals in the second phase, they'd adapted for it.

Uma flipped through the pages. "But the adaptations in the second phase -"

"They delayed it. By half a year. No more."

We'd wiped out that whole series of code. There was no other indicator for it. That should have been enough.

"Do you need me for anything else?" Carole asked.

"No, I'll take a closer look and let you know. Actually,

wait." Uma considered whether Carole might have tracked the correlation to the enzyme production, but then she remembered that Carole was only in implementation. She'd have no more insights than anyone else. "Sorry, go ahead."

Carole nodded and closed the door behind her.

Uma stared at the pile of reports.

How can the children want to kill themselves? Where does that impulse come from? We already removed the conflict between the stac1 gene and the malonase enzyme. That should have done it. But it's only delayed it? There's nothing left to remove, no indication.

Uma shook her head; they'd gone through all this before. First phase and second phase. That should have done it. It should have fixed it.

But it hadn't.

And now there was nowhere left to go.

If only Lucius were here. He'd see it. He'd see what we've missed. But Roman will never hear of asking him back.

Uma opened her top drawer and popped a cough drop in her mouth.

He'll have to hear of it. There's no way around this. Even Roman has stretched beyond his limit.

"Miss Uma?"

"What? Who are you?"

"Ma'am, I'm Loala of the fifth line. From the cleaners, I mean, I'm a cleaner."

"Yes, I see that."

The woman straightened her uniform. "Ma'am, we've been waiting for your review."

Uma looked at her watch.

"Damn it."

"Would you prefer I dismissed the cleaners?"

"No, no. I'm coming. Get back to your station."

"Yes, Ma'am. Sorry, Ma'am."

Uma grabbed her clipboard. Her mind was not working as she needed it to. Hundreds of staff would be waiting for her around the Tower, and meanwhile, she was trying to stop a catastrophe.

I've got to find Roman this afternoon. This can't wait.

Uma rushed to the ground floor to start with the Guard assigned to the Tower.

"Hello, Miss Uma, all set here for your review," Luo Gillard lifted a stack of papers onto the counter in Reception. "The entry forms are here for non-cardholders."

"I'm not looking at those today Gillard, I've got limited time. Just hand me the log."

"Oh, alright, Ma'am. I did get them all ready for you though. That's what you usually like, right?"

Uma closed her eyes. The Gillard line remained the most effective in Guard capacity, but Luo missed a few cues.

Someone was getting sloppy in the redesign.

Uma looked at Luo, her large eyes wide and sad, like a twenty-five-year-old massive child. Her shoulders were almost double the width of Uma's, her chest firm and legs thick with muscle.

I do miss Jan Gillard though. Shame she only made it to forty-two years old. We have to balance better. I'll only have just gotten Luo trained up as I want her and then she'll be the next to degrade.

"Usually, yes. But today is not usual." Uma dropped the logs back down. "That'll do. Back to work."

"Yes, Miss Uma. Thank you, Miss Uma."

Uma felt panic rising in her throat.

I'd really don't have time for this.

She opened the door to Logistics; Laure had the women already lined up. Uma nodded and Laure brought over the contingency plans developed over the past month.

"And for the East Fields?"

Laure snapped her fingers and another woman brought

over a file. Uma flipped through it. "Irrigation contamination?"

"We've almost got it under control."

"Like the last time?"

Laure cringed, "No. Not like the last time. We've included additional controls."

"Such as?"

"Tests both at source and in delivery channels. We're dumping the first thousand gallons after each treatment."

"A thousand? That's a bit excessive."

"Unfortunately, not. We've found evidence of the bacteria in the second five hundred gallons which is why we've doubled it."

"Second five hundred. Well, then you're right." Uma closed the folder. "Anything else?"

"Some warning signs from Rainfields, but nothing worthy of reporting yet."

"Such as?"

"Radiation. But thus far it's still within natural levels. Even so, we should track it."

"Yes, fine." Uma looked up at the women, who suddenly each snapped taller. "Where are your amulets?"

The women fumbled to pull out the pendants from under their uniforms, each holding it up in the air.

"Good. Remember. The work you do here is a blessing from the settlers' time. We owe it to all those who came before that we have the lives we have today. Now carry on."

Laure nodded and Uma pushed through the swinging doors into the service hallway. She leaned against the concrete blocks, a sinking feeling growing into a rock in her stomach.

This is such a farce. Review Day. None of this matters. I've got to get this news to Roman.

But then Uma remembered the value of routine, the principles she'd spent the last almost thirty years building. After the complete mess of five years earlier, the crackdown on back-room men and betrayers from their midst, Uma was even more convinced of the need to sustain discipline across the Tower. She was feared and she was respected. The Review Days reinforced it across the staff.

She stretched her arms high and then took the stairs two by two to the next floor.

Sequencing technicians, bioinformaticians, various specialists, she flew through the next five floors without fuss. Opening the heavy service door to the fifth floor, she immediately saw Sara in the hallway.

What's she doing here?

Sara looked up from the paper in her hands and saw Uma. She dropped her hand to her side, a little too quickly, Uma thought.

"Uma." Sara gave a quick nod.

"You're far from your office."

"Just checking in with the lab. They owe me structure on 7531."

"So you make house calls?"

"They don't always prioritize well. I have a deadline."

"Right." Uma gave a quick, inauthentic smile. "In that case, I'm sure I'll see you again back on the sixteenth."

"I'll be there."

Sara turned on her heels and walked away.

Something about her. She says everything right. She never missteps. But there's something about her that I just don't trust.

Uma's instinct had served her well over the years; though when it was wrong it was very, very wrong.

I never saw it coming with Adam. I had thought he was too dedicated to the Male Program, but I never would have guessed he was plotting behind the Queen's back.

Former Queen. I don't know if I'll ever get used to Queen Maeva being former Queen.

Uma continued the review across the lower floors, but only half her mind was in it. She went through the motions, watching the staff startle at her arrival and freeze at her questions.

All was as it should be.

Maybe we haven't been comprehensive with the incubation phases. We need more samples. We'll have to conduct more intrusive analysis if we're going to be able to save any of them.

Uma felt a sense of satisfaction knowing she could bring an action plan to Roman alongside the reports. She tried to stay solution-focused.

If we can identify the outlying features, then perhaps there's a therapy to address it. Perhaps it's only surface after all. We can recalibrate with drugs -

The knot in her stomach started to settle. They were far from a solution, and the drugs would still have to target a specific part of the sequence that they had so far failed to identify. But it wasn't impossible.

She took the stairs, two at a time, gathered up the charts, and headed straight for Roman's office. She took the elevator. It was important that she be seen after a Review Day. That would keep the staff on edge, right where Uma liked them.

9

———

U ma wasn't telling him anything he didn't know already. The concept of further samples was interesting, but they still needed the capability to read what they gathered. And so far they hadn't found a way into the data.

Roman looked over the report. "Have you consulted with Carole?"

"No, but she'll implement as we see fit."

"Still, she may know something about the social arrangements the subjects are in which would affect this plan. Bring her up."

"Fine."

Then again, Carole will botch this up if we're not careful. She's the least subtle of all of them.

"Uma, wait."

Uma turned, an eyebrow raised.

"Bring Sara too."

"Sara? Why?"

"To begin, because I asked you to. But also because she has certain... skills. We will need those skills if we are to move forward with your idea."

"I really don't see - "

"I wasn't asking your opinion."

Uma nodded and stepped out the door.

She may not like it, but Sara will be able to access the children without causing widespread chaos in the Homes. Carole risks throwing the Homes into total disarray. The last thing we need now is a wave of staff transitions. Those housemothers have it hard enough as it is.

Uma opened the door without knocking. Roman knew it was her way of protesting.

She still hasn't gotten over the fact that I used to be her subordinate. But it was her own fault. She's the one who rides the edge a little too closely. I hadn't intended to catch her in Cork Town, but clearly she'd been up to something she shouldn't have.

Roman had thought at the time that it might have been the opie drugs, but more than ten years later she showed none of the telltale signs. Perhaps it had been something else entirely. Whatever it was, it was enough for Uma to lay low and Roman to speed ahead of her in the Tower.

Sara stayed near the door while Carole stepped forward. "I just want to reiterate that the data is clean. We wouldn't have raised this without a thorough secondary review."

"I'm not challenging the data," Roman felt his trousers sliding below his waist. He tightened his belt.

"Good, because it was an intensive effort to - "

"We're not here to discuss data."

Uma cast Carole a look. Carole raised her hands and stepped back.

"We will go with Uma's recommendation."

Uma smiled.

"Carole will prepare the logs. Sara will gather the subjects and conduct the tests."

"Sara?" Carole's jaw dropped.

Uma's eyes narrowed. "What does she know about it?"

Sara stood still, her face didn't change. She stared forward at Roman.

"She has better social skills than both of you combined. Carole, I'm not going to bring up the subject of your previous reconnaissance missions. I've decided. It's Sara."

Uma stepped closer and spoke softly, "I don't think that's a wise choice, Roman. There are others - "

"She has the technical skills. And the ability to keep her mouth shut." He turned to Sara, "Since you left the Male Program, how many social collections have you managed?"

"Three hundred and twelve. Sir."

Roman shrugged. "Obvious choice to me." He walked behind his desk, pulled his belt a notch tighter, and sat down. "Uma, I need this written up for my briefing to the Queen at sixteen hundred. Carole, I gave you your instructions. Sara, pass off your current load to Lab D."

"Yes, sir."

Uma nodded. Carole turned and walked out without another word.

"Sara, stay for a minute."

Uma waited. Roman cocked his head, silently asking what more she wanted. Uma gave that quick smile he so despised and walked out.

Roman looked down again at the charts, the truth only becoming clearer to him.

We're going to have to take this to Lucius.

"Sara," he took a deep inhale through his nose, unsure if she really was the right one for the job. If she were at all arrogant or condescending, Lucius wouldn't put up with her for a minute.

"Yes?"

"What do you know of the previous Great Geneticist?"

He watched Sara's cheeks drop and her eyes widen. A look of both fear and reverence on her face. He sat back in his seat.

Yes, she'll be perfect.

10

─────

I rene listened to every word that Roman muttered in his briefing, but her eyes were glued on Maeva.

"We've been unable to remove whatever characteristic is causing this anomaly. Whatever it is, it's well hidden. We will be able to adapt it, that's no question. But we moved to implementation too early." He took a deep breath. "I can only say that with hindsight. I consider myself responsible."

The young Queen, still only twenty-three years old, listened carefully to Roman's bleak explanations, her face giving nothing away. It was impossible to tell whether she was angry, despairing, or confused.

But Maeva was a different case.

Maeva's lips were in constant but silent movement, speaking to someone or something with every bit of news that Roman gave. Her eyes were wide, and when Roman had said "suicide", Irene thought they might bulge right out of Maeva's head.

Of course, she considers herself responsible. This had been her decision after all. One of her last before handing over the throne.

How much Maeva had changed. When she'd been Queen, any failure was someone else not fulfilling her command. Now that she had no formal role to play, her body had shrunk, her shoulders pulled forward. She could still stand stately and proud, but in the quiet moments, she was a different woman. Irene felt a pang of regret at seeing her this way, though she couldn't identify why. She was the Commandante, dedicated to Lower Earth's well-being, dedicated to the Royalty who led it to prosperity.

Maeva has become my kin.

The thought came as a surprise to her.

Irene hadn't allowed herself to think of kin since she was first called to serve in the fortress. The concept had seemed rigid and outdated. The Lower Earth they were becoming sought common relationship across the peoples, not kinship.

But looking on Maeva now, in this state, Irene knew that behavior could only be adapted to a point. Maeva was her friend, her kin, and she felt loyalty to her even if she wasn't Queen anymore.

Roman's voice broke Irene out of her trance. "We continue, and we will find it, but we may need to use some unorthodox measures to have a breakthrough."

The young Queen stood and walked to the window, just as Maeva used to do, Irene couldn't help noticing. She looked out over the square, her eyes scanned and for a moment Irene wondered if she truly understood the implications of what Roman was saying.

Five years of incubation births, and it seemed they were almost all flawed. Flawed in ways that nullified their purpose. Several thousand girls, and they were all genetic outliers. They could not become the army they were intended to be. They could not become anything at all. The program of mass incubation was thus far "inconclusive" in Roman's words, with thousands of children born from its failure. What were they to do with a generation that had no place in Lower Earth's structure? No Willing Mothers could take them on permanently, and there were far too many for dispersal in the outer counties.

Queen Ariane turned back to the room, "Mother?"

Maeva's eyes refocused, "Hmmm?"

"What have you to say to this news?"

"This *news*? I don't call it news." A flame rose in Maeva's eyes. Irene recognized it. It was Maeva as she used to be. "I call it thorough incompetence."

Roman stepped forward, "We were always going to face challenges in implementing - "

"Challenges?" Maeva tilted her head, "You think this is a challenge? You've created a subset of society. That was rather out of your brief, don't you think?"

"I was unprepared for - "

"Clearly, you were unprepared. When I promoted you into the title you so desperately wanted, did you think that it permitted you to make foolish mistakes? To run amuck, *laisser faire* with my commands? The Great Geneticist always had to work within limitations. You let the glory of your position go to your head."

Roman's face reddened. "I was doing as you commanded."

"I commanded a generation who could defend Lower Earth. Have you done that, Roman? Have you really accomplished what I asked of you?" She walked to Roman, her face nearly touching his. "I still hear you over there. I may have passed along my title of Queen, but my ways have not changed. You take liberties, Roman, and you overstated your abilities. Perhaps you even let yourself believe you could do what you could not. And now look where we are. All because you didn't have the humility to admit your limitations. Now they are cast into the light for everyone to see." She opened her arms wide and dropped them to her sides, walking away from Roman, leaning against the stone wall. She closed her eyes.

"Seems my Mother has already said everything for me," Queen Ariane continued. "Now I want to know what you're going to do about it."

Roman spoke quietly, his eyes lowered. "We have a plan in place. We will gather more samples, conduct randomized tests. The samples will be more intrusive but I've assigned someone skilled at such collections. We won't rattle the Homes. We'll make sure this stays as quiet as possible, as we have done. We've attributed it to behavioral development, kept the focus on disciplinary measures and confinement as well as drug therapies. So far the Homes believe it's activated in the children under their supervision; they don't suspect, as far as we know, that it's related to the genetic makeup of the incubates."

The young Queen nodded. "And once you have these samples?"

Roman inhaled through his nose. "Then we'll take the sequences to Lucius."

Maeva's head snapped upright. "Lucius? No, no."

"We have to, Maeva," Roman's voice softened, "You're right, we've surpassed our abilities here."

Maeva pointed her finger at him, "He'll trick you. He'll trip us up. He'll turn this into his own little experiment at the expense of' - "

"Mother, " Ariane walked across the room. She put her hand on Maeva's shoulder. "You're too close to this to be objective. Roman's right." She turned back to Roman, "I want to be informed every step of the way."

"Yes, Queen."

"Daily."

"Yes, Queen."

Irene saw the shimmer of sweat on Roman's forehead. He'd done well, keeping his cool.

He's made such a mess of this, no wonder he feels the heat.

"You're dismissed, Roman. We have to discuss all you've reported. Leave us now."

Roman bowed low and walked out quickly.

When his degradation begins, who will take over the Tower?

As far as Irene knew, there were no obvious candidates. It had been held by a man since its inception, a way of staving off criticism and rebellion by backroom men.

But soon there won't be any men left. Isaac's gone; he might have been a contender but he was always going to die before Roman. A few on the lower levels of the Tower, but none sufficient for this level of responsibility. Never mind their capabilities. They don't hold a candle to Roman.

She hadn't considered the implications before of having a woman leading the Tower. It had felt like an institution and a cultural truth that men would have their place in the Tower while women ran the rest of Lower Earth.

Change. Change is coming.

She watched Roman's back as he left.

Ariane closed the door. "This is a complete disaster."

Maeva muttered, but Irene couldn't hear the words.

"Stop it, Mother. They have no answer for us now. You got us into this, not them."

Maeva looked up at Ariane, but her lips kept moving. Fast wisps of words spoken only to herself.

"I said, stop it. Mother, stop it." But Maeva continued, if anything, her lips accelerating.

"Stop it!" Ariane slapped her mother with such force that Maeva flew to the floor in a bundle of velvet and leather.

Maeva looked at the floor, but her lips were still.

Ariane panted, her lips parted, the air audible.

Irene blinked. She couldn't help Maeva up, that would be an insult. Ariane would not have it either. Irene couldn't speak. Any word she uttered would be an affront, regardless of its intent. She waited.

"Pack for your trip, *Mother*. You leave tomorrow." Ariane looked up and saw Irene. "And you have a clear-out of Cork Town to prepare."

Irene bowed and left and the room, clicking the door shut behind her.

11

Priyantha brought her a tray of fruits to break her fast. Three days of intensive prayer. Three days of visions, dreams, and ideas. Leadon was full of the words of the ancients. The sound of the tray placed on the floor was jarring. She wanted to stay in that meditative, prayerful state as long as possible. She found such peace there. In that place, there was no death, no fight, no politics. No imposter Queens. No lost childhood friends.

The array of fruits, beautiful though they were, signaled the end of her sabbatical. She was back in the earthly world.

Where has Aria gone? She can't be on the Forgotten Islands; we would know about it. Is she on another island, alone? Starving? Abandoned?

She shook the thought away. Anxiety rode up her throat. Every time she thought of Aria she went down this path, ending at a place where Aria was suffering and Leadon could have, or should have, done something about it.

Her teeth sank into a pear, the flavor cascading over her mouth and she found herself drooling. How delicious, how fulfilling, how consuming was the taste of the fruit.

Someone opened the curtain at the entry of Batrasa's hut.

My hut. I must come to call it my hut.

"Yes?"

"I come with good wishes for our new Chief."

"Enter."

Before Leadon was the woman who had stood around the fire, Ahnira, the very one who had spat insults and ridicule. Leadon felt her spine straighten at the sight of her.

She said she has good wishes. Hear her out. Perhaps she's had some change of heart. Or perhaps she's realized she made a horrible misstep in insulting the future Chief.

The woman kneeled.

"Please," Leadon said, "You're in my home. You do not need to kneel here. Those who enter are my friends."

The woman stood, shifting her weight from side to side. Her discomfort was palpable.

"I am Ahnira."

"Ahnira. I know your name, but not from your own lips. It is good to meet you."

The woman shifted again, "I felt compelled to come. But now that I'm here, I'm not sure what to say."

Leadon waited. She also didn't know what to say to this woman who had been so clear in her disdain for her.

Replica.

"If you do not know what to say," Leadon picked up, "Then do not speak, but come sit with me and have some fruit. The pear, in particular, is delicious."

"No, no, I cannot."

"Please, I insist."

Ahnira sat down and Leadon held out the tray. The woman looked at it.

"I feel disgusted."

Leadon lowered the tray, wanting to ask why but afraid of the answer. So she waited.

Ahnira continued. "I have complete faith in Batrasa. I

know she never would have led us astray. Since I was a child, I idolized her. I dreamed of one day becoming the Keeper, giving training, having some authority but always in service of Gana."

"It is a worthy dream to have."

"I don't know that I ever intended to fulfill it, but I tell you because I want you to understand how deep my loyalty was to Batrasa."

"I understand. I see it in you as you speak."

Ahnira's face twisted. "I never expected to be here, in this position. I don't have to tell you that I said things. About you. And to you. And all the while, Batrasa knew you were to be the next Chief. I feel - I feel *disgusted*. Because my loyalty was shallow. Because it was directed at Batrasa and not the good of Lower Earth."

Leadon felt her heart beating harder as the woman spoke. Leadon valued truth, but she also felt a desperate need to run away from this awkward conversation that brought all her insecurities to the surface.

"Chief," Ahnira continued. "You have my loyalty because you are Chief. But my loyalty is shallow. Please do not punish me for it. I am only just realizing my own shortcomings. I will change. I will grow from this. I already have." Ahnira took Leadon's hand and brought it to her forehead as she bent over it. "Forgive me, even for the thoughts I still harbor now."

"Ahnira. Ahnira, please lift your head." Leadon waited until she was upright again, "Do not be fooled into thinking I do not have flaws. My flaws are many. I, too, am learning." She was careful with her words. She wanted to be honest, but not reveal so much that this woman saw just how frightened and uncertain she actually was. "This is our journey. I forgive without condition. But I do hope you'll change your mind about me. I never was all you said that I was."

Replica.

Ahnira stood and bowed her head low. She then walked out of the hut without another word.

Leadon let out a breath she didn't know she'd been holding.

If only all the others could be so forthright. I should value the discomfort she gives me. But still, I'd rather not have it at all.

Leadon remembered Batrasa's words. The Chief was one who had to stand up against the women's words, one who would rise above their partisan beliefs. Leadon began to better understand why she was the one chosen, even if she still didn't fully grasp the enormity of what was before her.

She stood and walked into the midday sun. After three days in the dark hut, it felt good to have the sting of sunshine on her face. Priyantha was waiting for her.

"How was the transition phase?"

"Illuminating."

Priyantha smiled. "I think that's how it's supposed to be." She took Leadon's arm and they strolled together towards the river in silence.

Once at the river's bank, Leadon let Priyantha's arm fall. She put her hands in the water. It was icy and fresh. She brought two handfuls of it to her face. The rush of cold water on sun-stung skin awoke her senses and she smiled.

She and Priyantha continued their walk along the river's edge.

"I must make a trip." Leadon turned to Priyantha. "It will be my first as Chief."

"Of course. To the Dark Counties, I imagine? The traders off the north coast? Shall I see authorization from the Ministry of Displacement?"

"No, I'll go to Geb."

"Ah, I see." Priyantha nodded.

"I need to see Irene."

"That's to be expected, I suppose."

Leadon wasn't sure what she meant, but she didn't want to ask. "There is some history that needs to be clarified for me to better understand our direction."

"Know where we've been to know where we're going?"

"Exactly."

"It's probably more relevant for you than for any of us."

"Priyantha," Leadon couldn't contain it anymore, "Will the women here ever see past my face? Will I ever be something other than the first genetic model in Gana?"

Priyantha took a deep breath. "Leadon, I'm not sure how you can be anything other than that; I'm not sure why you'd want to be. It's who you are."

"But it's not all I am."

Priyantha shrugged. "That part might take more time."

"Yes," Leadon continued walking. "I believe you are right."

"I'll come with you to Geb." Priyantha jogged to catch up.

"That's not necessary."

"Perhaps it's not necessary, but it's desirable. Your position has changed, Chief. You are not a warrior priestess like the rest of us anymore. You may have need of someone while you're there."

Leadon knew Priyantha was right. Nothing was as it was the last time she made the trip to Geb. It felt like years had passed, not a couple of short weeks.

"Alright. You'll join me."

Priyantha smiled wide, "I've always been curious about the capital." Her face grew serious. "But you have my word, while we are there, my commitment is entirely to you." Priyantha's face was so earnest that Leadon had to smile. She took Priyantha's arm.

"Let's stroll while we can, and then prepare the horses. The world is changing around us. We may not have much time for simple joys anymore."

. . .

THEY TIED THEIR STEEDS AT THE ENTRY OF GEB AND STRODE into the city in their traditional garb. Last time Leadon had wanted to be invisible in the crowds of the city.

Now she wanted to be seen.

She walked with her shoulders back, the traditional bodice jingled as she walked through the streets. Priyantha wasn't far behind.

She approached a woman serving soup on a corner. "Excuse me, do you know where I find the East Counties rooming house?"

The woman looked at Leadon, serving spoon in hand, frozen in place. Her mouth was open but she didn't speak.

Leadon looked back to Priyantha, who shrugged.

"Excuse me, madam." She spoke slowly and clearly. "I am looking for the East Counties Rooming House. Do you know it?"

The woman gave a quick nod, her mouth still open, her arm still held in midair with the ladle of soup.

Leadon leaned forward. "Are you alright?"

The woman blinked and then finally lowered her arm, letting the spoon slip into the pot. "I've never seen anyone like you so close. You're the spitting image of-"

"Yes, I know. I also come from Gana."

"But the resemblance."

"Uncanny, isn't it?" Leadon smiled. "Now would you please tell me where I find the East Counties Rooming House?"

The woman pointed deeper into the city. "Over there."

"Would you mind being more specific?"

The woman shook her head as if she was woken up. "Of course, of course. It's down this road, then left onto Fifth Road B, it's easy to find because A is to the right. It's a few blocks down there."

Leadon smiled and looked back to Priyantha who nodded.

"Thank you for your help."

Leadon and Priyantha began down the road.

"Wait!" The woman called after them, "I'm so sorry, I've lost my mind. You're so tall, so striking, I just lost myself. Please wait." She rushed back to the pot and ladled two bowls.

"Please, take these with my good wishes for your time in Geb. Just bring the bowls back anytime, I have plenty."

"Thank you," Leadon and Priyantha bowed in gratitude.

The woman swatted the air, "Oh, it's nothing. A great recipe though. Full of nutrition, and that isn't easy these days. I use the fortification powder, too. Helps you grow strong, not that you need any more strength! I mean, just look at you! And you can be sure of the quality. No risk of poison, heavens no. Not like what you might find over in Cork Town." The woman slapped her hands on her apron. "Well then, goodbye, now."

Priyantha and Leadon exchanged a glance and sipped the soup on their way to the rooming house. Their arrival was greeted with basic efficiency. The host had been friendly if skeptical, her first question asking when they would be leaving.

"Now what?" Priyantha asked as they dropped their satchels in the room.

"Now we go to the fortress."

"Already? We just arrived."

"That's why this is the best time. If we wait longer, then word might go through the city of our visit, and rumors cannot serve us well."

Leadon didn't say that the longer they waited the less courage she would have. She wanted to waste no time and ride the thin bravery she'd been able to muster thus far.

They walked through the city, letting the women watch them pass by. They returned the soup bowls to the seller, who offered a wide smile and deep bow. Clocks were mounted on every function building; seventeen hours was approaching.

Soon the streets will be filled with women heading home. I don't even know how to find Irene.

The fortress rose black into the blue sky, streaks of pinks starting with the sunset. It appeared out of place next to the concrete blocks that surrounded it, and ancient across from Central Tower. Leadon took in the sight of it now that the square was empty but for a few strolling women. There was nothing welcoming about it. A fortress from pre-Mist days, so vastly different from anything in Gana. Gana *was* ancient. The fortress merely a leftover from an earlier settler period. New peoples.

How many waves of change will we see before the earth is finished? Ancient times, settlers. Final war, more settlers. And if Upper Earth comes?

Leadon shook the thought away. She had to focus.

I must prepare myself. Irene might come into sight at any moment.

But she didn't. An hour passed as Leadon and Priyantha watched life evolve in the square. The timekeeper's ringing bells. Women came and went. Conversations. Mary on the screen declaring the end of the day and a new curriculum soon to be applied in the Girls Homes.

Still no Irene.

Priyantha whispered to Leadon, "Do you know she's here? Could she be away?"

"I don't know anything for sure."

Perhaps they wouldn't see Irene that day at all. They sat on two concrete blocks that framed the entry to the fortress. Waiting.

Another hour passed. The square was empty. Dinners were prepared, served, cleared. Leadon felt pangs of her hunger mounting.

The sun had nearly set, the square nearly in darkness, and Leadon finally saw Irene enter the far end of the Geb City Square, making the turn from behind Central Tower. Four guards surrounded her, all Geb women. Together they were a fearsome block, their uniforms catching glint just as the perimeter lights came on.

Leadon and Priyantha stood.

Irene appeared consumed by the conversation, the Guard listening to her every word. Pointing and hands gesturing. Their faces were all severe.

Something is wrong.

Leadon looked to Priyantha who nodded, and she felt encouraged. This was what they'd come for, she couldn't shy away now.

Halfway through the square, Irene appeared to see them. She lifted her hand to stop the guards from speaking. She turned her head and said something. All the guards stopped, waiting in the middle of the square as Irene approached.

Leadon spoke before Irene arrived, calling out the traditional Ganese blessing to her.

"Lassa Irilena weh."

"What are you doing here?" Irene's eyes were on fire. She leaned forward. Leadon suddenly felt very young.

"I need to speak with you."

"Did you learn nothing from Batrasa? Do you not know how this process works? You can't just show up in the capital like a rogue weasel. There are customs that dictate these ways."

"I didn't know - "

"Of course you didn't because you remain rash and self-concerned."

Leadon felt heat growing up her neck. Irene didn't bother to lower her voice; the guards could hear every word.

"Irene, this is important. Perhaps I still have much to learn of custom, but my reason is intact and I must speak with you about Gana's condition."

"You'll speak with me about 'Gana's condition' when you've followed protocol." Irene rubbed her forehead and approached

Leadon, finally speaking only to her. "You have no idea what I'm managing right now. I really don't have the patience for whining discontent from Gana. There are larger concerns on our horizon. So go, Leadon, and don't show your face in the capital without a better approach, or else you'll receive no welcome from me."

Leadon was about to interject, even though she didn't yet have the words.

But Irene was gone. She turned and marched into the fortress, the guards silently following in behind her, casting a condescending look to Priyantha and Leadon as they passed.

They stood silently. Priyantha finally inhaled and breathed the air out through her lips. "Leadon - "

"Don't speak to me right now."

"You're right to be offended."

"Don't speak."

Leadon wasn't offended, she was humiliated.

My first visit to Geb in my official capacity, and I already made a laughingstock of us.

"We leave for Gana at sunrise. And Priyantha, I need you to gather any woman who ever served Batrasa, any who ever came to Geb. Any who served in the checkpoints. This must never happen again."

Leadon watched Priyantha swallow hard and nod, knowing she was as much to blame as herself. Leadon would never let her people come to such shame again. She vowed it, even knowing that Irene could have invited her in now. She could have taught her their ways. She could have mentored and supported her.

But she didn't.

Leadon stormed back to the Rooming House, grateful that Priyantha stayed behind. She wanted some time alone. She needed some time to breathe.

12

Sara adjusted her satchel, making sure she had all the entry papers. Security was tighter at the Cork Town entry than it used to be. Just a few years ago she could have flashed her Central Tower badge and that would have been sufficient. Not anymore. The commune was now held under close watch.

She'd never really understood why. The Cork Town residents were by-and-large benign. Many of them had mental and physical defects that would prevent them from mounting any kind of large-scale rebellion. Even small rebellions had been easy to quench in the past. Backroom Men had always been tracked. Even Isaac. The screens said it was for their protection. No one outwardly challenged that. But inwardly was a different story, at least for Sara.

When Roman asked her about Lucius, Sara had thought she might die on the spot. Her heart was going to run off the rails and her palms turned sweaty. There was no way Roman could know of their history, could he?

Sara hadn't seen Lucius in years, but he had been the one to tell her Adam was gone. Disappeared. Vanished. And her body had been covered with samples from their genetic experiment, everything Lucius needed to keep their project alive. But had he? Had Lucius been able to make any advancement on 4957 over the past few years at all?

She'd had a massive lump in her throat that she hoped Roman couldn't see.

But somehow her panic pleased Roman; she saw his face relax and he went on to explain the mission he had in mind for her.

The whole time, Sara's brain had been running like mad. She could only nod to Roman as he went over it.

Now it was happening. She was going back to Cork Town. She was going to see Lucius. She was going to try to save the incubation program from utter failure. The stakes were high.

She looked at herself in the mirror and shook her head.

I never thought, of all of us who worked on the old program, that it would be me who would survive. Or maybe I did know. I was the woman after all.

She stood a moment longer, taking in the sight of herself - brown hair, green eyes, olive skin, just like the Directive required. Her personal qualities overlaid on top of the basic model. Delicate facial features. Slender shoulders and slender hips. Not made for the Willing Woman program, she was made for research. Not only was she made for it, she enjoyed it and she was good at it. But Roman was right - she was better with people than most of the others in the Tower. He was right to select her for the sample collection.

But this side trip to Lucius, she wasn't sure. Convincing Lucius of anything was like melting a glacier with a match.

She threw her satchel over her shoulder and began the eight-kilometer walk to Cork Town. The residence for senior-level Central Tower researchers in Geb was almost as far as possible from the Cork Town limits.

"Papers?" the guard demanded on her arrival at the checkpoint.

She handed her the official documentation.

"Who will you be visiting?"

"The former Great Geneticist."

"For what purpose?"

"That's above your pay grade."

The guard gave an unfriendly smile. She had thick shoulders and a short haircut. Sara guessed she was from the Gillard line. They held most of the positions that required strict adherence to guidelines. Only a few of them ever strayed from the rules laid out for them.

The guard shifted her weight. "Nothing is above my pay grade when it comes to access to Cork Town. So speak up or go back home."

Sara sighed loudly. "You see as well as I do. That form has the stamp from Roman of the First Line. And unless you want to find yourself outside the regulations, you'll let me pass without further hassle."

The guard stared Sara in the eye. Then she looked back at the page.

Thrusting it back at Sara, the guard turned to open the gate.

"Out by timekeeper's bells. No reason for you to stay beyond seventeen hundred. Understood?"

Sara knew she wasn't bound to a timeline when she had Roman's stamp, but this wasn't the time to get into a power struggle with a Gillard.

"Understood." Sara walked through the gate and heard the loud clang and click behind her of the lock closing.

"People of Geb," Sara could hear Mary's voice on a screen, but she couldn't see it, and the quality of the sound was poor. Mary's voice crackled in a way that it never did on the screens in Geb Center. "I remind you that the upcoming session for potential Willing Women will take place in less than two weeks' time.

Are you ready to dedicate ten months minimum to the gift of Lower Earth's next generation? Gestation period remains at four months, with a possible post-natal period of six months before the child qualifies for one of the homes. Be sure to bring your latest physical results with you for initial screening. Regarding crop killers, we have news that County D in the north has seen some success with the use of refined fertilizer from Central Tower. Great news in the combat against the most current strain!"

Sara walked deep into Cork Town and Mary's voice faded away. Only one screen in Cork Town, not like Geb Center at all.

Sara knew a shortcut through the side alleys, but she had to stay on Cork Row until she was well out of sight of the guard. Her familiarity with the commune would only draw even more attention to her. Already there were more eyes on her than she wanted.

She walked along the main strip, the gravel crunching under her feet.

This used to be paved. Only the alleys had gravel.

The old cork factory rose up beside her. The stories told of it being a bustling hive, of cork being the center point of life in the commune, back during the time of the first settlers. It had long since been converted into smaller manufacturing. Some sewing, some carpentry, some welding. The front service doors appeared rusted shut, only the single doors for staff showed any sign of life.

Sara turned down the eighteenth alleyway, eager to get off Cork Row. The narrow alleyways comforted her, even if the last time she'd come had been with tears streaming down her face.

Five years. How does time pass so fast and so slow? We've never mastered our understanding of time's passing. The relativity of it, even within a single person's consciousness. Five years.

She made a turn and almost tripped on two women who were sat against the wall.

"Oh, sorry, I didn't see you - "

Sara stopped, the women were still, didn't even react at her kicking their feet. Their eyes stared straight ahead. After a moment, one of them looked up, and then the other.

"I'm sorry, excuse me," Sara repeated.

The women said nothing. Their cheeks caved in. Their eyes all but dead.

Opies. Poor women. They look far along now.

Sara stepped away from the women and continued down the alley when voices rose around her. The apartment buildings were all close together; sound echoed and bounced between them.

"You promised," she heard.

"And I couldn't do it," another woman's voice joined.

"But you promised!"

"Screech at me all you like, they won't take us anymore! Do you know what it took just for me to get permission to leave Cork Town?"

"We have nothing left! You brought the kid in. You have to make this work! I'm not going to starve just so that *she* can have a full belly. It's not fair. I didn't want her, and now you're letting us down. You're lazy and thoughtless."

"You're not hearing me, Rhonda. They won't take me. They won't hire anyone from Cork Town anymore."

"Then you're kicking the kid out."

"No!"

Sara reached another corner and quickened her pace. Central Tower had put a policy in place a few years ago. No more cleaners, servers, or runners from Cork Town. Even at the time, Sara wondered what that would mean for the commune's residents. So little was actually produced in Cork

Town and almost none of the manufacturing plants or other industries were based within the commune's walls.

She wove through the alleys, finally arriving at the twenty-ninth alleyway. The apartment jutted out from the main building, an unremarkable ground floor studio. From the street, it looked like any other extension on a building. The oddity of it didn't stand out in Cork Town. In Geb, the buildings lined up, even if they were built across several generations after the Mist. There was an understanding, an urban plan that unfolded as the city grew.

Cork Town had no concept of apparent organization. There was the main road and then side roads, and then alleyways that sprung off each other. They were like tree branches overlapping so that the main artery was the only visible connection between them. Even the alleyways blended into each other, new buildings popping up as the population of Cork Town had grown. Fewer genetic outliers were moved to the outer counties; more and more of them were kept under lock and key in Cork Town. The scare from Upper Earth's scouts those years ago had resulted in many knock-on effects across Lower Earth. The further ghettoization of Cork Town had only been one of them.

Sara approached the studio, her heart picking up in speed. She was quite certain Lucius would recognize her. But would he accept her in? Would he hear her out?

More importantly to Sara, had he made any progress on 4957?

She rapped with one knuckle on the door.

"No," she heard from inside.

"Lucius?"

"I said no."

"Lucius, it's Sara of the seventh line. Please let me enter."

"Sara." She heard the sound of shuffling and furniture

moving. "A minute." Papers rustled and there was a bang like a chair falling over.

The door opened.

"Hello, Lucius."

"Sara. I can't say I was expecting you. Perhaps if this were a few years ago."

"The rules on Cork Town access have changed."

"Changed. That's the euphemism of the decade."

"May I come in?"

He walked away from the doorway; he'd taken up every inch of the opening and more; leaving the apartment would be a logistical challenge for him to maneuver through. His body was still in an advanced stage of degradation, and yet he didn't go the way the other men did. His wheelchair waited by the table and there was a pseudo-wall that could slide closed to make a bedroom, and the entire place was a disaster. It appeared that he'd made a brief, feeble attempt to organize thousands of papers into piles - on the bed, on the countertop of the small kitchen corner, across every visible surface.

"Is anyone else here?"

"You can see every inch of the apartment from where you stand. Do you see anyone?"

"Rose has a way of hiding in corners where no one can see."

"Rose left a long time ago."

"She did?" Sara remembered the deformed face of the girl-woman well. Something very soft in her, but also something very persistent. Her dedication to Lucius had been unquestionable, as though Lucius were her father. And where does a genetic deviant go if they manage to get out of Cork Town at all?

"It's good to see you, Lucius," she finally managed.

"Don't give me that. Why are you here?"

"I mean it. I didn't want to stay away, but it wasn't worth the risk of exposing - "

"Don't speak of that here," Lucius hissed, holding his hand up.

Sara nodded, "I'm here on business entirely unrelated to - to that."

Lucius cocked his head, "Oh? Now, this is getting interesting. I can't imagine you having any sort of business for the likes of me."

"I was equally surprised." She remembered again the moment Roman mentioned Lucius' name.

Looking at him now, little had changed. The more she took in Lucius' spread, his waddle to the wheelchair, the way his body seemed to sink into the earth, the more she realized he had not changed at all in five years. Even she was beginning to feel the years on her. Lucius, who must have been well past ninety, seemed to have stopped somewhere along the line and remained at that age, even with his advanced state of degradation.

He'd broken through the gate of time.

But physically, he was still struggling. He lowered himself into the wheelchair, apparently the same he'd had for more than thirty years, and wiped the perspiration off the side of his face.

"Sit."

Sara sat.

"Tell me everything."

She did. She started with the incubation birth numbers.

Lucius gave a low laugh. "That'll have consequences."

Sara was startled.

How could he know that already? I haven't said anything about it.

She went on to tell of the adaptations they'd made with each phase, the samples she'd collected in the social environments, the behavior tracking, the initial reports. Lucius nodded, making circles with his hand that she understood to mean she should go faster.

She came to it. "We can't identify the cause of the behavior; the reports are coming in at higher rates than we ever could have expected. The children are in advanced states of depression without cause and none of the traditional therapies work. We can't code it out of them, and now we have a dual problem. How do we end the pattern for future incubation phases? And what do we do with the thousands already born with the anomaly we can't seem to treat?"

She sat back in the chair, her eyes glued on Lucius. Everything was riding on him. She was pretty sure he knew it. He had that way about him.

He pursed his lips, nodding slowly.

"Which treatments have you tested?"

She gave the list.

"Yes, that does sound exhaustive. I don't know why anyone would have thought that Q-enzyme would work."

"We were desperate. We thought perhaps the molecule - "

"There was no reason to believe the molecule for primase enzyme would have any effect. It's a red herring." He inhaled deeply, and Sara heard the sounds from his body, a grumbling growling from somewhere deep within. "Would you turn on the fan?"

"Sure." She got up and had to weave between his chair and the bedroom door. Squeezing past she tried not come into contact with the back of Lucius' head, but her breasts grazed his ear and the chair. She closed her eyes and sucked in further to go by.

"Turn it up to three." She snapped the knob up a notch. "That's better." Lucius had never lost his hair. Thick and black, peppered white, it blew in the fan's breeze.

She inhaled and sucked in, passing back to her seat. "So?"

"So what?"

"What do you think?"

"You can't expect me to respond just like that."

"I thought you could."

"It's not a question of could. It's a question of custom. Protocol. You come to my home, burst in with your business demands, meanwhile, you haven't had a word to say of our history nor any concern for my well-being."

Sara saw something of a glint in Lucius' eye.

Is he toying with me?

If he was, she had no choice but to play along. She was not in a position to bargain.

She folded her hands on the table. "How have you been, Lucius?"

"You don't care about how I've been."

"I do," she meant it sincerely. "Not just because of - of *that* - but because the time was so charged. Adam..." her voice trailed off but Lucius didn't interject.

Adam. His body in her bed the night they decided to take on the project. The night they passed in each other's arms. On the one hand, nothing of note had passed between them. Certainly nothing like what they talked about in the textbooks about the old ways between men and women. Those base sexual needs that had since been carefully out-coded from their sequence. No, nothing like that.

But something else. Something worse.

She loved Adam.

She loved Adam more than she loved herself. And she'd known it in that one night together, seen it in his eyes. Those eyes that flashed blue though they were deep brown in midday sun.

She'd always believed that Adam would be the one to change their human history, to bring them back to their natural state. To invigorate the DNA of boys who could become men who would populate the world again with new commitment to their future. A future of peace. A future of life's fullness.

She'd never thought he'd be called out as a traitor.

Some said he'd been disappeared to the Forgotten Islands, but Sara had known from the start. He was dead.

It was the risk they knew they were taking. She just wished it had been her instead.

She looked up at Lucius and tried to swallow, but a rock had lodged in her throat.

"Adam's absence is felt. Across the Tower. But especially here." She put her hand on her chest. "I miss him, Lucius."

Lucius' face flashed an emotion that Sara didn't recognize.

"Don't get teary on me now," he looked out the window.

"I do miss him. He could see through the numbers to patterns that no other could identify. He was so - so human compared to the others."

"The other what?"

"You know what I mean."

"Say it."

"The other men."

Lucius sat back in the wheelchair, looking at her sideways.

She felt heat coming up her neck. "It's not a criticism, it's a fact. Most men in Geb had become obsessed with the Male Program. There was nothing else for them, they couldn't see beyond it. The good of Lower Earth - "

"What good is there in Lower Earth for a dead man?"

"They weren't dead."

"They are now. Dead."

Sara bit her lip. So many had gone. Degraded. The numbers dwindled. Live births of boys were almost at zero.

Lucius stood back up, and Sara thought he might march straight to the front door, open it, and insist she leave. She steeled herself for it. The truth was that she wanted to stay with him. Wanted to talk about Adam. The subject had been taboo from the time he'd been disappeared, and with Isaac's degradations so soon after, she'd been left on her own to navigate Central Tower.

Lucius was the closest thing to an old friend that she had now.

He crossed in front of her and she held her breath, keeping the disappointment at bay. But the feeling snuck into the muscles under her eyes. She felt them twitch.

He approached the front door and then turned back to her. "Come." Lucius moved alongside the wall to the place where it met the separation with the bed area. It couldn't be called a bedroom, though there was a sort of partition between the spaces. Sara stood, not knowing what he could possibly be leading her towards.

Lucius turned on the bedside lamp and then bent one knee resting his hands on the bed for balance. He pointed to the divider wall, "Slide the door shut."

She slid the cardboard-like wall, giving privacy from prying eyes, but not more than that.

Lucius struggled to get his other knee to the floor, but eventually he folded it under himself. His body spread on the floor as he pushed a small rug from under the bed.

What has he got under there?

Lucius lifted a plank. And then another. And another. Little by little he revealed a gap, wide enough that he could maneuver himself into the hole. A stairwell led to the basement.

"You go first," he gestured melodramatically. "It will take me a while to get down the stairs. I should have built them larger while I'd had the chance."

Sara sat on the floor letting her legs drop into the hole. Her feet touched the first stair. She could only see the first few stars that were lit from the bedroom's light. She felt her way down, one foot at a time. She reached for a banister but found only open air. She stepped more gingerly after that. Eventually her foot hit a floor without anywhere further to descend.

"Some light will help," Lucius said from above. She heard him pull on a string that brought the room into a yellow glow.

She glanced around the room, the sight of it answering questions she'd had for years.

A laboratory. That's how he does it.

On all four sides around her was equipment, cabinets, a sink. Several long tables that ran the length of the apartment and then further under into the adjacent apartment building's basement.

"No one ever noticed this?"

"There's no one to notice. I put up a triple-thick wall beside the main apartment building's basement. Anyone down over there wouldn't know the difference unless they were digging for the foundations."

Unlike the apartment above, the laboratory was spotless. She ran her hand along the first table. Stainless steel gleamed back at her.

"This is incredible, Lucius."

"Fortunately, I'd thought ahead. Had I not installed this when I was still the Great Geneticist, there's no way I could do it now." He tapped his forehead. "Not just book learning up there."

"What are you working on?"

"This and that. My involvement is relatively defunct since Rose left. She'd always been the one to bring me active files from the Tower. I knew I was dependent on her, but I still manage to make a breakthrough here and there."

"But is Rose coming back?"

He ignored her question, "So I've thrown most of my energy into a single project."

Sara's heart jumped. She stopped admiring the microscope, which was nearly vintage but of a quality they didn't have in most of the Central Tower labs. She looked up to him, saying a prayer in her head that he would say what she thought he would say.

She could barely find her voice. "What project, Lucius?"

He pursed his lips and looked at his hands.

She cleared her throat. "What project, Lucius? What project?"

He looked up, meeting her eyes.

"4957."

She left Lucius after all his explanations, feeling in a daze. Her feet worked despite her brain. She was consumed.

How could he have made such advances, all alone? How did he find the code behind it? How, I don't get it, how did he isolate the chromosome's secondary genes?

Fire ran through Sara's veins, a feeling of being alive that she hadn't had in so long. She remembered Adam's touch, the way they'd held each other, innocent and guilty at once. The way he'd grabbed her with joy when he first found out that 4957 was viable.

She didn't walk; she floated down the alleys of Cork Town. She was well ahead of the local curfew, even though it didn't apply to her. Still, she'd be pleased to cross back through the gates without further rebuke.

But she had one more stop to make before she could leave the Cork Town commune. It was the only thing Lucius asked of her. She couldn't possibly say no.

She wound her way down the gravel of Cork Row, through the vendors in the market who only had half-rotten vegetables in their baskets. The stench of them invaded Sara's nose. Every sensation was heightened in her. Her chest rising and falling with her breath. The sound of the air as it entered and then exited her nostrils. Her pulse in her wrists, her thumbs, her neck. The gravel crunching under her shoes, sliding to the side as she stepped.

Her destination, according to Lucius, wasn't far off the Third Road, down the Second Alleyway. She would know it by the swinging wood door, the only part of the building that stood out. She saw it further down the alley and couldn't help but walk faster. There was no sign, no lights, no indication that anything particularly was there.

Sara pushed open the swinging door and stepped in, the low ceiling and single window giving the impression that she was already underground.

Some women were sitting around one of the pub's tables, another woman standing with one hand on her hip and the other holding a rag. All eyes turned and any conversation came to a complete stop.

Sara walked in further, her eyes adjusting to the dark. She approached the standing woman. "Are you Trudith?"

"Yeah, who're you?"

"A friend of Rose."

The women around the table all shifted uncomfortably in their seats. Trudith's eyes narrowed as she watched Sara's face. "You're a friend of Rose?"

Sara swallowed hard and nodded.

Trudith looked to the women around the table, though no one spoke a word.

Finally, Trudith grabbed a chair from a nearby table.

"Well, then you'd better sit down."

13

Trudith had just finished preparing the foods for the following day. The beans were soaking and the grains were put away. She'd had to become more creative with their meals; the variety at the market was at the lowest she'd ever known it. She hadn't been able to get soup fortification powder in weeks. The bland beans and grain would have to do, even though she knew the crops had become less and less nutritious.

"Didn't you see the market today? It's horrifying. Don't think for a second they eat like this in Geb." Yala's voice carried across the room, though there wasn't anyone else to hear than the group who came regularly. The pub had become their spot to dream, complain, and plot against their rulers.

Today, they were back on the topic of the conditions in Cork Town. Trudith was growing tired of it. There wasn't anything they could do, even if they wanted. Yala was particularly vocal. As usual.

"Trude!" Yala called, "This ale is worse than the sewer water they force us to drink!"

"Low on barley again," Trudith didn't lift her eyes. "I'm

making due. Drink tomato juice, if you don't like it. I have plenty of tomato juice from the West Fields overproduction."

"Too acidic! Overproduction, you see?" Yala turned to the group around the table again. "That's the best they'll give us here, what's left from overproduction."

Yala's head twitched.

"Don't get worked up now," Anna spoke gently. "You'll have another episode. Remember how long it took you last time to recover? I could have sworn those guards were going to beat you to a pulp, the scene you were making in the square."

"It's the injustice, gets me every time." She twitched again.

"It's not the injustice, it's your damn neurological condition," Matilde drawled. Matilde's cleft palate was the only visible sign of her deformity, though they all knew she couldn't eat more than three bites in a meal or else her digestive system quit on her. It was why she was hardly more than skin on bones.

"But the injustice sparks it. It gets me all riled up."

So why bother? Trudith thought *I'd rather put my time towards something that will bring out change. Politics is a deep, dark hole.*

But she let them use the pub. She wasn't unsympathetic after all. Trudith had never known how seriously to take them. On the one hand, simply for the words they shared over the table in her pub, they could all get disappeared, or at least a good beating. Trudith, too, for allowing it to happen. On the other hand, they were so far off from planning anything real, so out of proportion with anything they could actually do, that Trudith couldn't take them seriously.

"Did you see them the other day, doing rounds on Cork Row? They had their batons out before they had anyone to use them on." Matilde wiped the saliva that was dripping down from the side of her mouth.

"They found someone though, didn't they?"

"Rishelle."

"Poor Rishelle."

"I think they sought her out, they knew she'd have an episode. That's her genetic problem after all. They use it as an excuse."

"Is she alright?"

"Define alright."

"Last time I went to give blood, they took so much I almost fainted," Anna spoke from the corner. She wasn't one to talk much. "I really hate the mandatory blood collection."

"*For our own good*, they say."

"*Protecting us from future viruses*. I don't believe it for a second."

"Look, we need a different approach." Yala leaned forward. "I have an idea. We could sabotage the checkpoint."

Trudith couldn't bear it anymore, "You'll do no such thing unless you have a wish to be disappeared."

"We could do it from afar."

"You overstate your abilities." Trudith grabbed the broom from behind the bar. She had to distract herself or else the women would get her all worked up.

"What do you know?" Yala stood up. "Why do you always think you know everything, huh, Trudith? Why do you always have the last word?"

Matilde stood up. "Yala, come back here. She lets us use the place, that earns her some rights."

"I'm not trying to dampen your spirits," Trudith went on, "but don't you think you'd do better to find methods within your reach?"

"And what does that look like, Trudith, knower of all?"

"Trude the prude," Krescencia spoke up.

"There's a reason I'm a prude," Trudith said, "I've come this far and it's all gone pretty well. I've got this pub, and it gives you all a place, doesn't it? I'm here, I'm standing. Most days that's enough for me."

"It's not enough for me," Yala continued. "I had a job, I'll remind you. A good job. Honest. I worked hard, I cleaned those laboratories like they were my own children." She sat back hard against the chair, "And what good did it do me. The minute they wanted to be rid of all the outliers, we were the first cut. The first."

"I was in Logistics."

"I worked in the Western Counties Rooming House."

"All we wanted was to earn our keep." Yala punched the table, "And they even took that away from us."

"Of course, you're angry," Trudith softened her voice. "You have a right to be. I'm only suggesting that you take steps that stand a chance of making a difference, not creating more havoc for the rest of us. You mess around with the checkpoint, and who do you think will suffer for it? Imagine you're sly about the whole thing. Imagine they don't know it's you. They'll come for all the rest of us. We've seen it before. People will be hurt, disappeared. Killed. And then someone, under the duress of who knows what torture, will speak your name. Think it through!" Trudith felt her temper rising from her gut. She closed her eyes and took a deep breath.

They are just playing with ideas, but the game is too dangerous.

The pub was quiet for a few minutes, but for the sound of glasses lifting, lips sipping, and glasses setting back down.

How long will they try to find some magic breakthrough, some brave act that will undo generations of buildup? A hundred years of segregation. It's true, this must be the worst period in history for us. But with this new Queen, nothing can possibly get better any time soon.

Trudith wanted change too. She was disgusted by what she saw around her. Good women who tore at the seams. No wonder so many turned to opie. What else had Geb left for them?

The door swung open and the group of women all swung to look at it. Trudith's heart jumped. If they'd been spied on, they could easily be called out for violating the principles of loyalty.

The woman was slender, unimposing. From Geb Center. Though she was small in stature, she carried herself stately. The woman looked around the pub, at the group of women, and then to Trudith.

"Are you Trudith?"

Her heartbeat accelerated. What could this woman want with her?

"Yeah, who're you?"

Trudith's stomach seemed to jump into her throat.

"A friend of Rose."

Rose?

How she missed Rose and her little presence. A full-grown woman trapped in a pre-pubescent body. It wasn't hard to see why she'd be sent off to Cork Town.

She hadn't heard Rose's name in years. Once she'd left her job at the pub, suddenly and without warning, most of the patrons forgot she'd ever been there. She'd mostly hid in corners, cleaning and sorting, preparing, shopping at the market. But for Trudith, she'd felt like family. Rose was always there. And she'd always been the one who was there. No risk of Rose being disappeared, she kept herself well out of sight. But she'd been a pillar too. Trudith always felt there was more to misshapen, red-haired Rose than anyone knew. Though she couldn't put her finger on it.

"You're a friend of Rose?" It seemed unlikely. It felt like a trick. Trudith wasn't ready to believe it.

The woman nodded, her eyes staying on Trudith's. The woman didn't waver.

Maybe it's true. We'll have to find out.

"Well, then you'd better sit down."

The woman took a few more steps in. "Maybe I can sit at the bar?"

"Wherever you like."

"What I'd like is to talk to you," she whispered and again Trudith's heart skipped a beat.

"Me? Why me?"

"Serve me whatever it is you serve. I'll talk and you can tell me what you think."

Trudith saw the women at the table try to start a normal conversation, something about market days and weather. She poured a glass of ale.

"There you have it." Trudith set the glass down and put her hands on her hips but it felt unnatural. Everything felt unnatural. She needed the woman to just say what she had to say.

The woman leaned forward against the bar. "I knew Rose, a little. I knew her guardian better."

"Lucius?"

"Yes."

"The Great Geneticist?"

"Yes."

"I see." Trudith tried to look nonchalant. "And what about Rose? Where is she? What's she doing?" She hoped she looked relaxed. She felt like she was in a cloud of panic.

"I don't know."

Trudith's heart sank. She didn't realize how much she'd hoped this woman would give her good news.

"I've come for a different reason."

Trudith wiped down the bar. She couldn't imagine what reason there would be for anyone to see her.

The woman looked back at the table where the others appeared engrossed in their discussion of former blowouts, though Trudith knew they were listening to every word.

"We need your help."

"Me?"

"You know people."

"Not really."

"You know hundreds who come through here."

"I don't know them."

"Hear me out." The woman sat up straighter and explained.

Trudith tried to keep her focus but the sounds swirled around her head.

They need a woman? A woman to carry a child undercover? But that could get someone disappeared just for considering it. Outliers can't be Willing Women. I thought it was chemically fixed that way. That's what they said. But don't I know better, not to believe anything they say?

"It needs to be a sturdy woman. Someone who physically is up to the challenge without needing much care during the gestation period."

"The what?"

"The pregnancy."

"I see." Trudith sighed. "Actually, I don't see. How can one of us giving birth make any difference? There are thousands of births happening every day."

"I get it." Yala stood and walked towards the woman.

The woman stood up, the stool falling behind her. Trudith could see the scare across her face.

"It's okay," Trudith whispered. "They're alright."

"We can start undermining their system." Yala continued, "You want to challenge Central Tower. You want to throw their one-sided, prejudiced, blindly-loyal research program into the wind."

"I wouldn't put it that way."

The pub went quiet. Trudith watched the woman's hand tremble. Yala looked her down and up.

Trudith couldn't bear the silence.

At last, Yala spoke.

"We'll help you."

14

H*ow irresponsible they've all become. A Tower full of mindless scientific cronies.*

Lucius emptied a bag of pasta into boiling water.

Of course, this was Maeva's plan all along, back in the day. Build up her army. Willing Woman campaign, that's what she said. I should have guessed she'd be unsatisfied with that. Too much screening, too many variables, too much time. She wanted her army.

Well, now look at what she's got.

He watched the water boil, the little wheat spirals making a whirlpool in the pot. They were his own fortified blend he'd made in the lab below.

He let out a long, audible sigh, though there was no one to hear it.

She could never do anything the way I told her. Never. I suppose that's the prerogative of a Queen. And I'm the one who designed her, so that's what I get.

If only he could go back and never start incubation in Lower Earth.

It had been his own greed and ambition that had driven him to do it. But didn't he have ideals? Wasn't it supposed to be for the betterment of Lower Earth? Wasn't incubation going to replenish the male population, even if it did have an unacceptable mortality rate among infants?

He tried to shake the memory, but it doggedly came back. Too much talk of incubation. He knew the vision of it would haunt him for months, or years, to come.

Rainfields had been a perfect choice to set up the thousand-strong incubation boxes. The sun's reflection created more than enough heat off the lava rock to provide ideal conditions. They harnessed the natural heat and channeled it without any advanced technology required.

And there was something poetic in it all.

Rainfields - where the first settlers arrived after the Final War. Rainfields - where men would be born again.

Queen Idia had been the most unpredictable Queen Lower Earth had seen, and he had still been young at the time, under thirty when the Great Geneticist had died and he'd taken over the job. Martin. How he'd degraded into something inhuman. Lucius had watched it all happen before his eyes.

Martin, the father of modern genetics. And yet I surpassed him on every single measure. He designed me well. He did.

Even the thought of Martin degrading on that hidden hospital bed couldn't drive the image of Rainfields away. The beauty of the day he'd seen the glass boxes laid out across the land had been so powerful, so energizing. He'd felt the image burn into his mind at the time, and as he expected, it was alive in him until this day.

Though it was over seventy years ago.

Seventy years. What does that put me at now? A hundred and seven. How about that. And I used to worry that I wouldn't get past forty.

The glass boxes, a sea of them, row on row with the staff lined up through the channels. How striking the women looked in their white uniforms. Twenty-four-hour surveillance. His dream, the male embryos of various designs, finally they would test at scale. He was prepared to lose half of them. Or more. They just had to find the ones that took, the ones that endured. The ones that beat the odds.

They'd manipulate that genetic sequence until they broke through and had the one that would work. Replenish the male population. Bring the world back into balance. His plan had been perfect.

How naive. How idealistic. How clueless.

Then there was Queen Idia's smile at his arrogance. Idia's gentle touch on his arm. Idia's destruction of his dream.

No boys, not one.

She'd changed his perfect plan. Instead, every box was filled with the code of Queens.

The Queen's code, multiplied by a thousand, each a little life in each little box. And for what? For Idia's sick gladiator games. To find her true successor.

To find Maeva.

There had never been any love in Idia's heart for anyone. Something snapped, broken in her. It had to be. How else could she have taken the code he'd perfected and pervert it so deeply? Thousands of incubated possible queens, all of the same code?

Look how that went. Look how there was only one left standing. Look at the mark it left on Maeva's soul.

Maeva knew it. She knew it was the incubation program that had made her into what she was. That was why she dismantled it so soon after taking reign, even if she was only eighteen years old at the time.

Dismantled is not the right word. She destroyed it. Smashed and tore it. She purged the world of it.

And then she brought it back.

Lucius turned off the pot, the pasta swollen into gobs. He'd overcooked them without noticing.

Incubation. Using the common code of women. Incredible. Did she not think it through at all? Of course, they are clinically depressed little things. The code needs human contact. Humans are social beings, genetics 101! If you don't code it out, you deprive every incubate of the human contact they require. They need the mother's blood. They need to capture the sounds of the mother's heart. Without it, what are they? Loners. Worse, loners without boundaries, but whose need for fetal contact will never be satisfied. No wonder they jump off bridges.

They're raising thousands of children who will never know what loyalty means. They cannot even be loyal to their own survival.

Lucius dropped the bowl of overcooked pasta on the table.

What a disaster. What a complete disaster. How will Maeva try to fix this one?

He stopped.

She won't of course. It'll be Ariane.

Lucius felt something cold go down his spine.

I thought Ariane would be the last incubation birth we ever did. I designed her sequence for it. But the Central Tower cronies couldn't have known, none of them know what I compromised in her sequence to make it work. To make her sequence work.

Lucius had been wondering over the past few years if he'd compromised too much. Ariane's tolerance for Cork Town was frighteningly low. The Guard called it policy and treachery and a variety of other words, but Lucius knew what was behind it. Ariane.

It's my fault. Like all of this, my fault. The curse of my mind, that I see solutions. But I could never see the consequences.

He beat the table with his fist, his pasta falling out of the bowl. He picked up the individual noodles and popped them into his mouth.

One chance. Maybe my last chance. I will do this right. I will get 4957 right.

15

—————

Roman stood from behind his desk. "What do you mean, he said no?"

Sara shook her head, "I don't know what to tell you. You know what he's like."

"I selected you, Sara, because I had confidence you could get through that exterior. It's just an exterior. He's a man like the rest of us, and his dedication to Lower Earth exceeds most of us." Roman couldn't believe what he was hearing. He'd selected Sara specifically. Lucius would have seen the code he drew up in her, the scientific genius and then he would have been charmed by her kindness. Roman knew Lucius. Knew him well. "Did you impress upon him the consequences?"

"I did."

"This doesn't make sense. What did he say, exactly? Tell me word for word."

Sara took in a deep breath, looking at the floor. "He started with sarcasm."

As he would, Roman thought.

"And then he went into a long speech about how he could

have seen this coming. How we didn't take sufficient precautions, how this was something we brought upon ourselves."

That part I know. He would love to gloat over this. But then what? He should have finished his arrogant speeches and then relished the opportunity to come and save the day. He loves that. Especially because he'd have recognized that no one else could do it.

"Get to it, Sara. What was his refusal? How could he refuse! That's not Lucius. Tell me quickly, my patience is getting low."

Sara swallowed, she looked nervous. "He said that he's not the Great Geneticist anymore."

So that's what it's about. His demotion to common Cork Town outlier.

"And?" Roman leaned forward on his desk.

"And that if it mattered so much to the Great Geneticist that this was sorted out, then it should be the Great Geneticist who lowered himself to ask for help. He shouldn't send a half-wit, low-level, cookie-cutter sequenced technician to be the picture of humility before him." She exhaled. "Those were his exact words."

So he saw through it. Maybe I could have seen that coming. He'd love to see me beg.

"Anything else?"

"No. I was not welcome to stay, so I left."

Roman sighed. "Disappointing, Sara. Speak of this to no one. Dismissed."

Sara turned and left without another word.

Roman rubbed his forehead.

I guess I'm going to Cork Town.

"You've got some gall." Lucius had barely opened the door.

"Hello, Lucius. Nice to see you too."

"I didn't think you'd come."

"It's been a long time."

"You've been comfortably promoted."

"You're still alive."

"That's about all I am."

Roman shifted his weight. "May I come in?"

"I don't see why you'd want to."

"You know why I'm here."

"Not hard to guess once I sent that pony-ass girl flapping back to you. You thought just because she was R-type that I'd crumble? Become putty in her hands? You're out of touch, Roman. I thought you knew me better."

There was no point trying to cover it up with Lucius, that wouldn't help him get what he needed.

"Bad call, right?"

"Very. Now in addition to being flabbergasted by the liberties you've taken since stealing my job, I'm also offended. That doesn't bode well for your asking for favors."

Roman held his hands in the air. "I won't say any differently, Lucius. We're beyond that now. Not that it's easy for me to say. Don't take it lightly. Having to show my credentials at the entry to Cork Town was humbling enough."

"The Guard didn't accompany you?"

"I didn't want them to know I was coming."

"And the checkpoint didn't let the Great Geneticist slide his way in?"

"They didn't recognize me."

"Ah, that must have been awkward."

Roman gave a little laugh. Lucius had not changed at all. "Please, may I come in?"

Lucius opened the door. "Since you said please."

"It's the incubates." Roman looked for somewhere to sit. A folding chair was against the wall. He brought it to the table and sat down.

"Have a seat, why don't you."

"Lucius, I don't have a lot of time."

"You had time to send me the girl. She already explained your not-so-little problem, remember?"

"The behavior is all off-track. We're going to lose Willing Women over it. Housemothers are at a loss. If we don't do something soon, the error will become very public knowledge. So far no one has put it together but - "

"Error? Developing thousands of fetuses in incubation who were designed for womb birth is an 'error'? How many of them are there?"

"Fourteen thousand."

"*Fourteen thousand?* I can't be hearing you correctly."

"We went straight to scale. Births are on a rolling basis. We're preparing for several contingents."

"Stop, stop, stop. Fourteen thousand?"

"We had precedent."

"You had no such thing."

"We saw reports from Rainfields."

"The Rainfields official program never saw more than a few hundred, and they were experimental, closely monitored. And even so, several have found themselves in Cork Town. I have a neighbor who - "

"The Queen - I mean, Maeva - said there were records held in Royal archives, that you had experience you hadn't filed in Central Tower. She said it was feasible."

"Feasible. Oh, Maeva." Lucius let out a sigh. "The girl who came never mentioned fourteen thousand."

"That's over the last five years."

"You quadrupled the regular Willing Woman birth rate."

"That was the point."

"And you didn't pause to assess their viability, I see."

"We were moving at scale.

"Moving at scale. Moving at scale. Stop saying you were moving at scale! You were reckless. Careless. And worse, you were idiotic. You know better. Queen or not, you know how this is done. But your ambition got in the way. Was that when she offered you the title? I know Maeva. Look the other way in exchange for position. And you would have done it. What am I saying? You did it. You don't have to tell me. I know. You traded your integrity for an engraved brass plate." Lucius stood up from his wheelchair, leaning in front of Roman, his face and hot breath too close for Roman to focus. "And now look what you've done."

Sweat dripped down the side of Lucius' face. He turned back to the wheelchair and dropped himself in, the floor creaking around him.

Roman's voice was stuck in his throat. He managed a whisper.

"Lucius, I've made a terrible mistake, and I can't fix it. I need you."

Roman took in a deep breath, hoping this would give Lucius what he wanted. Maybe now they could start talking about the cases at hand. He watched Lucius' face go from bemusement to something like shock, and finally his eyes lit up, but not in the way Roman had hoped.

"You don't need me. You still don't get it." Lucius shook his head and hit the table. "Use your brain, Roman! There is no fix. The problem here is not scientific. You have traumatized these children. *Fourteen thousand* children with dissociative, disorganized attachment disorder. They needed warmth, they needed connection. They needed a bond, and you gave them a box. There is no treatment; this is social. And that's far beyond the ability of Central Tower to fix. I can't fix this, Roman. For what you've done, no science, no genetics, no medication short of tranquilizers will have any effect. And from what I know, tranquilizers do not help an army fight against an invading force. Your soldiers against the so-called invasions from Upper Earth are compromised."

Lucius sat back in his chair.

"Therefore I couldn't help you even if I wanted to."

I don't believe him.

Roman's gut was twisting, but he wouldn't give up. He had to make some progress. Lucius had to come around. He needed Lucius to at least try.

"Alright. I see what you're saying. I need to think about it, but I hear you, Lucius." He stood from the chair and moved around behind it, leaning forward. "Let me present you with a different challenge then."

Lucius blinked, his mouth agape, but Roman continued.

"Put the existing phases of incubates aside. I recognize now my failings in it. I'm not trying to smooth that over. But thinking about the future - "

"Don't tell me you want this to continue?"

"We have no choice, Lucius."

"You are completely brainwashed."

"Upper Earth is not so far away."

"Do you hear yourself?"

"We will continue our munitions programs, but we need soldiers."

"You need to leave."

Roman heard the pitch in his voice mount, but he couldn't do anything about it now. "We have to be prepared!"

"We don't even know that there ever will be such an invasion. And even if there were - do you know who's in Upper Earth, Roman? I know you do. You know it as well as I do. Men. You want us to fight against our own?"

"They'll kill us off."

"You don't know that."

"We'll lose everything we've built, everything Central Tower has accomplished, everything you have - "

"Don't bring me into this."

"The Queen - "

"The Queen is wrong."

"She intends to have an army to fight them off."

"The Queen is wrong!"

"She may be wrong, but she's Queen!" Roman lowered his voice. "What do you want me to do Lucius? Tell me, I'll do it. Nothing is as it was supposed to be. Just tell me, and I'll do."

Lucius looked at Roman for a long time. Roman could hardly bear to hold his gaze, but he did. Because he had to. Because he needed Lucius to understand. He needed Lucius to come back to the Tower.

Lucius brought his hands to his face. He rubbed his eyes and then rested his forehead in his palms.

"Go, Roman. Please just go. I'll think about what you've said. I'll send word when I've had time to process all this. Please."

Roman waited, hoping Lucius would change his mind. Hoping he would say something, anything, that Roman could action.

But Lucius didn't say another word. He kept his face in his hands, his chest rising and falling over his gut.

Roman stood, giving Lucius one last look before clicking the door shut.

16

Lucius knocked over a Petri dish and it smashed on the concrete floor of the lab.

Damn it, he's thrown me all off now.

Lucius worked in a frenzy. He hoped the familiar smells and challenges of the lab would wipe away the past hour he spent with Roman.

He knew what Roman was trying to do. He knew he was appealing to Lucius' sense of duty, his former failures, and the opportunity to redeem himself. And he knew it was a farce, a trick. He was being manipulated.

Or am I?

Roman doesn't know anything about what really happened at Rain-fields. He doesn't know the depth of what I've done. I can't be held fully responsible for the chaos of Maeva's birth among the thousand other Queen infants, though it wouldn't have happened without me.

Lucius swept the glass shards into a corner. He couldn't bend over to sweep them up. There was a collection of dust and broken pieces of various equipment in the corner. It hadn't occurred to him to install a vacuum down there. The corner was an otherwise fine resting spot.

He sat on the oversized stool; *that* he had thought of in advance. He threw all his thinking into the chromosomal structure of 4957. He'd always hoped 4957 would be his redeemer. It was supposed to be Adam who would be his redeemer, but since Adam was now dead, 4957 was his only chance.

Sara thinks Adam was disappeared. Just as well. The truth would shake up their delicate balance.

He looked up from the structure, thinking of Sara.

I don't have the heart to tell her. She's better off this way. The girl loved him, even if we had done everything to scrub individualistic loyalty from the code.

He let out a long breath and felt something deep inside his body. Something different. Something unexpected. And he couldn't identify it.

What's that about now? I can't be further degrading already?

He thought back to his genetic modification cocktail, how long ago had it been that he'd administered the therapy? It prolonged life, but not indefinitely. Degradation would come for him eventually. Like Martin. Like every other man.

Stay focused on the structure, Lucius. No point in being distracted by the inevitable. If anything, I'd better speed this up.

He examined his newest modifications to 4957. He'd taken a different approach. Nothing like they originally envisaged. The original plan had come up empty, the child would die like the others when the organs grew into their full size, the acceleration too advanced to then be slowed down. He hadn't been able to crack it. A child with a vastly overgrown heart and impending liver failure was not going to be the *coup de grâce*. It wasn't good enough.

He looked at the sequences for 4957-208.

Something in the fourteenth gene isn't looking quite right, it might inter-fere - but it's close.

He scanned the enzymes, the proteins, the chromosomes.

He compared them against 4957-207, which had felt so close before falling apart entirely.

The conflict with the nucleotide sequence is solved; the structure must be corrected now.

Lucius looked up from the papers for a moment, his heart beating faster.

If I just adjust the eighth chromosome can that be right? Yes, it's in the eighth, I see it clearly now... and if we include a tunable cancer cell to ensure ongoing growth, that will counter any effect from the anomaly in the fourteenth gene, for the most part anyhow.

He felt the idea strike him like an anvil to his head.

If I blend it with the common code of men...

He almost couldn't let his mind take it any further, the excitement of it bubbled in him like champagne. His head became light.

With the common code of men...

He rested his elbows on the stainless steel table and let his head drop into them.

We just might be able to overcome the sequence of advanced degradation.

Keeping his head resting on his hands, he looked at the sequence on the table between his elbows.

I've got it. I've got it. For the sake of every man on Lower Earth, I think I've got it.

Lucius lifted his head. The breakthrough breathing new life into his veins, his brain snapping into action, swirling and speeding faster than he could consciously follow, he computed probabilities and scenarios. All of them were possible.

He had to try.

He thought his heart might burst at the finding, a discovery that had the potential to change the face of Lower Earth. He stood from his stool and grabbed his lab coat. There was no one to tell, no soul with which to share his elation. He put his face in his coat and screamed with joy, muffling the sound as best he could, this was not the moment to have his lab found out.

He let the coat drop to the floor, his heart beating in his head and his breathing quick.

Do I contact Sara? No, too risky at this point. I cannot seek her out; she has to come back to me. I'll prepare the serum. I can do most of it without Central Tower.

He couldn't have known he was this close to breaking the code, to finding 4957-209. Had he known he would have used Sara for more, had her do the next stage of recruitment. But there was no telling when she would be back.

This couldn't wait. Lucius couldn't wait.

I have to find a woman to carry it.

He closed his eyes. There was only one way.

Trudith would help him.

What he would have done to have Rose with him now. How he missed her. How she could have helped him. He spoke quietly into the air.

"My little fairy, wherever you are, you be safe. You come back to me. I have news you won't believe. Or maybe you will. You always had more confidence in me than I deserved."

Lucius changed his clothes. Washed his face. Tried to do something with his hair. It had been so long since he'd had to face the good people of Cork Town. He hadn't left his apartment in nearly three years.

He stepped into the dwindling light of day. The timekeeper's bells would ring soon.

Perhaps that's just as well, I can move through the crowds less noticed.

But the concept of a crowd made Lucius' throat close.

I'll get through it. They're just people. Only in a larger dose than that with which I've become accustomed. That's not their fault. Focus on the objective, Lucius. Just get to the pub and figure out the rest as you go.

He stepped out onto the gravel of the Twenty-Ninth Alleyway off the Fourteenth Road. He'd always been so pleased to have found a spot, near-invisible, in the far end of Cork Town. But now he had to walk into the heart of the commune with his cane, and he cursed the distance. He took a step. And another.

Don't think beyond the next corner. You'll get there when you get there.

He had reached the far end of Cork Row when the time-keeper's bells clanged. He caught glimpse of the woman with her bells, walking up and down the roads and alleys of the commune, taking the exact same route every day, for fairness. It seemed like that was the only thing in Cork Town for which the principle of fairness was applied, and the people were insistent on it. Days when the timekeeper walked at a slower pace, or heaven forbid a replacement covered a day, the people were up in arms. He could hear it even from the Twenty-Ninth Alleyway. Voices of protest in the street walking by saying things like, "She went down Sixth Road first, can you believe that?"

He moved further along Cork Row, women emerging from the different buildings around him. The few small factories, several small shops, a processing plant for Geb's sewage in the distance. Women filled Cork Row.

He saw the Guard ahead of him. He'd expected it, what with the various crackdowns that had taken place.

Two guards looked in his direction, but he couldn't tell if they were looking at him or the crowd more generally. They looked to each other and then began walking towards him.

They're coming for me. Not a surprise, I rather stand out. Just have to play cool.

"Lucius."

"Ah, you know me. That makes this easier." He tried to give a little smile.

"It's been a long time we haven't seen you on Cork Row."

"It's been a long time since I came."

"Why today?"

He gestured towards his legs, "Degradation coming. I have to move while I can. Soon I'll be completely confined to that wheelchair."

"So you go for a stroll during the control hour?"

"Control hour?" Something tinged in Lucius's stomach.

The guards looked again at each other.

"Your papers, Lucius."

"Papers?"

"You can't expect us to believe you're roaming at this hour without your papers."

"I thought papers were for visitors."

"Have you been living under a rock?"

"Figuratively."

"When was the last time you came out, Lucius."

He inhaled and looked up, "Approximately eight hundred and forty days ago."

The guards just looked at him.

"I didn't know anything about papers."

"Don't you listen to the screen?"

"I live on Twenty-Ninth Alley. I can't hear it from there."

"Someone must have told you."

"No one visits me, at least no one who says anything about any control hours."

One guard looked to the other. "I believe him."

"We can't make exceptions."

The first guard looked back at Lucius. "Do you have papers?"

"Of course, stuffed in the back of a drawer. But I can find them."

The second guard lifted her chin. "Head home, Lucius. Go for your stroll tomorrow. With your papers."

"Be more mindful of conditions in Cork Town, or you might find yourself in real trouble," the first guard added.

"Yes, of course. I'll take the back roads home so as not to

make a scene. I wouldn't want to put you in an uncomfortable situation in front of others. Good day." He nodded deeply, knowing they were staring at him.

He turned left, down Sixth Road. From there, if they hadn't changed the layout, which was always possible, he could cut behind and get to the pub. Assuming they didn't follow him. Assuming he didn't come across any others. Lucius' heart beat harder and faster than he knew possible.

He walked, weight heavy on the cane now, turning the last corner before the pub's alleyway. He saw it, so close, and he let out a breath that he felt he'd been holding since meeting the guards.

He pushed through the swinging door that was almost unremarkable on the street. His eyes had to adjust to the darkness inside the pub. It appeared to be a black hole in front of him, though he knew he was inside, knew the layout. He had been there many times before, but that had been before all of this. Before, when he was the Great Geneticist. Before Cork Town was enclosed and when Rose went there daily. Before Cork Town became a ghetto.

He blinked and began to be able to make out some shapes. Ten or so women sitting around a table.

And they were all staring straight at him.

"Good evening, ladies. Please, don't let me interrupt."

"Lucius?" A woman behind the bar stepped out and walked over to him, wiping her hands on a rag.

Lucius smiled. "How've you been, Trude?"

17

Trudith leaned against the bar and rubbed her arm where they had taken the blood in the mandatory rounds. The place in the fold of her elbow was already bruising. She listened to the women speak. For ages, they had been coming into the pub after the timekeeper's bells and after the controls. How many years had they complained, conspired, and made grandiose plans?

But that had all changed since the woman from Central Tower had come. Sara, her name was, with a story that seemed part possible, part fantasy. A story of secrets underway in Cork Town and possibilities for preserving humanity. She'd made it sound so large, so important. Trudith could hardly believe she'd come to the pub to seek out support.

Now they've become more selective, less sensational. She gave them something, some kind of hope, that they could be a part of something bigger. This is dangerous. It's very, very dangerous.

But Trudith understood why they wanted it. Even she was not immune to the treatment in the streets, the hardening rules, the growing barriers in front of them. Sometimes Cork Town felt like a noose that was tightening.

Things had been easier when Rose had been around. It wasn't that Trudith needed help with the work, she didn't. The clientele had reduced over the past years, everyone afraid of doing something that might cross a line. Even just a visit to the pub. Trudith could handle management and operation of the pub on her own. But Rose had more presence than Trudith realized. It seemed as though she hid in a corner on most days, at the time Trudith felt like she rarely saw her at all even though they were in the same room. But Trudith realized now that it wasn't the case. Rose had been a constant, ever-present, dare she say, friend? Trudith knew so little about Rose; she felt ashamed now for not taking a greater interest. She had made many assumptions because of Rose's condition, her disfigurement. More than she should have. Rose had been there when things had first gotten noticeably hard in Cork Town. The market raid. Trudith shuddered at the memory. The sight of blood and the taste of fear in her mouth. Metallic. She'd been in the market when it happened, looking for barley, as it had been a bad season with the viruses. A bad season that had turned into a bad period and now a seemingly permanent condition of modern life.

Seven years since that day when they beat the man in the market, and look where we've gone since. I never would have imagined. I never could have guessed.

Trudith touched her pocket where she kept her papers and then brought her hand to the lava amulet around her neck.

Could we have fought the changes? Could we have stopped things from becoming this bad?

Trudith absent-mindedly wiped at the bar, even though she already had her answer. It had been within six months of the new Queen's coronation that things had turned for the worst. They didn't see it at first; the arguments had been logical, even if now they made no sense at all.

They put limitations on food consumption and access. And still, nothing has improved for us here. Wasn't that the point of all this? Wasn't that how the directive on carrying identity papers came to be, to assure equality, fairness? It had seemed so reasonable. Even necessary. And now? Mandatory blood collection. The end-of-day controls. It wasn't supposed to be like this.

Then Rose had left. She hadn't shown for work in three days, which hadn't happened in the three years since Trudith had taken over the pub. Rose had come with the pub. She was as much a fixture in it as the countertop under her fingers.

And then, just like that, she was gone. Trudith had found Rose in the morning, behind the pub, waiting for her. "I'm sorry, I have to go," were the only words she'd said. But Trudith somehow understood. She couldn't place the feeling, but she understood. Was it because Rose was among the most disfigured in Cork Town and would experience greater persecution than others? Or did Rose see the crackdown coming and couldn't bear to live in it? Or...was it something else entirely?

Maybe Rose was right. We live this half-life now and we don't even know why. The screen tells us nothing of our actual conditions. Sometimes I'm sure Mary is outright false. Soil viruses? I don't buy it. It's an easy answer for the lack of resources in Cork Town. Too easy an answer. Something isn't right. Someone is lying.

But there was nothing to be done about it. Not now. Maybe not ever, with this Queen.

Queen Ariane. I thought things might have gotten better with her. At least Maeva used to come to Cork Town. She tried to show solidarity, even if times were hard. But Queen Ariane?

Trudith rubbed the amulet between her thumb and forefinger.

I'm not sure what the Royalty even stands for anymore.

"If I have to watch one more guard push a child into their house, I just might lose it. What's wrong with them playing on the street in off-hours? They've reduced the schooling time.

Magda of the sixth line, you know, the one three doors down from me? She must be sixteen years old. And she can't read. Not because she can't. But because they're not teaching it anymore." Krescencia sat back in her chair. "Not teaching reading."

Heads around the table nodded.

"It's all part of some plan they have."

"And it's working."

"I'm sure it's part of the reason for limits on circulation. Forget all that blather about crop killers. There's no way that's related to us. They're just looking for a scapegoat."

Trudith heard the door swing open and her heart jumped. Her eyes darted at the door in silent prayer that it wasn't a guard.

Please tell me this isn't how everything ends.

Trudith couldn't believe her eyes.

She'd thought of Lucius a few times over the past years since he'd gone quiet, but she never expected him to show up in her pub again.

And then Sara had come.

Of course, Lucius would send Sara to the pub, straight to her. Though Rose had few things to say, she spoke kind words of her guardian, the former Great Geneticist. Trudith still remembered when he held the title though he was already degrading and living in Cork Town. She'd had some misplaced hope that his living in the commune meant their lives might somehow integrate with Geb again. When Lucius was stripped of his title, her hopes disappeared with it.

And now he was standing right in front of her.

"This is a surprise," Trudith managed to say. "We had the woman you sent over here just a couple of days - "

"Yes, yes, I know. Trude, do you have something cold to drink? I've had to walk a long way with this cane, never mind the guards who got my blood pressure up."

Trudith noticed there was sweat rolling down the sides of Lucius' face. "Yes, of course, sit down why don't you?"

He nodded and hobbled past the table of women. They'd shut up as soon as Lucius walked in. It was one thing for them to see Sara, a woman, even if she was from Geb. But Lucius? This would have their heads scurrying. Trudith knew it.

Yala hissed across the table, but loud enough to be heard. "Did you hear that Isabel disappeared yesterday?"

"Isabel of the fourth line?"

"No, third."

"Oh, thank god. I just saw Isabel of the fourth line two days ago. She was yakking about how her building had been raided. I thought maybe that's why they'd take her, for blabbing about the raid."

"No, it was the third line, I'm sure of it."

"Isabel of the third line had it coming. Just couldn't keep her mouth shut, not in the same way as the fourth line Isabel. Third line had a problem in the head. She truly couldn't tell when to shut it or not."

Yala looked over to Lucius and then back to the women. "Maybe we should change the subject."

"Don't let me stop you, ladies," Lucius said, "These are worrying times indeed."

"Is that why you sent that woman here?"

"I didn't send her, I asked her to come."

"She had some real concerning things to say." Yala slowly stood from the table.

"Yes, she did."

"But she had some ideas too. Ideas that might affect us directly."

Trudith watched Yala's verbal dance. Throwing some hints out, watching Lucius' reaction. She wasn't bad at it, considering that Yala had a tendency to speak harsh words too quickly.

Trudith brought over iced lemon water. She couldn't keep much ice, but she felt Lucius deserved it. He lived on the far side of town. In his condition, hobbling to the pub might almost put his life in danger. Though it was true he'd survived longer than any of them so far. She didn't know how old he was, but she knew he was very old. His face didn't give it away. She could see something in him, when she took off the years and effects of the degradation. He had been a very beautiful man, at one time. But it must have been a long time ago.

"Sara is a very good woman," Lucius wiped his forehead with his arm. "Trustworthy."

"Yeah, I thought so too. But when she started talking about one of us being a Willing Woman, you know, in secret," Yala walked towards Lucius, "That's a pretty frightening prospect you know. Could get us disappeared, you know."

What's she going to do? Is she going to threaten him? There's something in her swagger.

Trudith stepped out from behind the bar, concerned that her pub might become the sight of something unseemly if Yala made a wrong move.

"Yala," she said, "What are you doing?"

"I want to talk with the Great Geneticist."

"So talk from back where you were."

Yala raised her hands as though to show she had no weapon. She must have heard the worry in Trudith's voice. She picked up a stool and took it to Lucius' table while the other women sat with their mouths open.

"Speak, old man. Sara was supposed to be the one to come back. Why are you here?"

Lucius cocked his head.

"Come on, out with it," Yala's tone was somewhere between threatening and curious. Trudith stood nearby.

"You're right to be suspicious," Lucius said. "Today was the first time in nearly three years I've set foot on these streets. Much has changed. And not for the better."

"Three years?" Anna said. "How could you stay inside for three years?"

"I have a lot to occupy my mind," Lucius tapped his forehead. "And I'll tell you all about it. I don't have secrets to keep from you, not anymore. I don't need secrets, I need allies." Lucius looked straight at Yala. "You want to know if you can trust me. I want to know if I can trust *you*."

The pub went quiet. Trudith looked from the table of women who had been meeting there for months now, back to Lucius who seemed to be offering something that was what they'd all been looking for. A chance to take action. Something to do. A way to be useful. A way to undo what had been done to them.

"You can trust me," Trudith said.

Yala's eyes narrowed, but something in her softened.

Lucius nodded, "You already know we will need a woman. But this one woman will need a team behind her. You need to know what you're getting into here. I don't have much to lose anymore. I don't know how long I have left. I'll never go back to the Tower, but my work is not yet done. I need a woman to give birth, and this will not be a regular child. I couldn't let Sara tell you everything. No, I need a woman to give birth to a boy. I have designed a boy. And I think he will survive."

The women looked from one to the other, necks snapping. Even Trudith did not expect to hear this. *A boy?*

"It'll be a boy, building on the common sequence of men, but he will have sequences from women who have - skills. The gestation period will be longer than it is for Willing Women, this is a long-term commitment. I'm not willing to accelerate it. It has to be as it was before we first began altering the sequences. Nine months."

Trudith swallowed hard.

He's taking a great risk coming here, speaking like this. Any of the women could report him.

Trudith looked at the faces of the women around the table, all with an unexpected expression. Calm, assured.

They won't report him. He's giving them something to live for.

"You want to save the men," Anna said.

"I want to give men a chance." Lucius raised his hands in the air. "But there's no more to say unless there's someone among you who would be ready to risk her life for this. This isn't just about getting disappeared anymore. This is so much more than that."

"We could get disappeared any day," Matilde spoke. "They're looking for reasons now. It could be any one of us, any day."

Anna held the amulet, twisting it with her fingers. "This isn't a greater risk than us being here right now with the conversations we've been having."

Yala stood up. "A boy? Yeah, I did not see that coming." She looked to the women and back to Lucius, " We trust you. And you can trust us."

Lucius let out a big breath of air. "Trude, would you get me another one of these divine drinks? Nothing ever tasted so wonderful. And we're going to be here for a while. We have much to discuss."

18

The cool night air invaded Leadon's hut, settling across her skin. She inhaled deeply through her nostrils, letting the smell of the fire fill her up. She closed her eyes. Even over the crackle, she could hear the six women standing with her, a circle around the fire. Their breathing, shifting positions. She opened her eyes and scanned them. They all kept their eyes tightly shut.

Joom, Rianh, Adanni, and Ahnira had all accepted her invitation. She already knew that Priyantha and Miliah would come. She was winning them over, slowly. It would take time. She had trust to build after decades of them believing she didn't belong among them. Seven women in whom the Ganese blood was strong. Not just in their physique, though the black hair, dark skin, and tall feminine figure were common between them, but in their belief that all they were living now had come before.

Leadon looked at Rianh who had come from the West. Leadon smiled. She intended to bridge the divide that had emerged between East and West Gana in these recent years.

Leadon sang at the fire, a low prayer for unity. The others

repeated after her. They all closed their eyes and lifted their hands in the direction of the smoke, up higher and into the next world, where all who came before would infuse their wisdom within them.

They sang, each her own individual song, the voices mixing and colliding into a beautiful wild call to the beyond. Leadon felt compelled to open her eyes to look on the scene.

That's when she saw Irene standing in the doorway.

They locked eyes and held them. Leadon softened her face, hoping the invitation to Irene would be apparent. Irene didn't see the invitation or paid it no mind, for she stayed in the doorway, unmoving, eyes on Leadon.

The women finished their song and let their hands drop to their knees. They opened their eyes, one warrior priestess then another looked to Leadon. She felt their eyes on her, but she did not break Irene's gaze. The women followed Leadon's look to the door. All eyes were on Irene now.

And still, Irene didn't give any sign. Finally, Irene took in a deep breath. "Your prayers are important. But they are insufficient."

"I do not argue for their sufficiency." Leadon stepped toward her. "You have come during a sacred moment."

"I wish I could have seen you doing something more indicative of our peoples' way."

"More indicative than prayer?"

"We are *warrior* priestesses." Irene spat, her shoulders pulling her taller, her head grazing the top of the entryway. "It's time you acted like it."

Leadon felt something stirring in her, a foreign feeling. Not the shame that had blanketed her in Geb. This was different. She was on her soil now. She was making progress. And Irene had no right to stand there laying judgments.

She speaks out of turn.

"Warrior priestesses," Leadon continued, "I thank you for

your communion. Please continue your tasks as discussed. I will remain here so that I may speak to the concerns of our *friend,* Irene."

These women had better leave quickly, for I am now beginning to understand why the Ganese distrusted my genes. Irene is closer to Royalty than she is to us. Too close to this imposter Queen.

It's time she answered for it to her people.

19

Irene wanted to kick the fire, rush the women out of there like children, chastise them for their laziness, their passiveness.

Everything that's happening in this world and they are standing around praying.

It didn't matter that Irene understood that it was part of their tradition, and an important part. Something in her had hoped she would arrive in Gana to find the women in frenzied activity, training, preparing, strategizing.

Not singing around a fire.

She didn't know how to impress upon them the precipice on which they were all walking. She feared it would fall on deaf ears even if she did. Irene knew her position in Gana was tenuous. It had been that way since Maeva had first called her from the tribe to serve in the fortress. But how could she have said no?

Irene knew the call to the fortress would likely mean the end of her kinship with the Ganese, just as had happened for Sahna when she'd left Gana to serve Maeva all those years ago. The warrior priestesses had always been wary of their own moving off to serve another master. It was written across their history, and it never ended well. Even Sahna had found herself ejected from all communities. That's why she'd established the cult of the Sisters.

And yet the Ganese had withstood every trial. When their leaders had negotiated with the new peoples who landed before the Mist, when modern life threatened to take away all they had developed over thousands of years, the Ganese remained. When the settlers came and rearranged their land, politics, and power, the Ganese remained. Even the procreation wall that had been thrown up with the death of the Ganese warrior priests - their husbands, fathers, sons — still they had found their way through by negotiating with Central Tower. One-to-one birth rate with normalized Ganese genetic code, that was all they asked for in exchange for predictions on land and crop health. That had long been in the Ganese blood. They knew the land better than anyone since the first settlers had arrived.

They were the original peoples of Lower Earth.

And what will our people come to with Leadon at the head of it all? Her, of all people! What game was Batrasa playing? What was she thinking?

Irene waited until the other women filed out, leaving her alone with Leadon. Irene had never grown accustomed to seeing her face on another's body, even if she understood why. Even more so, she didn't recognize herself in this other person. Leadon, so far from her own character. Meek, gentle, kind. Needy.

Irene couldn't wait any longer. The last of the women filed out of the hut.

"What strategies do you have in place, Leadon?"

Leadon's eyes betrayed no hint. "Strategies?"

"Yes, strategies. Negotiations with the other peoples. Negotiations with Geb. Agriculture development. Warrior preparation. What are you putting in place?"

Leadon crossed her arms. "I am starting with cultural evolution."

Irene nearly choked.

"Cultural what?"

"We have a divide in our people, Irene. It's unhealthy. It will only become a larger gap within Gana. I am unifying East and West."

"Is this a joke?"

"It's no light matter."

"Worse than that, it's irrelevant."

Leadon's eyes narrowed. "When did you last live in Gana, Irene?"

"That is not - "

"Relevant?" Leadon sighed. "Let me explain. We have many trials on the horizon, natural and human-made. Many are already on our doorstep. The crop killers, the viruses, the changing seasonal patterns. Divisions in Lower Earth are becoming more acute. The threat from Upper Earth remains a current underneath it all."

Leadon walked to the main door of the hut.

Irene followed behind, stunned still at the idea of *cultural evolution*.

Leadon gestured into the women who mingled in the pathways in front of her hut. "Do you see how they demarcate themselves? At first, I thought it was only those who wore the traditional garb from the West, but then I started watching more closely. There are greetings that Westerners give each other. There are styles of speaking used by the more permissive Easterners. They live together, but they are not *one*." Leadon looked back to Irene. "They are on the verge, Irene. If we come to a great test, as our ancestors did - be it starvation or war - we will crack down the middle. Our seams will split. It will be the end of Gana. Batrasa saw it, but she laid her hope on Aria being the one to unite all of Lower Earth. And now look where we are. Look," Leadon paused, "Look how our *Queen* plays on the divisions in Lower Earth. Gana will be no exception."

Irene controlled her questions.

She called her the Queen, she didn't call her Aria. What does she know of Aria? She can't know that she's dead. She must believe the Queen is Aria, or does she?

Irene didn't know how far to take the questioning. It wouldn't change the course of their conversation and it wouldn't change the course of Leadon's chieftainship. Irene would not test those waters now, lest Leadon become suspicious.

"You underestimate our Queen," Irene tilted her head. "You have so little knowledge of what goes on beyond these borders."

Leadon stepped forward, "And why is that, Irilena? Where were you, my kin? When I needed this guidance, when I needed friendship, when I needed someone to buffer the masses who judged me for the condition of my birth, where were you? Nowhere to be found. Hardly even returned, and when you did, I was like a scab, a parasite you flicked away. I have much to make up for now, and I'm learning quickly. All the times I asked so little of you, and now you come to cast judgment." Leadon shook her head.

Irene felt her spine pull up, "You were common. There was nothing you needed from me. You were not and were never intended to be Chief of our people."

"So you're jealous."

"Jealous? I am doing everything within my power to work within a system our ancestors despised. This was no choice of mine, but I will represent our people with pride."

Leadon whispered, "Irene, you don't even know who these people are anymore. We're in a crisis here. Never mind Geb, never mind the rest. I have to start here because those who came before and those who *left* have given me no choice but to rebuild."

"Your *cultural evolution*."

"Yes."

"You are a naive child." Irene could stand by no more, humoring Leadon's ways would only encourage her deeper along this mistaken path. "Look at these women. For generations, they have been allowed to become soft. You want a cultural evolution, start with our roots, Leadon!" Her voice was getting louder, the sound coming from somewhere deep within, saying words she'd held back for so many years. "We are warriors first, my misguided genetic kin! Forget this talk of garb and greetings, we must go back to who we were, who we've always been." Irene put her hands on Leadon's cheeks. "You grew up in the fields, your privileged country lifestyle. You know nothing of the world we are becoming. You may be able to lead your little cultural evolution, and then where will we be? Singing around a fire as the land burns around us. We will be conquered without seeing the enemy coming. You play at leadership while the *Queen* has all of Lower Earth riding on her shoulders. You'd best watch your loyalties. First to Gana, then to Queen."

"To Queen Ariane? You'd have me pledge my loyalty to Queen Ariane?" Leadon's shoulders pulled in. Irene couldn't understand the tone of her question.

"You've been playing as you've always played. But no more. You must abandon your childish fantasies if you are to prevent the Ganese from falling to ruin and extinction."

Leadon stepped close enough to Irene that she could feel her breath on her face. "Go back to Geb, Irene. You have spoken many impermissible words, and I will forgive you for them, but I cannot stand to look on you now. And for the moment, I am Chief and you are in my hut. I will call upon you when I am ready to hear of your ideas for my people. For now, get out of my hut."

Irene felt her temper nearly about to explode, but when she looked on Leadon, she recognized the same fire in this sister-self across from her; the power of their genetic bond was too obvious for her to ignore.

The realization was a bucket of water on her rage. Her breathing slowed.

"I am going, Leadon. But Maeva is coming. I don't know when, but soon, and on order of the Queen. Don't ask me her objectives, I couldn't tell you if I wanted to. What she'll do when she finds you here with your friends, circled around the fire with your hands to the sky, I do not know. But she's coming. Be smart. Be ready."

Irene turned and walked out of the hut without another word. She would return. She always returned. And next time she would be smarter. She would say it in a way that Leadon could not ignore.

20

———

Rose opened her eyes, hearing Irene leave the hut several hundred feet away. Rose's red hair flew across her face in the evening wind. She climbed the tree under which she'd pitched their little tent. She pulled herself up easily, climbing to the highest point that would support her weight, scanning the landscape from along the Gana border. Her eyes found Irene, six hundred feet away. She focused on the distant woman, the retina of her eyes adjusting as required. The Commandante was pounding the ground as she went, her steps heavy with emotion. Rose could see it written across her face.

Commandante retreating, Leadon full of pride. Her position in Gana assaulted. She is raw. Now is a good time to see Leadon at last.

She came back down the tree, hand over hand as a monkey would. She'd always been adept at hiding.

Rose landed on the ground where her little traveling companion was waiting for her. Rose smiled, but she received a scowl in return.

"Are you going?"

"I have to go," she said in low tones, "but I won't be long."

"I don't like it when you go. I don't like it."

"I know you don't. That's why I promise to be as quick as possible. This is an important meeting. I want us to finally have a home." She kneeled down and put her hand on the child's face. "You do as you are supposed to do. No wandering." The child's lips pursed at her. "I mean it. We have to conduct your treatment tonight. You cannot go far."

She let her hands stroke the soft cheeks, seven-year-old cheeks, and the feeling blazed inside her. Such love she never knew she could give. Such love she never knew she could receive. She didn't have to birth a child to feel the pull; ever since she had run into the depths of the Dark Counties and pulled the toddler from the sacrifice table, she knew they were bound together until the end of time.

He was her life.

He was her meaning.

He was the only boy in Lower Earth.

She straightened a lock of hair that had fallen into his face. The long hair was essential so that he would be mistaken for a girl to anyone who may catch sight of them during their travels.

He put his hands on her cheeks, their ceremonial goodbye. He didn't mind the way her skin pulled in multiple directions across her face. He'd never judged her for her disfigurement. He loved that her hair was the color of the fire from which he'd been pulled. He'd been so petrified when she found him that no birth defect could have struck him any deeper into fear. Ever since then, he would run his fingers over the folds of her face, around her widespread eyes, over her protruding ears. He never asked about the accident of her birth. He never knew she died before she was born.

He accepted her as the one who gave him new life.

His mother.

Even though she still felt such longing in her - for the life she was supposed to have, for her sister selves, for those who had died and for those who were estranged - Zev gave her new hope. Rose had been a lost soul, full of anger, full of right-eousness. She still had those feelings, but she tamed them. They had been destructive, eating away at her, breaking down her being. When she arrived in the Dark Counties and heard the voices of the people in hushed tones speaking of their plans to kill the boy, those feelings all dropped aside. Who was behind it, Rose couldn't tell. It wasn't the women themselves, she could hear the hesitation in their voices, but someone had planted the superstitious idea, and it only took one to commit the act.

Her longing remained, one day it would rise again in her. But for now, she was satisfied, fulfilled even, whenever Zev laid his head on her chest to sleep. She stood taller than him, but the day would come when he would far surpass her. She hadn't grown after the age of twelve. All part of her gene sequence, which had been unnaturally modified.

Her DNA was a mosaic.

She inhaled deeply. If she were to go to Leadon, she would have to call up old memories, painful memories. She steeled herself for the words she would have to say.

"Don't be long," Zev repeated, pulling Rose back into the moment.

She smiled and touched his head before running at a speed that only Rose - and the few with whom she shared her original DNA - could.

She paused outside Leadon's hut. She had heavy news to share, and she wasn't sure how the new Chief would take it. Leadon had been a friend to Aria.

Aria, beloved sister. How the world would have been different had you become Queen.

And Ariane, sister of Strangelands, where have you gone? Did you throw yourself off the Rainfields cliffs like so many who came before? I no longer feel you. I can't sense your heartbeat anymore. Are you dead or are you away? Will you ever come back?

It still struck Rose as sick how four daughters had the code of one mother, and all had been given the same name.

Mother played it dangerously, laying bets across daughters, playing with life circumstances as a test for future resilience. It was wrong, Mother. You were so wrong. Look at us now.

She centered herself. Rose looked up at the rising moon and touched the pelt over the entry. Fox fur, it had the same color hair as her. Rose pulled the hut curtain aside and entered.

Leadon was seated on a stool, her face resting in her hands. Rose stepped, quieter than sound. She let her hand run along the wall of the hut to catch Leadon's attention, not wanting to surprise her, trying to gently rouse her from her thoughts. But Leadon didn't stir.

Rose looked down at herself. Her cape hid the worst of her deformity, the hood pulled low over her face. Her height was an advantage in these situations, most believed her to be a child. When she was with Zev they appeared to be two girls in the countryside, not an unfamiliar sight in the Outer Counties. It was only Geb that was off-limits. Rose knew they'd be found out within moments of their arrival. But Gana was safe. Leadon was safe.

Rose whispered.

"Leadon?"

Finally, Leadon's head rose from her hands. "Child, why are you here? Who allowed you to enter?"

"Forgive me, I need to speak with you."

"I am not in the spirits for speaking."

"I know things you must hear."

Leadon cocked her head to the side, her black hair falling over her shoulder. "If you have things that I must hear, then I must hear them." She gestured for Rose to approach. "Remove your hood, child."

Rose hesitated. "I will, but let me first begin my story."

Leadon opened her hands in front of her in the Ganese way, inviting Rose to begin.

But the beginning wasn't evident. Rose had thought it over many times but now that Leadon was in front of her, beginning was harder than she'd expected.

"You knew my sister," Rose began.

"Who is your sister?"

"She spent time here, much time. She grew here. She loved Gana though she was foreign to its ways."

Leadon's head pulled upright.

"I have come because my sister has been wronged. So very wronged. There is no saving her from the wrong she has been done. But there needs to be right in our world."

"Who is your sister?" Leadon's voice was barely above a rasp.

Rose swallowed.

"Tell me, child, who is your sister?" Leadon was leaning forward now, the hint of it pulling at her. Rose could see that Leadon sensed it. She heard Leadon's blood rushing from her heart through her veins the blood pumping and the beat accelerating.

Rose slowly removed her hood.

Leadon's eyes batted to clear but she did not recoil at the sight.

"I am no child. I call myself Rose, because I must. My birth name is charged, my birth name is borrowed. My sister was my sister-self, a parallel to your experience with the Commandante. But different. Deeper. And broken." She watched Leadon's eyes darting trying to keep up with the information. "We have much to discuss, but let me be clear with you in a way you cannot help but understand."

Rose paused, breathing the secret one last time.

"Aria was my sister."

"Aria?" Leadon pulled herself forward off the stool onto her knees. "Come, come closer, Rose. Let me look upon your face."

Rose hesitated but knew Leadon needed this. She stepped forward to the kneeling Chief and closed her eyes. She felt Leadon looking at her, from crown to foot, heard her breath move in angles.

"Rose, what you say is near unbelievable."

Rose opened her eyes.

Leadon continued, "I believe you."

Rose inhaled, relief washing over her like a waterfall.

"Rose, please, tell me. Where has Aria gone? Where did they take her? Can I find her? Can we bring her back? The Queen is false. I knew it the moment I laid my eyes on her. This cannot continue; Aria was meant to lead this world. She was born for it, raised for it, she had goodness in her and the ancestors of Gana infused in her, even if she was not of our blood. Please, Rose, where is she?"

Rose's mouth hung slightly open. It hadn't occurred to her that Leadon would think Aria was still alive.

"Leadon - " the eyes beseeched Rose and her heart broke again for the sister-self she'd lost. "She's dead."

Leadon dropped deeper into her knees, a whimper escaping her lips. "Dead?"

Rose watched the realization roll over Leadon, heard her blood pump hard into her brain, and then slowly calm. Leadon blinked and then nodded her head.

"I understand."

Rose stood still, letting Leadon process it as she sat back onto the stool.

"Rose, you must tell me everything."

Rose straightened her spine. It was all moving ahead as

she'd hoped. "I will. But first, you must call me by my birthright. My name is Ariane."

Leadon listened with wide eyes as Rose took her through it all from beginning to end. Rose felt the pull to go back to her little tent, back to her waiting child, so she glided over details, eager to give Leadon only what she needed. There would be time for the rest later. This was only the beginning. Leadon would have to process this first layer of the story. Rose knew that to those who lived outside it, the concept of multiple genetic copies of the Queen was enough to take in already.

"So you are four?"

"I believe we are four. Aria is dead, Ariane of the Strangelands has vanished. Then there's me and the Queen. A mass of tragedies and social experiments."

"But could there be more of you?"

"I do not believe so."

"How do you know?"

"I have no sense of any others. I always had a sense of the three. Memories I couldn't place, lived moments that weren't my own. I can't easily explain it."

"But you were the first, the Queen's first child. How could you be denied the throne?"

"Look at me, Leadon. Imagine my newborn body emerging from your womb, knowing that you had already killed me inside you and then brought me back to life. The consequences were unknown. I was afraid even of myself. I didn't know then what I know now."

"What do you know now, Ariane?"

Rose relished the sound of her name. "I come from the code of Queens, and I was designed to lead this land. I know that the woman who claimed the throne is a modified version, a redesign of perfection. The result of my mother's own insecurity." Rose turned and looked out the door of the hut, the dark of night fully upon them now. "I know that Lower Earth will suffer under her." She looked back to Leadon. "The current Queen Ariane was designed for a world that never came to be. She was meant for a world at war. She lacks the very humanity that Lower Earth most needs in these times. She will make decisions of precision, mathematical logic, and all at an emotional distance. She'll see half of Lower Earth dead to save those she thinks most worthy." Rose felt the anger boiling, as she had since the day the new Queen emerged on the balcony for her coronation. "That's what *she* was designed for."

Rose opened her lips and took in a cool breath of night air. She felt it touch the back of her throat and down into her lungs. Cooling the fire.

"Leadon, we must be allies. As much as Aria was myself, I consider you my sister."

Leadon looked deep into Rose. "You are sincere. I do not have the experience of my genetic kin, but I have more awareness than she. And I know you are sincere. You have Aria's eyes."

Rose smiled, "She had *my* eyes."

Leadon smiled.

Rose looked over her shoulder, but she sensed no one in the vicinity of the hut. "Leadon, I need a place to stay."

Leadon didn't hesitate. "Gana is your home."

"I have a child."

"A home for you both then."

"My child, like me, is an outcast. Unsafe, the world is unsafe for… for my child. I did not give birth, it is not a child by blood, but yet as much deserving or more of life."

"Of course." Leadon's earnestness did not comfort Rose. She didn't need comfort, she needed safety.

"You offer us home, but all I ask is a hiding place, away from Ganese eyes. They will not understand."

Leadon looked at the ceiling for a moment and then met Rose's eyes. "I know where you can go." Leadon's face softened. "It's perfect actually. Far on the edges of the other side of the river. No Ganese dares to disturb the place, believing it to be the abode of a Queen." Leadon smiled, "Aria's hut."

Rose smiled, "It will be perfect."

Leadon's face darkened. Rose heard the blood accelerate in Leadon's brain, she tried to understand the sudden change, but there had been little to hint of worry or danger until now.

"Maeva is coming," Leadon said, her voice low.

"Maeva?" Rose froze. "Here, she's coming here?"

"Yes, I do not know why. It can't be related to you, can it?"

Rose scanned her memory. "No, it's not possible. She hasn't known of my movements since I left Geb on the day the new Queen was crowned. I have felt her at times, but - " Rose stopped. She didn't know how to explain the sensation to Leadon. The years she and Maeva had been connected despite their separation. The pull they both felt to one another. Code of mother perfected in the daughter, but for a moment of weakness that had changed everything before her birth. A moment that had warped Rose into the woman she'd become.

Rose took Leadon's hand, her white skin glowing against the rich earth color of the Ganese Chief. "I will be careful. I have always been stronger than her. I just didn't know it until I had to."

"We have much to discuss, Ariane." Leadon leaned forward, her hand squeezing Rose's tighter than anyone had done before. "This is just the beginning."

"Just the beginning," Rose whispered in affirmation. So much richness between them already, Rose knew this was more than a union of allies. She bowed her head and then ran out of the hut. Out into black night, running faster than eyes could capture, she ran back to her tent in the trees, back to the home she'd made in her child's heart.

He would be waiting for her.

21

Maeva rode on the donkey's back. She'd refused to take a coach and refused to be accompanied directly. She would ride as a commoner to show her unity with the people. It would show her humility, her simplicity. It was a strategy that Ariane found laughable before waving her hand and sending Maeva back to her little room on the second floor.

At first, the beast was hard to manage. Her trip past the East Fields had been difficult and long. She'd begun regretting her choice. By the time she'd gone to the Lakes District a few weeks later, she understood better the donkey's way. Rather than trying to manage the animal, she had to not manage it at all. She just had to ride. She'd passed nearly two months winding around mountains and coast, through the various settlements. The donkey was her constant companion. Once she'd surrendered to the animal's gait and given up trying to direct it, the gentle sway was surprisingly soothing, more so than that bumpy coach she had taken on all her official visits.

For the unofficial visits, she had always run. It was faster and more covert than any coach.

Many of her senses had begun to numb with time, though

they were only in their very initial stages of decline. Maeva had at least another forty good years. Idia had died at shortly over a hundred years old. Maeva intended to outlive her mother.

Though she wasn't sure she wanted to.

She distracted herself with the donkey's sway. The landscape evolved. The dust of the Central Mass turned into rocky terrain with swatches of green in the distance as she headed east. She came closer to Gana, a day's ride away. The green fields extended for as far as she could see, agricultural fields for as far as she could smell. She arrived at the last checkpoint before Gana, surprised to find her legs stiff from disuse.

I could have made the trip to Gana in just over a day on foot. But I cannot trust myself and now is not the time to have the people catch on to our ways. Ariane would have my head.

"Madam Maeva, you are most welcome at checkpoint A6."

Madam. I don't think I'll ever get used to being called Madam.

A broad woman with standard brown hair and green eyes bowed. Maeva waved absentmindedly.

"Yes, fine. Hello. Where am I to stay?"

The guard stood up and Maeva could finally appreciate the size of the woman. Wide shoulders and thick thighs, she'd obviously been designed for the Queen's Guard.

"Are you a Gillard?" Maeva asked.

"Yes, Madam. Helen Gillard."

"I see. Do you compete in the summer games?"

"Yes, Madam."

"I think I saw you last year."

"I won at discus."

"Yes, I remember now."

Helen Gillard's shoulders drew back with pride. "I'm honored. I was most pleased to enter the Guard under your reign, Madam. That had been a good period for the Guard."

I wonder what she means by that?

"Yes, well, times change and we must change with them."

"Yes, Madam."

"Now take me to my sleeping quarters."

The mattress was common, lumpy, and stiff. Maeva didn't sleep. The thought of going to Gana, where Aria had spent so many years, made something flutter in her stomach. How many times had she traveled to Gana to see Aria? She couldn't count. Was it Gana that had given her such depth of character? How could she have turned out so differently from the others? It had to be the nurtured aspects of her life, for the nature of them was identical. Especially with the Strangelands one, of course. They were more than identical. A single existence living in two bodies.

Maeva attempted to regenerate to fill the time. She sought out the cells from the inside, sensing where there was weakness.

She saw through her veins to the center of her arteries. Blood moved well and healthy. No blockages to be concerned about, not since that time around the coronation. How lucky she had been to find the clot, hiding within the curve of her hip. She had arrived upon it through her internal consciousness like a boulder.

Imagine if that had been allowed to progress. I must take better care. It could have killed me, or worse. Left me handicapped, dumb, mute. What horror that would have been. I must be more careful.

She arrived upon her abdominal muscles. They had always been taut and toned. Her core was essential to her state of mind as well. Kept her upright, kept her mind clear. Her posture erect.

She sent the blood to her abdominal walls, thrusting in, splitting the cells, and creating anew. The flesh welcomed the birth of new life within. She strengthened the muscles with a conscious and targeted application, breaking and re-growing the fibers stronger than they had been before.

She remembered watching the two, Aria and Ariane of the Strangelands, as newborn babes, passing between them the innate knowledge of growth. As one developed a new skill, it transferred to the other. The other grew muscle and skin and flesh, it was soon reflected in the first. The two had held each other with eyes so captivated, each consumed by her perfect infant double, there had been no place for Maeva as Mother between them.

That was how she knew the two had to be separated.

And that was how she'd had the idea.

Three Future Queens. Three separate upbringings. The true Queen would emerge the stronger of the three. One in East Gana where the tradition of raising Queens was old and strong. One in West Strangelands where she would remain a secret amongst the sisters, in isolation so she would be dependent on no one but herself. And one, born as an incubate, like herself, to stay close to the capital and the women within it.

It had made so much sense.

So how did it end up so very, very wrong?

Lucius. It all came back to Lucius. There never should have been two in her womb. One natural birth. One incubate. The decision would have been easy, Maeva had thought. One would be more adapted than the other.

So she'd thought.

And then Lucius had interfered. A double womb birth, all his idea. All in the name of saving Maeva. All in the name of preventing another disaster. All to prevent another "Rose" from occurring.

Rose. It had all been Maeva's fault. None of the three should have been born. It should have been Rose. The first Ariane. The Queen Child had been alive and well in her pregnant belly when she'd jumped off the cliff at Rainfields. She hadn't intended to, hadn't wanted to, but the call had been so strong, the voices so full of lies, the mirage calling her forward so real.

She'd fallen over the edge, not even realizing it before it

was too late. She'd prepared for her fall, knowing she would regenerate her broken body. She had no fear for herself.

But the child.

Oh, how that child suffered. She suffered in the fall and she suffered as I rebuilt her inside me. And she's suffered her whole life because of it. Deformed face, deformed spirit, deformed life. Red hair like the fire that has burned my heart ever since.

Maeva couldn't blame Lucius for everything. She'd been the one who'd killed her first Ariane and brought her back from the dead. There was no escaping the consequences.

The first Ariane calling herself Rose now, the name suited her. The softness of petals. Red like Rose, not red like fire, blood, anger. Rose.

Maeva closed her eyes.

Where are you, sweet Rose? Where have you gone? It has been so long you have not appeared through the window. I don't feel you anymore. Come visit me again, Rose. Come back again, my precious first-born.

A streak of light entered the tent where Maeva was lying in the checkpoint. Morning entered in red hues. Maeva prepared her overnight satchel and left for Gana before breakfast.

She paused before the gate into formal Gana territory. That gate had been Aria's limit. She recalled seeing Aria's face through the bars as she'd approached. Aria, always waiting for her. Always wanting her there. Maeva never questioned that Aria loved her.

There were no lookouts along the fence; they'd always been more for show anyhow, but it was unusual.

The time of day where the lookouts change, perhaps? Or an event in Gana of which I was unaware?

Maeva didn't know what event it could be, but then again she had been surprised by much she had seen on her travels. In the five years since she had been Queen, the landscape had evolved across Lower Earth. Mortality rates had risen, some counties hadn't received food stores in months and were living off rations. The administration of the country had slipped. Maeva had noted it all for her report to Ariane.

Ariane had been right to send Maeva; the people relished the opportunity to entreat the former Queen with their pleas and requests. Arms reached out to her, asking for healing, though she had no such power for them.

She could heal herself, that was the gift of her code, the element of the sequence that had been added from generations earlier. Send new blood, split healthy cells, grow and strengthen from within. But it was a gift for her alone.

She realized now that it was a selfish gift.

A selfish gift whose consequence was the voices of the past that lived in her. The voices had little to say on her tour of the counties. Maeva wondered how the Queens of old had led in such troubled times. Previous generations certainly had it worse on Lower Earth than they did now. But when she sought answers from within, the voices were uncharacteristically quiet. Maeva wondered if the old queens had ever traveled outside of Geb at all. Or perhaps the suffering of common people had not been a concern of theirs. There was no asking such a concrete question of the voices; she would never know. What she knew was that she was on her own. They would offer no help in interpreting the conditions of Lower Earth. She had to rely on herself to propose something that would be acceptable to Ariane.

The task was not self-evident.

Gana was her last stop before her return to Geb.

She scaled the entry gate.

Her feet landed firmly on the dirt behind, and a wave crashed over her, a sensation so strong that she was struck, nearly thrown down to the ground.

Rose?

Can it be? Rose in Gana?

It couldn't be Aria; any scent of Aria was gone years ago along with her cold body, tossed into the ocean for her watery, silent funeral rites.

Am I recreating this? Why would Rose be in Gana?

Then again, why would Rose be anywhere? Maeva had tried to locate her, made delicate inquiries on the sighting of any deformed children. Despite Rose's more than thirty years of age, others would see her as no more than a girl. Maeva was certain she was no longer in Cork Town, but then where, and what for? Rose had no business, no calling, no reason, which made her sudden departure all the more perplexing. And finding her - near impossible.

Perhaps she felt in Queen Ariane what I only came to know after. Rose always had been more sensitive than I to people's true characters.

A gathering of Ganese was underway a hundred feet in front of her. She walked to the crowd of about fifteen who dispersed just as she approached. They were a sight. Fifteen towers of women, their thick hair carrying them even taller, they walked with the grace of deer. Their piercing dark eyes. How long it had been since she'd seen dark eyes in Geb except for Irene. It had become too easy to forget that Irene had hailed from Gana. She had adapted to the Geb lifestyle as though she had always been there.

A woman approached Maeva, her head cocked. "You appear to be looking for someone."

"I am."

"Are you a visitor?"

"Yes," Maeva nearly laughed, "I am Maeva, the former Queen of Lower Earth."

The woman in front of her stumbled backward. "Queen Maeva? I must find the Chief for you. I will find her right away. But the gate is shut. The gate *is* shut, isn't it? We lock it during our briefings. How did you - "

"Please find the Chief immediately. And send someone for my donkey. He's still waiting on the other side."

"Yes, yes, Queen. Former Queen." The woman ran, her hand on her head.

Maeva strolled further into the center of the village. Nothing had changed. The dirt under her feet kicked up in the same way it used to. The vines continued to grow up the trellises. Pines provided shade. There appeared to be more West Ganese in the village than she remembered. They stood out. She only ever recalled seeing a few wandering in amongst the more modern Easterners. Now the population appeared nearly equal.

Curious. They are blending. I always expected that the West would want to branch off on their own. Irene was supposed to quench the bubbling rebellion, but she'd lost any credibility with Habana by then. And Batrasa only sparked the spirit of independence further amongst both sides of Gana.

A woman wearing the light-colored pelts of feral deer strode slowly on her way. Her legs were long and her shoulders relaxed. The leather glowed against the dewy shine of her dark skin. There was no mistaking who she was.

She was the spitting image of Irene.

Yes, exactly like Irene at the age when Maeva had sought her out from Gana.

Maeva felt like she'd gone back in time thirty years. She had to remind her heart not to flutter at the image of young Irene before her.

She is not the same woman. She does not love you as Irene does. Do not be confused by the identical glint in her eye. It is borrowed from strong genes.

"Maeva. I am Chief Leadon."

"Indeed you are. I know your face."

Leadon tilted her head. "Will you be staying with us?"

"Yes. I will stay for at least one week."

"I see. Let's walk."

Leadon led her through the village. Curious eyes looked up at that from various daily activities, plucking chickens, sharpening knives, and swords over a fire, a woman doing the wash. Maeva tried to smile at all of them, but she didn't know if it came across as genuine. She was distracted.

Rose. I feel her. It must be her.

"Have you been to the river, Maeva?"

"Many times. Aria and I often met there." She hadn't wanted to mention Aria. That was not the purpose of her visit. Discussions of Aria could derail more than she was ready to manage. Queen Ariane, as far as the Ganese knew, was the Aria they had watched grow within their borders. She had been careful to keep the story alive amongst the Ganese. She had to be careful not to shatter the illusion she'd spent so long building since the coronation.

Leadon was quiet at the mention of Aria. Maeva watched the Chief's face as they walked closer toward the river, but it gave nothing away.

Just like Irene.

The rush of the river came closer with each step.

"I knew Aria," Leadon finally said.

"Oh?" Maeva would be more careful with her words.

"She was a friend of mine."

Reinforce the Queen, the Ganese must remain on our side. She knew Aria, she will love Queen Ariane.

"Do you not consider her still a friend?"

Leadon looked at Maeva with an expression she couldn't read. "I do."

"A reigning Queen has many complicated relationships. I would know. Queen Ariane has not come to Gana, but that doesn't mean - it doesn't mean she loves you any less."

Prepare your words, Maeva. The girl is not stupid; she comes from Irene's stock. If you stumble, she will see it.

Leadon kept her eyes firmly on Maeva. "The Queen's sentiments towards Gana are ambivalent."

"This is only because she is managing at a level across Lower Earth. She cannot favor one county over another."

"We are not a county. We are a nation."

"Yes, yes." Maeva waved her hand, then slowed down her words. She was involuntarily becoming dismissive, and that approach wouldn't serve her either. "Of course. The Ganese have an exceptional role in the history of Lower Earth."

"And in the governance of Lower Earth. You'll recall it's our Land Sages who to this day predict the harvest."

"And with remarkable precision."

"We are not a relic of the past."

"I hope you read no such allusion in my words."

Leadon kneeled by the river. "There was a time this river was all but dry." She let her fingers drag in the currents. "The fish had changed their course to adapt to the more nutrient-rich tributary further north. It was Aria who brought them back."

"Aria?"

"As a child."

"How?"

"She put her fingers into the water, just like I'm doing now, but it wasn't so deep. Then she waded, up to her knees. I was so little at the time, I watched from behind a tree. She rearranged the river floor, moved stones, large stones but not so large that she couldn't move them. She was always stronger than anyone else her age. She rearranged the smallest of currents. And that was all it took. It had to be at just the right location, but she knew the spot. Our Sages never could have predicted it. The change was subtle, but profound."

Maeva looked down at the river rushing before them.

Leadon spoke slowly, "Aria is alive in this river. This is where she belonged." Leadon looked intently into Maeva's eyes, seeking something, though Maeva didn't know what. She hardened herself, not allowing her eyes to betray the truth within her.

Aria, alive in this river. It is the only place Aria could be alive. For one who dies at the hands of her genetic replacement, there is no place in Lower Earth but here.

Perhaps that was why the sensation, had struck her so strongly. Aria's soul, rushing through the Gana River. Perhaps it wasn't Rose at all.

I must ask. I must be sure.

"Leadon, do you have other visitors amongst you?"

"Of course, we manage the C8, 9, and 10 checkpoints within our borders. We regularly have people coming through from the Dark Counties, even the Strangelands if they are looking to trade."

"And no one else?"

"Who else would there be?"

"I just want to be sure of security."

"Gana is most secure. While we no longer maintain a protective presence along the border, which was my decision and one I believe is right for the free movement of peoples within Lower Earth, we remain a tribe of warriors. That training is part of our blood."

"You don't maintain the borders anymore?" Irene would be most displeased to hear this.

"Lower Earth is not owned by any people. The borders were erected at a time when we feared for our safety. This is no longer the case. Therefore, I have reopened Gana for access by all who wish to come through."

"So you do not monitor entry and exit?"

"No. We still have the lookouts, primarily for greeting and orientation. We close the gate during briefings, one hour a day. Unfortunately, that was when you arrived. I apologize for the cold reception you experienced."

Maeva couldn't believe what she was hearing. Gana just left open. It was unheard of for at least two hundred years. "There is nothing to apologize for."

A wave crashed over Maeva's feet and she slipped. Leadon grabbed her arm.

She's here, somehow she's here. My soul feels her, feels them. I cannot place the sensation; I have lost all my bearings. There is no landmark for the sensation to cling to. But someone is here. My Strangelands Ariane? She couldn't, she wouldn't. She left Lower Earth, I knew it in that moment.

"Maeva? Maeva? You are unwell."

"I am not unwell."

Rose, are you here? Rose?

The voices were building inside her now, hums of mother-hood and abandon, words she'd buried five years earlier.

"Maeva, you should sit."

"Yes, perhaps."

Leadon led her to a large flat rock, but she watched it from outside herself. The voices rose, words pulling out of the din of disgust amongst them.

"Queen Mother, killing mother, abandoning mother. How you became everything you despised. Everything you despised in your own mother you live again."

"Perhaps some water, Maeva."

"No, no."

"You will feel them wherever you go. You have reopened the wound. Our wound. How we all suffered, how we tried to tell you not to do it."

"You told me nothing."

Leadon cocked her head, "I have told you only the truth."

Maeva realized her lips were speaking in spite of her. She pulled it all back in, pushed with force the voices deeper, knowing she would pay consequences for it in the night. Her feet would carry her away from Gana, she knew it. She would wake while already on the path to Rainfields. She had to hear everything from Leadon now, anything that needed to be reported to the Queen, or else she would have to explain her absence and eventual return.

"Excuse my exhaustion, it has been a long and difficult voyage. I have recovered now. Let me explain what has brought me here, why I have traveled across Lower Earth for the past two months." Maeva inhaled deeply, "The Queen has concerns for the conditions in which people are now living. In Geb, she receives reports that cannot begin to uncover the full truth of her people's suffering. So I have come. I speak with the Queen's voice when I say you must tell me everything about conditions in Gana. Whatever concerns you may have about speaking freely, or of sharing the truth about challenging times, be assured that I have already heard worse."

Maeva looked up, so many stories she'd heard over the past two months of mothers holding dying infants, of emaciated animals without strength enough to graze on the little grass there was. The stories swirled in her head. "Times are especially hard in the Minor Rainforest, the Lakes District and the Sisters in the Strangelands have been disproportionately affected. So Leadon, do not hesitate. Pass to me the burdens you experience in Gana. The Queen will hear all. She will find ways to help. Gana is my last stop before returning to Geb."

"The Queen wants to help?"

"Yes, Queen Ariane intends to pivot aspects of the research agenda, manufacturing, and agriculture investments to support." Maeva hesitated, wondering if she should go the extra step to reassure this young Chief. It could only help Ariane, so she continued. "You remember Ariane from a young age," Maeva felt a pang in her heart at the lie. "You know the benevolence in her heart."

Leadon took in a deep breath through her nostrils. "I see. So Queen Ariane wishes to help the people of Gana." Leadon tilted her head. "Then I will tell you. I will tell you everything about our conditions."

22

"You want to go to the Strangelands? Why in Lower Earth would you want to go to the Strangelands?" Priyantha hadn't fully understood the implications of Maeva's words, even though Leadon had tried to explain.

"Did you sort out my transportation?"

"Yes, in secret as you asked. But the authorization, I haven't yet - "

"I have sufficient food for the entire trip?"

"Yes, but Leadon, why? The Sisters have a hate for us that goes back decades. From their very inception. What good can come from you going there? I hear they practice dark arts."

Leadon closed her eyes lightly. "Priyantha, sit."

Priyantha walked tentatively, visibly worried about whether she'd crossed some line.

"Don't worry, your question is natural. I just thought it would have been obvious to those who lived through Habana's time as Chief. Sit."

Priyantha sat.

"Maeva, like the Queens before her, was raised and trained in Gana - "

"Yes, I know this."

" - by Sahna."

"I know this too."

"Maeva left Gana while still a girl and she called Sahna to join her in the fortress as her mentor. You know that Sahna was banished from Gana after that? The well-known argument with Habana."

"Yes, but this is all history. I don't see what this has to do with today."

"Sahna established the Sisters amongst the self-isolating women who objected to Lower Earth's political structure. And then, she disappeared. Died, we can imagine."

Priyantha stood up. "What does the death of an excommunicated warrior priestess from twenty-odd years ago have to do with you going to the Strangelands today? You're not coming to the point, Leadon."

"The Queen's own words, 'The Sisters have been disproportionately affected'. The Sisters had some of Lower Earth's brightest among them. Those who couldn't dedicate their talents to this - the political structure. Everyone knows that the Sisters have many disillusioned Central Tower researchers. They've forged some of the strongest trading relationships and have agricultural abilities that match our own. Sahna brought our greatest knowledge there. So, if the Sisters are struggling, then there's something very amiss in Lower Earth. And I'm going to find out what it is. We have allies in the Sisters. They just don't know it yet."

Priyantha came closer to Leadon. "The Sisters have no sense of loyalty. They are individualists. That's why they went there in the first place. That's why Sahna was cast away. You must be careful about who you trust, Chief. Putting your faith in the Sisters is like trusting a bird not to fly away when its cage is finally open."

"Sahna was cast away because the fortress has an effect on one's sense of reality. I've seen it. All too intimately. Irene is no exception from its power to warp perception. What we know of the Sisters is only what we have been told of the Sisters. I will go and see for myself." Leadon looked off far, recognizing the limitations of her upbringing to prepare her for moments such as this. "There is much in Gana of which I am ignorant. It can't continue. I must know where Gana lies within its land. I'm going."

"I will seek the authorization."

"No, I will go in secret."

"In secret? Why would you take such a risk?"

"I feel the risk is greater if Geb knows I am going."

"I see. And I won't try to convince you otherwise," Priyantha said. "So instead I will come with you."

Leadon looked at Priyantha. She never would have expected that *this* warrior princess would be the one to attend to her so closely, but Leadon found she was relieved to have her company.

"Alright. You will come with me."

They arrived four days later at the edge of the Sister's commune. A makeshift fence rose high, though was not sturdy enough to keep anyone out who really wanted to come in. It was more esthetic than functional. The gate was a series of bamboo cuttings woven together. Priyantha took the donkeys to find a place to tie them, and Leadon stood before the gate.

So much I have seen in these four days across the center of the country. So much my imagination had never correctly pictured. The Central Mass stretches farther than I knew. The peoples spotted along the journey in their small hamlets. There's charm and there's isolation in it. Something poetic about living in the middle of nowhere.

She looked up at the gate.

And this is the end of nowhere. It's time to do what we came here to do.

She felt her heartbeat accelerate as she pushed open the gate. Priyantha came up behind her. A large expanse drew out before them, fields split into smaller plots with a variety of crops planted. But the plots were smaller than would ever be sufficient for feeding a population like the Strangelands Sisters. From what Leadon knew, which she was beginning to realize might all be wrong, there were several thousand Sisters across the whole of the Strangelands, with a main village and huts that dotted out from it towards the edge of the county.

Leadon and Priyantha walked slowly, looking for signs of Sisters, but all was quiet. They followed the main path that led to the village area, not so different from Gana except that the terrain was black soil and everything was less densely positioned. But clearly, Sahna had based its design upon the layout of the entry to Gana.

As they approached the village, a group of about ten women came out.

"Are they here to greet us or to threaten us?" Priyantha whispered, but Leadon kept walking forward.

"You are only two?" One of the women called, "Or are there more coming behind you?"

"We are only two." Leadon opened her hands to show they were empty. We have come to exchange information, nothing more than that."

"Who are you?"

"I'm Leadon, Chief of Gana."

"Chief of Gana?" A voice spoke from within the small group. The woman came forward. "What is the Chief of Gana doing visiting the errant Sisters, the disloyal and unwelcome castaways? We know how you treat those who you think have abandoned your values. Your narrow and closed-minded ways have long been spoken of here."

Leadon spoke slowly. "I can imagine why you have hesitation. I know your history. And I know the history of Gana. I cannot say I am innocent of it myself. What I *can* say is that I too have been a victim of it. Perhaps you cannot see it but my face is the face of another. I am the first genetic duplication in Gana."

"The Ganese do not accept duplication."

"I was a test."

"A successful test?"

"I am Chief. But that is on my own merit." Leadon looked to Priyantha and then back to the women. "Let me be honest with you. I'm not even sure if it is on my merit, but it is on something the Keeper saw in me. I, therefore, embrace my duty."

Another Sister spoke, "Why have you come?"

"I have information. I wish to share it and hear your views."

"It seems everyone is coming to the Strangelands to hear our views these days."

"You received Maeva?"

"How do you know that?"

"She came to us as well. It was her words that prompted me to make this trip." Leadon took a deep breath. "I believe we have more in common than we know."

The group of women looked to each other, seeming to relax a little. One of them stepped forward.

'I am Leesa of the fourth line. Come with me."

They entered deeper into the village, huts, so familiar in style, surrounded them. If it weren't for the color of the ground and the darkness of the sky, Leadon could almost imagine herself in Gana.

Leesa led them to a clearing where a woman was sat on a log. She appeared around fifty years old, small in stature, though her spine was straight and her green eyes gleamed with youth. While there was no common garb among the Sisters, this woman wore a brooch that shone even without sunshine against her long dress. Leadon understood that she was someone important, but she couldn't see this woman as the leader of the infamous Sisters. There was something demure in the woman's manner, her crossed legs and hands resting on her knee.

"Hello," she said. "Thank you, Leesa. You may stay if you want as I get acquainted with our - shall I call you guests?"

"Please do," Leadon replied.

Leesa stepped backward. "I'd rather leave you, Daphna."

"As you wish."

Leesa left the space. No bow, no ceremony at all. So different from Gana already. Or perhaps Leadon didn't yet know how to read their ways.

"I am Daphna." She nodded her chin.

"I am Leadon, Chief of Gana. This is Priyantha. We come with wishes for harvest and spirit."

"That's very kind of you. However, I suspect that you come with more than that."

Leadon nodded. "I have information."

"And what do you intend to do with that information?"

"I intend to share it."

"In exchange for what?"

She comes straight to her point.

Leadon considered her answer. "Insight."

"Now why would a Ganese warrior priestess Chief ever want insight from a Sister."

It was spoken as a statement, not a question. So Leadon waited.

Daphna scratched her cheek and looked at the sky. "You should know that I don't have the same profound mistrust of the Ganese that is held by most of the others. Perhaps that's because I lived most of my life in Geb. There are fewer grand tales of the warrior priestess there. But the folklore surrounding your people is well known in the outer counties. I think they enjoy having a people on which to cast their superstitions. When blaming the Queen is punishable by disappearance or death, the Ganese make a worthy scapegoat for the horrors we are experiencing."

Leadon stood silent. She'd never heard of any such rumors. But then, she'd never set foot on the Central Mass before this trip, and that was on her doorstep. Daphna was right, the ways of the Ganese could be interpreted in many ways. She needed to know more.

"I have said much already, and I can see that you are surprised by this bit of information which is such common knowledge across most outer counties."

"You are right. I didn't know the Ganese were being blamed - and I still don't know what for."

"Sit down, please." Daphna gestured to the logs in front of her. Leadon and Priyantha sat. "Leesa? I'm sure you're not far."

"I am here," Leesa emerged from behind a hut. Leadon understood she was watching to make sure nothing went awry.

"Would you be so kind as to bring our guests some tea? I imagine they've had a long journey, there isn't much for them on the route from Gana."

Leadon gave a small smile, hoping the sentiment would be communicated.

Daphna looked back to Leadon. "You said you had information to share. I also have information. But what we don't have is trust. You'll have seen that with your greeting committee. I asked them to be gentle. You appeared to only be two warrior priestesses. If you were to attack, as you are known to have done in ages past, I was certain you would come with more than two."

"We wouldn't attack other counties in Lower Earth." Leadon was confused by the statement.

"You've done it before."

"It was a different world in pre-Mist days."

Daphna leaned forward. "I'm not talking about pre-Mist days. I'm talking about these days."

Leadon looked at Priyantha, but Priyantha gave a small shrug.

Daphna tipped her head, "Leesa, can you come back here please?"

After a moment, Leesa reappeared. Leadon understood now, Leesa was never far.

Daphna lifted her chin. "Leesa, have you seen Lana today?"

"Of the fourth line? Yes. She was on duty in the test garden."

"Good, it'll only take her a moment to join us then. Have her come immediately." Leesa left and Daphna turned back to her guests. "Lana comes to us from Geb, where she held a very privileged position."

"In Central Tower?" Leadon asked. Defectors from Central Tower notoriously made their way to join the Sisters.

"No," Daphna looked between the huts beyond where Leadon sat, "The fortress."

"The fortress!"

"And she will tell you about it now."

A young woman stepped from between the huts, thin but with large eyes. Her shoulders hunched forward, but Leadon saw strength in her stride. She walked with consistent steps, not slowing on her arrival.

"You asked for me, Daphna?"

"Lana, do you know these women?" Daphna gestured to Leadon and Priyantha.

Gale turned and cocked her head to the side. "Unmistakable. That one is Leadon, the bottom feeder chief of the treacherous Ganese. An obvious replicate of the Commandante. The other one is unknown to me."

There was no shame in her voice, no fear of repercussion.

Leadon stood, ensuring her full height was apparent to the woman, who only reached to Leadon's chest.

"You call me bottom feeder?"

"Your reputation is worse than that."

"On what evidence?"

"Your acts are well-known to the Queen."

"The Queen says such lies?"

"The Queen watches your depravity with resigned concern for Lower Earth's future. Such grave acts you commit on the rest of our land."

Leadon sensed a strange tone in Lana's voice. It was as though she was a parrot, repeating words without emotion or belief.

"And you, Lana?"

The woman gave no sign of reaction. "What of me?"

"Do you believe these words?"

"I am amongst the Queen's enemies now. From great friend to great villain. I'm certainly she replaced me swiftly. Such is the Queen with her waiting women." She turned to Daphna. "May I go now?"

Daphna nodded and waited as Lana left their meeting place. Then she turned back to Leadon. "Now you see how such mistrust has been planted."

"But what is its purpose if we are innocent to the rumors?" Leadon still couldn't find a reason for the accusations and lies.

"Do you not have strict limitations on your movements?"

"Strict limitations? No. We must register our travel with Geb in advance, for the purpose of tracking possible virus transmission, just like all the other counties. But we have no limitations."

Daphna stood up from the log and walked around behind it.

"So you cannot move at all without authorization?"

"The Free Route to Geb is of course open, as it has been since the first settlers. But otherwise, the rest is on authorization, a simple registration process. To protect us from accidental transmission, to trace contact in case of new outbreaks. We remain primarily within our county lines, but not because anyone told us - "

"And did you 'register' your trip here?"

"No."

"Why not?"

Leadon paused. They'd come this far, and here was a chance to build the elusive trust that was so needed between them.

"I didn't want Geb to know I was coming here."

Daphna walked to where Leadon was seated and kneeled in front of her.

"Leadon," she paused, tensing her lips, "No one else has such restrictions on movement. I don't need authorization. Nothing is being tracked, not officially anyway. It's only you. Only the Ganese. And when there are attacks, or poison, or vandalism in the fields, we are told it is the Ganese. Rogue Ganese who are terrorizing the counties."

"What?" Leadon couldn't wrap her head around Daphna's words and didn't know if she could trust them. The story seemed far from plausible. "That's not the Ganese way. We do not attack in the night like bandits. And we certainly do nothing like poison - I don't understand what you're trying to say, Daphna. And I think you'd better be clearer in your denunciation."

Daphna put her hands on Leadon's knees, the touch was gentle and warm. Leadon felt no hate in it. "Leadon, I'm telling you that the Ganese have been blamed by Geb for acts across Lower Earth, and amongst the very Sisters with whom you share your space now. Acts that make your skin crawl. And the Queen says it was your people. *This* is why you are so hated here."

"Hated?"

"Despised. The stories say that you resent the other peoples on Lower Earth who have taken over your land, and hence you use terrorism to make their lives miserable."

Leadon looked again to Priyantha, her heart beating stronger in her chest.

"Daphna, we have been used."

Daphna stood from her kneeling place in front of Leadon. "Yes, Leadon. I believe you have."

Daphna walked again to the other log and sat down. "The Sisters wouldn't have me speak with you, but I knew I must. I lived in Geb. Do you not see my green eyes? I was in the Tower. I saw the current Queen, on several occasions. Beautiful, benevolent, awe-inspiring." Daphna leaned forward, "And I never could shake the feeling that there was something evil in her. Your visit here today confirms what I always knew."

She could be disappeared for that statement alone. No wonder she left Geb.

"Leesa will show you to our guest lodgings. They are very basic."

"We appreciate the welcome. We don't seek anything more than basic."

"I imagine the two of you have things to discuss. Leesa will collect you for dinner. For your own sake, I recommend you stay in your tent. The Sisters are not yet ready to accept you among them. I would hate to see something unexpected take place."

"Understood."

Leadon and Priyantha stood, bowing their heads low as Leesa reemerged with her arms crossed.

"This way. Your tea is in the tent."

THEIR TENT WAS SEPARATED FROM THE REST OF THE VILLAGE. Leadon was glad for it. Not only did it give them a little more privacy to speak, but she had grown wary of the Sisters' accusing eyes in the village.

"Leadon, this is crazy. The Ganese blamed for all this? What is happening, can it be true?" Priyantha spoke with her voice hushed.

"It could be true. But I'm not certain yet. I'm not sure why Daphna would be so willing to share such information. Perhaps she means to destabilize us."

It had occurred to Leadon as they'd been walking to the tent that perhaps there was no truth in Daphna's words. That it was a ploy to prevent Leadon and Priyantha from feeling comfortable. Or worse, it was intended to spark tensions between Gana and Geb. The relationship had always been tenuous, but over generations, they'd found ways to live together. Daphna's words could change that entirely. There could be other motivations behind it.

But if Leadon relied on her instinct, which had served her well until now, and which had been the very reason for her selection as Chief - her instinct said it was true.

"She has no reason to lie about the movement restrictions. If they don't need authorization, well, there's no disputing that. We Ganese have stayed within our boundaries for many years now. All because of the fears instilled from Geb, agreements made with Habana and those who came before. I cannot go back in time to know what lay behind those agreements, but why else have these limitations on us? Or is it that the existing limitations made us an easy target for blame?"

"Poison, attacks, vandalism? No warrior priestess would stoop to that level."

"We have to consider it possible. But what isn't possible is the widespread nature of it. There's no way that could happen without someone knowing. But we have been kept in the dark for so long... so insistent on the old ways of insulating ourselves..."

Irene's words came to her. The new threats facing the Ganese. Even back more than twenty years, it was Irene who had suggested the Ganese begin genetic duplication. She'd been the first to offer herself for it. Irene was the one who'd been worried Gana would be left behind while Lower Earth moved on. Leadon was beginning to understand that Irene's fears weren't just about culture, and not just because of the threat from Upper Earth.

There are threats to us on our own doorstep, and we are completely unaware of our enemies.

Leadon and Priyantha passed three days in relative isolation but for meetings with Daphna. The Sisters barely approached them, limiting all interaction only to the most basic of exchanges. But Leadon found an unlikely peer in Daphna.

"We're being attacked. Regularly." Daphna lowered her voice. "I believe it is biological."

"A weapon?"

"A virus."

"From Geb?"

"Who else but the Tower has the ability to create such a thing? My departure, three years ago now, was closely monitored. I wasn't in the higher ranks. But that doesn't mean I didn't know some of the secrets within the Tower's walls. I had always been a troublemaker in their eyes. I asked too many questions. I know others felt the same as me; they had their ways of seeking out answers. I wasn't afraid to voice my concerns, even if it did limit my career. My career had never been my priority; it had always been the science. And then, it wasn't long after Queen Ariane was crowned, the death of one of our male lab leaders, Jakob of the eighth line. I found something in the autopsy. It was out of my remit; I was supposed to be focused on analyzing tissue breakdown for the purpose of lengthening tissue life among women. But when I saw the results of the autopsy, I couldn't make sense of it. Though I saw something wasn't right. And you know what Roman of the first line told me?"

"Roman of the first line?"

"The Great Geneticist."

"Lucius is the Great Geneticist."

"Not for four years. They really have been keeping you in the dark out there in the east."

This is impossible. How can we be so removed? How has so little information reached us?

"Well," Daphna continued, "When I told him what I found, he said, 'Not your job.' Just like that. End of story. My supervisor was right there, so her hands were tied. I was dumbstruck. 'You heard the man,' she'd said, 'Back to work.' So I took the report and dropped it on Uma's desk, Uma is the secondary overseer, and I walked out. Just like that."

"And you came straight to the Sisters?"

"No. I first went to Cork Town. This was just before the real embargoes on Cork Town began. I'd heard some whispers of women meeting there through a couple of allies in the

Tower. I hoped I could find them, and I did. They met in a pub, about once a week. Backroom women."

"There's backroom women now. I see."

"They were relatively new, didn't call themselves that, of course. They were shocked to see me, I'll tell you. Didn't trust me at first. Long story short, my stay in Geb was becoming tenuous. I just had a sense of it. Sooner or later I was going to be disappeared. There'd be some story about leaking Tower secrets or some other such propaganda. I wasn't about to wait and find out. That's when I decided I needed to come here. And it was just at a time when they needed someone like me. No Sisters had come from the Tower in several years, they needed an infusion of research power. You probably saw the test garden in the front?"

"When we first arrived, yes, we saw it. We wondered why you'd have such small plots."

Daphna smiled, her green eyes catching a glint of light, "Those are all experiments. Modifications of various common species. Several of them are showing promise. We might be able to self-sustain. Given all the seasonal changes and crop killers hitting the rest of Lower Earth, we're hoping our species will withstand the test of time. That's if we can stop Sisters from dropping dead."

"It's as serious as that?"

"It is. Attacks women of late middle-age. They should still live a long time, and then all of a sudden, they drop. The thing is that it's not pervasive. It's perhaps one a week. But one a week, of an unnatural and unexpected death, is one too many. We can't get Geb to do any analysis. They claim it's natural, that other counties have the same, and we're no more special than anyone else. But I've been to the other counties, Leadon. It's not the same. It's not the same at all. And I can trace it back, I think I can – a woman who joined us, her stay was fleeting. She fell ill, and then she was gone. Vanished. But there was something in her illness that seems to be of the same root as that which we see now. Accelerated atrophy of internal organs."

Leadon nodded, feeling fortunate that no such thing had afflicted Gana.

Not yet.

Could it come to Gana? Could someone bring it to Gana? Or is this truly a targeted attack on the Sisters for their transgressions over the years?

Had someone told Leadon before she'd traveled to the Strangelands that the Ganese were receiving harsher, more monitored treatment than other counties, she would have dismissed the claim as not credible. But the rules across Lower Earth seemed to be changing. There was so much she didn't know. So much she needed to know.

Leadon lifted her eyes to Daphna. "I don't know how to help you."

"I don't think that you can. Not now. We will continue working towards a cure in our own labs, despite their insufficient equipment. In any case, I am confident you are not behind all that the rumors claim. We all fear what we do not know. The Sisters have long had mistrust for the warrior priestesses. It's not hard to see why, given our collective history. But now I know you. I see who you are. And if I may be honest, as have been from the start, I think you are frightfully ill-equipped to lead Gana through this next phase." Daphna stood up. "I don't mean it as an insult. Consider it rather an invitation to educate yourself."

Leadon also stood. "Had those words come from any other source, I would have dismissed it as something between venom and jealousy. But from you, I accept the invitation. And I thank you for the blindness in me that you have already lifted."

Daphna walked out of her cabin and led Leadon back to the tent where Priyantha had packed the few items with which they had traveled.

"Go back safely."

"We have a Ganese blessing that seems appropriate for you. It translates to 'May you fight and lead well with the blessing of the ancestors upon you'."

"I accept your blessing." Daphna looked long and hard into Leadon's eyes before finally saying, "Goodbye, Leadon."

23

Maeva closed her eyes and steeled herself for what she knew would be one of the hardest conversations she would have in her life. She blocked out the sound of the flute on the screen and rushed through her mind before Mary began her morning diatribe. She needed quiet to think it through.

I must find the right words to reach Ariane. I was the Queen. Certainly, I can find a way to speak to my own daughter so that she will listen. Then again, I raised her to be systematically independent. Wasn't that the whole point? So that when Upper Earth came, she could make the hard decisions that would need to be made and not shy away from them?

But Upper Earth hadn't come, not yet. And management of Lower Earth dominated every aspect of the fortress. Ariane was fixated on population control, both socially and demographically, and even more so on Cork Town. Population control had never been on Maeva's mind when she'd told Lucius how to design this Ariane. The fourth Ariane. And yet that had come to dominate the past few years of management across Lower Earth. There were ways to sustain life across all counties; that had been the Queen's very commitment from the start. It was half of the Tower's reason for being. Fortifying the soup had been an important first step in overcoming the crop failures; there was now more than enough to feed the masses. They could arrange it so that everyone could live. And yet Ariane insisted that Cork Town was a parasite. It didn't make sense. Cork Town was their own doing, the results of their genetic experimentation, lives that still had a reason and way to make themselves in the world. Why fixate on Cork Town any more than the other counties, when with Central Tower they could find ways for everyone to live?

She doesn't want *the deviants to live.*

It hit Maeva like an earthquake.

If she doesn't want the deviants, and it's not a question of resources, then I need to change my approach entirely.

Maeva dressed in her habitual velvet gown, pulled her long brown hair into a tight bun, and looked at herself in the mirror.

"I still look like a Queen."

A knock on the door and Maeva's stomach jumped. She cursed herself for being too absorbed to hear it coming.

"Madam, the Queen will see you now."

Maeva looked one more time in the mirror and nodded, as much to herself as to the waiting-woman.

"Always slow-moving, Mother," Ariane's voice reached her ears, and for a moment Maeva wished she couldn't hear a voice from halfway across the fortress.

Maeva didn't respond. She would speak to Ariane on her own terms and not before. She wanted to look her daughter in the eye when she gave her reports on the suffering on Lower Earth. She wanted to know if her words would have any effect. She wanted to know if Ariane cared at all about what was happening across their land. They had to adapt some of Central Tower's work to address those critical issues. Not just incubation.

The Queen was lounging across her armchair, velvet

cushion against her velvet dress, and Maeva was struck at the image of herself fifty years younger.

"So you've returned, Mother."

"You didn't think I would?"

"I thought it would take you longer."

"I fulfilled what I set out to do."

"Then you must tell me. Come," Ariane stood and stepped away, opening her hand to invite Maeva to take the chair. She walked to her bureau and took the wooden seat, placing it across from Maeva. "Tell me, have you been successful in rebuilding relations with the outer counties?"

"I believe so, but not without trials."

"Oh?"

"They are struggling, Ariane."

"Ah yes, they are."

"It's not just scarcity of food."

"Illness too, I imagine."

"Yes. And terrorism."

"Mmm. I heard murmurings of such."

"The rumors are widespread. Fingers pointing in multiple directions."

"Suffering has that effect on a population."

Maeva paused. Ariane was leaning forward in her chair, her brow furrowed. For all she could tell, Ariane was deeply engaged. Concerned. Absorbed.

Have I been misreading her? Misinterpreting her?

Ariane sat back and looked out the window. "And what of their dedication to Geb?"

"They are reliant on Geb."

"Reliance and dedication are not the same thing."

"True, but with the conditions under which they are living, basic survival is their greatest focus - in some counties. Not all counties."

Ariane sat back in the chair. "I can understand this assessment, even if I find it displeasing. The Tower is working nearly twenty hours a day trying to resolve the crop viruses, modifying grain, adapting them to new conditions. I don't have to tell you that. Do these people not see how much we are dedicated to them?"

"I never saw it as 'us' and 'them'."

Ariane waved her hand, "You were always too poetic about it. I'll read your report in detail, have no concerns about that. But now I need you to get to the heart of it." Ariane pulled the chair even closer and took Maeva's hands in her own. "I know there is discontent. So who will it be? Who will rebel? And will they attack directly, or will it be subtle? Is it the Sisters? I have long felt that with their skills and insight they could pose a great risk. I feel tension in the air, I smell it with the morning dew. Treachery mingles with the first rays of sun, every single day. But I need to know who it will be. Is it Gana? Which county will dare first to make an offensive move on Geb, or on the fortress, or on me?"

"On you?"

"Tell me, Mother. You've seen them all. Is it the Sisters? The Ganese? They are the most powerful, but the Dark Counties have always had ways about them ever since the first settlers arrived. Who will it be?"

Maeva shook her head slowly, "No one is preparing any attack."

"Not yet. But they will. It's the natural order of things during times of shortage. We saw it in the pre-Mist days and we'll see it again. You have gone around the country unbiased in a position of observation. You have built some trust. I know you have. And now I'm asking you for the simple task of assessing those you reviewed to identify who will be the first, given the right conditions, to rise up against us."

She's looking for an enemy where so far she has none.

"Tell me, is it the Sisters?"

"The Sisters are in a weakened state. There is an illness amongst them that is affecting those with the greatest experience. Daphna is a researcher, her only experience coming from the Tower. She puts it to use in their fields."

"Daphna has an ingrained disdain for all we stand for. She *hates* the Direction of Lower Earth, each one of us. No wonder Lana ran off to her."

"You did not offer much alternative to Lana. And Daphna is concerned for the well-being of the Sisters. Rumors are that the illness is planted. They suspect it is from the Ganese." Maeva paused, wondering whether she should reveal her suspicion. But to hold it back wouldn't serve her. "I, however, am quite confident it is not from the Ganese at all."

Ariane's face didn't change. "Oh?"

"It looks like it came straight out of the Tower to me."

"I see."

"The Sisters are in no position to launch any kind of attack."

"Illness or not, they are the very antithesis of Geb. The Sisters' reason for existence is to oppose the very institutions which are keeping us all alive. I don't have to remind you of that. They pose a threat."

"I can understand your concern, but this will not be realized any time soon. They are consumed with their own problems and seek someone to blame for them."

"That is your assessment?"

"It is."

"Fine." Ariane stood, pacing. "And the Ganese?"

"Irene's genetic duplicate was an unexpected choice for Chief. But Leadon is simple. She's focusing on the needs of the Ganese. She doesn't look outside her borders. It's as planned."

"If Leadon is anything like Irene, we could find ourselves in grave danger. It would just be a matter of time."

"She has some of Irene's qualities, that is undeniable. But

their characters are so different. In the little time I spent with her, other than looking upon Irene's face, I heard words no previous Ganese would have said. Not in our lifetimes."

"Explain."

"She is concerned about the divisions within the Ganese."

"East and West? Or more political than that?"

"East and West."

"Hmmm," Ariane looked up at the ceiling.

"They continue to follow instructions. Few move outside Gana boundaries. It was well instilled in them to remain. Any requests for further movement have been denied on grounds of health and safety, and the requests they'd made weren't out of necessity anyhow. They were learning expeditions. Easy to deny without consequence. They hardly use the Geb Free Route except for the planned exchanges."

"Queen Idia did well containing them."

Maeva shuddered at the sound of her mother's name. She'd never heard it on Ariane's lips before. She kept the voices at bay; they too were upset by the sound. "It's true she instituted measures which continue to be respected to this day."

"And the Ganese are not any wiser to the purpose of the restrictions?"

"They have no reason to be. They have their sacred lands, that's what they always wanted."

"Ambition among the Ganese would be dangerous."

"The words I heard from Leadon were of seeking peace internally among her people, and eventually to prepare them for the war with Upper Earth."

"Prepare for war?" Ariane marched at Maeva, "How could you leave that out, Mother! If they are going to prepare for war they could just as easily redeploy it against us."

"Daughter, they are far from any such position."

"These details are important!"

"I will detail everything for you in my report, and then you will see how insignificant they are."

"Hurry then. Tell me of the other counties, and then focus on preparing this report."

Maeva went through each of the other locations. Pests in West Fields, water diseases in the Lakes Region. Crows dropping dead in the Dark Counties, which the people took as an omen.

"Ariane," Maeva measured her words. "The Tower needs some additional strategies. Much of the discontent can be mitigated with targeted programs. If the people see some small improvements, and we attribute them to your dedication, the counties will give greater loyalty in return."

Ariane cocked her head and looked out the window. Maeva could see the thousands of ideas running across her eyes, the possibilities and scenarios measured in sprints. The Ariane who became Queen always had the greatest abilities to assess among the four.

"You are not wrong, Mother."

"Let me address it with the Tower."

"No."

"No?" Maeva felt her temper rising. How could her offspring tell her no for such a reasonable and logical action?

"You haven't finished."

"I have told you everything, unless you seek the details of each location."

"You haven't said anything about the other one."

She means about her sister.

"You mean the other Ariane?"

"I mean the imposter who wears my face somewhere in this country."

"She's been gone since the day you were declared Queen." Maeva used every tactic to keep her blood from rushing at the question. Ariane would hear it. Maeva was not about to tell her what she felt in Gana. That would not bode well for the Ganese, nor herself. She quieted her heart. "I suspect she's left Lower Earth."

"You don't feel her?"

"Do you? You were always more sensitive to her than even I was."

Ariane looked Maeva straight in the eye. "No, I don't."

"Nor do I."

"She couldn't have just disappeared into thin air. She's hiding somewhere."

"I've always believed she went to an island, off the southern coast, where no one would seek her out."

"Or she's right here in better hiding than we believed her capable of."

"I saw nothing of her. Felt nothing. Heard nothing."

Ariane paused, her eyes ticking again as Maeva knew she was running the scenarios. "Fine." She took the chair back to the desk and sat down. "While I await your report, advise Irene that the Ganese must have stricter supervision. Further limitations on any movement. No one coming to Geb unless permitted, close down the Free Route. The checkpoint should now be managed by the Guard. Make sure it's someone who will report everything. I will consider your proposal about the Tower. That will be all." Ariane turned back to her desk, opening a file.

Maeva backed toward the door, pausing a moment to look on her Queen Daughter, but Ariane showed no sign of continuing the conversation. Maeva lifted her chin and set her shoulders before walking into the corridor.

24

Sara hardly paid attention to the pages before her. Activity around the Tower was as usual, everyone had their heads in their own business. She was left relatively alone but for the occasional intern who dropped another report on her desk.

She stared at the report in front of her on the rate of nutrient value of post-natal umbilical cords, but she was looking through it to somewhere far away. Deep into Cork Town. Her mind was in Cork Town with a woman who they'd been able to successfully confirm as pregnant.

Pregnant with 4957-209.

She laughed in spite of herself and quickly darted her eyes around, hoping no one heard her. She made up a quick back-story regarding conflicting genes that she'd unearthed, in case anyone asked.

She remembered the look on Lucius' face when the test came out. In his smile, his gleaming eyes, she could see the man he had been.

We've gotten this far. It's a miracle at all that we've gotten this far. We've finally done something, and we never could have done it without Adam.

Her heart swelled, she could feel it inside her. She thought of Adam, his eyes, brown, flashing blue, the morning sun as it rose red across their bodies, though all they had done was sleep in each other's arms. How fulfilling it had been. How natural even though it was forbidden. Natural, even though she knew well enough that desire had been coded out of them generations earlier.

"Oh, Adam, you'd be proud."

"You're talking to Adam?"

Sara spun around, her heart stopped and her stomach in her throat.

"Uma, I didn't hear you come in."

"Adam." Uma looked past Sara. "I haven't thought about Adam in a while." She looked back at Sara, "I should have caught on sooner. I never would have guessed he was planning a revolt, among the backroom men of all things. I'd always thought he'd stayed away from them. Goes to show that after years of working together, you don't really know someone. You see what I mean, Sara?"

Sara read the threat in Uma's tone. Her mind raced for any reason, any excuse.

"I was reviewing the conflicting genes." She grabbed the report from her desk. "Adam was the first to show me how to find them. He'd mastered their identification."

Let that be sufficient. Let her believe it.

The way Uma looked at Sara made her feel like she should say something more, but she didn't have anything more to say.

"He was your friend?" Uma asked.

"He was my mentor."

"You were close."

"We worked closely, but like you said, you never really know someone."

Uma pursed her lips and passed a page to Sara. "I need

your best work on the incubation revisions. Stay focused, understood?"

"Understood."

"No more muttering to yourself about disappeared men."

"Hadn't even realized I'd done it." At least there she was telling the truth.

Uma nodded, turned, and left the lab.

Sara sank into the chair and closed her eyes. Her head was spinning. She quickly pulled together the pages she'd promised Lucius and slipped them into her sack before anyone else could wander in. Lucius asked for so little in return for all he was doing, she'd made the promise to bring the old files on the Male Program without a second thought.

But the rock in her stomach warned her to be more cautious. She was far from innocent now. Anyone who checked her records would see the additional trips to Cork Town. Everything was documented. She had a backstory. But a backstory wasn't worth the air on which it was told if someone really wanted to challenge it.

She zipped up her sack and let her head rest in her hands.

25

———

Uma leaned against the corner, keeping herself hidden, as she watched Sara put the papers into her bag. In itself, it wasn't unusual. But coupled with the utterance about Adam, Uma was getting a sinking feeling that there was more happening than she could see.

Sara put her head on her desk and Uma walked away. She'd seen enough.

I have to report her. But what for? For taking her work home with her? For whispering the name of a dead man, a traitor, during working hours?

When Adam had been revealed for what he was, Uma had gone back through all the records. There had been no concrete sign of his treachery. Even if Adam had always been among the smartest in the Tower, still, he couldn't possibly hide all his tracks. The only known associate of concern was Isaac of the first line, and he'd been so near degradation at that time, and his association with the backroom men so well-known and tracked already that there wasn't any cause for concern with him. He hadn't lasted long after Adam went. Died while waddling his way to the Tower, his degradation complete. He nearly toppled over his own gut.

When the Queen had announced Adam's transgressions during an assembly at the Tower, Uma had felt she might throw up. It wasn't just that Adam had been found out.

She feared for herself.

What if Roman decided to talk about her secret excursions to the blowouts? What if he told about what he'd seen?

The memory of it brought red shame to her cheeks. Hot shame. The woman had been an opie, desperate for a hit. She'd only wanted a few credits, she'd do anything for a few credits, she'd even… she'd offered… she'd reached out and touched Uma, and Uma didn't recoil. She let it happen. Innocuous to most who might happen to walk past; a stranger would dismiss the scene of two women huddled together in an alley corner as opies on a trip. They wouldn't see what was happening under the fabric, the waistband of Uma's standard-issue suit pulled away. No one would see it and no one would suspect anything.

But suddenly Roman had appeared in the entry to the alley.

She'd seen him. And he'd seen her.

His shoulders had been hunched, but he was a man, and he walked with the telltale hunch that had been Roman's for as long as she'd known him. He'd stayed, watching for a while. Uma kept control of her breathing as the woman continued, uninterrupted and unmoved by Uma's distraction. Perhaps it had only been a minute, but it felt like hours passed before Roman finally stepped away. Uma passed a credit to the woman but her whole being was numb.

All of it had transpired years ago, before Cork Town was closed off, but the fear lived in Uma's veins. Even now, she couldn't be sure just how much Roman knew about what he'd seen, but it didn't matter.

He'd seen her, and that was enough.

She'd had to lay low after that. Toe the line. Be invisible.

That's when Roman had shot up the ranks in the Tower. He'd flown right past her. The years she'd dedicated didn't matter. She watched his glory as he became second in command to Lucius, then the *de facto* Great Geneticist when Lucius went into exile, and now he held the title she'd always thought would be hers.

She prayed for his degradation, but it was slow – too slow – in coming.

Adam a traitor. Uma verging on deviant herself. Something wild that lived behind Queen Ariane's eyes. So long she'd had the strange feeling that something was going on right under her nose, and she couldn't figure it out.

She had that feeling again now.

With Sara.

I've got to trust my instinct. Carole never liked her and Carole sniffs out disobedience like a hound. But even Carole has never been able to artic-ulate it. I need to put it into the right words. Roman seems to have some kind of a soft spot for her. I better get it right before I report it to him. Maybe Carole can do it. She'd relish the opportunity, anyway.

She called Carole to her office immediately. She couldn't wait. Uma wouldn't sleep with this on her mind. She just had to do something, however little. Get the wheels moving.

Carole arrived in a flurry, quickly closing the door.

Uma felt something bad was coming. Her instinct rose bile into her throat. "Carole? Why are you so flustered? What's going on?"

"You haven't heard? Maeva is here."

"Maeva? Doing what?"

"How am I supposed to know, but she's been walking up and down each of the floors, scanning desks and nodding at staff but not saying a word."

"Did Reception ask what she wanted?"

Carole put her hands on her hips, "You really think Reception is going to question the Queen Mother who has just walked through the door?"

"Where's she now?"

Carole walked out of Uma's office to the central corridor, where she could see each of the levels down from the open column that stretched up the full height of the Tower.

"Looks like twelfth floor, judging by the bodies rushing around."

"Are the upper floors in order?"

"How should I know?"

"Carole - "

"Fine, I'll check on them."

Uma's heart raced.

What does she want?

Or has she come for someone?

Should I report Sara before the Queen comes?

What if she senses my apprehension? Maeva always read deeper into all of us than we ever understood.

Uma gathered the results of the recent review; Roman would want those close at hand. She pulled the incubation report and the files on West Fields that had recently been updated.

She rushed up the two floors to Roman's office, silently praying that whatever Maeva was looking for, it was something Uma could give.

26

Maeva relished each second. The eyes on her, full of wonder, surprise, and fear. She recalled the many times she'd walked through Central Tower as Queen. How her words inspired activity. Just a single word, and an entire floor would rush into action.

It seemed they were still sensitive to her presence. With every room she entered, a wave rolled over them, bodies stood to attention on the sight of her. She walked up and down the rows of desks, tables, laboratory equipment all covered in pages of code, sequences of different colors, Petri dishes with varying forms of life in various stages of growth.

Silence cast over each floor as she passed. She heard blood accelerating, veins throbbing in foreheads as she paused to look over their work. Breathing became shallow, perspiration beaded.

So few men. There used to be so many here, this was their den. How quickly the population of them has dwindled.

She was in no rush. Eventually, she would find her way to Roman, if he didn't come down to meet her first. But he wouldn't. He would wait for her arrival. He was probably preparing for a variety of scenarios.

I don't need Ariane's permission to check in on the Tower's work. I'm not her prisoner. I will just check in on certain programs. My attention on them alone will spark Roman into closer management.

Maeva smiled to herself.

Let that daughter of mine chastise as she wishes. It's time she treated her Queen Mother with greater respect. My role here is not yet finished.

She arrived on the fourteenth floor and immediately felt someone's throbbing neck. The pulse accelerated. The floor had sixteen offices on one side and a series of labs on the other. And someone was in a panic over Maeva's arrival, more than she should be.

"Hush, it's Maeva!" she heard one of the lab techs whisper, but she was not the one Maeva sought out. As on the other floors, those who had been at their desks, heads down, with magnifying glasses or turning pages of reports, all stood on seeing her. She felt the normal scurry of rushing blood at the sight of her as she walked through the rows of glass offices, looking into each one, occasionally taking a step inside and inspecting, though not for anything in particular.

But this one woman was different. She still felt it, the shallow quick breathing, the tension. Out of place.

She is more nervous than can be explained by simple surprise.

Her dress stroking her legs as she walked was the only sound on the floor.

The heartbeat of the woman in her ears grew.

I am nearly upon her. Who are you? What have you done to inspire such anxiety?

She looked from face to face, but so far each was as expected.

The heartbeat grew louder still.

I'm coming, whoever you are, I'm coming. And we're going to find out what this is all about.

She approached an office with a slight woman inside. At first glance, she was like the others, perhaps a little less muscular, a little shorter, a little smaller in the hips.

Designed for research. So what has you this panicked?

Maeva entered the office and looked the woman in the eye. The woman kept her spine erect, her eyes on Maeva, but not in opposition.

You mask it well to the common eye. But my eye isn't common, woman.

Maeva came to the desk and picked up a report. The incubation program. She rustled through the papers, all the while the woman's heartbeat pumped and her blood rushed like a waterfall. Maeva saw her identification and gave a small knowing smile to the woman.

Seems I remember something of you. And it seems you have been taking liberties where you should not. We just have to find out what they are.

Maeva inhaled deeply, turned, and left the office, hearing the woman's inner workings tumble over themselves with a rush Maeva knew to be relief.

Enjoy it while you can, Sara of the seventh line. Things are about to get much worse for you than you expect.

She continued her observations of the Tower, but she put her original plan to one side. She'd thought she was coming to assert herself, to lay the groundwork for a plan that Ariane would later execute. Instead, she came to unearth a traitor working at the very heart of the program they'd all come to count upon - and which was failing.

Could she be responsible for the problems we've seen? Could this be why my demands for incubation have gone awry? Fourteenth floor, she very well could have planted something in the genes that would be responsible for the madness we've seen in the incubates' behavior. Yes, she very well could be. Perhaps it wasn't at all that they rushed to scale. Perhaps it was

*doomed from the start by a Willing Woman hardliner right within their
midst.*

Arriving on the nineteenth floor, Maeva headed straight to
Roman's office. The administrative management in the other
offices could do nothing for her now.

Roman was waiting for her. "Maeva."

"Call the Primary Overseer."

"Uma?"

"Call her now."

Roman stuck his head out the door and called to one of the
admins. He rubbed his hands together. "I wasn't expecting
you."

"Of course you weren't, I didn't tell you I was coming."

"To what do we owe - "

"Seems you've been running a lax operation, Roman."

"What?"

"How closely have you been monitoring the staff?"

"We do all the regular checks, per protocol - "

"And are you satisfied with what you've found?"

"I'm not following you."

"Roman?" Uma knocked on the door.

"Come in. Your timing is impeccable, Uma. I was just
telling Roman about how you've allowed yourself to slip."

Uma snapped her head at Roman, who shrugged.

"Your ignorance is yet another sign of your incompetence."
Maeva walked to Roman, bringing her nose almost to touch
his. "How could you allow a traitor to be working on the incubation program?"

Roman recoiled, his shoulders pulling in, "A traitor?"

"How could you allow this to happen? How could you! I
placed all my faith in you, right from the beginning. It wasn't
just about the promotion. It was about something far greater
than that. This program - you hated it from the outset, didn't
you?"

"No, never - "

"You paid it such little mind that now there is a woman, smack in the center of it all, who has been sabotaging it right under your nose." She swung to Uma, "What kind of affair are you running here, Uma? Where is *your* loyalty? Perhaps that's the question I should be asking."

Uma recoiled. "Madam, I have always invested everything - "

Don't start with your meager defenses. Explain how there is one among you, one you have assigned, who has been allowed to play with our future like it's a child's game? I can't tell you if it's the genes or something else in the sequence. I have no idea what it is, but I can tell you that the moment I saw her it was written plain as day on her face. Reeked of betrayal. That rank, sweet stench. And you couldn't see it among your own direct reporting staff? This is more than shame, Uma."

Roman stepped forward, "Maeva, please, who are you talking about? Let us deal with this as we must, and have no doubt, we will. Immediately."

"No Roman, this is out of your court now and squarely in mine. Call the Guard and have her arrest Sara of the seventh line immediately. I want her dragged to the fortress before I even have time to advise the Commandante of what you've been permitting between these walls. Sabotage. Betrayal. Roman, you might have ruined everything. I just hope we can salvage what's left of the incubate program before all of Lower Earth finds itself at the mercy of the enemy. Go! Call the Guard! And consider yourselves fortunate I'm not having you arrested alongside her. I truly believe you were reckless enough to deserve it, being blind to her treachery."

Electricity wove through Maeva's body as she marched out of the office and ran down the back stairwell of the Tower. She did not want to see anyone, not now. Life was coursing through her veins and she remembered all she had been born for, her great mission, her reason for being. All she had sacrificed, and now she had a chance to salvage it from the wreck yet again.

She would take it to Ariane, certainly. But not before she'd had Irene wrench the truth from the traitor.

27

Irene marched through the fortress, the recent notice crumpled in her hand. She stopped and uncurled it again, disbelieving the ink before her.

"Stay-Within Order - Immediate effect: On Royal command, all ethnic Ganese are required to stay within the negotiated boundaries of Gana until further notice. The Free Route is hereby closed, the pathways off-limits for any travel, whether logistical or political in nature. The first checkpoint shall be overseen by the Queen's Guard and the Ganese currently in place are to return to Gana boundaries. Geb hereby assigns a representative for ongoing management, communications, and negotiations, and shall remain in the checkpoint, thus requiring lodgings and sustenance to be provided by Gana. This order remains in place until Royal command releases it. To be distributed to all ethnic Ganese."

Irene clenched the notice in her fist, her nails cutting into the flesh of her palms.

This is going too far. I have always been supportive over the years, but now, to close down the Free Route? There is no justification for it. I cannot sit by and let them cut Gana out.

She went through the East Wing, Main Fortress, and South

Wing, opening each door, finding meetings underway or empty spaces, but Maeva was nowhere to be found.

She has no reason to be elsewhere, Ariane has not given her permission for any further expeditions. Where is she?

The fire burned hotter in her. While she knew she had to approach the situation with political acumen, the affront was more than she could bear.

It felt personal.

This young Queen who thinks she can undo generations of negotiations. Her arrogance reeks like rotten flesh. That she demands my complete loyalty while offering nothing in return. There is no love from her. Even Maeva, for all her faults, her violent temper, and mercurial nature, even she knew the importance of relationships. Now it is Maeva who must teach her Daughter Queen a lesson about how to inspire loyalty in her people.

Close the Free Route and she invites every offense Gana might muster.

"Maeva!"

Irene saw the Queen Mother entering the Fortress.

"Irene. I need you. In the underground chambers. Now."

"No, it is me who needs you. I need you to explain this ludicrous order!"

"Not now, Irene." Maeva clenched her teeth, "You come down to the chambers with me, this instant."

Irene wouldn't move, not until she had some kind of answer. This was her time to make demands, not take them.

"These restrictions will have consequences, Maeva, don't you see that? The relationship is managed right now, but it's tenuous. Leadon is an unknown quantity. We cannot be confident in how she will respond. She could react in ways that jeopardize all we worked so hard, all these many years to build." She held up the order, "For what? For a Queen whose own paranoia creates her enemies in the outer counties? You saw it, you know what I'm talking about Maeva."

Maeva stepped close to Irene, both were breathing heavily, Irene felt the emotion rolling off Maeva, strong enough to meet her own, but she would not lose her ground. She lifted her chin and looked down at Maeva, "You must explain this."

Maeva's eyes alit, wild and wide. "We have problems far greater than this right now, Irene."

"Greater than a civil war?"

"You exaggerate." Maeva's teeth clenched, "So a few priestesses won't be able to come to Geb for a while, they hardly traveled anyway, this will be no loss to them, the condition is temporary while their new Chief settles down."

"That is not the point! The Free Route has been the basis of the relationship with Geb from the first settlers. What's being asked here - not asked, *ordered* - is to violate the very premise of how our peoples came to live in mutual prosperity."

"Mutual prosperity?"

"The Route is necessary for impregnation, for trade, for ceremonial relations - "

"Irene. Shut up. Listen to me. Events are overtaking us. We cannot stand here a moment longer. Your concerns for your *people* have been noted. But now you must rise into your role as Commandante, because all that we have been working towards for the past five years is about to come to nothing because of the traitor planted deep in Central Tower. And she's being brought here right now. I don't know what she's done, but I know that she's done it. And if *she* is the one responsible for the failings of the incubation program, for the program I set in place myself, then we have far greater issues than excursions by the Ganese to the capital. We're talking sabotage of the genes of what is now a generation of fourteen thousand. Fourteen thousand possible deviants, possible betrayers, and possible ruin of all we planned - they were to be our *army*, Irene. Do I have to remind you of this? The *army* you so desired, the thousands needed to prepare for the colonization that still will come, will one day come and within their generation. Irene, this is it! This traitor might be at the center of its demise, and you - *you* - must pull it out of her. So do not stand here for another second with that piece of paper in the air when I am about to deliver to you the woman who might be the undoing of everything!"

Irene's heart was beating faster than she could control, her ears throbbed with the sound of it. Maeva's words penetrated her. Her whole spirit shifted; an answer, a possible answer at last to how things had turned so wrong.

The order fell from her hand, the paper floating to the ground.

"Where is she?" Irene whispered.

"The Guard is collecting her. You need to prepare the chamber."

Irene nodded. There would be time for the order later. Maeva was right, it paled beside the chance to finally uncover the truth behind the mess the incubation program had become.

THE LAST TIME IRENE HAD USED THE CHAMBER HAD BEEN FOUR years earlier when they captured the last known Upper Earth scout. The woman had gone mad, eyes bulging as Irene thrust her face again and again into the bucket of water.

But she'd never cracked. They had no more intelligence than when they'd started. No news on Upper Earth's plans. No sense of when they were coming. Not even an idea of why they'd sent the women when it appeared they would never be going back to Upper Earth. The scouts had integrated wholly into Lower Earth's population, almost exclusively in the Dark Counties, but a few had migrated to Geb, playing at being the regular traders who came to the capital for simple business.

Irene looked at the chains mounted on the wall and vowed.

Never again. I am a warrior before I am a priestess. This is my gift. I will never again allow a prisoner to outmaneuver me.

She mentally prepared her list of tactics. A woman from Central Tower would have a very different constitution from a scout. Irene would have to read her movements, listen to what she didn't say.

She heard feet scuffling down the stone steps towards the chambers. The fortress clearly had been built at a time when they needed many prison cells. Irene had only ever used three of the thirty on the underground level. She heard the prisoner struggling, but without saying a word. Feet slipping and dragging, while heavier steps moved forward at a regular steady pace.

Two guards framed the woman, each dragging her by the arm. The prisoner didn't stand a chance against them.

This is the woman? This tiny sliver of a woman is the one who may have undone all our plans?

It hardly seemed possible, but Irene watched the woman's eyes. She watched as the woman scanned the room, taking in the dimension, the implements, evaluating Irene herself.

She is assessing every detail, eyes darting as information assesses the risk and measures the possible outcomes. I should not underestimate her. She is not made of the same mettle as a scout. She is made of something else entirely.

Irene opened the folder in her hands. "Sara of the seventh line. I see you have made several unexplained trips to Cork Town recently. We have much to discuss."

Irene walked past the woman and slammed the heavy wooden door to the chamber. Irene had selected the chamber in the center of the underground maze. No one would hear the woman's screams.

28

———

Leadon moved in between the rows of warrior priestesses conducting the morning routine. Their bodies moved as a single unit, the flow between stretch, strengthen, and assault was near invisible.

Lea smiled.

As it should be. Their ability is evident; it's only a matter of increasing their skill.

Across the village, women conducted the exercises at sunrise. No one complained. The enclosure of Gana had ignited renewed discipline.

We had become strong as priestesses, but we are only half ourselves if we are not warriors.

"I believe we are ready for a more challenging routine," Priyantha joined Leadon in her inspection. "They are excelling."

"I agree, on both points." Leadon looked at Priyantha, "Have you spoken with Yon?"

"She says the Westerners are feeling more integrated than ever."

Leadon closed her eyes and let out a long breath. "I cannot tell you how relieved I am to hear it."

"You should feel more than relieved," Priyantha stopped on the outskirts of the women's configuration, "You should feel proud. You made that happen."

"No, " Leadon continued walking. "I did not. I only saw the divide and knew it served neither East nor West for us to consider ourselves as one or the other. We are Ganese."

Priyantha smiled, "Exactly."

They continued the inspection, turning around the village square to where Anyook was leading the exercises. Anyook saw them coming and waved them over.

"Leadon, did Priyantha tell you?"

"That you're ready for the next level, she did, and I agree."

"Excellent. I've prepared sparring routines."

"Where do you see that fitting in with the other exercises?"

"After, definitely after. We can use the midday sun to increase intensity. Eventually, we can move to midnight assault practice."

"After this, we should attend to strategy, at a more universal level."

Leadon nodded, "Yes, we have to complete our designs. We can build upon those which we already have from the ancestors, but new threats call for new approaches."

"Agreed."

"Let's meet on that with the council in four days. That will give Anyook enough time to launch the new sparring training and we'll be able to identify the possible weaknesses we need to overcome."

"Four days is plenty," Anyook added. "We could do it in three."

"Fine, keep me informed."

Anyook nodded and then ran back to her station to lead

through the next series of exercises. Leadon looked across the organized crowd.

How quickly the women were able to pivot into their blood's calling. And I worried that galvanizing them would prove a challenge. I underestimated my people. I must not do that.

Leadon heard footsteps that were out of time with the others. The thousands of women in exercises moved with each other, the rhythm predictable. These steps were running. Leadon turned to see a lookout running in her direction, waving. Leadon walked at a fast pace to meet her.

"Leadon, Chief. It's the Commandante. She's coming."

"Irene is coming? Why?"

"I saw her in the distance. I don't know why."

Of all times, after the betrayal of her own people, after I told her not to come back until I called for her - she has audacity. Unwise, ill-timed, audacity.

"I'll come to the gate. I don't want her to see the women in training, not yet."

"Yes, Chief."

Leadon turned to Priyantha, "Prepare a contingent. Just in case. If we need to make a show to send a message, I want us to be ready to do that."

"Yes, Chief," Priyantha ran back to Anyook as Leadon headed towards the main gate.

Leadon walked towards the entry, the lookout waiting for her. "Close the gate." The lookout did as she was told.

"Should I lock it?"

"That won't be necessary. We will be opening it, but just not right away."

"Yes, Chief."

Leadon waited, the leather of her bodice slapping against her thighs in the wind. Her hair brushed across her face. Leadon suddenly realized that all her senses were heightened. She could hear the steps of the donkey approaching, the women deep in the village training, the trees rustling. She felt the dirt flying into her cheek and her eyes drying in the breeze.

Irene dismounted and walked the animal toward the gate. She didn't say a word. Leadon saw her own face, aged a further thirty-five years, approaching without a sign of the shame it deserved to wear.

A flame lit inside Leadon.

That she dares to walk with her head high - she doesn't even know the offense she's causing simply by her arrival. Be wise in your words, Leadon. She lays her loyalty away from the ancestors and toward Geb now.

Irene came to the gate, her face inches away from Leadon, but still, she didn't speak. Both women waited, neither moving nor speaking. Their eyes remained fixed, their towering height identical.

They spoke at the same time.

"Why would you come?"

"You have to understand what's happening."

"What?"

"You have to understand."

"I understand perfectly well."

"You don't."

"Haven't you read the order, the one your own Guard delivered?"

"Of course I have, but it's what's behind it - "

"The motivation is rather evident, I know the blame that's been cast on the Ganese, and unjustly so."

"That isn't related."

"Do you take me for an idiot?"

"It isn't related, I'm telling you, Leadon. Now open the gate and let's talk."

"The Free Route is closed. I won't accept visitors."

"I'm a Ganese."

"No. You're the Commandante before you are a Ganese. You've made this clear for decades."

Irene didn't respond. Her chest rose and fell with each breath, waiting.

Leadon stepped away from the gate and turned to the lookout. "Let her in." She looked back to Irene, "We will walk by the river, and I will hear you out. You will not interrupt the women as they prepare."

Irene stepped through the gate. "Singing at fires again, are they?"

Leadon didn't answer.

They followed along the border of Gana, a route Leadon had followed near daily before.

Before. That was before everything changed. Evolved. I should consider it evolved, not changed. We are becoming what we ought to be, neither more nor less.

When they were out of earshot of the lookout, Irene spoke, her eyes set straight ahead.

"I have come not as Commandante. I wouldn't dare say as much in front of anyone, but you must know. Things are heating up in the capital. The Queen seeks out her enemies while also making plans to - to cull the population."

Leadon looked at Irene. She was prepared to listen, but she wasn't yet sure whether or not to believe anything Irene would say.

"Cull? What does that mean?"

Irene ignored the question. "You must be careful. This stay-within order is just the beginning. Suffice it to say that when I first saw it, I was incensed, but I was corrected, had to put it into context. You can't see it, but the blood of a traitor is still on my hands, I have just come from the underground cells of the fortress. There is an undercurrent running across Geb, and maybe across Lower Earth."

"I know it. I have seen it."

Irene looked at Leadon, her brow furrowed in question. Leadon weighed her options.

She decided it was time to take a risk. "I've been to see the Sisters."

"You have?"

Leadon nodded.

Irene inhaled deeply. "I suppose that was wise. Especially to do it before the stay-within order came down. Yes, it was wise. I would have done the same."

She seems sincere.

"The Queen sets her eyes across Lower Earth, Leadon. She's looking for anyone who may undo the delicate political balance in place. Like in the Strangelands. The Dark Counties too. And who knows what will happen in Cork Town once the clear-out really begins."

"Clear-out?"

Irene raised her hand, "It's not just Cork Town. Many plans that have been in place for years are crumbling. Ariane will have to take strong measures, great leadership. And someone in it all is going to lose. Don't let it be Gana, Leadon. Don't stick your neck out now. Ride low, wait it out. You have nothing to lose from that approach and everything to gain. Otherwise, you'll put the Ganese in the center of the Queen's target."

"Sit and wait? This is your advice to your fellow warrior priestesses?"

"It's temporary, it's protectionist even. Anything else and you risk attracting the Queen's attention just at the time when she's seeking an enemy."

She doesn't speak as a Ganese now. Now she speaks from the fortress. No Ganese would advise that we 'sit and wait'. This has never been our way.

Leadon looked into Irene's eyes. Her dark eyes implored, her lips terse.

She doesn't want to say the words she's said. Her instinct advises against it. And yet, she has become the Commandante of 'sit and wait'. She must be reminded of the stock from which she comes.

"Follow me," Leadon led her back towards the village, then through it. They strode in silence. They passed the forest, arriving on the exercise field.

"What is this?" Irene whispered.

The women were between sets, the timing was ideal. Leadon led Irene to the head of the field where Priyantha and Anyook were standing. Priyantha had her hands on her hips, watching every move they made towards them. Anyook's arms were crossed. She scanned across the thousands of kneeling warrior priestesses, waiting for the right moment.

Anyook has a strategy. She's waiting for us to arrive at the right angle where Irene will see it all in action.

Leadon smiled to herself. Priyantha glared at Irene, not speaking a word as they arrived at the platform. Leadon stepped up first, Irene followed.

At that moment Anyook let out the assault cry and the thousands sprung to their feet, their bodies twisting into the different forms, kicks, punches, attacks from all angles taken on invisible enemies.

Leadon looked at Irene whose eyes had widened at the sight.

We have surpassed her expectations.

The warrior priestesses cried out with each imaginary hit, the sequence identifiable but adapted by each woman. The cries echoed into the late morning sky until the set had finished and they retook their defensive positions in silence.

Anyook shouted out the rest position and the sea of bodies relaxed.

"You are progressing," Leadon called out to the women. "In this short time, your discipline is paying off. Dismissed."

The women slowly scattered back to their daily duties in their individual quorums.

Irene's eyes stayed on the field even as the women were abandoning it. "This is a terrible idea, Leadon. Imprudent. Reckless."

"It's not an idea. You saw their state. We advance further every day. We will reach the level of the Guard - "

"You are foolish!" Irene hissed.

Leadon saw Priyantha call the women to her side

"Where is your loyalty, Irene? Is it with your people, or is it with our oppressor?"

"You make distinctions like that and you will invite opposition."

"Which is it, Irene?"

"You know me, Leadon." Irene leaned forward, "I have always had to keep one foot in the fortress while the other was here. That was not a choice I made, it was a command that I was given."

"And now you've been gone long enough to forget that there are ways things are done here which have served our people for thousands of years."

"In thousands of years, we've never faced this before."

"We've faced worse and you know it. We are warriors, we have our history to rely on, and more than that, we have trust within us. Did you see the warrior priestesses? West and East as one, of one mind. And you'll recall that as long as you're here, you obey the Chief and the Chief had told you not to come back until you were invited. You were *not* invited, Irene, and you come with advice that we never would take. Your counsel is poisoned by the woman you've become. Now you will leave Gana, escorted by these fine warriors, and I will try to swallow the shame I have at wearing your face. You should be proud that you share yours with a Ganese who remains unafraid to be true to her blood. Now leave. And if you come back, be prepared to meet with the consequences."

Leadon kept her eyes set on Irene as the six women behind her stepped forward. Irene raised her hands.

"I'm going. You are foolish, and you are steadfast. I only hope it's not a vow you come to regret." She walked away, the contingent following behind her. Leadon watched until they were out of sight.

Lea turned to Priyantha, whose gaze hadn't moved from Lea's face.

"Her heart is with the Ganese. Only her head is not."

"I have no choice to but believe you."

"You always have a choice, but you are right to believe me on this." Leadon felt the power of Priyantha's loyalty rolling off her like an ocean wave. "Your faith in me is strong."

"Because you are worthy of my faith."

"And yet you are not afraid to voice your concerns."

"Because you listen to them."

"Because they are wise." Leadon paused to take in a long-awaited breath. "And this is why you will be Keeper of the Chief. My Keeper."

They stood in silence, holding each other's eyes. Spines pulled tall, the leather of their bodies flapped in the wind. But all Leadon's could see was Priyantha's jaw set and her eyes soften before she gave a long, deep bow.

Leadon waited until Priyantha's gesture was complete before taking her arm and led her back to the hut.

.

29

U ma felt like her throat was closing. It had been stuck in that position for days. Ever since Maeva had commanded that Sara be arrested, a boulder had been stuck in the middle of her esophagus and there were moments she felt she couldn't breathe at all. She went through the motions in the morning.

No one expected her to be at the Tower before sunrise, but she had a specific mission now. There were hundreds of pages to pore through, and they weren't in any particular order. Not in any scientific order, that was. Rather they were stacked in the order in which they'd been written. Hundreds of pages of code, gene properties, revision strategies.

From beginning to end of her interrogation.

Sara's last testament.

The acid from her stomach rose, even though she hadn't eaten anything.

When did I last eat? I should eat. I won't be able to think straight if I don't eat.

She grabbed a few things from the kitchen and set out for the Tower just past four in the morning. The Tower came into her sights, the glass walls catching the small rays of reflected light that remained from the full moon. The Tower reached deep into the sky, seemingly standing taller than the clouds, the stars, and whatever was beyond.

Could there be a place beyond where we find ourselves when this life is through? Could the Ganese have it right, that the ancestors are all there, waiting for us, advising us, even living beside us on another plain?

Where is Sara's soul now?

At the thought, Uma felt a breeze stroke her cheek and jumped. She didn't know what she expected to see, but nothing was there. She closed her eyes and inhaled the cold air of early morning before picking up her pace to the Tower.

She entered through the rear service door, knowing the Logistics department would already be in place, but she could avoid them. She didn't want anyone asking questions about why she was unlocking the front door at this hour. The alarm would beep and the residences surrounding the Tower would hear. Normally that wouldn't bother her, but this wasn't normal. She wanted to enter in peace without anyone asking any questions. She wasn't sure how she'd respond to them.

She hesitated in front of the elevator and then opted for the stairs. The exertion would do her good. Clear her mind. The concrete was hard under her feet and the air had a slight dampness to it. She took each stair at a steady pace, steadily moving up. She knew what awaited her there.

The door into the seventeenth floor felt heavier than usual.

She stepped into the carpeted corridor, the weight of her mission settling on her chest. She tried to swallow.

Her key stuck in the lock. She jigged it until it hit the right angle. Her office door creaked as she pushed it open and she suddenly had the sensation that it wasn't her office at all, that she was trespassing into someone else's work, spying, thieving. Stealing into the mind of someone else, ideas that had been torn away in life's last moments.

A wave of shivers went up her spine.

Get ahold of yourself, Uma. The task is clear. Don't muddy it with ethics now.

The desk got bigger in her vision as she stepped closer. Every movement was amplified, her senses turned on.

A pipe was being hammered somewhere in the building.

Who is hammering a pipe at this hour?

A crow called from outside the window.

This isn't their season, how has a lone crow found its way to Geb?

She sat at her desk, her body not recognizing the shape of the chair.

In front of her, the pages stacked high, but in disarray. Some were crumpled, the colors of the paper weren't uniform. It was as though someone had scavenged through the fortress for random sheets, here and there. Two different pens had been used. Some of the pages she'd seen had become wet. Uma didn't ask herself what had moistened them. They'd been in the chambers, after all.

Perhaps it was simply dew off the walls.

She cut off the thought.

Uma closed her eyes and inhaled deeper than she thought her body was capable. She opened them again and continued where she'd left off the previous day.

The first page was soft in her hand, the writing quick but even. She recognized the sequence from the West Fields virus of two years earlier. It had emerged after a mutation of the previous variant. While the pathogenicity had been reduced, the virus had become more resistant to heat. They used to rely on the summer season to kill the virus off, but it had lasted long into autumn.

Uma dug more deeply into the notes scribbled along the side. Remarks on possible proteins that had influenced its evolution as it became a new crop killer, and a few comments Uma couldn't read. She scanned the rest of the page, but it was sparse compared to others. She walked to the table where she had classified the other pages she'd already assessed. There had been another page that outlined West Field viruses from an evolutionary perspective.

How did she keep such a variety of information in her head, able to recall it on command?

Uma shook her head.

And I'm still in the first fifth of the stack.

She added the page to the previous one, clipping them together. She looked back at her desk and then up at the clock. Five forty-five, activity in the Tower would soon pick up. And she still had days' worth of analysis in a muddled pile on her desk.

There was no time to waste, especially with the incubation program hanging in the balance.

She sat back at her desk and continued.

Tissue strength.

Monitoring data on gene mutations for womb development.

A case study on immunity to influenza.

A small tap came on her door and she saw Roman on the other side.

She lifted her hand. "I'm working on it. There's a lot to get through. It's not classified at all. Not at all, Roman! I have to crosscheck it with the activity logs. It's a manual process."

"Hey, hey, now." Roman entered. "I haven't come to urge you on or to criticize. Quite the opposite. You're making good progress, and faster than I could. You have always been closer to implementation. I wanted to know if you'd eaten anything."

"Eaten?"

"It's two in the afternoon. I know you've been here since before sunrise as I came by then and you had your head deep in it already. You didn't even see me there, did you?"

"No. I saw nothing."

"I'll have an admin bring you some food."

"Fine, fine." Roman was ruining her concentration; she needed him to go. She'd agree to anything.

"Come up to the nineteenth floor at seven o'clock, latest. Give me a report then. Oral is fine. Don't spend time noting your assessments yet."

"Fine."

Roman nodded and stepped out, closing the door behind him.

She continued. Page after page, some of it looked like nonsense, other pieces were relevant but already well documented in the incubation program. She didn't bother looking at the clock anymore, she went page by page into the evening.

She turned to the next page. Her eyes couldn't register what she saw, but her body did. She felt it coming up from her gut and managed to grab the trashcan in time before the burning vomit came. She didn't even know what she had in her to throw up, the substance thick. Her throat stung. She closed her eyes and willed the nausea to leave, letting the words coalesce in her head.

Accept it, Uma. This is just the beginning. The next pages will only get worse.

She looked back down at the page, halfway down the handwriting pulled to the right. On top of the ink was a stain of dried brown blood. It covered much of the code on the bottom half of the page. Uma had to hold it up to the light to make out the writing beneath it. The penmanship was growing erratic, the words varying in size, at one point letters were missing from the middle of words.

Uma didn't let her imagination recreate the scene in which the page was written. She held it up to the light and steeled her stomach, forcing her eyes to focus on the writing and nothing else.

"Uma."

"What? Can't you let me concentrate?"

"Uma," Roman started gently. "It's eight o'clock."

"What?" she looked at the wall, ticking two minutes past eight. "Sorry."

Roman looked at her desk. Uma had made good progress but there were still more than a hundred pages left.

"Go home, Uma. Come at it again tomorrow. One more day isn't going to alter our course."

"But the Queen - "

"The Queen knows you're human."

"We *need* to know, Roman - if it's here, if she's said anything at all, I'll run it through to the deepest level of analysis. I'll analyze the - um - I can find through the lab techs the different experiments that cover - "

"Uma, you're tired. You'll start making mistakes. You'll miss something. I'm not asking, I'm telling you. Go home."

Uma closed her eyes and her head began spinning.

He's right. And I can't afford to make a single mistake. Not now.

"Alright. I'll go."

"Find me tomorrow when you've finished, obviously I have no greater priority than to hear your analysis."

Uma nodded and Roman left. The door shut again. Uma let her hands rest on the pages in front of her, which were outlining the next stages for reducing the gestation period for Willing Women. She lowered her head onto Sara's script and immediately fell asleep.

Tapping on the windowed wall woke her.

She jolted her head upright, stars sparkling in her peripheral vision.

Carole opened the door. "Roman sent me."

"Mmm."

"I'll take you home."

"Not necessary."

"Roman says it is."

Uma lifted herself from her desk, her toe catching on the carpet as she tried to walk. "Fine. Let's go."

She jimmied the key in the lock and looked one last time at the nightmare on her desk.

Nightmares. My whole night will be filled with nightmares.

SHE AWOKE BEFORE HER ALARM. SHE GRABBED THE CLOCK, HER eyes adjusting to read it.

Five in the morning.

She stayed for a moment, staring at the ceiling, a single strip of light sneaking through the curtains from the street-lamp. She blinked her eyes, having forgotten the day that lay ahead of her. It rushed back into her consciousness and quickly threw off the covers, hastily dressing. She grabbed two pieces of bread and tossed them in the toaster. She tied up her shoes, but the laces felt foreign in her fingers. She almost couldn't tie the knot.

Snap out of it, Uma. Today's the day.

She swallowed the toast without tasting it as she rushed to the Tower. The front door was already open.

"Hiya, Miss Uma," the Gillard guard saluted.

Uma nodded without making eye contact. A young woman was waiting at the elevator, the doors opening just as she arrived.

"Take the next one," Uma said to the woman, who stepped back from the entry, nodding quickly at Uma.

The elevator felt painfully slow.

8-9-10...

She was convinced she'd climbed the stairs faster than the elevator was delivering her.

14-15-16...

At last, the doors opened on the seventeenth floor. Carole

hadn't yet arrived, nor had the admins. She had the floor to herself.

She stuck the key in the lock, shaking it until it took, closing it firmly behind her. She pulled down the blinds on the windowed walls.

This is it.

She sat down, knowing that in addition to the information scratched out on the pages, she would see the evidence of Sara's interrogation.

I can't let it shock me. I am a scientist. I'll observe it and file it like any other input.

She looked down at the next page of code.

Roman crossed by her door. She continued.

The door creaked as Carole peeked in. She continued.

Roman and Carole were speaking, she heard their voices. It was early afternoon, but she was too deep in now. She'd just started seeing the pages she'd been waiting for from the start.

The pages which detailed the adaptations made on the incubates.

Finally, they got it out of her. How many days had she written before she cracked? How much had she endured? Never mind that, Uma. This is what you need. Stay in it. This is what counts.

The initial pages were all known modifications, the conflicts they'd found in the first phases.

Come on, Sara. Get to it. This is all standard, though the guards forcing it out of her wouldn't have known that.

On the first page, there was a reference scribbled, the beginning of something Uma recognized from the Male Program but which was out of place here. But the sequence wasn't finished. Uma couldn't make sense of it. The sequence was unknown, and it seemed to contradict itself. Uma compared against Sara's activity log, but it didn't match up.

It's not incubation, the reference points aren't even close. What is this? Was she starting to go mad? Did she have a side project that none of us knew about?

Uma flipped to the next pages, hoping it would put the code in some kind of context.

It didn't.

But what she found jumped out from the page. It was what she was looking for. It couldn't have been planted by Sara, but it appeared that she knew about it and hadn't reported it. At least, not reported it in a way that anyone had noticed.

Inconsistencies in incubate sequence - is this the first of the window or the middle? Must be the first - position A - when the signal starts is when the reduction is... it's synonymous. The reduction in variability. It's picking up the first position and the twenty-fifth.

Uma sat back in her chair so hard it bounced behind her.

There is an overlapping gene.

She scanned further, there was much to interpret, but she had enough now to go to Roman with something concrete. She felt everything inside her release, like the darkness she'd felt stretching before her had transformed into a fertile green field at sunrise.

30

———

Uma passed Roman the page.

He didn't want to take it.

He knew what had been done to produce it. Knew the torture Sara had endured. Maeva had detailed it without hesitation.

He looked at the page Uma held out, the writing hardly legible, the edges of it crumbled. Spots across it that he couldn't identify and didn't want to.

He slowly stretched his arm and took it from her.

"It's in the second half." Uma's eyes had fire in them. Roman was worried about her mental condition. She'd pushed too far these last days. He wasn't sure her analysis could be reliable in her state. "Look, look." She came around beside him and pointed, "Position A is the beginning of the coding sequence. But Position H reads in reverse." She squinted at the page, "From what I can tell."

He looked it over, and then back again.

She might be right.

"So you think it's a regulation sequence?"

"I haven't taken the analysis to the next stage yet. Could be regulation sequences to transcribe the gene, but it could be a splicing enhancer or even a promoter sequence. There's a chance it's a functional RNA, but that's unlikely. Still, I haven't gone any further yet, I don't have much left to review, but I wanted to tell you immediately."

"Yes, as you should have." He looked up at Uma, her hair sticking out and her collar pulled wide. "You've done well, and you look ill. We can't take it to the Queen with you in this state."

"Me? I'd take it to the Queen?"

"Of course you would, it's your discovery."

"But I haven't completed the analysis."

Roman walked to the door, opening it for her. "You go home. You take a couple hours of rest. You don't have to sleep, but you have to at least clear your mind. Bring me the remaining pages before you go, " he felt his stomach drop, but he had no choice. It was his turn to face what had happened to Sara. "I'll review what remains and we can do a deeper analysis tomorrow, based on the Queen's response."

"Yes. Yes, fine." Uma walked out the door and Roman watched as her shoulders relaxed. She walked in a trance to the elevator. She forgot to push the button. Roman shook his head. She eventually realized it and quickly thrust her hand at the panel. He closed his office door and sat at his desk, preparing himself for what was coming.

THREE HOURS LATER WHEN UMA CAME BACK, HE WAS NO closer at advancing the theory than when Uma had brought it in.

"It's all confused," he said to her before she'd even come through the door. "It talks about one potential variation and then flips to another. I can't make any sense of it."

He couldn't tell if it was intentionally written that way by

Sara to throw them off the scent, or if she didn't know herself, or worse.

Is this just the scientific musings of a dying woman?

Uma came and looked over his shoulder. She was a changed woman from who she'd been just a few hours before. Her skin was fresh and her clothes pressed. Her hair shone in the light of the setting sun.

She shook her head. "I can't tell. Not without comparing it to the original sequences."

"That could take weeks."

"For me, yes. For you, yes. But for Lucius - "

Roman cut her off, "Don't say it. Don't say his name."

I've already been on my knees before Lucius and he might as well have kicked me like a dog. This code won't change that. If anything he'll be furious about Sara's capture and - and the method of extraction of this information.

"We've got to figure this out, Uma. We don't need him. We have to try."

Uma stood up and shrugged. "Maybe you're right. Maybe with time, we can fix this. But the next phase of incubates is about to be launched. They are already in month five."

Another phase of incubates to be born. If only we'd known five months ago what we know now.

Roman internally prepared himself for a conversation he couldn't imagine. "Get ready, we're going to see Queen Ariane."

"There is a message superimposed on the gene," explaining the science was proving more difficult than Roman had expected. "That's the one we're concerned about."

Maeva stepped forward in front of Queen Ariane. "And you couldn't have found this before?"

"We're still not even sure of what we've found, if it's there at all."

"This is ridiculous, Roman. So you've come here to tell us of something perhaps you've found but can't interpret it?"

"That's right. And we never would have had any idea of what to look for without - " he didn't know the right words to describe it, "without the insights the Commandante provided through her, um..."

"We all know what you're trying to say," the Commandante stepped forward. "So this is all a result of analysis of the intelligence provided by the betrayer?"

"Sara of the seventh line. Yes. It's our interpretation of those pages."

The Commandante nodded, and Roman couldn't help thinking that she looked satisfied at hearing it.

'Would you all please sit back down." Queen Ariane had not moved from her armchair at the head of the room. Roman had never been in the meeting hall before. While the surface wasn't large, the walls extended up at least two stories, completely stone. No windows. There were in the very heart of the fortress where prying ears couldn't happen upon them by accident.

Maeva retook her chair, as did the Commandante. They were in a circle where all the seats tilted toward the Queen.

Ariane rubbed her temples. Everyone waited. "You have a concept, but no real evidence yet, is that right?"

"Yes, my Queen."

"You have fourteen thousand live births over the past five years."

Uma cleared her throat. "Fourteen thousand births, but only twelve thousand, nine-hundred alive."

"How's that?"

Uma looked at Roman quickly before turning back toward

the Queen. She straightened her shoulders. "The others were involved in incidents."

Ariane didn't flinch. "They killed themselves."

"Yes."

"Incidents," the Queen echoed shaking her head. "Central Tower is gifted at creating euphemisms."

Uma shifted in her seat. "Within one week's time, that figure will be fourteen thousand, nine hundred."

The Queen sat forward in her chair, her green eyes catching the candlelight from the chandeliers. Her voice came out slow and precise. "Explain."

Roman knew it was his turn. "This is the sixth phase."

"You conducted a sixth phase?"

"Yes, this was before we had identified the pattern."

The Queen, Maeva, and the Commandante all spoke at once.

"You didn't see the pattern?"

"How could you continue with a failing program?"

"This is the disgrace of Lower Earth," Maeva stood. "I cannot sit down. I cannot take any of this sitting down!" She marched to Roman, "I cannot comprehend what was going through your mind!"

"We were operating on orders."

"You mean *my* orders."

"You were Queen."

"You were the Great Geneticist. It was your responsibility to do it right, I gave you no timeline."

Roman bit his tongue to keep from saying something that could have repercussions. "We weren't ready for the order you gave."

"You said you could do it."

"We had the ability to implement. We had the equipment, we had the common sequence of women which was getting closer to exceptional levels of resilience. But we didn't test it. We immediately operated at scale."

"Lower Earth needs soldiers, not warm bodies that throw themselves off bridges! It was your design, not my command, which has left us in so sour a position. The flaw was in the design."

"It was never designed for the incubation program you ordered. There were unforeseeable social consequences. We couldn't have identified them in the design."

"Nearly fifteen thousand?" The Queen whispered. She stood, gesturing with her hand for Maeva to sit back down. "Fifteen thousand? And you cannot guarantee the long-term effects, nor create a treatment for them?"

"We cannot treat it. It's social in nature, not biological. The very fact of their incubation birth has already done irreparable damage to their brains."

"Fifteen thousand," Ariane whispered.

Roman felt like all the air in the room had been suctioned out. He wasn't sure if he was breathing, and couldn't tell if anyone else was either. He heard the air go into the Queen's nostrils. She parted her lips and the air sighed out. She nodded.

"You have all created a very unfortunate situation for me." Ariane closed her eyes.

Maeva whispered, "It was based on the intelligence of the time, the scouts-"

"SHUT UP, MOTHER!"

The sound of the Queen's scream tore at Roman's ears, the screech almost inhuman, he'd never heard anything like it. He covered his ears but it passed. Maeva was sitting far back against her chair, all color drained from her face.

"You," Ariane stepped toward Maeva, "You have put us in this position. Do you see what you have caused? You tell me to bring compassion to our people, and yet you have given birth to a generation who would rather die than serve you." She walked down the middle of the circle to the Commandante. "Irene, I will be holding a Tuesday Briefing," she turned back to Maeva, "Does that please you, Mother? Look at how I take your advice."

The voice sounded like venom and Roman's stomach turned.

The Queen turned back to Irene. "Every soul across Geb must be in attendance. Every Willing Woman, every soup seller and field dweller and Central Tower lab tech. All of Cork Town, you hear? Every single person must make their way to the center of Geb and have clear, unobstructed access to a screen. The message must be unambiguous and every ear must hear it from my own mouth. There will be no rumors, only the truth that falls from my lips." The Queen turned, "Am I clear, Irene?"

"Yes."

"I can't hear you!"

Irene stood. "Yes! My Queen!" Irene bowed deep. "It will be done. Every guard will be dedicated to this one goal until the Tuesday Briefing."

"Do not let me down, Irene."

"I will not!"

"You are all dismissed. You all have much to discuss, much to prepare, much to do. And I can't bear to look at any of you anymore. Leave. Now."

Roman didn't remember winding through the corridors of the fortress, he only remembered the sound of his breath between his ears until finally he stepped into the sun of the Geb City Square and marched to the Tower, his mind concentrated on one task and one task only. Remedy the code of incubates, or feel the weight of Lower Earth crush him into his grave.

31

Trudith and Anna tried to settle in the crowd, but shoulders were pushing and feet inevitably stomped on theirs as the thousands moved from Cork Town to the Geb City Square. Despite the number of people in movement, few voices dared to speak. They didn't need to be told something was very wrong; the fact alone of their being herded like cattle to the Tuesday Briefing was enough for alarm bells to sound in Trudith's mind.

"We haven't even had a Tuesday briefing since Queen Ariane's coronation," a woman said. "Whatever this is, it can't be good."

Trudith agreed. Anything that brought together the entire population of Cork Town with the Geb City population was going to rock the world they knew.

"I still think it's Upper Earth," a voice said somewhere behind Trudith, but she couldn't turn around to see who it was. The waves of people forced her forward. Trudith didn't know Geb City much at all, and in these conditions, it was downright unrecognizable.

"Maybe we're moving to a system of rations. I always thought that would be what came next."

"Like with vouchers to trade for food?"

"Exactly."

"Trudith?" Anna held her hand so they wouldn't get separated.

"What?"

"Are you sure you can't tell?" Anna didn't dare use the words 'that I'm pregnant', though Trudith knew exactly what she meant.

"I'm sure. I said it before and it's still true now. But you've got to stay focused here. Forget about that." If Anna had some kind of panic attack or went into labor early, it would be disastrous for all of them. She looked over at Anna whose face was serene and remarkably calm.

Maybe she can handle this after all.

Trudith set her eyes straight ahead, the crowd still pushing forward, though it was all very well organized. The guards flanked them, making sure everyone stayed in a kind of intense procession, and guards at the rear made sure there were no stragglers. It was exactly as they said they would do. And so far, no violence.

The Queen has made good on her promises so far. That this is a time for critical information to be shared and not for a crackdown on behavior. Not that I want to put that to the test.

"Stop! Stop there!" Trudith heard ahead. "Cork Town Residents take these two roads, fill them, and be sure you have access to a screen!"

The same words were echoed behind her, each guard saying the same.

"Be sure you have access to a screen!"

And quieter in the distance behind, "Be sure you have access to a screen."

She and Anna stood still. They had a good line of sight on

a screen that was mounted on an angle of a street corner. Trudith looked at Anna, who looked back at her. Trudith tried to give the most encouraging face she could, but she wasn't sure it came off right. Anna blinked and looked back to the screen.

She's not far off from the full gestational period now. Just don't let it be today. Don't let there even be any signs of it coming.

Trudith tried to make a plan for how to handle it if something went wrong, If Anna experienced pain or - curse the thought - went into labor. Normally Trudith liked having back up plans. But there was no way to back up this one. It just had to go according to plan.

Someone somewhere behind them shoved forward, and bodies waved outwards from it with a variety of grunts. Trudith caught her balance and automatically reached out to hold Anna up.

The screen clicked on. It showed the main city square, stuffed full of people in every direction. A sea of brown hair with the occasional dot that must have been someone from the outer counties, though Trudith couldn't see the details. Each head was barely the size of a pinprick. The screen changed to show views down side streets, alleys, anywhere there was a screen. It wasn't just the roads where the Cork Town folk gathered that were full to the max, it was everywhere in Geb. Trudith's eyes were glued to the screen. She'd never heard of Geb being like this, much less seen it with her own eyes.

And still, the voices were hushed.

Anna squeezed her hand just as the Commandante appeared on the screen.

"Guard. Positions. Set."

A singular clack echoed throughout the streets as the Guard moved into the same stance; Trudith could see the guard nearest to them, her legs outspread and hands on hips, the same position as the Commandante.

Over the screen she heard footsteps; the camera focused in on the balcony of the fortress.

One step.

Then another.

Step. Step. Step.

It felt like forever.

Where is she? How can she keep us waiting like this?

And then she appeared.

Her gown was the same one she wore at her coronation, the collar pulled high up her neck as her chest opened out to the people, her skin smooth. The black velvet caught the midday light and rippled with it like diamonds across a night water. Trudith was transfixed, like every other pair of eyes in Geb.

The Queen lowered her head, her shoulders lifting with heavy breath. When her head again rose, Trudith saw pain in her eyes. Even over the screens, it was palpable. Her green eyes shone with it, and without knowing why, Trudith felt the sadness with her.

Could we have been wrong about the Queen? She hasn't even said a word and yet everything in her speaks volumes more than what we've thought.

Her lips parted, mouth suspended in time. Trudith felt everyone around her stopped. It seemed like they'd all stopped breathing, only a collective heart beating between them.

The Queen began.

"People of Lower Earth."

The sound echoed out from the screens, over their heads, like four queens were speaking at once.

"You have come today because you have been called. But you will leave with one mind. Every one of you is experiencing individual hardship. I know it. I see it. I hear of it every day. And my heart breaks for you."

A tear crested in her eye but didn't fall.

"The settlers who came gave us life when our planet was failing. When men had all but destroyed everything, the settlers gave us life anew. My ancestors, my family. How grateful I am to them for their sacrifice. When they landed on the lava rock – the very rock we wear around our necks as a reminder of their hardship – they did not know what would become of us. And yet," she leaned forward over the balcony, taking in the crowd, "Here we are. We stand tall. We stand, alive and fighting!"

She paused, putting both hands on the amulet, her lips moving as though she were speaking to it. Trudith noticed that she too was holding her amulet in her hand. Tightly.

If only the settlers could see what's become of us.

She didn't have time to continue the thought. The Queen began speaking again.

"We have the best among us working in the Tower, day and night they slave to find solutions to the scourge you experience. The illnesses, the crop killers. They are the ones who developed the very fortification powder that keeps many of us going. They try everything to predict the changing weather patterns so that we do not experience another period like the second generation. They do their best, but this world is a difficult one to predict indeed. My gratitude to them is infinite. I may be Queen, but I cannot do as they do. My gratitude to you, those of the Tower."

She bent her head low. Trudith found herself doing it too, without really knowing why.

The Queen inhaled through her lips, and exhaled, the sound of her breath alive in Trudith's ears. Trudith's breath carried the same weight. It could have been her own breath she heard across the crowd of millions. Her eyes remained fixed on the screen.

"My friends, my family, my people. I must tell you now why you are here and I must say it quickly lest I lose my courage. More information will come. You will forgive me if it seems

I've brought you all here with such ceremony for the briefest of announcements. But you will understand. I know you will."

The Queen blinked, the tear breaking free and rolling down her cheek.

"There is a virus amongst you."

For the first time, there were murmurs across the crowd.

"Do not speak! Listen. Listen and then you will have every opportunity to discuss. Indeed, you must, for we must resolve this together, as one." She looked straight out. "It runs amongst the youngest of us. The weakest of us. Our children."

She paused, everything was silent.

"So far we have no evidence of it being transmitted to those who were born more than three years ago, but we could be wrong. It afflicts the respiratory system, attacking the most basic functions, and it's not visible to our equipment until it is too late. It causes great distress in the bearer. Our children. Our poor children."

The Queen stopped, and then lifted her chin high, the streak where the tear had fallen caught the sunlight and gleamed on the screen.

"We will find a cure! Of that, you can be sure. But until then, we must protect them, and we must protect ourselves. The degradation of the children's vital systems is evident. We have already begun preparing a place where they can be comfortable, continue their studies, and a dedicated team of the Tower's best are working on a cure. A vaccine. A treatment. They will find it. And in the meantime, we will protect our most vulnerable from exposure to other illnesses that could compound their condition. And we will protect the rest of Lower Earth from exposure to a virus we still know so little about."

Her chin set itself straight again. "Listen to me carefully, Lower Earth. We will not allow women to go the way of men. We will overcome this virus; we will find those responsible for propagating it. We will locate the birthplace of this enemy and we will cut it down at the quick!" Her fist shot into the air. "The children will be taken in the coming days to their quarantine. The rest of you must now move with the resolve of which I know you are capable, back to your lives, back to your duties. Speak of this. Understand it with us. We hold nothing back from you and we invite your questions. But first, we must set our operations in place. We will have time to discuss, to challenge, to explore. But first, in these coming days, I ask for your solidarity, as your friend. And I demand it, as your Queen. As you are mine so am I to you. Move away in silence now, following the Guard. They will lead you home."

The Queen turned and walked back into the fortress.

Her steps echoed again across the crowd.

Step.

Step.

Step.

The screen cut to black.

Trudith looked at Anna. Their hands were squeezed so tight that Trudith felt the imprint of Anna's nails as though they were her own.

"Leave as you came!" The Guard cried out, each one echoing the one who came before across each section of the crowd.

"Leave as you came!"

"Leave as you came!"

Still, no one spoke. Trudith could feel the heat coming off Anna's body as they walked in measured steps back to Cork Town.

32

The insistent knocking was drilling a hole in Lucius' head. He'd tried ignoring it, but whoever it was, she was not satisfied by his silence.

"I'm busy!" he finally yelled from bed.

"Lucius, let me in. It's Trudith. From the pub. Please let me in."

Lucius sat up as quickly as he could, nothing in him moved fast enough anymore. He managed to get himself off the bed and over to the door, opening it just wide enough for Trudith to enter.

"What are you doing here?" he hissed at her. "You're putting us both at great risk, never mind the girl."

"I came straight from the Briefing. We have to figure out what to do."

"What to do about what?" Lucius was losing interest now. If Trude was on his doorstep, he'd figured it was because the girl was going into early labor, or something worse, with 4957-209. "I'm not interested in politics anymore."

"Politics? This isn't about politics. This is about what they are going to do. With the children."

"With the children?" Lucius was getting a sour feeling in his stomach.

"Weren't you at the Tuesday Briefing?" Trudith's eyes were wide, the whites of them glowing under his naked light bulb.

"Of course not."

"What do you mean 'of course not'?"

"I told you, politics don't interest me."

"But the Guard came - "

He wasn't about to show her his hiding place. It was bad enough that he'd revealed it to Sara. If ever she was captured, he couldn't be sure she wouldn't reveal everything about it.

"I have my ways. Now, until you have something relevant about 4957-209, the girl, that is, then it's best you never come back here again."

"Lucius." Trudith crossed her arms. "You'd better sit down. I have more than politics to tell you."

A virus. So that's how they've explained their botched incubation program. And I thought they'd release them all into the sea, run them off the Rainfields cliffs, or some other such poetic violence.

Trudith had told him everything in quick delivery, bullets of information shot at him as he struggled to organize it all in his head. And then in a moment, it all made sense. He gave Trudith a sufficiently condescending pat on the back and told her not to worry about it, that it didn't affect their plans, that they had to stay the course as they'd promised to do. And she'd nodded as if she understood.

But Lucius knew. This changed all their plans.

'Children under three years' is a ruse. They'll up it to age five with time. Just didn't want to call attention to it too soon. Didn't want people making the connection between the campaign, the births, the coronation. I wonder who helped prepare the communications plan. Maeva could have,

but she'd be too flustered at the whole thing to think clearly. The Commandante is too blunt.

Perhaps it was Ariane all on her own. She has the cunning to pull it off, that's for sure.

He looked back to Trudith who was rapt before him, waiting for something, though he wasn't sure what.

"You look like you have a question, Trude."

"A question? No. I don't have a question. I have panic, deeply carved into the middle of my body. A question." She shook her head. "Lucius, they said the virus could transmit. And who do you think it'll transmit to? It won't be the women of Geb center, and it won't be by accident."

"You're getting a little too much into conspiracy theories here now, Trude." He needed her to calm down or the guards patrolling would smell her out like a rat. "There have been viruses in the past. Quarantine is not so unusual."

"Then why call all of Cork Town to the briefing? Why not just broadcast it on the screen in a loop? We'd get the information that way. Why bring us in, Lucius? *Why bring us in?*"

"Shhhhh," he pulled her deeper into his apartment, worried that her rising voice might catch more than one eager eavesdropper. "Trudith, we have to play it cool here. None of this will be happening overnight. We watch. We observe. We track with the changes just as we've done for the past few months. And we respond when the time comes in a way that preserves us."

"You've always been about 'preservation', Lucius. I don't want to preserve *this*. This is no life, under constant scrutiny, constant fear. This is why women go to the Sisters. I would if I could but I don't even have the right to leave this hole of Lower Earth unless it's under the watchful eye of the Queen's Guard, and only to bear witness to the Queen's announcement of an upcoming quarantine. For a virus. One that might already be loose in Cork Town. I don't want to preserve any of this, Lucius."

Lucius racked his brain, seeking out the right words to console Trudith, to bring her anxiety down a notch.

But she's right. How can I reassure a woman whose anxious intuition is correct?

Lucius nodded, "I see what you mean, Trude. Your panic is not unfounded."

"That's right, it's not."

"But it's all a question of timing."

Trudith cocked her head, and Lucius felt confident he'd distracted her from the main point just enough to bring her down a level.

"What has timing got to do with it?"

"There are times when if you act, you get your immediate satisfaction – and then you're disappeared. And then there are times to act which have a longer-lasting effect, a slower burn. And those moments transform in small steps, over time. So you're not wrong. But you have to consider strategy. And timing."

Trudith looked at the ceiling and nodded. "Yes, timing makes the difference."

He put his hands on her shoulders. "Look at me, Trude. Now is not the time to jeopardize Anna. She's relying on you and she's relying on me. We provide her with reassurance and confidence, and she provides Lower Earth with a rewritten future. We have to stay the course, Trudith. *You* have to stay the course. Don't cut out on me now."

"I won't."

"Good girl." He patted her shoulders. "Now take a round-about route to go home. One where no one can guess you came from here."

Trudith nodded and slipped out the door.

Lucius double-locked it behind her and sat down hard in his wheelchair. He was suddenly feeling his age.

33

All through the Briefing, guilt clawed at Maeva's gut. It took every ounce of her energy to look up at the balcony from the fortress entry, to not scream out at the madness it had all become.

And now she was going mad in her apartment. It felt like the stone of the walls was caving in on her from all four sides. The more she tried to think clearly, the more claustrophobic she got.

Why is there no air in the room? I just need a minute to figure this out!

She opened the window, a gust of air washing over her. The sensation distracted her just long enough that the voices took advantage of her guard being down. The voices of Queens past rolled over sounds and bubbled up, though she did everything to keep them muffled. Their advice would be toxic in a situation like this. How many times before had she heeded their warnings in times of distress just to be led down the wrong path?

They are responsible for the birth of the four. The death of Sahna - oh, how I miss you, my mentor! If only you were here now. Archer, I had so much fear of Archer because of them and the poison they spoke of him.

And for what? He's in the ground having done nothing but attempted to fulfill my horrible commands. Even the culling among my daughters was their idea.

My daughters.

I was supposed to be better than my own mother. I was supposed to take her code and be the Queen Mother she should have been to me.

But I am exactly the same as her.

The exact same.

Maeva punched the stone wall and the rock crumbled under her fist. She stood, trying to quiet her heart, trying to ignore the voices.

But they wouldn't let her ignore them.

"A virus?"

"This is the beginning of chaos."

"Millions of people have heard it."

"Civilization will regress as they try to protect themselves."

"Maybe you can control Geb, but the outer counties?"

"You set these wheels in motion, Maeva."

"You pushed Roman into the incubation program. He tried to tell you it was too soon, but you wouldn't listen. You insisted. And he had no choice but to obey. You didn't give him any other choice."

"And now, fifteen-thousand - "

"Fifteen thousand of your subjects - "

"Your people! Just children!"

" - will suffer because of it."

"Because of you."

"Your dreamed-up army is a generation of deviants."

"And you know Ariane doesn't take well to any kind of deviance."

Shut up. Shut up. Maeva closed her eyes. *None of this could have been foreseen.*

"You picked the daughter who was ruthless in her execution."

"And now she will execute."

I didn't know, I couldn't have known.

"Such are the decisions *you* have made in your reign, when you had it."

"Where is Upper Earth? Where is the great war you so eagerly prepared for? The reason for every decision you made? Where are the men, Maeva? Where are the Upper Earth men you so gravely feared? WHERE ARE THEY?"

"Enough!" Maeva threw her body against the wall, anything to shock them into submission. She needed them to stop, stop, stop.

Blood trickled down the side of her face and she felt the wound throbbing on the side of her skull.

Her door opened.

"Madam! Are you alright? There was a horrible noise!"

"Leave!" Maeva shouted.

The woman shrunk back and shut the door.

Maeva felt the droplet of blood rolling down her cheek. The little white hairs being absorbed on its path. It gathered more blood, the wound not yet closing.

She didn't let it close. She held back the cells, prevented the healthy blood from rushing to the place, though her physiology screamed at her to heal.

The sensation was tender, the caress of the blood, her skin reacting with a gentle wave of tingle. Bumps rose over her arms. She lifted one to watch the hair stand on end.

She dropped her arm back to her side and let the cells rush to the spot. They split, healed, closed the gash on her scalp, healed the crack on her skull. Three minutes passed in the state of healing. It had never taken three minutes before.

My time is coming. I am less and less able to direct my own body.

She walked to the mirror and touched her soft cheek. Her sixty-seven years of age were lost in the semi-smooth skin of a forty-year-old.

But it wouldn't last.

I must make Ariane understand the consequences of my decisions so that she will never do the same. The voices are alive in her, they will direct her if she is not able to control them. Aria and the Strangelands one had been stronger. Lucius was right to have designed them as he did, but I couldn't see it then. I didn't let myself see it then. If only it had been Aria as Queen. It all would have been different with Aria.

But I'm crying for a future that cannot be.

The tear's path made a parallel journey alongside the line of blood.

Maeva washed her face and changed her robe.

She breathed into the center of her body and muffled the voices back into their resting place. If she was going to confront Ariane, she needed every resource available to her. Any scent of weakness and Ariane would smell it on her before she walked through the door.

Lucius designed her precisely as I demanded. And now it's me who suffers because of it.

She smoothed her long brown hair with oil.

Rose. If only it had been Rose from the start.

The voices are responsible for Rose's condition; it was they who called me to Rainfields. Them who played the hallucination across my eyes. Them who made me believe I could walk on air without consequence. What if I hadn't jumped? What if her infant body hadn't smashed to pieces in my womb? What if I hadn't been forced to pump her heart back to life as she died in my body?

Oh, how the world would have been different. It would have been as it should have been.

Rose, Queen. I, her Queen Mother.

Rose! My daughter. My beautiful soul. Where have you gone?

The guilt is mine until the day I die for what I've done to her.

She looked deep into her reflection.

I didn't do it just to her.

I did it to the entire world.

Under Rose, the world would have been what it should have been. And it is my fault that it's not.

The weight of it crushed her lungs and her head fell forward. She tried to keep breathing, tried to inhale but it came in coughs as her muscles pulled her into herself, her chest contracted and she was choking on air.

I will drown. I will drown in my own chamber on air poisoned by my guilt. This is my own doing. They will find me and Ariane will blame the virus. And Lower Earth will explode.

No. I cannot allow it to happen.

Her lungs loosened, her shoulders began to lower.

If I die now, I allow it to be.

She lifted her eyes back to the mirror.

I will be the Queen Lower Earth always needed me to be. It's not too late.

A drop of blood crested on her nostril. She dabbed it away. She pulled her hair back into a tight bun and looked herself in the eye.

It was time to see Ariane.

She heard Ariane before she saw her.

She's not alone.

Ariane's voice carried across the fortress to her ears, "When this stage is complete, and only once the information is diffused throughout Lower Earth, only then can we move to the next phase. Talk of the virus must be on everyone's lips."

Maeva pushed the door, which opened with a distinctive creak. Both Irene and Ariane snapped their heads to see her enter.

"I didn't send for you, Mother."

"We need to talk."

"I'm occupied."

"I'll wait."

Ariane's lips tensed, but she looked back to Irene. "Don't forget the Ganese, not that you would, but I want to reinforce that they are as much a part of this as anyone else. Clear?"

"Clear, my Queen."

Watching Irene's deference to Ariane made Maeva's stomach turn. Why didn't Ariane assign a new Commandante instead of stealing Irene as her own? Maeve knew why; Irene's unique status as both warrior princess and loyal to the fortress would not be something Ariane could develop anytime soon. It took years. Maeva knew it, for she'd done it herself when she'd plucked Irene from the village.

Still, to see Irene take the same posture with Ariane as she had once done with Maeva felt like a slap in the face. Of course, Irene had no choice. No choice at all. She would do as told, that had been one of her most redeeming qualities. She had opinions, she had ideas, and some of them were good. But most critically, Irene could make happen what Maeva could not. That wasn't lost on Ariane.

So Irene is to be the mouth of the Queen now, transmitting the news of this false virus to the counties. Perhaps I can convince Irene, perhaps we can combine to convince Ariane -

But Maeva knew it was futile. Even the words in her head fell flat as she thought them. There would be no changing Ariane's mind.

Independent thought. That's what you wanted, and that's what you got in this Queen Daughter.

Ariane sighed and walked to the window.

"Leave us, Irene. We can deal with business later. I sense that my mother wishes to speak with me alone."

Irene looked to Maeva who gave a quick fake smile. Irene walked out, closing the creaking door behind her.

"Well?"

Maeva had to come right to it. Ariane wouldn't allow for

small talk; if Maeva tried, that would ruin any chance she had of getting her to listen.

"A virus is a dangerous proposition."

"I agree."

"It will spark thoughts of the Mist."

"It will."

"It will create terror across the counties."

"I think it might."

"Why do you take that so lightly? Terror will not serve Lower Earth, and it won't serve you."

"And why not?"

"The people will become unpredictable. We saw it in the second generation, and in the seventh."

"I don't need a history lesson."

"But there are lessons in our history." Maeva's arms reached out in front of her, and she was cautious that the pitch in her voice had become sharper. She lowered her arms slowly and spoke directly, "You see a set of effects from this choice. Certainly, you do or you wouldn't have used the tactic."

"Thank you for giving me the benefit of the doubt, Mother."

Maeva ignored her tone. "I offer to you my own experience. I don't know where the idea of a virus came from, but if you are anything like me, and alas, you are much like me whether you want to hear it or not, then your own voices have been murmuring to you that a virus, or rumors of a virus, would serve your ambition."

"Not ambition - "

"Your plans. It would serve your plans. But Ariane," Maeva's brain ran to find the right words, "The voices provide and the voices betray. You'll have many challenges before you in your reign; this is but the first of many. Perhaps the voices guide you well. This time. But perhaps they don't. Let me help you. I have made so many mistakes and I did what I did so that your reign would be free. Let me help you hear the voices and put them in context."

"You did what you did so my reign would be free?"

"Yes," Maeva whispered, ghosts of daughters flooding her memory. Blood and panic, running, disappearing daughters into the distance. Daughters lost to time.

Ariane walked slowly toward Maeva. "I have a generation of children who must be executed, because of decisions you made. This is my freedom? This is the reign you wished for me?"

Maeva blinked. "That not what I meant, I meant - "

"I know what you meant. But I'll remind you that it wasn't your hands on Aria's throat. You didn't look into your own eyes and watch yourself die in your own hands. I felt her die, my lungs burned as I cut off her air. My heart shriveled as hers stopped. This is my freedom? You've made many mistakes, Mother. You are right. But I am the one who has had to pay the price for it."

The voices in Maeva's gut rolled over each other; Maeva gasped as they hissed up to her ears.

Ariane walked close to Maeva, standing beside her. She laid her hand on Maeva's stomach. "You hear them now, don't you?"

Maeva could only nod. Ariane had never touched her like this, the warmth of the hand on her stomach radiated upwards and the voices quieted at the shock.

"You suffer from them, Mother." Ariane stepped to face Maeva, "I do, too."

Ariane's face changed. The edges softened. Her lips parted and Maeva saw the child of twenty years earlier before her. The child she'd watched grow in the incubator. The Queen child who had been her last hope at the time.

At the time. She was so smart from her first moments. So cunning. She'd seemed so perfect.

The Queen before her still had that child inside. Maeva had to be her mother.

"I never wanted you to suffer as I did. I'd hoped you'd escaped them."

Ariane took Maeva's hand and placed it on her own stomach.

"They are with me, right there, every moment of every day." Ariane closed her eyes. "It's torture."

Maeva placed her hand behind Ariane's head, caressing the thick brown hair that fell in long waves. "My child. If I could take it away, I would take it all. I would silence them for you if I could."

"Mother." Ariane opened her eyes. "We must go. Together. We must go to Rainfields and face them. Together we will overcome them. Then I can finally reign with the freedom you wish for me. Together we are stronger than them. Will you come? Will you come with me?"

Maeva felt the shock of panic throughout her body. She didn't know if she could withstand Rainfields in her condition. She was weakened. But Ariane's eyes implored. Eyes like her own. Eyes that were her own. And there was only one answer.

"Yes."

THEY LEFT WHEN DARKNESS FELL. THEY RAN AS ONLY THEY could run. They had never traveled together before. The countryside passed in blurs. Maeva glanced at Ariane beside her, but her face was unreadable. Focused.

She knows this will be challenging. She knows there will be some consequence for our joint arrival at Rainfields. But maybe she's right. Maybe together we can rewrite our code. If we stand up to it as one - me supporting her, she supporting me. It's a possibility I'd never considered.

They passed the first night in a makeshift den just beyond the boundaries of West Gana. She watched Ariane resting, her eyes open to the skies. She willed herself to stay awake, to watch her child in a way she'd never seen her before. Ariane's eyes were wide with wonder up at the stars. Maeva wanted to ask what she was thinking about, but she feared she would break the trance and the tenuous connection between them. So tried to keep her eyes open, but physiology overtook her. Her eyelids batted shut under the gentle night breeze.

By the time they reached Rainfields, the sun was just disappearing off the horizon. The sound of the wind through the channels of rock sung in low tones. It used to frighten Maeva, but having Ariane with her, she heard a different song. A sad song, but not a threatening one. It sang of all those who had found themselves on the rock's surface, so many souls lost, lost in so many ways.

The settlers who first arrived here after the Final War were the embodiment of grief. Rainfields sang their trauma, but it was only the beginning of their hardships. If only they had known... it was only the beginning.

They arrived near the site of the original incubation program and Maeva felt a shiver. She didn't know if it was her imagination, but the air grew colder against her skin and her body trembled.

"What is it, Mother?" It was a curious question, without emotion.

"This place, right here. It's my birthing place."

"I saw that in the records."

She's been in my records. Only I have those records. I didn't give them to her, did I? I gave her some, I couldn't have been so careless as to give her those - could I?

Unease grew in Maeva's stomach, but she couldn't trust the feeling. "Why did you bring me here?"

"It seemed the right place to confront these old Queens of ours."

"Yes," Maeva looked around, "You might be right."

She could still see the place as if everything was still there. All the equipment, the laboratories, the rows upon rows of incubators designed to pull the heat from the lava stone in the height of summer. The retractable awnings. The women in their lab coats. Cold white and stiffened cotton was her only comfort. She had vague recollections of her first days and the way the cotton scratched against her cheek. The coats had never been designed for nurturing.

The glass boxes that haunted her still. The memory alone was vivid enough to choke her. Born in a box, with so little touch, surrounded by thousands of others, drowning in the sound of their cries, dying as each one died, feeling their cells shrivel, their hearts slow to a stop. The staff preferred to snap necks. Easier to clean.

A thousand possible queens across a sea of glass encasements. Glass wombs that became glass coffins. From the time she could walk, it had been made clear to Maeva: there would only be one queen.

It had to be her.

When there were only four infants who remained, Maeva had made the decision. Nighttime rounds by the carers were few and far between. They were left unchecked. She'd waddled to each of her sister selves and did what none of them could have done. She was made of something different. She would be Queen.

And she was.

"So much death," she whispered at the empty expanse.

"You fought for your position."

"I didn't have to fight," Maeva turned to Ariane, "I just had to be willing to do what no one else would."

Ariane looked deeply into Maeva's eyes. "This I understand."

Maeva looked out again at the place. She couldn't see

where the lava plateau ended and the cliffs began, but it wasn't far. Ariane moved to leave, but Maeva couldn't. Not yet. She needed to get through to Ariane about incubation, and this was the moment.

Perhaps she feels the same chilling in her bones as I do, being in this place. She must understand that I was wrong. Let her hear my words, don't let them fall on deaf ears.

"Ariane - " she reached out her hand, not knowing if Ariane would take it.

Ariane walked back to the place where Maeva stood. And took her hand.

"You will lead as you will lead. I do not intend to influence you. But I would be doing you a great disservice if I did not impress upon you the gravity of my choices. Incubation. It was a mistake. Perhaps it's worth investigating the possibilities in small groups, but not at the scales we have implemented in our lifetime. I knew it. I regretted my own birth, and still, I fell into the trap. I can't tell you why. In my memory, I was motivated by real dangers, visceral and actual risks. But now - " She looked past Ariane, "Now it all seems to have turned to smoke. Enemies that were built of smoke."

Maeva lowered her head to her chest, the song through the rock channels singing louder with the growing wind.

"Come, Mother. Let's leave this place. Leave those memories behind. Bury the pain in the sea." Ariane walked away.

Did she hear me? Did my message land? I cannot ask. I don't want to hear her answer. Maybe it will become clear as we move ahead. Maybe with the last phases of incubates safely transferred into confinement, we can truly retire the incubation program. Forever.

Maeva stepped forward, now several paces behind Ariane, but Ariane moved slow, not rushing to the cliff edge. The voices pulled at Maeva's gut. They alone were the reason for Rose's condition. Maeva had faltered all those years ago, and Rose had paid the price.

Rose has suffered so greatly. Rose… and my heart. I will never heal.

The sight of Rose's broken unborn body still haunted her, for though Rose had still been in the womb, Maeva could see the death that had washed over her infant child.

So the voices came at her again now, with words that were lost in the crashing waves against the cliff. Still, they were present. Like dull knife blades, they scraped away at her, desperate for her to give them space to scream, power to control.

She wouldn't. Every time she'd let the voices reign they left behind immeasurable regret.

She'd seen it in her mother, her mad eyes bulging white as she screamed at herself on the cliff edge. The rain had poured down and Maeva, desperate to do something without knowing what, had listened watched in paralyzed horror as Queen Idia shriveled into a slave to the voices. And then Idia had thrown herself over the cliff edge.

The gnarled knife of rock that shot up through her chest.

Death without dignity. Death without ceremony.

And such was how Maeva's reign began at the age of eighteen.

I was too young. I knew nothing, nothing!

She fought the voices back down again. The risk of the cliff edge loomed, though they were still a safe distance away.

"I hear them too, Mother. But together we are safe. We overpower them."

Maeva's body twitched. She wouldn't give the voices space to speak out, but still, they battled for her consciousness.

"I see them in you," Ariane came closer, her eyes growing worried. "They are strong in you. But you are with me."

"Yes," Maeva tried to agree but her body twitched in spite of herself.

I will not give in to them. I hear their rumblings, a cry of warning in one while screaming for quick death in the other. They contradict themselves and I will not give them space.

Maeva inhaled deeply, "I can overcome them. I have done it many times before."

"We can use them."

"When I have tried, daughter, they led me astray. They led us all astray, especially in this place." Maeva leaned toward Ariane. "Do you have the memories within you? Do you see the old Queens die in your memory the way I do?"

"I have the memories, Mother. So many memories that don't belong to me."

Maeva at once felt grateful that she was not along in her experience of it. She'd always felt so alone. "Each of Lower Earth's Queens, each death off this cliff edge, it's all because of those echoes. That's all the voices are, Ariane. Echoes. The voices do not speak to us; they are only echoes living in our blood. You cannot place your faith in them."

"I have no faith. But I do listen. They speak of such incredible things. Do you ever take the time to listen to them?"

"Far too often."

"I mean, really listen, to find the truth within them. To weed out the noise and focus in on the one that truly knows the current situation. It is there, I can find it now. It took me time and I had no guidance as a child, no way of interpreting them. I had to find it on my own."

I should have been there. But by my own program, I couldn't. She was to raise herself, find her way rather than be guided. That had been her test.

Suddenly the setting sun was glaring bright and stronger than was known in this season. It slapped at her skin, intensifying in the moment, the heat pulled into the lava rock.

"I wanted you there, Mother, when I was young. I needed you." Ariane's green eyes caught the light. The green of them so crystal, so clear. Eyes that saw so far and so much. Eyes that told Maeva of the pain she had caused.

"I didn't know."

"You say that as though you didn't, but you did. If I had been your beloved Rose, things would have been different."

Maeva's heart skipped at the truth in Ariane's words. "You were the one I chose."

"To be chosen is not to be loved. You showed your face to me on a regular basis, but in it you gave me no love."

"I loved you."

"You didn't. You couldn't. I understand that now. How could you, when you had four daughters across the land, and only one could be Queen. Of course, you couldn't. I understand now, Mother, but I didn't understand then."

Her eyes are looking down to the very part of my soul I never wanted anyone to see.

Maeva felt a hot tear gathering in her eye.

Ariane's chin lowered, but the skin of her cheeks softened. "You said you wanted to be a real mother, more than your mother ever was. We have that chance now, perhaps our last chance, to bond as we should have."

"That's all I want, Ariane." She meant it. Ariane was the product of what she created. Perhaps Lucius had designed her, but it was all on Maeva's demand. The incubation birth, the hardened resolve. Her persistence. Her single-mindedness.

Maeva looked at Ariane.

She is everything I had asked her to be.

"I do love you, my child. You are exactly the Queen I had always hoped you'd become."

Ariane put her hands on Maeva's shoulders.

"Then let's do it. Dive into the voices with me, Mother. We must conquer their lies, let the truth emerge. We must seek them out. We must *cull* them. Cull until the single voice is so clear that we have only one choice to make."

She doesn't know their power. We ride a dangerous edge.

"Ariane, we risk failing."

"We will not fail. We are together. We will not fail. I will not have your blood on my hands." Her eyes drove into Maeva, the logic seemed weak but the power of it too great.

Maeva inhaled and pulled her shoulders taller and closed her eyes.

"Yes, Mother, strengthen yourself. Go in, go deep into them, and then allow them to rise up. Listen - "

You are a great fool, Maeva!

And you listen to the beast Queen you created?

How can you dare to call her daughter after everything that's happened?

How can you trust her?

You never knew what was best for your own well-being.

Never knew what was best for Lower Earth.

You're no better than your own mother.

Maeva snapped her eyes open.

"Stay with them, Mother. Don't quit."

The madness of your little game, you are full of delusion.

Worthless.

Lower Earth ought to be rid of you.

Lower Earth would be better without you.

All the trust of the ages, all the wisdom we've had to share.

We, your sisters, your mothers, your friends.

And you trust the box-born beast more than us?

We know it, we've seen it all before.

Before this, before Lower Earth, before the Mist, before men turned it all mad.

Maeva's body twisted.

"I'm here, Mother" Ariane's voice whispered in her ear. "Let them rise up."

"They speak truth and lies," Maeva managed to say as words flew across her brain.

"Stay with them, we both dive in, I'm there with you. I listen. Listen, Mother, listen."

You continue to play this game? You gamble more than we knew!
You gamble with the future! You are not worthy to lead!
You are not worthy to live.
Not worthy at all.
Listen, Maeva, you have done such wrong, such damage, it cannot be undone.
You will only continue to ruin the spark of Lower Earth.
"Their words, Ariane..."
You cannot continue. You know you cannot. You knew it long before coming to this place.
And now here you are, the poetic death you deserve. The death of a traitor. How many have been thrown over these cliffs against their will? Why do you think the Queens come here to end their reign with the end of their life?

Maeva's feet pulled her toward the cliff edge though she willed against it. The words confused directions, the voices encouraging and chiding at once.

"What do they say, Mother? I am here. Tell me what they say."

She is no daughter to you.

"They say you are not my daughter."

You are unworthy of her.

"I am unworthy of you."

You have done everything. Your time is through.

"My time - they say..."

Ariane brought her lips to Maeva's ear. "Listen to them, Mother."

Dive.

Dive as the swan into the void.

Release everything.

No healing.

No need even to try.

Let it end.

"Ariane - their words..."

"I hear them too, Mother."

Maeva pulled back to look at Ariane's eyes.

Ariane nodded, "I hear them too. I hear their truth." Ariane pulled her in close, an embrace so full that Maeva could almost dull the call of the voices.

Dive Maeva.

Let her watch you go.

She will lead as she must.

She is you.

You won't die.

You live in her.

"Mother," Ariane whispered. "Listen to them. It's time."

Maeva pulled out of the embrace.

Ariane nodded, her eyes with shards of sunlight and the crashing waves below. "You have done what you had to do. Now you live through me."

Dive, Maeva.

The water and rocks call you.

Join all those who came before.

Dive, Maeva.

Die, Maeva.

"Go, Mother, go. I am here, you do not leave me behind. We will always be together."

Maeva stepped to the cliff edge, the blades of rock below.

"Go, Mother. I am here. You can go at last."

She was falling. She didn't remember jumping. The air pulled at the skin of her face and the rock tore at everything inside her.

She let it.

Maeva watched as the sunset across the water turned black.

34

I rene heard the fortress door slam shut as the Queen whisked in. From where Irene was standing on the main staircase, she could see the frays in the Queen's dress. Her hair was flying in wisps as though she'd just survived a great storm.

Irene came down the steps, trying to focus her eyes on a sight she'd never seen since Ariane had taken the throne.

She's disheveled? They were to discuss strategy in the cottage. There's no way she's been to the cottage, arriving back in this state. Where's Maeva?

"My chambers. Now." Ariane's voice cracked.

Irene squinted her eyes, trying to think through the possibilities of what could have occurred during what sounded like it was to be a reasonable strategy review between Queen and Former Queen.

From the beginning, it was logical, even if it didn't make sense. Ariane never had time for Maeva's ideas. A 'strategy session' may have sounded reasonable to anyone who didn't know them, but now...

Irene followed behind Ariane who moved so quickly that Irene, despite her longer gait, could hardly keep up.

She walks like her mother. I shouldn't be surprised. That's what comes with a genetic duplicate.

"My Queen - "

"Do not speak until we are in my chambers."

Irene picked up her pace. Ariane threw the door open with such force that the aged wood bounced off the stone wall behind it. Irene tried to slow her heart as she closed it; she didn't want Ariane picking up the sense of panic she felt brewing.

"This cannot wait any longer. I have been desperate to put the steps in motion."

"My Queen. You appear to be in a state. Are you alright?"

"I'm fine, this isn't about me. It's about the incubates."

"You discovered a solution during your retreat?"

"During my retreat? What is the matter with you, Irene?"

"With me?"

I cannot get defensive. I know this glare in her eyes. How often I saw it in Maeva. I must ride out the wave of whatever she is saying. She will have it no other way.

"I apologize, my Queen."

Ariane closed her eyes briefly, "Yes, you are right. I am tired. I have spent days thinking this through." She opened her eyes, bright green and sharp, she stared into Irene. "I have prepared these words carefully, so listen. Take note. I expect you to act in most immediate terms."

"Yes, my Queen."

"The incubates under age three are to be gathered. They will be transported up north." Ariane paused.

Irene had been considering the options already. "My Queen, I have already researched some possible locations. They are discreet and far from any neighboring community."

"That's perfect," Ariane's eyes lit up. "We will gather the children and move them in groups while those who accompany them wear protective gear. They will move in caravans. I don't want to use up fuel for this. Instead, horse or donkey-drawn."

"I will begin the procurement process."

"Good, good." Ariane walked to the mirror. "Oh. This is how I look?"

She seemed to be speaking to herself. Irene didn't reply. Ariane tried to smooth the wild wisps of hair that went in every direction, but they sprung back immediately.

"I should have a bath."

"Would you like me to leave?"

"No! Not yet. We must finish. This must begin before anything else." Ariane walked to her bureau, sat down, then stood up immediately and walked to the window.

She is restless, distracted.

"Are you writing this down, Irene?"

"No, my Queen. I have committed it to memory."

"I will write it down." She ran over to the desk and sat, pulling open a drawer and placing paper on the desk. She stared at it, white and empty for a long moment. She opened another drawer and took out a pen. She wrote furiously in large script, turning page after page as Irene waited, though it wasn't more than a few minutes. Ariane kept her eyes on the pages, "I have it now. Now it cannot be lost. Now it is written."

Irene waited. She didn't dare test the Queen's sanity. She'd seen Maeva in such states many times over the years, but this was the first time Queen Ariane had been taken over by such a manic need. Not that Irene would challenge it.

Ariane stood, leaving the pages on the desk.

"So you will arrange for the transport."

"Yes, I'll make sure the lists are organized, accompanying staff mobilized, provisions for the trip, and accommodations on arrival."

"Accommodations?"

"We will have to mount them quickly, but I am confident the Guard can manage it."

"What will they need accommodations for?"

She's distracted, she's not thinking straight.

"For the children on their arrival. And for the staff. Those who will supervise and perhaps eventually those who will educate them. We will ensure all is in place."

"You've misunderstood, Irene."

Irene's chin involuntarily tilted. She felt she was missing something, or the Queen was, and she couldn't identify the gap.

Ariane's eyes narrowed. "Ah, I see. Yes, the - *preparations*. Please. Do explain it this way to all who may ask. Use only your most trusted guard to accompany the children. We begin with under three's and then we'll move to all incubates, once we are ready to announce the virus among them."

Whatever I am missing, it is big.

"And what are the accompanying guards to do with the children?"

Ariane pursed her lips. "I believe the most efficient would be to throw them over the cliffs. If it is done at Rainfields we can be sure that no one will find them. Those lands are still in Royal territory."

Irene thought her heart had stopped. Her ears muted and her eyes suddenly had the sensation of sand as she blinked.

I cannot be hearing this correctly. This cannot be -

"Don't look at me like that, Irene. This was because of Maeva. There's no other solution left for us. Only the most trusted of the Guard must go." Ariane walked to the window and looked out for only a second before turning and marching at Irene. "Don't let me down, Irene. Not now, not on this." Irene stared at Ariane, she didn't know what to say. "Don't look at me like that! This was *not* my doing! I didn't want this! I am doing the best I can, and this is the best I can do for Lower Earth."

"Yes, my Queen." She barely managed to get the words out. Her throat was closing.

"Don't let me down."

"I won't."

"You will report to me on each step of the way."

"Yes, Queen."

"Speak of the place you mentioned. Let that be the people's story. The girls are going to their countryside quarantine. They will rejoin when a treatment is found. Dedicated researchers working on-site, whatever. Give me the lines. Make sure Roman is across it."

"Yes," she couldn't command her mouth to say "Queen". How had it come to this? How could Maeva have allowed this to be the conclusion of their strategy planning together? Maeva would have objected to every word falling from Ariane's lips.

But Ariane hadn't said a word about Maeva.

"Please, my Queen, Ariane, where is Maeva?"

"She's dead." Ariane's eyes widened, the whites glowing as Ariane stepped forward and leaned into Irene's face. "Killed herself. Just like her mother."

35

___

"They are improving in assault skills," Priyantha continued, "But generally there is still a problem with stealth operations. It's a mystery to me given that this has been part of our hunting ways for as long as we've all been alive."

Leadon looked up from the most recent training report. "Could it be the pressure?"

"The pressure? Is there more pressure than the hunt?"

"Generally the deer won't kill us if we miss. Perhaps we're trying to solve the wrong problem."

"So it might be psychological?"

"I think it could be."

They both turned their heads towards the sound of a woman running in their direction. Murrani, the lookout, was headed their way at a speed that said her message was important.

She was out of breath when she spoke. "It's the Commandante."

Leadon felt heat flame up the back of her neck.

"What's she doing here?" Priyantha asked the lookout.

"I don't know. Mitam took over the station as soon as I saw

her so that I could come tell you. She'll be arriving any moment now."

"Assemble a unit, in case we need support!" Priyantha shouted to Anyook as she already was running in the direction of the gate.

Leadon was only a pace behind her.

That she would come here, after all that's happened, after all we discussed, and after all I made abundantly clear to her - the gall. She must be taught a lesson. She cannot give affront after affront and expect there are no consequences.

Leadon prepared the plan in her mind as she ran. She was out of breath, not from the effort, but from the emotion she fought to contain.

"Are you alright?" Priyantha asked, "You suddenly look unwell."

"I am unwell. I am unwell with disgust and anger and I won't let this continue." Leadon could see Irene arriving, fifty steps away now, her image growing in her approach.

Priyantha nodded, "What will you have us do?"

"Where's the contingent?"

"I can see them making the turn onto the path now, they'll be here in a moment."

"Fine."

Irene's hair sat in long braids down her back, bouncing with every step. Her face had no specific expression. Leadon felt another flare of temper at the sight of Irene's resolute calm.

She has no shame. No sense of what she's done. As ever. When has she ever thought of anyone but herself? She insults my authority. Worse than that. She treats me like a dog. She pushes me too far.

Leadon paused. Suddenly she realized she'd lost sight of the larger issue.

This isn't about me. It can't be about me, nor the insult she's cast upon me. If I make this about me, then I'm no better than her.

Leadon's shoulders relaxed and lowered. She took a deep breath.

This is about what her fortress has done to Gana, to her own people. What they will continue to do if their power evolves unchecked. She is as much a part of that power structure as the Queen.

This can't be about me.

Lea's lungs filled with cooler air and she felt her head clear.

"I see you've brought a party to greet me," Irene spoke through the gate, still no sign of any emotion.

Leadon looked at Irene, scanned down her body, and back up. She did not appear changed, though something in her posture told Leadon that Irene was tired.

"Open the gate," Leadon said in a low voice to Murrani, who obeyed, the gate clicking as she lifted the lock bar and slowly swinging open.

Irene stepped in, back onto her land. But where Leadon was now firmly in charge.

She's in my territory, not hers. And as much as this is about Gana, she must also know how to treat us with respect.

Irene inhaled, "I must speak with you, Leadon. Alone."

A long pause followed and Leadon could hear the warriors behind her growing tense at the silence. Leadon turned to them.

"Arrest her."

"*Arrest* me?"

"You have violated my commands." She turned back to the warriors, "Make sure she has good food and drink, and a comfortable mattress." She tilted her head toward Irene, who's mouth was agape. "I will speak to you when I'm ready." She nodded to the arresting warriors.

"You don't understand, Leadon. Things have changed. I must speak with you. I shouldn't even be here. You don't know what I had to arrange in order to come."

"You will explain everything to me. Later."

"It's going sour, Leadon. Let me speak with you."

"I will. Later."

"This is ridiculous!" Irene threw her head back and broke her arms from the warriors. She pointed at Leadon, "Play at Chief if you want, but this isn't about all that. It's not about me and it's not about you."

"I agree with you entirely on that. You'll tell me all it is about. Later."

Leadon turned and walked to her hut without stopping. She feared she would lose her nerve.

Have I been too hasty? Of course, she wouldn't come simply to flout her authority like a peacock. That was never Irene's way. The conditions in which we are kept here with their planted "representative" is already enough to show Geb's superiority.

She's come for another reason, and I have no idea what it is.

Leadon cursed herself for deciding in haste, even though it had seemed appropriate. For the warrior priestesses of Gana, Irene's arrest would send a good message.

Perhaps it's not bad that they have seen this. It makes our role clear. I do not have the information about why she has come, but this solidifies something in the women's way of thinking. That we are not victims to the whims of the fortress.

But still.

Lea waited an hour.

That was long enough for the message to be clear. And she couldn't wait a minute more. She walked to the reinforced hut where Irene was being kept. It took a moment for her eyes to adjust to the darkness inside, but Irene's outline was there, right in front of her, standing in the middle of the cell.

"You throw me in like a thief, like a common rat."

"Come, Irene. You didn't give me much choice." Leadon's voice was calm now. Calmer than she even expected to hear her voice.

Irene's face tensed - and then relaxed. "You're right."

Both women looked at each other, the sounds of the training outside underway.

"They are improving." Irene looked to the small brick-sized window.

"They are."

"We must speak."

"I agree." Leadon unlocked the cell. "But not here. Let's walk."

They walked at a quick pace towards the village's boundaries. Warrior priestesses stopped whatever activity they were doing as they passed. Two women of the same face, thirty-five years between them, the future of Gana and the iron fist of the fortress. Leadon saw that the women knew how important this meeting would be. They didn't interrupt. They cast their eyes back to their respective work, albeit moving more slowly upon seeing them.

They reached the far end of the village limits, the sound of the river growing before them. Irene stopped, and Leadon stopped with her.

Irene looked at Leadon and then looked at the sky. "I have been charged with an impossible task."

"Little is impossible for you." Leadon meant it.

"This is different." Irene kept her eyes set straight ahead.

They walked a while further before Irene continued.

"Maeva is dead."

"Oh." Leadon didn't know what else to say. She'd had such little interaction with Maeva other than as a child and then during her visit just a few weeks earlier. She had seemed distracted and unfocused, but Leadon never would have guessed she was close to death. "There's been no announcement."

"Exactly."

Leadon didn't know what to make of that. "And this jeopardizes your position?"

Irene looked into the distance, "That's not why I'm here, though that may be true." She sighed, "And if it is, then I can't imagine Ariane allowing me to simply retire to the Gana countryside. It's also why I had to come immediately. What she's planning, what she'll have me do-" Irene swallowed, words seeming to get stuck in her throat as Leadon watched her struggle to speak. "Thousands and thousands of girls, Leadon. Babies. She'll have me kill them, Lea."

Leadon looked hard at Irene. "That makes no sense. Why? Why would she - "

"There's a problem with them. They were born in incubation and the effects of it seem to be life-long. A clinical depression. No medical intervention seems to reverse it. They're in a wretched state. But to kill them? That's not who we are. That's not the Lower Earth I serve. We are about preserving life in the face of everything the Final War threw at us." Irene's chest inflated and she pulled her shoulders back. "I have to serve the world we should be. Not the one the Queen commands it to be."

Leadon could only bring her voice to a whisper, "She wants you to kill children? Thousands of them?"

"Infants, toddlers. First all those under three years, but soon it'll be all under five. I'm to make it look like a quarantine that is so secure that no one sees them again. Certainly, in some time she'll announce that they've been reintegrated into different counties and no one in Geb will be the wiser. And meanwhile, we'll have committed a genocide as bad as, or worse, than any which came before the Mist."

Leadon closed her eyes, a dizziness invading her.

"Why have you come here to tell me this?" Leadon's stomach turned.

Irene grabbed Leadon's shoulders. Her eyes were wide with desperation. "Because we have to find another way, Leadon. This is *our* land. Lower Earth is ours. Our ancestors built this society out of love for one another, even for those who were different from us. Even when it brought misfortune on our own people. That is what we stand for. Strength and perseverance, care for one another, no matter how hard. These girls are not ethnic Ganese but they are as much a part of our Lower Earth sisterhood as anyone. Even more so because they are *just children*. There is no one protecting them. *We* are warrior priest-esses. This is our greatest calling, and I'd be insulting the gener-ations who came before, every ancestor who took any risk to save the life of another if I didn't do everything in my power to save them."

"Thousands," Leadon whispered to herself. Her mind was blank. She sought some kind of message from beyond, a sign, a feeling, but inside her was vacant. The thought of thousands of girls being led to their death hit her somewhere deep. "It's not possible, not without the Queen knowing - "

"Don't tell me it's not possible." Irene pointed in Leadon's face and then paced, her hands on her head. "We have to find a way, Leadon. Geb is going to become an ugly place. The clear-out of Cork Town will turn worse soon. Not just disap-pearances of the known betrayers; that's been accepted as normal. No, this will be a culling. A *culling*. Those are the Queen's own words. A culling of those undesirable, those who take resources without giving. I can't fight her on that. The animosity against Cork Town is already great, brewing for years as the rumors circulate of the deviants causing havoc, stealing, and never mind the opies. I can't do anything about Cork Town. But there must be something to do about this. "

The river rushed by them, the sound filling Leadon's head as it masked their voices. She brought her hands to her face, rubbing her temples, hoping a solution would come, a way to do it that didn't risk all of Gana, something that didn't put their very existence in danger. But every thought came back to the same conclusion.

The moment the Queen finds out, she'll come for us.

Torn between dedication to Gana and shock at the inhumanity, at the very idea of thousands of incubated children being marched to their death, Leadon felt her blood drain.

"It's horrible, it's horrifying. Everything you've said, which I accept as truth - "

"It is the truth - "

" - makes my stomach turn. But Irene, what can possibly be done? How could we even begin without risking a massacre of our own people? Irene, it can't be done."

A voice behind them stepped out from the trees.

"It can be done. I'll do it."

36

Rose recognized the voices long before they arrived near the river edge. And more so, she recognized the cruelty in Irene's recounting of the plans for the incubates. She knew it was true of the Queen. There was no question to the truth of her story. Rose had felt it in her sister Queen from the moment she'd first been announced on the balcony of the fortress.

There was something dark in her from the very beginning. The way she could detach herself from those around her, those who loved her, from those who could have loved her. Anyone who can kill her sister, kill the one who wears her own face, has something broken inside. But I never thought this - I never imagined it could come to this.

Rose waited, hearing out the story.

Irene is right. This cannot be permitted, we cannot stand by and watch a generation of children be led to die for a decision that hadn't been their own.

Leadon cannot do it. She risks too much if she is at the helm. And what of Gana then? She's only just begun to bring East and West together, only just begun to unite them as a single people in the vision of their ancestors. No, Leadon can't do it.

But I can.

Rose stepped out from the trees, knowing the shock it would have on the discussion. She had seen the Commandante many times since the coronation, but the Commandante hadn't seen her.

"It can be done. I'll do it."

The two faces, the same face but in two, snapped toward her.

"Rose?" The Commandante's eyes narrowed while Leadon's relaxed.

Rose nodded.

The Commandant approached her, "But you're... limited. Rose. I certainly didn't expect to see *you* here. You hide well and hear everything. You did inherit certain abilities from your mother."

"You said she's dead."

"She is."

"Ariane killed her."

"I don't know that."

"I do. I didn't have to see it to know it."

Irene nodded slowly.

Rose continued, "Leadon cannot leave. Not now. But I can. No one knows where we - I - am." Rose blinked at the memory of Zev. He would support this decision, there was no doubt. But she would be putting him in harm's way. "I will need help - "

"The warrior priestesses will not hesitate to support you." Leadon bowed.

"Wait, wait, wait." Irene stepped forward. "Rose, you hide in shadows. You have never grown past the body of a girl. I'm not trying to be cruel here, but this is a serious matter that can only be handled by those with great resolve and courage in the face of what could be death. You are kind. You are gentle. You are - "

Rose ran at Irene, knowing she could move faster than

Irene could catch with her eyes. She leaped and grabbed Irene's throat, pulling her to the ground. Irene coughed, the air knocked out of her.

"You know nothing of who I am." Rose stood, allowing Irene to regain her footing.

"And so I continue to be wrong." Irene shook her head and looked at Leadon, "There was a time when I was so sure. So sure of myself, so sure of our direction." She looked back at Rose. "I don't know anything anymore."

Rose lifted her chin. "Don't fall into the mistake of believing that you ever did."

Irene bowed her head low and then brought her hands to her hips. "I have an idea."

Rose listened carefully, curious at the sincerity in the Commandante's voice. There was no doubt that what she was proposing could get Irene disappeared. She could be publicly flogged, and then worse. Rose could see it. Ariane would enact incredible horrors upon her. She would feel she had to, in order to send a message. And a part of Ariane, that false Queen, would relish it.

She only ever lived to have an enemy.

Irene outlined her plan. It was simple - it had to be. The logistics of moving nearly fifteen thousand children would be challenging enough. The rest had to be as easy as possible.

Leadon spoke as Irene finished, "If we are to make this work then we'll need to set up a collection point from the location in the Central Mass you already suggested to the Queen. The less you change now, the more likely she is to accept it."

"I agree. Once I leave here, I cannot sway from the plan in place. She'll hear it in me the moment I open my mouth to lie. I must only speak truth. I must commit myself to the plan. The rest will be up to you."

"The island must be prepared in advance," Rose whispered herself out of her thoughts.

Lea spoke up. "I'll send a group ahead. There are several warrior priestesses who can be trusted with the task. And they shall stay on as educators and carers. No one else attends to that island. Once they pass the Forgotten Islands, the rest is truly forgotten until Upper Earth, and we know that is several thousand kilometers away."

"We don't know that," the Commandante added, "but that was the best intelligence we ever got from the scouts."

Rose nodded. She hadn't heard talk of the scouts in years. Upper Earth had become a forgotten enemy like the island on which they lived. There had been a time when Upper Earth consumed the consciousness of all peoples across the land.

And now? Those women scouts were as real as any. It was not an invention. But the fear of an enemy on our shores has faded into the enemy that lives upon our own land. The enemy who leads our land.

Rose stepped close. "We have much to prepare."

The Commandante nodded, "Rose, I shall not see you again."

"Never again."

The Commandante lowered her head. "May the wisdom of the ancestors be with you." She kneeled.

As did Leadon. "We bend to you, Rose. You carry the blessing of our ancestors. You embody their values as much as any Ganese."

Rose brought her hands to her heart and then placed one on each of the kneeling Ganese warrior priestesses' shoulders. "We each have our duty to fulfill. This one is mine. My restitution for the Queen. I cannot undo all she has done. But I will not let her do this."

And with that Rose ran, unconcerned at what the double faces would believe at her leaving. She needed to see Zev. She had to explain to him their mission. And she had to prepare herself to fulfill the meaning of her life.

37

Queen Ariane's eyes widened. Roman had known they would. He had known she'd be displeased, but there was no hiding any of it from her anymore. She had to be told and Roman had to face the heat.

She flipped through the pages Roman handed to her. He stroked the lava amulet without realizing he was doing it.

"You need to know just how far behind we've become. I know this is disappointing."

"So you've made no advances on any of the new crop killers? Not the rice crinkle disease, nor the bacteria in the water of the Dark Counties pipeline?"

"None."

"You've got some guts bringing this report to me. You don't need me to tell you that the ratios don't work. I'm doing simple math here, Roman, and our arable land is decreasing on a monthly basis. I *told* you that the newer generations in Willing Women had to be less dependent, able to manage with fewer natural resources. You haven't solved for that, and meanwhile, the viruses continue to run rampant across the fields. Over four hundred active viruses, am I reading this right?"

"This is precisely why I've brought it to you, and why I've brought it now."

"Roman, do you understand that what you've put before me is not just unacceptable, but it is a travesty and an insult to my intelligence?"

"No, my Queen, never. Quite the contrary. This is what I've been trying to tell you. We've pivoted to work on the incubates. And now we've reached the limits of our resources in the Tower. We're spread too thin. The biologists and statisticians and bioinformaticians working on the viruses of West Fields and East Fields are the same we need working on the revised incubation program, as you commanded. We can't be in two places at once. We've tried prioritizing and we've tried strategizing but ultimately we've come up against a wall. The resources in the Tower are insufficient to meet both the demands of the incubation program and the issues of climate evolution and virus proliferation." He closed his eyes, not knowing how she would take his next words. "If we are going to solve every angle of the problem, we need to do some things differently. And this is where I need your help, my Queen."

Ariane exhaled loudly through her nostrils. "My help." She walked past him to the window of her office that looked into the square, the Tower across the other side. "I should commend your transparency if I weren't so frustrated by your inadequacy."

Roman let his breath out. He was fine with being called inadequate. In the circumstances, even he felt his own inadequacy. He'd slaved over the code of the incubates. And still, their progress was barely incremental. Certain drivers had to be dialed back without affecting the overall viability. He felt like they were right on the cusp of it now, having recognized the overlapping gene. They could adjust the levels of dependency on basic needs while sustaining muscle growth, resilience, and baseline vitals. But the adaptations to adjust for the psychological impacts of incubation - that was beyond him. It was beyond Uma. It was beyond the entire eighteenth floor.

"What is it going to take, Roman?"

He'd prepared himself for this question. "We can implement. That's not the question here. We've found enough mechanisms through our existing tools to define the structure and solve through experimentation."

"You're not answering my question, and now I'm starting to lose my patience."

Roman's heartbeat quickened. He knew she heard it. Her eyes narrowed in on him and his palms began to sweat. "We need Lucius."

"Lucius?"

Roman nodded, "I'm the last one to want to have to say this, which only attests to my recognition of my own limitations."

"You are full of words today, Roman, and yet short on meaning."

"Lucius is the only way we can overcome this. His abilities surpass the collective intelligence of Central Tower. We cannot resolve the incubates DNA problem without him."

Ariane looked back out the window. "I can't say that I'm happy to hear this."

"I'm miserable that I have to say it. That man -" Roman checked his language, "He is infuriating and arrogant. Frustrating and obstructive." Roman lifted his hands in defeat. "But I can't do this one. I can't do it without him."

"You think he can identify the weakness in the current design of incubates?"

"I suspect he already has."

"And he can address it so that they are psychologically stronger for the method of their birth?"

"I would lay my bets on it."

"Would you lay your life on it?"

Roman knew his words now would define the rest of his time before degradation began. "Yes. I would."

"Fine."

Roman closed his eyes.

"Waste no time, Roman, bring him to the Tower immediately."

"He won't come if I ask."

Ariane marched to her desk and flipped open a blank piece of paper. "I'll prepare the summons. Then you can deliver it."

"He won't come. Even with that, if he sees me at his door he'll have it decided before I even have a chance to pass him any letter."

The Queen put her pen down. "The Guard then."

"You risk making him hostile. I don't think that will serve us."

Ariane stood up. "You want me to go there."

"I think it's the only way he'll come willingly."

"You want me to walk into that virus-infected, deviant and deformed, outcast-laden ghetto? Expose myself to the dangers of those who plot behind my back, give them the opportunity to access the one they hold responsible for their conditions - me - when *they* are the ones who've been plotting, planning, and preparing for my demise?"

She can't be serious. Her paranoia is out of control.

Her nostrils flared. "All this because you couldn't convince him yourself."

"It's our history - "

"It's your *failure*. You reek of it, Roman. He's smelled it on you for years." She swiped her arm at her chair and it flew into the wall, a leg cracking against the stone. "You leave me no choice. But I'm not going without the Guard, don't you try to convince me otherwise or else I'll begin to suspect there is more behind your entreaty than simple inadequacy." She pointed her finger into Roman's face. "Watch yourself, Roman. You are on notice."

He wasn't sure he was still breathing. Her face was red and her chest lifted and fell in quick succession under the velvet gown.

"Send Irene to me now so that we can prepare. You'd better hope I can be more convincing than you."

38

———

Lucius heard her coming. The Guard had always been less than subtle when trying to make a point. He inhaled deeply and looked in the mirror before they arrived.

Would have liked to bathe before the great confrontation. I've known this was coming for years. I couldn't have guessed it would be over incubation, of all things. But here we are.

He tried to smooth his hair down, look a little less the mad scientist, and perhaps a touch more the man he used to be. Not that Ariane would know what he used to look like. She was born well after his degradation had started.

She only knows me in this case of a body. Such a shame. We would have made quite the family portrait back in the day.

He laughed at himself as he shook his head; the distaste of his humor was wearing even on himself.

A knock on the door.

"Yes?"

The hand on the other side turned the handle, but it didn't give.

"Open the door, Lucius."

"Who is it, please?" He giggled again, his stomach rising and falling with it.

"This isn't a laughing matter."

"Nothing is, dear. Nothing is. I'm coming."

He opened the door, the vision of his Queen daughter with a group of guards behind looked ridiculous in his corner of Cork Town.

All this for me? What did they think I would do? Sit on her?

"Afraid there isn't room for all of you. There's hardly room for one of you. So who will it be joining me for afternoon tea?"

The first guard behind Ariane moved to step forward, but Ariane held up her hand, entered, and closed the door behind her.

"Hello, Lucius." Ariane strolled around the small apartment, looking into the bedroom area.

"Daughter."

"You consider yourself father? Not grandfather, perhaps? I certainly don't know what to call you."

"I designed the one who came before you, and I designed you better than her, but of the same code. I see it in you right now. You can consider yourself set apart from Maeva, but you are the same. Exactly the same."

"You birthed us in boxes just the same."

"Ah, now I cannot take responsibility for that. At least, not for Maeva. I didn't know that was how she would come. You, however, are a different case."

"And this is why I've come to see you."

"To talk about your birth? You were a beautiful baby, cooing gently and giggling without a care. What a time that was. Surely you remember it."

"I remember being cold and alone inside a glass prison."

"Ah, you remember that? Shame. I'd hoped that might fade into the past."

"It didn't, but I got over it. These ones don't, and I want to know why."

"These ones of what?"

Ariane sighed. "I don't want to play games, Lucius - "

"We've never had the pleasure of playing games, *Ariane*. I must say, I never liked that she gave you all the same name."

"Shut up."

"Something morbid in it all. You must feel their blood running through you. That foreign sensation, an invasion. None of it was ever supposed to happen this way. But then, had everything gone to plan, you never would have been born at all."

"If everything had gone to plan then men would still be running the world and you wouldn't be rotting in a studio flat in the Cork Town ghetto."

Lucius sat back in his wheelchair and pursed his lips. "Touché."

"Now that we've played your game, we need to get serious."

"I can't see why."

"You can run Roman back to the Tower with his tail between his legs, but I won't go so easily."

"I'm not asking you to go."

Ariane leaned forward in her chair, leaning her arm on the table in a way that made Lucius feel they were just having a chat about the weather or the status of banana crops in the East Fields.

"This virus is running rampant across the incubates. It's horrible to watch. The impact of their own code driving them to self-destruction."

"We both know there is no virus."

"I fear for the future of the incubates program."

"Rightly so."

"We cannot allow it to continue."

"I agree. Stop incubation."

"I mean the illness among the incubates. Stop playing games with me and come back to the Tower."

Lucius sat back. "Just stop using incubation and you don't even need me, your problem will be solved."

Ariane's eyes narrowed. "Incubation is the way of the future."

"The Willing Woman program was and is the only future for Lower Earth."

"You've become an extremist?"

"I'm not an extremist, nothing like it. But, *like you*," he emphasized, "I want the richest future for Lower Earth. It can never be with incubation. It violates a basic rule of our humanity."

"I was born in one. And I am Queen."

Do not speak the words you're thinking Lucius. Do not say it.

And you will be the downfall of Lower Earth.

Lucius exhaled, relieved he managed to only say it in his mind.

"And even you, Daughter, have seen the limits of a birth that occurs in a glass case."

"It is the very thing which has prepared me for what we must now do."

"What must you do, Daughter Queen?"

He saw her twitch at the condescension in his tone.

"We must bring forth a generation able to withstand a changing earth. Fewer caloric needs. Greater growth on reduced nutrition. Even stronger ability to withstand bacteria in the water. It's only going to get worse, Lucius. We are only just at the beginning of all this. If we are to survive it, then our women must be physically able to withstand it."

"But will they be mentally able to withstand it?"

"That's your job. You must code it in."

"I decline."

"You can't decline."

"I decline."

"I SAID YOU CANNOT." Ariane stood and the chair fell behind her. The guards flew open the door and Ariane screamed at them, "Get out! I didn't call you in here. Get out!"

The guards backed out and slowly clicked the door shut again.

Ariane closed her eyes. When she reopened them, her cheeks relaxed. Her jaw slackened and her lips parted.

"There's no one I trust, Lucius. No one but you now. I have to trust you. I need you. I never thought I would say any of this. Not to you. But I am doing my best, and it isn't good enough. Lower Earth needs better than what I have to give. Please, Lucius. Please come back."

Lucius found himself weakening. Something in his resolve lost its luster. Her green eyes sparkled even though there was hardly any light in his apartment. Her shoulders hunched over, far from the proud Queen who stood on balconies or made grand declarations.

She looks so little. So small. I can see the resemblance with Rose when she looks at me this way. She's still only twenty-three. Too young to have taken any of this up. Just like Maeva.

Her eyes implored him and he started to question his determination.

And then he remembered her code. His spine stiffened but she leaned forward, eyes wide, glazed. He thought she might even produce a tear.

She's doing it on purpose. This is how she manipulates the masses. There's nothing soft in her, I didn't put it there. That was intentional. This is all learned behavior.

Lucius felt the realization smack him straight between the eyes.

She's a sociopath. My designed daughter - the Queen of Lower Earth - is a textbook sociopath.

He spoke slow and deliberate, knowing he was inviting a battle. One that would be hard for either of them to win.

"I'm not coming."

Ariane didn't move. Not her eyes, not her lips, nothing in her face flinched for a moment. She sat back in the chair.

Time passed. Lucius didn't know how long, but long enough that he knew it was about to get much worse for him.

Ariane stood. She stepped to him slowly, her head cocked to the side. She leaned in and Lucius tried not to flinch at the sight of her face coming into his line of vision. Her breath was sweet, sickly sweet like rotting prunes.

She brushed her lips against his cheek, not in a kiss but something that resembled it. Lucius could tell she'd never done it before.

She stepped back, turned, and opened the door to the waiting guards.

"Arrest him."

39

———

Anna whisked into the pub and ran to Trudith, her lava rock bouncing against her chest. Trudith took one look at her and thought it was the moment she was going to give birth.

"Anna! Slow down, we have to follow Lucius' instructions now, remember?"

"No, no, no, no."

"What do you mean 'No, no, no'?"

"It's not that, it isn't. Trudith!"

"What!"

"They're rounding people up."

"Who?"

"The Guard."

"No, who are they rounding up?"

"I don't know. They have a list."

"A list of what?"

"I don't know!"

Trudith took it in for a moment. Changes had been underway in Cork Town ever since the announcement, quiet movements of people. Not like before, not the disappearance of people who she knew had been up to things they shouldn't have. This was different. It was the older ones who were being led away, not dragged. Two weeks it had been going now and it was impossible not to see the change. Cork Town was quieter, people weren't talking. An electric sensation had been running among them ever since the Tuesday Briefing and the announcement from the Queen.

Trudith grabbed her satchel. "Stay here. Don't move."

As Anna sat down, trying to catch her breath, Trudith tiptoed outside. She didn't mean to tiptoe, but she couldn't seem to make her feet walk normally. She heard her own breath louder than any other sound as she walked toward the market area. Before she turned the last corner, she could hear voices before she saw them. The voices were calm, low. No panic or hate. She turned to see on one side of the square a group of guards, and on another side of the square, a group of older women. Older, but not so old.

A large caravan being pulled by four horses pulled away as she arrived. Trudith could just catch a glimpse of the people inside.

There must be fifty of them in there.

A face at the back of the caravan looked at her. She didn't know the woman. An older woman, her back hunched, she lifted a hand as a greeting or goodbye. Trudith couldn't tell which. She lifted her hand back. The woman lowered her head as the caravan bumped away toward the main entry to Cork Town.

Trudith looked back to the square. People were milling around, but not in their usual way. They stayed along the edges of the square avoiding the group of women in the middle. About twenty of them huddled together, none of them speaking.

In the group, Trudith saw the scarred face of her favorite vendor from the market.

She'll tell me what's going on. She always loves to gossip. But this doesn't feel like gossip. Where are they going?

Trudith walked over to her. The woman's face lit up but then she waved her arms madly.

"Stay away, Trude." She hissed from fifteen feet away.

"Why, what's going on?"

The woman's face relaxed, the scars running from her hairline down her neck. She'd been that way as long as Trudith had known her. The woman's head cocked to the side, "We have the virus, Trude. We got it."

"What? How?"

"Seems it goes for young and old. The most vulnerable among us. Just like the Queen said."

Just like the Queen said.

"So what are they going to do with you?"

"We're going into quarantine, like the little ones."

"Are you going to the same place? Do you know where it is?"

"I don't know anything. I just know that I never thought I'd die from a virus. I saw lots of other possibilities, but not a virus." She scratched her arm. Her skin was raw and red, scars running up and down her arms like her face. She was sensitive to any kind of light. "You take care of yourself now, Trudith. You've always been a good one."

Trudith nodded her head and backed away, walking like in a trance back to the pub. A guard stepped in front of her.

"Name, please?"

Please? Did a guard just say 'please' to me?

"Trudith. I live on Fourteenth Road."

"Trudith of what line?"

"I don't know."

"You don't know?" the guard looked suspicious.

"I've never known." She lifted her long skirt to show her gnarled legs. They never gave her trouble anymore; she'd learned how to walk in spite of them. No one had expected she would. "Had these legs from birth, was brought here while I was still an infant."

"I see." The guard looked at her list and then flipped the pages back to front. "Carry on."

"I don't have the virus?"

"You're not on my list."

"How many are on your list?"

The guard looked down at the papers again.

"Many."

Trudith nodded and turned to continue back to the pub. It was as though she'd lost her peripheral vision. She could only see the very next step she was going to take. She had to get back to Anna, who hopefully was not putting herself into labor with the anxiety of it all.

And then it hit her.

She ran back to the guard. "Excuse me, I'm sorry, Excuse me - "

"Yes?"

So polite, I cannot get used to this.

"Do you have Anna on your list? Anna of the - um, I think she's fourth line. Maybe third actually." Her heart was beating like a gong.

Please let her not be on the list. Please, please.

The guard shuffled through the pages.

Please, she can't be there, not after everything we've risked. Not with her being so close. What would the virus do to the baby? Please tell me she's -

"No Anna on the list. Not of any line."

All the blood drained from Trudith's head and she thought she might faint from relief.

She smiled, trying to keep it small, trying not to draw attention. These kind, polite guards were putting it on. Best not to catch their attention. She'd seen them at their worst.

"Thank you, sorry to trouble you."

She turned, feeling the guard's eyes on her as she left.

Don't turn around, Trudith. Don't do it. Don't let her see you.

She pushed open the door to the pub and Anna rushed at her. "What is it? What's happening? Why are they so quiet? Why are the guards so quiet?"

Trudith explained as much as she could.

"Is it true?" Anna's face turned into doubt. "How could it be that there's so many more with the virus than they thought? We give our blood weekly. They could have caught it sooner."

"Maybe they didn't know what they were looking for. Maybe this is something completely new." Trudith didn't believe a word out of her own mouth, but she wasn't about to let Anna know that.

"What do we do, Trude?"

Trudith thought about it. She'd been thinking about it ever since the woman on the caravan gave her a wave that felt like a forever goodbye.

"We're going to have to leave, Anna."

"Leave? How can we leave? Leave. You say it like we just walk out the gate like it was any other day."

"We'll ask Lucius."

"Yes, we should ask Lucius."

They walked out of the pub without another word.

They avoided walking through the main square by taking side roads, but they could see into the activity from each street as they passed. A woman was climbing into the caravan.

They must have sent another. How many have gone already? It's all been done so quietly.

But a woman in the square was not so quiet. She was pulling on an older woman's arm as the older woman tried to climb into the caravan.

"Don't go! Don't get in there, Ba! It's a trick, it's all a trick!"

"Let go of me, dear. I have to go. It's to protect you and the others."

"No, I don't believe it! They said children only. Please!"

Three guards stood by, watching the scene with their arms clasped behind their back. They watched closely, attentively, but they didn't intervene. Still, Trudith could see that they would if they had to.

The caravan clicked into movement, the horses pulling ahead. The younger woman threw herself at the caravan. Letting herself drag behind it as the old woman halfheartedly swatted at her.

"Go, girl. You'll be fine. I'll get better. We all will. You let go now."

"I'm not letting go! I'm not letting go!" Her feet dragged in the dirt as the horse picked up their pace.

A guard was suddenly there, her large body leaning over like a crane, dislodging the woman from the caravan. The woman screamed and kicked, but the guard had a solid hold on her.

"Don't go! It's a trick! Ba! Wait!"

Trudith and Anna watched as the guard finally put the wailing woman down. Her legs crumpled underneath her as she sobbed in the middle of the square.

Several other older women were already being gathered on the other side, waiting for the next caravan.

"Come on," Trudith took Anna's arm and they moved faster in the direction of the Twenty-Ninth alleyway.

TRUDITH SAW THE APARTMENT JUST AHEAD OF THEM, THE strange studio that had been built into a wall. It looked more like a garbage enclosure than the place where someone lived.

Lucius will not be happy we're here. He'll have some harsh words for us. But things are changing. He must have seen it too. Or maybe he hasn't yet. I'll tell him. He'll know what to do.

Trudith felt a rock in her stomach as they approached the studio.

The door was open a crack.

Trudith pushed it open, revealing the studio apartment in complete shambles. The bed overturned, every drawer and cupboard open. The place wasn't big, but it had been turned inside out.

And Lucius was nowhere to be seen.

40

R oman opened his eyes, the sense of dread heavier than the wool blanket under which he now slept. He got shivers in the night, his whole body trembling, shocking him out of deep sleep. Then it was sweats. Then he was somewhere between the two, alternating between a sense of frozen hell and blazing like he was too close to the sun.

He inhaled the sight of the rising morning, his chest pushing against the blanket, though it felt like there was an anvil in the middle of his gut.

But he had to get up.

At least of that much he was sure. He had to get up. Get dressed. Make himself presentable. That's what a Great Geneticist does. And he was the Great Geneticist.

If only being clean-shaven and persistent were enough to succeed.

He'd felt the limits of his intellect. It was a dark place. He arrived there and knew it had to go further, but all color and substance turned to black. He needed insight, he needed to see consequences, he needed to apply previous sequences to over-write the failing ones. And he couldn't do it. He knew the answers were there, sometimes he caught a glimpse of an idea, but it never came fully into view.

And they were all suffering because of it.

If only we'd focused our attention on solving all the crop killers. Or even on combatting the Elgin bacteria. If we had sorted out the water shortages, then we wouldn't be in this position, desperate to design a population that can withstand a world we allowed to become uninhabitable.

He ate his breakfast because he had to. His body needed the nutrition. Already he was starting to see the signs of degradation. He'd been lucky so far. Born in a generation where they still had something like a fifty-fifty chance of survival to age fifty.

The symmetry wasn't lost on him. And he was fast approaching his expiry date. He turned the lava rock around his fingertips.

Why don't I just let it all fall apart? Why don't I just let go and watch them figure it out for themselves? Maybe they don't need me at all. I could live out my last years in the Dark Counties, watching the ocean crash against cliffs in peaceful solitude.

As if she would let me. Maeva never would have allowed it, and Ariane won't either. They are indeed too much the same, even if Ariane is the more pragmatic one. At least with Maeva, I never questioned her motives.

The flute played on as Roman slipped his feet into his shoes. They were too tight. He took his foot out and looked at it, compared it with the other.

Swollen. Maybe it's the sweats?

Or maybe it's degradation coming for me at last.

He shoved his feet into his shoes and pushed the thought out of his mind. Mary would shortly be announcing everyone into positions. He headed to the Tower.

Uma met him in the lobby as he walked through the swinging glass door.

"Finally. Had a leisurely morning? I've been waiting for you for an hour."

Roman rubbed his forehead. He needed to get to his office and review the files. He'd decided on his way to focus on the Elgin bacteria. If they could counter that, then some of the other after-effects could be mitigated. Until the Queen called him in, hopefully because Lucius had returned, he would stay focused on the things he always should have prioritized.

"I'll call for you later, Uma. I have other things on my mind right now."

"You have to come with me."

"Not now."

Uma's voice changed. It lost the edge. "No, you're not understanding me, Roman. We have to go. The Queen has called for us."

Roman felt a jolt through his body. "Called? For us?"

"We have to go."

"Yes, yes, of course."

Uma led him back out the door he'd just walked through and into the main city square. People were buzzing in every direction.

Mary's face dominated every street corner, her voice filling the air. "Clear skies and sun in Geb today, temperatures warmer than usual but with a fresh northerly breeze," Roman tried to block it out. "Settler's Day next week should be a glorious one! Hold your lava rock close, we will remember with solemnity and celebration our first peoples who arrived and the gift of life they bestowed on us. Their sacrifice gave us what we needed most then, and resulted in our savior today - the Queen! We will give thanks!"

They were waved in through the front gate of the fortress and arrived in the main hall, where Irene was waiting for them.

"I was waiting for him," Uma said lowly. "He didn't know about the summons."

Irene looked down on Uma, her body seeming to stretch even taller. Roman tilted his head up to see her, arms crossed, brow furrowed.

She turned and walked away, "Come with me."

Irene led them down a series of corridors, deep into the fortress.

We must be within the cliff now, there are no windows.

Moisture beaded on the stone. Irene opened a door to a stairwell heading down. She had to duck to avoid hitting the entryway, though Uma and Roman passed without difficulty.

Two or three stories down, Roman couldn't tell how far they'd gone as there was no light to guide them, Irene turned onto a landing. She opened another door which led to yet another corridor. Roman took a deep breath and tried to calm his growing sense of dread.

Another door opened and light burst out from inside, Roman blinked in temporary blindness. He could make out a figure at the other end of the large room, but he couldn't tell if it was human or animal.

And then his eyes adjusted.

He spoke but only air came out, "Lucius?"

"He has three days," Irene turned back to Roman and Uma.

"Three days before what?" Uma asked.

"Three days to solve the incubate - problem."

"What happens after three days?" It sounded like Uma didn't want to ask it, but did anyway.

Irene didn't answer. She turned to Lucius. "Would you sit up?"

It was a command, not a question.

Lucius was sat on a chair but hunched far forward, his head resting on the mass of his gut. His shoulders looked so small by comparison. Roman remembered when Lucius used to stand tall, his shoulders strong, athletic. Now they were scrawny, stunted against the rest of his body that had expanded wider than his shoulders had ever been. Despite his size, he looked frail. Breakable.

Lucius lifted his head.

"Roman. Well, isn't this a delightful reunion of Lower Earth's greatest minds."

THREE DAYS. WE'VE GOT THREE DAYS. IMPOSSIBLE.

Roman watched Lucius working.

They'd been given a different room in the fortress. Roman hadn't had to insist much with Irene. A dungeon hardly seemed the right place for a scientific breakthrough. Instead, they were in a kind of turret room having climbed no less than five stories of stairs. Roman had worried Lucius might have a heart attack right there and fall backward like a boulder onto all of them who followed.

But he didn't.

Their room was small. A table, two chairs. Two windows. And a chamber pot. One story below was an even smaller room with a single mattress on the floor. Lucius' quarters. A far cry from his previous quarters in the fortress when he'd been the Great Geneticist.

When Roman had taken over the title, he hadn't been invited to move into Lucius' old chambers. And he was just as glad for it. He wouldn't have been able to refuse, but he had no desire to be any closer to the Queen than he had to be.

Uma arrived from Central Tower, her third trip of the morning, her arms again full of reports. She dropped them on the floor in the corner, which was still within arm's reach for Roman from his seat at the table.

"I think that's it. Everything that's relevant anyway."

Roman nodded, but she didn't leave. "You're not going to stand there for three days, are you?"

"Orders are to remain at hand. In case you need anything."

"Can't they send a messenger?"

Uma pursed her lips and tilted her head.

"Right, we shouldn't involve anyone else."

"What am I going to do anyway?" Uma whispered, "It's not like I can get anything done while the two of you are up here."

"Would you *shut up*?" Lucius lifted his head from the page of code, magnifying glass in hand. "I'm trying to concentrate on something rather important here."

"You should go out, Uma. Just go down a floor or two maybe."

"Here," Lucius passed him a page of code, "Find the gene anomaly responsible for the lymph system decompression. If you're smart, you'll see what's missing. I can't believe you didn't catch it before. And you, *shoo*." Lucius waved Uma away, and she went.

"She's on our side," Roman closed the door.

"I don't have a side."

Roman did the initial scan of each page before passing it to Lucius. Hopeful he might catch something they didn't see before. Inevitably, Lucius was waiting for him on each pass.

"What about that girl?" Lucius asked as Roman reviewed the code's arterial resistance.

"What girl?"

"The one you sent to me."

"Sara?"

"That's the one."

"What about her?"

"Where is she?"

Roman looked up. "Gone."

"Gone?"

"Leaked secrets."

"You believe that?"

"She could have. She had secrets to tell." Roman had his

suspicions. Why would Sara go to Cork Town with forged papers? Was it really to participate in meetings of backroom women? Could she have started a riot, and would she have? It wasn't her way.

But Lucius - she could have gone to see Lucius again. Roman didn't know why, but Lucius could have convinced her to do something for him. Lucius always had a way of getting what he wanted.

"I suppose we all have secrets," was all Lucius said before turning back to the code. "Move faster, I'm ready for the next one. Three days won't be enough if you keep slowing me down."

IT WAS WELL PAST MIDNIGHT WHEN LUCIUS ROSE WITHOUT A word, his half-eaten dinner mixed with the sequences for eyesight and amylase enzyme production. Roman heard him struggle down the stairs.

"Go home," he heard Lucius say to Uma before closing the door to the little bedroom.

Roman descended. He and Uma left the fortress together without saying a word.

ROMAN ARRIVED BACK AT THE FORTRESS BEFORE SUNRISE. Lucius was already up in the room. Pages were everywhere. He found sequences for hair color mixed with structures of metabolizing factors. It was a complete mess, except that he knew Lucius knew what he was doing. If he discarded something, then there was nothing in it.

"Good morning," Roman said quietly.

"Is it? Get to it already. Seems your work ethic has slipped since becoming the Great Geneticist. When you were under my watch, you always showed up before me."

"Not always." Roman heard the sound of his voice like some kind of rebellious adolescent. Lucius looked up from the magnifying glass. Clearly, he'd heard it too.

Roman took his seat.

Lucius tossed a page his way. "Review the correlation between the fourteenth gene and the equivalent gene on chromosome four."

"This page only has the gene sequence."

Lucius didn't respond.

"Where's the exon-entron structure?"

"Over there." Lucius waved his hand toward the wall. Under the window was a stack of papers. Roman let out a sigh before seeing that it was right on top.

At first glance, there was no evidence of any relationship to the overlapping genes from the incubates. It appeared unrelated. "These two? But I can't - "

"You can. Just look closer. Or maybe farther. Now shush, I'm working."

"Morning," Uma whispered through the door.

"I said I'm working! Can't I get a damn minute of silence in here?" He beat his fist on the table. "Maybe you don't realize that I have a lot riding on the next thirty-six or so hours." He lowered his voice, "So please, *please*, let me concentrate."

Roman set into the gene sequence and representative views of the three-dimensional protein structure.

What did he see, and why don't I see it? How is it that Lucius can seek it out like a hound while I don't even know what I'm hunting?

The self-doubt felt metallic in his mouth.

And then he saw it.

The correlation was weak on first look, but the more Roman looked at it, the more the evident it became. The opening window of the sequence seemed to have the same attributes as the ending phase. Overlapping, but only in those two phases. It didn't seem likely that this finding was related to their current problem, but it was nonetheless valuable. If the incubates were to go through adolescence with this correlation in their genes, there could have been other consequences they hadn't yet adapted for, since it would be exacerbated during puberty. Likely an immune response that would attack the body.

Without Lucius, the sequence they'd created could have left them with further genetic illness among the incubates in ten years. Now they could treat it.

"Unbelievable that we missed this." Roman looked up from the page. "Unbelievable that you found it. How did you..."

"Don't ask. This is my first gift to your incubate debauchery."

Roman had Uma bring over other sequences of the Willing Woman program to compare and by early afternoon he'd identified at least four other designs with the anomaly.

Including the Gillard line.

The Queen will be very pleased about this. We should have done something sooner with the Gillards, assessed why some lines had normal levels of longevity while others prematurely degraded. But it was never a priority. If we had known the link across other designs -

How much have we missed?

Roman's mind raced. If the Willing Woman program, with all its controls in place, could still have what could only be attributed to 'human error' in the sequence processing, then it was no wonder they were downright failing with the crop killers.

Food was delivered to their turret hideaway; Roman didn't notice it come and didn't notice it being cleared. Lucius continued to thrust pages his way, but none had anything in them like the immune response.

Mary's voice called out through the streets, but the sound was just a muffled hum in the room. It became dark; Roman only noticed because the sequence before him was impossible to read. He hadn't seen the sun setting.

The light flicked on as Uma reached in a hand, and then her head, and looked around the little room.

"Well?" She whispered to Roman

"Don't you think you would know if we'd found anything?" Uma ducked back out and closed the door.

Lucius sighed. "It's not here, not yet."

"What isn't? What is *it* exactly, Lucius?"

"I don't know." He looked up at Roman, "I'll know it when I see it."

Roman's eyes took in Lucius' face under the single light bulb. His cheeks drooped, as though there wasn't enough muscle even to hold his face in place. His brow fell deep over his eyes. His neck disappeared as his chin rested on the thick of his chest. Roman saw age in Lucius in a way that he never had before. Not in his face or his body, though the degradation continued its slow advancement toward death.

But it was in Lucius' eyes.

Eyes that had sparkled were dull.

"What?' Lucius caught Roman staring.

Roman shook his head. He was surprised to find that he felt pity towards his former mentor. He looked back down the pages, but his brain couldn't take it in. If he put his head down, he'd be out for the night.

"I'm heading home."

"Mmmm."

Roman left, waking up Uma who'd drifted off while sitting in the stairwell.

ROMAN WOKE, HIS CHEST AGAIN HEAVY HAVING PASSED THE night in trembles and sweats. He didn't notice that he'd dressed himself and eaten before leaving the flat. Everything was blurred into a single movement, no definition from one act to the next. He walked through the city to the square to the fortress to the room on the upper floor. Surely he'd seen people, even at this early hour, but their faces blended into the scenery behind them.

When he opened the door Lucius was standing at the window, a page in each hand, the circles under his eyes even darker than the day before. His lips were parted and one was bleeding from a crack. It struck Roman that Lucius might be dehydrated. He'd have Uma bring up water when she arrived. Lucius's eyes looked like they might walk right out from his head. Roman blinked and set down his satchel.

His voice was scratchy but clear. It rolled through space to Roman's ears.

"I've got it."

Roman froze.

He was sure he'd stopped breathing.

"You hear me, Roman? I've got it. It tried to hide between multiple levels, and I couldn't make sense of it, took me most of the night just to locate the polysialilated neural cell adhesion molecule, it had been useless out of context, and it wasn't as though the message was clear, you see? But it was mixed in between the lines, the neuroplasticity of the brain," he tapped his head hard with his finger, "Like the words spoken while a door creaks so you miss them entirely."

Roman's head was pounding. "I can't keep up, Lucius. Go back."

"Go back! I'm never going back!" He waddled towards Roman, "I only go forward from here, Roman, you see? Everything has its reason, and you'll get there, compare across them. Your overlapping gene, its opening window, the doublecortin alongside the common code. It's in the common code itself, Roman! Ha! Hidden in plain sight!"

Roman couldn't justifiably take it on Lucius' word, they

would have to verify it. The Queen wouldn't have it any other way. But at first glance, even to his eyes which were wrought and tired, he could see a hint of what Lucius was saying.

"Right there, Roman! Look!" Lucius slammed his finger onto the page in Roman's hands, tearing the corner.

"Relax, Lucius. I see it."

"*Relax*? You're a piece of work, Roman."

I think he's right. Good heavens, I think he's right. They line up, even though they shouldn't. They should be discreet sequences, and yet, the pattern is unmistakable. I'll have to double-check, but it looks good.

Roman looked up to Lucius whose face had already changed so much from the night before. Defeat transformed into relief. Shame into pride. His eyes had the old gleam.

But they were only at the first step.

"So, you've found the weakness. But we need a way to treat it, or at least a way to inoculate against it, or we're no closer to a solution. Just finding it doesn't resolve it."

"Of course it doesn't." Lucius shook his head. "But I'm going to need a big roasted duck with potatoes before I produce the next stage of the game."

"It's six in the morning."

"Get me a damn duck, Roman."

41

———

I rene watched as the caravan pulled away, extra bars across the back to keep the girls in.

They look like sheep packed in there. Lambs to the slaughter.

"That's the last one, Commandante."

Irene nodded. The heads of battalion waited for her next commands. She inhaled and assumed her position, standing with legs wide, hands clasped behind her back.

She didn't want the guards to see she was shaking.

"You've done well. Tell your guards that I am pleased."

The battalion leads nodded to her.

"You will all travel up next. You are my most trusted across the Guard. Preparations have already been put in place. The Ganese have mounted all the lodgings, rough though they are. You will not be comfortable, nor will you stay very long." Irene inhaled deeply.

This was the part they had to believe. She lowered her voice.

"The stealth team will come in the night. They'll start with the girls since they are more resource-intensive to maintain. The older women will be later. They'll move out fifty to a hundred of them each night. Some will die naturally in the conditions. That will speed the egress, but your guards should never, never interfere. Is that clear?" Heads nodded. "I need to hear from you that it is clear."

"Clear, Commandante," they spoke in unison.

She nodded and then continued. "If a child, or woman for that matter, decides to - " she hesitated, " - *remove* herself before we have a chance to move them on, they should be allowed to do so. Depending on the circumstances, we can attribute it to the virus. Understood?"

The heads nodded.

"You will not see the stealth team. This is intentional. Only the old women assigned as carers should be allowed to sleep in the quarters with the girls. We will provide them with treatment to "fight the virus", which will help them sleep deeply. You and your guards must remain innocent to the acts. We cannot have this coming back to the Guard. Am I clear?"

Heads nodded.

"Confirm: No member of the Guard will be involved in any acts of death against anyone in quarantine."

"Confirmed, Commandante."

"Fine. You will each rotate through in two-week shifts. This will also protect you from slander. You should each lead according to your own style, variation is fine. It serves the purpose. No one should be able to see the correlation between your presence and the dwindling numbers. The fortress will take care of the messaging. If anyone directs their questions to you, you pass them to me. Clear?

"Clear, Commandante." Every pair of eyes was glued on her. Irene ignored the sweat on her palms.

"I'll provide you with the shift allocations before the day's out. Dismissed."

Irene watched as the heads of battalion relaxed and started moving away, looking from one to the other, but not speaking.

They will not tell a soul. They know it could only ever come back on them.

Relief washed over her. That was the final step she had to take.

The rest was on Leadon now.

There's nothing more for me in this. It's all up to you, Leadon. May you have the courage and wisdom to pull it off.

Irene looked up to the high room of the fortress. She could just about make out Lucius' form in the window from where she stood in the square. This was the day he had to deliver. Turn the incubation program around. Find out what was causing the social disease and wipe it out.

Or else.

Irene's responsibilities were far from finished for the day. She marched her way to the high room, taking the stairs two at a time, eager and anxious to know their progress on the code.

And Ariane was likely already there.

42

"Here," Lucius pushed himself to stand, the pages of handwritten code with scrawled instructions in the margins crumpled in his hand.

Roman found the scene somewhere between ceremonial and farcical as Lucius did a bow while handing the revised incubation code to Ariane. They were seven people - Roman, Lucius who was the size of three people, Uma, Ariane, Irene, and two members of the Queen's Guard - stuffed into the tiny room around the table, with papers covering every inch of the floor. There was no room for the guards to enter; they stood on the stairs.

Ariane snatched the pages from his hand and leafed through them, though Roman knew well she wouldn't be able to interpret their contents.

"Have you confirmed this, Roman?"

"Me? No."

"Why not?" Ariane glared at him.

"He only just finished writing it. It'll take us time to review it and put it into testing." Roman backtracked, "From what I can tell, this sequence will prevent any physiological need to attach to a mother figure during the pre-birth phase, but I need time to verify it."

"Time. Fine. Everything around here takes time." Ariane let out a sigh and brought her hand to her forehead. "You had years Roman. *Years*. Now you very likely have the key to undoing the disaster you created, and you want more time?"

His heart beat in his throat.

Ariane looked to Irene, "Is this what the world was like when men ruled it?" The Commandante gave no reaction. "Everything needing more time. Can't possibly do it as demanded. Moving at a pace that suited them. Irene, how long did it take you to resolve the issues of relocating into quarantine nearly fifteen thousand incubates under the age of five and an additional four thousand over the age of sixty from Cork Town?"

"One week."

"One week. Well. And Roman, how long have you been working on the incubation code, implementing it with fatal defaults and unacceptable results?"

"Five years."

"Five years. Well." The Queen looked at Uma, "How long have you been working in the Tower, Uma?"

"Twenty-four years, Queen."

"What line are you, Uma?"

"Uma of the nineteenth line."

"A well-refined line. And early on, from the sounds of it. I'm glad to know there's a woman in natural succession for the Great Geneticist." Ariane looked at Roman and he felt his neck go hot. "I believe you have some reviewing to do, Roman. And if I were you, I would try to take less than five years to produce it. Even five days will be too long. Don't keep me waiting."

"And me?" Lucius spoke up. "I'm really missing my firm foam mattress in a back corner of Cork Town, despite all the hospitality."

"You stay." Ariane turned to Irene, "He doesn't go anywhere until we've confirmed that the code is good." She closed her eyes slowly and reopened them. "Now, if you'll all get out of my way in this horrid cramped stairwell, I have the rest of the country to attend to."

"Over to you, Roman." Lucius dropped into a chair that bent under his weight. "I'm going to finish up my roasted duck from breakfast and have a little nap, I think. Fine having you all around but I do like my privacy."

Despite the Queen's reprimand, Roman only felt relief as he walked back to the Tower with Uma close behind. The code on the pages in his hand felt heavy. He squeezed them extra tight to be sure they wouldn't float away. He didn't have proper control over his senses now. He imagined the code flying off in the wind as he chased behind it. He squeezed tighter.

Once inside, he spread the pages out on the table in his office.

Uma looked over his shoulder. "I'll get the sample structures for the proteins he references."

She'd already left the office by the time Roman said, "Fine."

The revised code Lucius had drawn up was a thing of beauty. Roman held it up to the light. In it was a complete slowdown of the problematic process of integration, the origin of the social issues among the incubates. In the new sequence, bonding with their carer would occur *after* the gestational period. The fetus would be dependent on the feeding tubes without any emotional development. That part of the brain would be stalled until the appropriate time, when they were placed with a carer, and then it would develop at an exponential pace to catch up. Without foreseeable consequences, thanks to the brain's plasticity.

It could work.

Uma sat down and ran through restriction enzyme sequences, only making the occasional grunt of surprise.

"Brilliant," she turned the page and pointed, "We can use that same period for heightened muscle development. We can apply it to the Willing Woman program. Those subjects can be mobile even sooner than the current design."

They continued running the sequence through the simulation.

She pointed to another section. "We can add a piece from the Gillard line here for resistance to salmonella. That worked well in their line, Gillards do much better when up against Elgin virus."

Night fell, and Roman sensed the need to sleep washing over him. It was all moving well ahead, and these last weeks were catching up with him. He looked forward to rest that wasn't troubled by nightmares, trembling, and sweats.

"Let's leave it here for the night, Uma."

"What? We can't stop now."

"You've slept over these past three days. I have not."

"We're close. I think we can be through it all within five, maybe six hours."

"It's past midnight. I don't have five minutes left in me."

Uma sighed. "I'll carry on."

"I'll be back first thing," he said, but Uma was focused in on the code.

He didn't notice the pavement pass under his feet. He climbed the stairs to his apartment and was asleep as his head touched the pillow.

BANGING ON THE DOOR WOKE HIM UP IN A SHOCK.

"What? Who is it?"

"Roman, come, come now."

"Uma?"

"You have to come. This can't wait."

He stood, still fully dressed. He opened the door; she began talking before he could see her.

"There's a problem."

"With the code?"

"It's in the common code of women."

"Why are you looking at the common code? You're working on the incubates."

"You have to come. I have to show you."

She didn't speak as they practically ran back to the Tower. He didn't know what time it was.

As they entered the Tower he caught sight of a clock. Four in the morning. He rubbed his eyes.

"Uma, can you please explain - "

"You have to see it. I'm not quite sure, but I'm close. You'll be able to tell, even if you were useless last night." She cast him a sharp look.

Uma never used a tone like that with him. Not since he had caught her in the alleyway of Cork Town. The Queen had propped her confidence.

They arrived on the nineteenth floor and Uma unlocked the door. It stuck. She thrust herself into it with her shoulder and marched straight for the table.

"The effect of the recombinant DNA. It appears to have a slowing effect before the acceleration in the post-gestational period in the incubator."

"Yes, that's what we saw yesterday." He controlled his temper. His patience was waning and he feared he might yell at her. He didn't need the Queen hearing that, not now. She always appeared when he least wanted to see her. Just like Maeva.

"Focus! Look at the page, Roman. This sequence, from the common code." She brought over another page from a printed file. It wasn't from the code Lucius had prepared; it was something else entirely. "Compare."

"Which version of common code is this?"

"Mine."

Roman looked at her.

"I have accelerated processing. I studied it in my fourth levels." She brought the two pages side by side. "Look at this piece of my code, and now look at it in what Lucius has drawn up."

"That's only in the base pairing."

"Which makes it appear innocuous. Insufficient for anything more than normal development, right?"

He sensed the trick. "But?"

"But that would be wrong. Look at the enzyme for the post-fetal stage."

Roman looked.

Damn it. She's right.

He looked up at her, his heart racing. "It'll accelerate."

"Rather than slow down."

Roman saw it now, plain as day. Lucius had built a switch into the sequence. "It's not viable. It's a contradiction."

"With a contradiction like *that*, we're not talking minor complications."

"The fetus will die before it reaches full growth." Roman closed his eyes.

"He did it on purpose, Roman," Uma hissed. "He set us up. He thought we wouldn't find it."

Roman wasn't ready to believe that. "Uma, you didn't see him the way I did. This isn't intentional. It's hardly even visible."

"You think Lucius didn't know exactly what he was doing?

He never wanted to save the incubate program. The Queen had to arrest him!"

"It's still possible that there's another control written in that offsets the contradiction. We haven't done a full analysis."

"Why are you defending him?"

"I'm not defending him. I'm defending the code."

"Why?"

"Because it stands a chance compared to what we have now!" His head throbbed.

"It doesn't, Roman. Look at it."

Roman tried to keep his eyes focused. A sense of resignation was washing over him.

Uma sighed. "If it hadn't been for the variation in my own sequence… if I hadn't known exactly what I was looking at…"

Uma looked up at him, but Roman still couldn't find the right thing to say.

Her tone of voice softened. "The longer I look, the more obvious it is. I spent two hours looking for another offsetting feature, and there's *none*. You and I might miss a contradiction. But Lucius?"

Roman knew she was right. "Lucius wouldn't miss it."

"I'm not happy about finding this, Roman." She leaned toward him, her voice barely above a whisper. "I don't want it to be true, and I don't want to know what Ariane is going to do to him when she finds out. But Roman…"

Dread filled his stomach, but he nodded. "We have to tell the Queen."

He closed his eyes.

She's going to kill him. She'll string him up in front of everyone. The Queen is going to have Lucius' head.

.   .   .

THE MIDDAY SUN BEAT DOWN ON THEM. ROMAN'S EYES couldn't adjust to it. He was in a constant state of blindness. He forced them to remain fixed.

Lucius, stripped naked, was kneeling in the center of the square.

The flesh fell over the sides of his legs, his form hardly recognizable as a man even from Roman's vantage point. The image on the screens was no better. The screens played out everything from Lucius' heavy breath to sweating back. His black hair fell over his face, but there was no dignity in it.

A guard stood behind him, whip in hand. The Commandante a few paces away. The Queen seated on the balcony above.

Crowds of people filled the up square, but they left a twenty-foot radius around Lucius. Even more were watching it broadcast across the screens. Perhaps all of Geb.

Lucius' back was already red in the sun. The white of the sides of his gut glowed in juxtaposition. His head remained lowered.

It seemed an eternity had passed since they'd reported their findings to the Queen and she'd called in Irene.

Then the screens called people to the square.

And the people came. By the thousands.

There they were now, a lifetime having been lived since the elation he'd felt the night before.

The crowd came to complete stillness. In all Roman's years, he'd never heard them so quiet. Even at the massive Tuesday Briefing feet had shuffled and breathing had been steady.

Now everything was stopped.

Time had stopped.

There had never been a public flogging in their lifetime. Irene's head turned up to the Queen, seven stories above in the balcony out from her chambers. Roman tried to look at her but the sun backlit her silhouette. She was a black figure against a blinding sky.

But Roman saw her head nod.

And he heard the crack of the whip.

Lucius' head rose for a moment but he didn't cry out.

It cracked over his back again. And again. And again.

Roman lost count.

Twenty? Thirty?

Lucius collapsed onto his hands, breath fast and shallow. The guard looked up to the balcony for instruction.

"Carry on."

They all heard it.

The whip came down, and Lucius's body bounced in reaction, like oil on a hot pan.

The guard started to look distressed, her chest heaving as the red skin broke open across the sides of his ribs, his back, his buttocks.

Irene stepped forward and took the whip from the guard's hands. She looked up to the Queen and then bowed low to her before turning back to Lucius.

Irene cried out, low and long, sounds from another world, a different voice from somewhere far beyond as she brought the whip down harder and faster than Lucius had so far received. Again and again and again.

A whimper came from the broken man's body and Irene stopped, arm in midair.

Lucius fell from his knees to his side, head smacking into asphalt square. Bloody, naked, sweating.

His eyes looked into the sky with the glaze of death across them.

43

L eadon and Daphna stayed at a safe distance from the quarantine camp, watching the final preparations before the first caravan would arrive. The location was ideal.

Ideal for the Queen, as it was far from any other town or road where unwanted eyes might happen upon it.

Ideal for the Ganese and the Sisters who were together about to destroy the Queen's plans.

Leadon had known the Ganese couldn't conduct the operation alone. She'd known it from the moment Irene had explained the horrifying plans the Queen had to assassinate the children. While Ganese priestesses could accompany the young to the island and be their caregivers, there was no way a Ganese could steal into the camp and act as Queen's-Guard-turned-assassins the way Irene had arranged. They'd be spotted and apprehended before they'd even reached the gate.

The Queen's Guard overseeing the camp expected to see guard-assassins enter in the dead of night to remove children, swiftly and effectively. Each assassin was to be one of their own.

No six-foot ethnic Ganese could shape-shift her body to play the role.

But the Sisters could.

The Sisters had a number of former Guard among them. They had those who despised Geb, who detested what the Queen stood for, who would do anything prevent something so wrong from happening in their land.

So Leadon went to the Sisters.

Daphna didn't have to be asked twice, and the Sisters themselves - a group of them who would play the role of Queen's assassins - were convinced beyond a doubt.

The relationship between the Ganese and the Sisters was at a crossroads. Leadon felt it and she'd seen it in Daphna's eyes.

But now the night when it was all to begin was upon them.

Leadon and Daphna had a perfect place to observe the operation, a brush forest up a hill, a quarter of a mile away. The camp below had been erected hastily. Tents were haphazard and Leadon doubted they'd last if there was a massive storm, which they were bound to get at least once before the end of their mission. Supplies were being brought in - cans of food, some fresh - and a silo was erected. Still, it obvious that the Queen didn't intend for it to be a permanent structure, not in the way that she'd told the whole of Lower Earth.

"How are they going to sleep all of them? Fifteen thousand children?" Daphna shook her head.

"Not quite fifteen thousand. And they are counting on several of them dying on the way."

"They really die… spontaneously?"

"These are children who were doomed before they were born."

"It will take incredible effort to undo that."

"The Ganese have raised children through all periods of history, including the worst of it. We have that knowledge in our bones and in our stories. We cannot do miracles, but we are ready to do everything possible."

"Look," Daphna lowered her voice, "The first caravan."

Six horses pulling the caravan crested a hill, no evidence of the cargo it carried. Of course the Queen wouldn't use precious fuel to transport the children to their death. Even they didn't stop on the way, if they rotated drivers and deprived children of any opportunity to relieve their most basic needs, the trip would still take days.

Leadon watched as it advanced and then a movement behind it caught her eye. "There's a second one." Depending on how tightly packed the children were, each caravan could easily take a hundred children. Perhaps more if they treated them like cattle.

They watched as it approached the camp and a group of guards stood from the enclosure's entry to receive it. They walked around both vehicles with clipboards before allowing them to enter the main gate of the quarantine camp.

The first vehicle entered, and Leadon caught her breath. Those who emerged were not small children at all, but women. "Who are *they*? Staff?"

Daphna slid forward a little more on her stomach, squinting into the distance. "Several of them are limping, I can't make out the detail, but those are not young women."

"It's supposed to be children, not women."

They continued watching as the Guard addressed the women, some of whom had paired up to support each other. A guard gestured towards the gate, and the first caravan exited. The second entered. The old women lined up behind the caravan as a guard climbed into it.

One at a time, two children were passed to each woman's arms. Some of the children could walk, others had to be held. The procession continued until all the children were off the second caravan. By the end, the guards were giving three to each woman.

"This is madness," Daphna whispered. "Look at how the women are dressed, how they stand. Some of them are even deformed. They're Cork Town deviants."

Leadon was at a loss; this was outside the scope of everything they'd arranged. "Does this change our plan?"

Daphna let out a large sigh. "We may have to adapt."

"Things must have changed since Irene came. Otherwise would have told us this was happening."

Daphna narrowed her eyes at Leadon. "You share her blood."

Leadon's heart beat harder. Was Daphna doubting her now? "We share DNA. Nothing more."

"Still. I know from my days at the Tower that there are some things within that which don't change from person to person. And all the more as you both grew in Gana."

"I'm not following your logic." Leadon wasn't sure what Daphna's tone meant, was she accusing Leadon? Was the trust between them that delicate?

Daphna leaned closer in toward her. "If you were Irene, and you learned there were to be women joining as well as children, what would be your plan? How would you communicate the assassinations to the Guard? What would be your instructions to them?" Daphna gestured to the Guard below.

Leadon sat back. She tried to clear her mind of the logistics they'd spoken through seemingly hundreds of times now. She tried to go back to the root of it.

What would I do if I were Irene?

Leadon knew.

"I'd tell them to kill the children first. They are higher maintenance and there are far more of them. The older women serve a purpose in caring for them. Kill the children first."

Daphna nodded. "That decides our plan."

"We start with the children."

They looked out together one more time as the women split into different tents with the children. They moved as ants in formation. No woman dared to do anything other than what was told. A child broke away from one woman, a child perhaps four years old, and she ran. A guard grabbed the child by the neck, carried her back to the old woman, and threw her down on the ground at the woman's feet. The child didn't move for what seemed like a long time.

Daphna looked at Leadon. "We start tonight."

Leadon nodded. "There's no time to waste. By the time news reaches her that the children have been taken from the camp, the Queen will be pleased to hear that her plan is already in motion. She'll be no wiser to their true condition." She spat on the ground in front of her, the taste of hate stuck in her mouth.

They walked in a crouch, out through the brush. They made their way to the hidden enclave where their horses were tied and they galloped back to their own camp. It was set inside a bamboo forest where no one would happen upon them by accident. The first shift of twenty Sisters was already there, having set up the camp over the past couple of days.

Rose and a Sister stepped forward to meet them.

"How does it look out there?" the Sister asked.

"Bad," Daphna said. "We have to move fast."

"We're ready," Rose replied, "We've gone over the possible scenarios together."

"Tonight will be the most difficult," Leadon said, "The Guard won't know what to expect and therefore might react in unexpected ways. If you come across any of them, you'll have to play your role well, while not revealing too much, lest you raise suspicions."

"We can do it," the Sister replied. "Many of us know the

Guard from days we spent in Geb. We know how they operate. We can do it."

Leadon nodded. "Without you, none of this could happen. I thank you, truly, on behalf of all the Ganese."

"Our greatest thanks will be knowing that the Ganese will meet us on the coast when we arrive with the children."

"We will be there," Leadon assured. "Several have already sailed and await you even now. My former quorum mate is preparing all the boats."

"I will accompany the Sisters tonight to the camp," Rose said. "My skills may be of service as we make the first journey. Then I will sail with the first boat."

Daphna put one hand on Leadon's shoulder and the other on Rose. "I don't have words that are adequate for this moment."

Leadon nodded. "I do. It's an old Ganese pact. Translated, it's '*Where you go, we will meet you there*'. And we will. On the coast of Rainfields as you deliver the children from the death that had been promised to them."

Daphna nodded and turned her head to the twenty Sisters. Rose and Leadon did the same. No more words were needed between them. Their mission was clear and agreed: Lower Earth needed saving from itself.

44

R ose waited. The nighttime was black. They hadn't been lucky with the clouds. Thick white cloud cover had rolled in before the sun had set, blocking any light the moon would have offered.

Perhaps this will be to their advantage. Perhaps they can enter more easily without undue questions.

Or perhaps this complicates their task.

Rose was two miles out from the camp, far enough that no Guard would catch sight of her and close enough that the Sisters could reach her without getting lost, even without the moon's light.

She tried to clear her mind. She tried. And failed.

So long she had put her blood's calling aside. From the moment she'd seen Ariane take the throne, when Ariane had stood on that balcony as though the world *ought* to bow to her... since then Rose knew Ariane would be the Queen to defile what Lower Earth's royalty had stood for.

But how she, Rose, could do anything about it wasn't clear until now.

She knew there was a new world called to her, calling to

Zev. Horizons unknown and future apart from Lower Earth. She'd seen enough of their land now to know that the depravity, the destruction, and the corruption would continue for as long as Ariane wore those velvet gowns. Rose heard it in her blood. The echoes of the old Queens had long known there would be dark periods in their future.

But the future was now.

And in the now, Rose had to accompany fifteen thousand or more to a new world, far off and more forgotten than the Forgotten Islands. Upper Earth was in that direction, but they would steer away from them. The place they were going to, whatever it would be, it would be uninhabited. They would have to do it all from the start.

Give birth to a new world in exile of the old.

But first, the children had to come. The Sisters had to fulfill their role.

And the dark of night was passing.

They are taking longer than we planned.

Rose's heartbeat accelerated and she wondered for a moment if she should run for the camp, to check in, but she quickly dismissed it. That would only expose the Sisters to greater risk than they already had.

And if someone saw her… their plans could be ruined before they'd even really begun. Rose steeled her nerves.

And waited.

She closed her eyes, letting her ears lead her awareness. Sounds from the camp reached her, but they were muted. No sign of their meaning.

She waited.

Shuffling feet, could be anyone. She didn't allow herself to become excited.

More feet, and breath, shallow, quick inhales, quick exhales. Young breath, young lungs extending and retracted with fear.

They're coming.

She waited.

At last, with the small glow from the sky, she could see them approaching from a mile away. Her face pulled into a smile, a grand and invisible smile in the dark of night, but everything in Rose awoke.

They had barely made it through the first of many trials to come, but Rose was sure, beyond any doubt or fear, that they would succeed.

The Sisters arrived, towering over their charges, small groups of them crowded around, held hands, and marched in silence to the place where Rose waited.

Seventy or so children stood silently around the ten Sisters. More than Rose had expected.

"Several more caravans have arrived," a Sister whispered to Rose. "We've brought who we could. The guards nodded us in and were nowhere to be seen as we left."

"As we'd hoped," Rose's cheeks burned with excitement. It was happening.

Her elation faded when she saw the faces of the children, some of them infants in the arms of Sisters, frozen in silent fear.

"We must walk now, children," Rose said to them. "We have a long way to go, but when we get there, I will tell you everything about the adventure before us."

Rose put her hand on the head of the girl in front of her, about three years old with wild brown curls. The child's lip quivered in quick shakes. Rose kneeled and took her in her arms.

"You are so brave, child. So brave. You must stay brave for a while longer." She released the girl and took her hand. "Let's go."

Rose led them down the paths she'd come to know so well in the previous years of her wandering in Lower Earth.

She knew the ways they could avoid foot traffic, avoid logistics routes. The safest ways to move with seventy children in tow.

Not a word was spoken.

The sun began to rise and they allowed the children to rest in a small canyon hidden by a natural rock wall. Just a few hours. They needed the children to make it all the way to the coast. There was a full day of walking ahead of them, and they only had the food they could carry on their bodies.

Rose watched them sleeping, chests rising and falling, the wash of innocence on their faces after all they had endured since they'd left the capital city.

Her heart broke.

She shook herself. No time for pity nor anger. The voyage before them was long and hard and barely begun.

Rose nodded to the Sister who'd taken the last shift as lookout, and they began gently waking the children.

They walked on.

The ground changed beneath their feet, from green to brown to black as they arrived at the Rainfields lava plains.

Rose kept her eyes straight ahead as the sun set.

The Ganese should be moving into position now. If everything has gone to plan, they'll be waiting for us when we arrive.

A Sister came up beside Rose, "What do we do if they aren't there yet?"

"We wait."

The Sister shrugged, "That's logical, I suppose. I just can't say I like the idea of waiting like sitting ducks."

"They'll be there." Rose nodded her head into the distance. "They'll be there."

Day passed into night and this time the moon was on their side. Bright and clear, they navigated the lava plains without difficulty in the dark. They still had the cliffs to descend, but Rose knew the places they could use. Natural cutaways served as switchbacks to climb down. Hopefully there would be some Ganese to help with the youngest.

Hopefully? Not hopefully - that is our plan.

The edge of the cliff came into sight and just off in the distance, in the water, a boat bobbed in the gentle waves.

Rose closed her eyes for a moment, feeling the wash of relief.

Four Ganese were already ashore, waiting for them. On seeing Rose at the top of the cliff, they trekked up, taking a child in each arm and one on the back, navigating down the cliff with ease.

They were built for this.

Rose sighed with gratitude that these would be her accompanying carers. Her partners. Her friends.

A few knees were scuffed and little hands scraped raw, but no great falls down the cliff and no broken bones. All children, ten Sisters, four Ganese, and Rose waited as the sailboat rowed in, not yet daring to lift the sails.

With the children all aboard, the Ganese rotated out, those on the boat staying behind to meet the next group and ride with them towards the island off the Forgotten Islands, farther than most had ever dared to travel. There they would begin anew. Some Ganese had already gone before them to prepare.

Rose paused to take it all in. The children lined the sailboat's edges, watching. The Ganese aboard stood tall in the moonlight, their skin blending into the black silk of the sky. The four Ganese on land stood with the Sisters, their eyes set.

This was the first night of a hundred. They would continue until they had taken all they could.

Rose saw the uncertainty across all the children's faces, though they did not speak a word. She raised her eyes to the sky.

They have suffered so much already and don't know what this future holds. Neither do I.

But I have to believe it will be better than whatever awaited them here.

She waded into the water and climbed into the boat where Zev was waiting for her. He took her hand and the boat pushed out. Lower Earth became smaller in the distance, but Rose could still see the women on shore, waiting for the boat to disappear into the horizon.

She led to the bow of the boat. The water cut smooth on the still surface as the moonlight made clear their direction. She stood behind Zev, her hands on his shoulders. The wind blew whispers of promise on the waves before them. No more looking back at Lower Earth.

Instead, they looked ahead, off into the silken night, off to the world they would create.

THE END

ABOUT EDEN

I started writing the Lower Earth Rising series at a time when I was pretty sure the world was moving towards a nuclear war. The news spoke of certain presidents of certain countries who weren't getting along.

I was panicking. What could I do to stop a coming nuclear war?

The answer, obviously, was "very little". But I needed some way to deal with the intense nervous energy it was giving me.

I imagined what the world might be like after such a war, and the land of Lower Earth took shape in my imagination.

And then the global pandemic hit.

I was stuck at home with nowhere to go and no one to see, so I dove into the world of Lower Earth to free myself from the everyday fear that was invading my life.

The world can be a scary place; I write to escape it.

~Eden